VIKRAMADITYA VEERGATHA
BOOK 3

THE
VENGEANCE
OF
INDRA

VIKRAMADITYA VEERGATHA
Book 3

THE
VENGEANCE
OF
INDRA

NATIONAL
BESTSELLING
SERIES

SHATRUJEET NATH

JAICO PUBLISHING HOUSE

Ahmedabad Bangalore Bhopal Bhubaneswar Chennai
Delhi Hyderabad Kolkata Lucknow Mumbai

Published by Jaico Publishing House
A-2 Jash Chambers, 7-A Sir Phirozshah Mehta Road
Fort, Mumbai - 400 001
jaicopub@jaicobooks.com
www.jaicobooks.com

VIKRAMADITYA VEERGATHA: BOOK 3
THE VENGEANCE OF INDRA
ISBN 978-93-86867-57-5

First Jaico Impression: 2018

Page design and layout: R. Ajith Kumar, Delhi

Printed by
Thomson Press (India) Limited
B-315, Okhla Industrial Area, Phase-1
New Delhi - 110 020

To
Vijayam mami, Chitra mami and Raghu mama.
Without you, Kochi, 1988, would never have happened,
and life wouldn't have taken such an interesting turn.

Index of Major Characters
(In alphabetical order)

Humans

Kedara	captain of the Imperial Army
Kalidasa	ex-councilor of Avanti
Kshapanaka	councilor of Avanti; sister of Queen Vishakha
Kubja	labourer at Aatreya's shop
Kunjala	physician at Avanti's palace
Mahendraditya	late king of Avanti; father of Vikramaditya, Vararuchi and Pralupi
Mithyamayi	Vismaya's niece; maid to Pralupi
Mother Oracle	Shanku's grandmother; head of the Wandering Tribe
Pralupi	sister of Vikramaditya; Ghatakarpara's mother
Pulyama	captain of the Imperial Army
Satyaveda	governor of Malawa province
Shanku	councilor of Avanti; granddaughter of the Mother Oracle
Sharamana	garrison commander of Musili
Subha	Second Captain in the garrison of Udaypuri
Suhasa	commander of the Imperial Army
Udayasanga	samsaptaka warrior
Upashruti	mother of Vikramaditya and Pralupi; second wife of Mahendraditya
Ushantha	mother of Vararuchi; first wife of Mahendraditya
Varahamihira	councilor of Avanti
Vararuchi	councilor of Avanti; half-brother of Vikramaditya
Vetala Bhatta	chief councilor of Avanti; royal tutor
Vikramaditya	king of Avanti
Vishakha	wife of Vikramaditya; Kshapanaka's sister
Vismaya	chief of the Palace Guards

THE KINGDOM OF MAGADHA

Asmabindu	councilor of Magadha
Daipayana	general of the Magadhan army
Kapila	second son of late king Siddhasena
Shoorasena	king of Magadha; elder son of late king Siddhasena
Siddhasena	late king of Magadha

THE KINGDOM OF VATSA

Chandravardhan	king of Vatsa; ally of Avanti
Himavardhan	brother of Chandravardhan; father of Ghatakarpara
Piyusha	Shashivardhan's bodyguard
Shashivardhan	son of Chandravardhan of Vatsa
Yashobhavi	councilor of Vatsa

THE KINGDOM OF KOSALA

Adheepa	general of Kosala's army
Bhoomipala	king of Kosala; ally of Avanti
Gajaketu	travelling musician
Kadru	courtier of Kosala
Kirtana	courtier of Kosala
Pallavan	envoy and councilor of Kosala

THE KINGDOM OF HEHEYA

Harihara	king of Heheya; ally of Avanti
Rukma	daughter of Harihara of Heheya
Sumayanti	queen of Heheya

THE KINGDOM OF MATSYA

Adri	garrison commander of Kasavati
Baanahasta	king of Matsya; ally of Avanti

The Anarta Federation

Yugandhara	chief of the Anarta Federation; ally of Avanti
Manidhara	chieftain of the Anarta Federation

The Republic of Vanga

Bhadraka	Vanga chieftain
Sudasan	chancellor of the Republic of Vanga

The Hunas

droiba	Huna shaman
Ga'ur Thra'akha	Kalidasa's Huna name
Khash'i Dur	chief of the Hunas
Zho E'rami	late Huna chief; Kalidasa's father

The Kingdoms of Odra and Kalinga

Abhirami	queen of Odra; sister of Veerayanka
Veerayanka	king of Kalinga; brother of Abhirami

Devas

Agneyi	apsara and chief of the fire-wraiths
Brihaspati	royal chaplain of the devas
Dasra	captain of the Ashvins; twin brother of Nasatya
Gandharvasena	a deva
Indra	lord of the devas; king of Devaloka
Jayanta	son of Indra
Manyu	palace keeper of Devaloka
Matali	a deva
Menaka	apsara of Devaloka
Narada	envoy of Devaloka and advisor to Indra
Nasatya	captain of the Ashvins; twin brother of Dasra

Shachi	wife of Indra; Jayanta's mother
The Ashvins	elite cavalry of Devaloka, led by Nasatya and Dasra
The Maruts	the seven sons of Diti
Urvashi	apsara of Devaloka and mistress of Indra

Asuras

Amarka	asura general; son of Shukracharya
Andhaka	the blind rakshasa
Chandasura	asura general; son of Shukracharya
Diti	sorceress and matriarch of the asuras
Hiranyaksha	lord of the asuras; king of Patala
Holika	sister-consort of Hiranyaksha and witch queen of Patala
Shukracharya	high priest of the asuras
Veeshada	the thief of the Halahala

Others

Ahi	the serpent-dragon
Betaal	the Ghoulmaster; lord of the Borderworld
Kubera	lord of the yakshas
Shalivahana	lord of the danavas
Shiva	the Omniscient One
Takshaka	lord of the nagas
Tribhanu	lord of the kinnaras

Glossary of Indian Terms
(In alphabetical order)

akashganga	the Milky Way
amlika	tamarind tree
angavastram	a stole or light shawl to cover the torso
apsara	a beautiful, supernatural female being in Hinduism
badi-maa	elder mother; a form of address
barasingha	swamp deer
chakram	a throwing weapon, circular in shape
danava	a mythical race in Hinduism
danda	a walking stick
devadaru	a species of cedar
dhoti	traditional men's garment
ghat	steps leading down to a body of water like a holy river
gurudev	master or teacher; also a form of address
jal-yantra	an Indian percussion instrument
kashayam	a brewed Ayurvedic medicine
katari	a fist dagger

ketaki	fragrant screw pine
kimshuka	flame of the forest
kinnara	a legendary tribe in Vedic India
mahaguru	grandmaster or teacher; also a form of address
mandala	a spiritual and ritual symbol in Hinduism representing the universe
naga	a legendary tribe in Vedic India
parijata	coral jasmine
pishacha	a mythical flesh-eating demon in Hinduism
pranaam	salutation
rajasuya yajna	ritual sacrifice performed by ancient Indian kings before being anointed emperor
raj-guru	royal tutor; also a form of address
rakshasa	a mythical humanoid being in Hinduism
roti	Indian bread
rudra veena	an Indian string instrument
salmali	red silk-cotton tree
samrat	emperor or overlord
samsaptaka	a tribe of mythical warriors
soma	Vedic ritual drink
suryayantra	a heliograph
tamalpatra	Indian bay leaf
teetar	quail
tilaka	mark worn on the forehead by Hindus
urumi	a longsword with a flexible whip-like blade
vaidya / vaidyanath	physician; also an honorific and form of address
vamsi	a bamboo flute
yaksha	a mythical spirit in Hinduism

Author's Note

When I began writing the tale of Vikramaditya in 2013, I had estimated that the story would spread over three volumes, which is why the series was titled and marketed as The Vikramaditya Trilogy. But by the time I was through with *The Conspiracy at Meru*, my publisher and I were left in no doubt that the series would end up spanning *four* books. The story had grown in its telling, and several vital and interesting sub-plots had emerged that needed space of their own to breathe and blossom.

Naturally, the series couldn't be called a trilogy any longer. I was dead against terming it a 'quartet', so after scratching our heads a bit, we agreed on Vikramaditya Veergatha — *veergatha* meaning a song of valour or an epic poem.

I bring this up because there is a degree of confusion among readers, some of who assume this is the last book in a trilogy. No, it isn't. This book is Volume Three in a *four*-book series and will be followed by *The Wrath of the Hellfires*, the final Vikramaditya book.

As always, there are so many people to thank for having supported me in the creation of this series. I shall reserve the roll of honour for the last book, but there are a few names that deserve special mention here. Blogger and reviewer Debdatta Sahay, for all her support and faith. My friends Ravi Balakrishnan and Varsha Naik, for reading the manuscript and sharing their thoughts and suggestions. My wife and editor Pragya Madan, for putting up with all the typos and tantrums. Lastly, the superb team at Jaico headed by Akash Shah, Sandhya Iyer, Sonal Surana and Vijay Thakur, for giving this series wings.

Contents

Rescue

*T*here was nothing to see in the inky-black sky, from where a cold, numbing drizzle had been coming down right after sunset. Still, Vikramaditya crinkled his eyes against the needle-pricks of rain and studied the great blot of darkness overhead. Somewhere above the stacks of rainclouds was the new moon, he knew, ready to inch into the sky like a shy bride.

A new moon that would usher a calamitous end to everything, should they fail in their mission tonight.

Fate had granted them this one chance to rescue Betaal and save Borderworld. This, scarily, was also their last hope of holding out against the savages from the Marusthali. Failure tonight would render everything that Avanti and its allies had strived for meaningless. The hard, stubborn years of resistance; the countless bitter battles fought to reclaim land from the invaders, inch by bloody inch; the martyrdom of so many of Sindhuvarta's bravest warriors — all of it would amount to nothing.

Dropping his head, Vikramaditya turned to his left where Kalidasa's form was barely visible in the dark, lying flat on his stomach. Everything hinged on their beating the new moon —

and beating the large Huna force massed between them and the banyan tree growing at the centre of Ujjayini's cremation ground, where Betaal was being held captive.

Everything depended on Kalidasa being able to get past the heavily guarded cordon around the droiba, the Huna shaman, and slaying him first.

"It will be done, brother," murmured Kalidasa, as if reading Vikramaditya's mind. "You focus on getting the ghoul out of there."

"Ghoulmaster," Vikramaditya corrected, his gaze returning to the dozen-odd fires scattered across the cremation ground. The light was sufficient to make out clumps of Huna warriors standing guard and the shapes of the horsehide tents pitched all around the ground.

The barbarians' bid to capture the cremation ground nearly a month ago had made little strategic sense to the defenders of Avanti. Since then, the Hunas had dug in and fortified their position there — sometimes at the cost of yielding critical ground to Avanti's troops elsewhere — and had proved impossible to dislodge. What merit the Hunas saw in holding the cremation ground was lost on Vikramaditya and his council.

Two nights ago, they had finally learned the answer. When it was almost too late.

"Ghoulmaster! What kind of Ghoulmaster lets himself be trapped by a shaman?" Kalidasa snorted in irritation. "Then, although he knows you are his only hope, he waits until everything is nearly lost before he starts seeking your help. How is he the protector of Borderworld? Don't they have anyone better for the job?"

Vikramaditya shifted and flexed his arm to maintain circulation. Under him, the grass was damp and uncomfortable. He feared an arm or a leg might go to sleep just when it was time to launch the attack.

"*To be fair to him, Betaal had been trying to reach out to me for nearly a week.*"

"*Umm.*"

Vikramaditya could tell that his friend was still most unimpressed with Betaal. But in truth, the Ghoulmaster had been striving to get through to Vikramaditya every day of the past week. Or every night, to be precise.

The first two nights that Betaal had approached him in his sleep, Vikramaditya had barely registered the occurrence, putting it down to just another dream. It was only after Betaal's third appearance in a row that its significance had dawned on him.

"*It is the thing with its hair made of fire, raj-guru,*" *he had told Acharya Vetala Bhatta on waking up.* "*The same thing that brought me back to the palace.*"

"*You mean...*" *The Acharya had looked at Vikramaditya sharply,* "*...when you were a little boy? The time you had brain fever...?*" *Seeing the young king nod, the raj-guru scratched his nose in surprise.* "*The Ghoulmaster. After so many years. If he is so persistent, he must want to tell you something, Vikrama.*"

That night, as the Acharya had kept watch, Vikramaditya had slept, and allowed Betaal to come to him again. And Betaal's account of all that had transpired — and all that would happen if he were not rescued before the night of the new moon — had left the king and his chief councilor shaken. The council was hastily convened, but with only one intervening night to the new moon, there was hardly time for deliberation. Decisions were taken, a course of action plotted, and as an outcome, Vikramaditya and Kalidasa lay on the sodden earth, staring at the Huna fortifications.

"*This* droiba... *did the Ghoulmaster describe him?*" *Kalidasa's gaze flitted between the burning fires.*

"*He wears a headdress made of vultures' feathers,*"

Vikramaditya said, trying hard to recall the details of Betaal's conversation.

"Many of these savages do that," Kalidasa grunted. "Anything else?"

"Yes. His face is painted blue. Blue streaks, I think."

"Blue streaks?"

Vikramaditya nodded and Kalidasa expelled his breath in exasperation. "How can I possibly find a face painted blue in such darkness?" *A moment's pause, then,* "Why couldn't the Ghoulmaster have been more specific about the shaman's whereabouts?"

Betaal had actually been generous with information, even if dread had made him a little incoherent. "The Huna shaman will sacrifice me two nights from now to take Borderworld," he had blurted out in fear and relief the moment he had Vikramaditya's attention. It had taken quite a few probing questions for the king to piece together the problem they were up against.

The *droiba* was cunning, for he had managed to trick Betaal into leaving Borderworld and coming to the banyan tree in the cremation ground. He was obviously powerful too, for not only had he taken Betaal prisoner, he intended offering the Ghoulmaster as a sacrifice, something that Betaal appeared powerless to prevent. Once the relevant Huna gods had been appeased, the shaman would assume control of Borderworld.

"Why does he want Borderworld?" Vikramaditya had asked Betaal.

"So that the Hunas can vanquish the kingdoms of Sindhuvarta," came the chilling reply. As Betaal revealed the Hunas' diabolical scheme, Vikramaditya had felt his skin crawl even in his sleep.

Borderworld, everyone knows, separates the world of the living from the world of the dead; a bridge, a space of transition. All dying things first pass into Borderworld, where *they are tended to by the ghouls under the Ghoulmaster, who dispose of whatever is physical before sending the spirits on their way.*

"When the dying come to Borderworld, they aren't alive, but they aren't dead either," Betaal had explained. "They are undead. It is my ghouls who destroy the flesh, so that these undead can cross into the world of the dead. But what if the undead aren't destroyed in the flesh, but are preserved and revived with the aid of sorcery? What if such undead are sent into battle against the armies of Sindhuvarta? Imagine, king of Avanti. By mastering Borderworld, the Huna shaman gets access to an endless supply of the undead, who can be used in war against you. Imagine losing troops in battle today and having them return tomorrow as the undead, fighting on the side of the Hunas. What chance do you and your allies have of winning such a war, good king?"

To avert such a catastrophe, Avanti's protectors had but one recourse available to them. By new moon night, Betaal had to be rescued and escorted back to Borderworld — but first, the shaman had to be killed to free Betaal of his influence. And the task of rescuing the Ghoulmaster and reinstating him in Borderworld fell on the young shoulders of Vikramaditya.

"I will be too weak to go by myself," Betaal had said. "You must take me back. You are the only one who can, because you are the only human who knows the way into Borderworld and back, king. You have been there before, remember?"

Vikramaditya remembered. He remembered stumbling feverishly through the cold fog, his small feet slipping and sliding in the wet, marshy soil. He remembered the strange apparition come out of the fog, with hands that had razor-sharp claws and hair that was a shock of orange flames. He remembered the skeletal face and the black, hollowed eyes with their pinpricks of red light, staring at him. He remembered being unafraid as the thing gently took his small hand and told him he wasn't meant to be in Borderworld, that it wasn't his time yet. He remembered it leading him back over the choked and sluggish river, up the broken steps of the bathing ghat, past the ruins of the city gate, into the deserted city of —

"Is that Amara Simha and Varahamihira?"

Kalidasa was already halfway to his feet, his body arched, his big muscles bunched, ready to launch into a run. His right hand gripped a long-handled axe, and he stared into the darkness at the far edge of the cremation ground. Vikramaditya followed his friend's gaze, and as if on cue, shadows sprang into form and battle cries burst from the night as the massive, bearded figure of Amara Simha charged into view. Close on his heels came Varahamihira, brandishing his sword. Behind him came a screaming wall of Avanti's soldiers.

"Let's go, Vikrama!"

Kalidasa shot out of the thicket and was already six paces ahead by the time Vikramaditya broke cover. More soldiers emerged from the surrounding brush and charged noiselessly after Kalidasa, now silhouetted against the fires. He was bigger and broader than most men Vikramaditya had set eyes upon, his long hair knotted in a high ponytail, the arc of his axe glinting in the firelight.

Pulling his father's sword free and feeling the texture of the hide-bound hilt under his palm, Vikramaditya covered the distance to the cremation ground in long strides, passing the men accompanying him and Kalidasa. He drew abreast of his friend just as the Huna defenders clashed with Amara Simha and his troops on the far side. With the din of battle shattering over the ground, Kalidasa and Vikramaditya exchanged brisk nods and parted, the former taking a long, curving route to the left, the latter cutting to the right at an angle. Behind them, the men also broke into two groups.

Vikramaditya ducked into the shadow of the Huna tents, flitting from one to the next, while holding a straight line as far as possible — a line that pointed to the tall banyan out in the middle. The scurry of his men's footsteps came after him.

The banyan was where the droiba *had imprisoned Betaal. And if the Ghoulmaster was to be believed, the tree and this entire cremation ground were extensions of the ancient banyan and the field of pyres in Borderworld. That explained why the Hunas had taken such a tenacious grasp of the cremation ground — their shaman had known that the place was crucial to summon and seize Betaal, Vikramaditya realized.*

A sudden movement occurred to Vikramaditya's left — a well-built Huna, drawn by the noise of battle, stepped out of his tent armed with a sword. The barbarian's eyes widened on sighting the king, but before he could attack or raise an alarm, a shadow with a raised sword slipped in behind him. A swift, expert thrust through the back, and the savage sagged without a sound. The Huna's killer stepped away and the light caught his face — Vararuchi. Vikramaditya nodded at his half-brother in appreciation.

Just then, cries rose from the far-left flank, the direction where Kalidasa had gone. Vikramaditya didn't know what to make of it, but it was clear that the element of surprise was over and that the Hunas were engaging with Avanti's troops. At that instant, five Huna warriors appeared from nowhere, straight onto Vikramaditya's path.

"We will take them, brother," Vararuchi shouted as he tore past the king. "Go get Betaal." Almost immediately, half a dozen of Avanti's men raced past Vikramaditya to join Vararuchi as he clashed with the Hunas blocking the way.

Vikramaditya breathed in deep, took his sword — his father's sword originally, now officially his — in both hands and looked towards the banyan. The tree was still some distance away, but the time for stealth was over. He had to get to the tree, hacking and cleaving his way forward if need be, praying he wouldn't be hopelessly outnumbered, and hoping

*that Kalidasa could somehow, miraculously and swiftly, find
and kill the* droiba. *Breathing in once again, Vikramaditya
stepped from behind a tent and broke into a run.*

The ringing and clanging of metal against metal, the roar
of fury intermingling with screams of agony and terror, the
sound of his own feet pounding in his ears as he ran, orange
firelight and black smoke — everything became a blur against
the banyan. Huna warriors came at him. The first one swung
a heavy sword at his head, which he ducked under. Slipping
past the Huna's raised arm, he drove his sword into the man's
midriff, slicing his stomach open all the way from front to
back. The next one to come was stopped by a stiff kick to the
chest. Vikramaditya followed that with a huge, arcing swing
of the sword that took the barbarian's right leg off from above
the knee.

Onwards he ran, pushing past an increasing press of
resistance. The savages were now appearing from everywhere.
He took two heads clean off the shoulders and skewered a
dozen more to death. His sword was slick with blood, but
Huna soldiers continued to throw themselves at him. Mild
fatigue was setting in, as was anxiety — the tree was still
depressingly far and the Hunas were firmly set on stopping
him. Vikramaditya rammed his blade into an exposed neck. At
the same instant, a barbarian slashed at his shoulder, opening
a deep cut. The king's step faltered, but he was grabbed at the
elbow and steadied by Vararuchi, who had ploughed into the
fray and already cut the assailant's throat.

"Go, Vikrama, go," Vararuchi urged, swiping at the
savages, beating them back.

More men from Avanti joined Vararuchi, clearing a path
for Vikramaditya. Far to the right, Amara Simha was fiercely
carving up a pile of dead Hunas, while Varahamihira was
driving a wedge through the Huna ranks straight ahead, forcing
the barbarians to turn and defend themselves. Vikramaditya

noticed that the savages finally had a battle to occupy them and keep their attention diverted from him.

Wondering if Kalidasa had found the shaman yet, the king neared the banyan. The wound on his shoulder bled freely, mingling with sweat to run down his arm, and Vikramaditya felt a little light in the head as he looked up at the tree.

Almost at once, he spotted Betaal.

Rather, he spotted the corpse, spread-eagled and strung from the tree's aerial roots, tied at the wrists with thick vine. Suspended halfway up from the ground, it hung cold and motionless, like a grotesque offering to some cruel, hungry god.

Ghatakarpara

When Ghatakarpara rounded the bend along the ragged, rock-strewn stream, his face fell on finding the grassy spot in front of the big boulder empty. In his mind's eye, he had been picturing Aparupa seated with her back to the boulder, awaiting his arrival. The anticipation of that sight had seen him through two strenuous rounds of drills in the morning and an inspection of a regiment of Frontier Guardsmen in the afternoon. Not finding Aparupa by the stream was anticlimactic, to say the least.

Ironically though, the prince also experienced a small wave of relief at her absence. These few extra moments of solitude were a favour from fate, he surmised, given to him to evaluate the situation once more before arriving at a decision. Not that he believed he could come to any decision, given the state of his mind. Everything was so terribly confounding, Ghatakarpara frowned, dropping into the vacant shade of the big boulder. Leaning back, he watched the stream meander past his outstretched feet.

It had all started on a whim, a mild fancy fuelled by the

fertile loneliness of the frontier. For the prince — far away from the palace, removed from family and friends, with nothing to fill his hours except drills and border patrols and troop movements — Aparupa had come like a breath of fresh air, a surprise blossom in this bare, parched land. Ghatakarpara still remembered the afternoon he had ventured across Udaypuri's festive streets to engage her in light banter; he had been craving company that day, nothing more. Yet, that one chance encounter had led to other planned ones, each progressively more surreptitious as both of them had grown bolder and more at ease in each other's company.

Although he had never intended for things to turn serious, quite suddenly, a couple of days ago, they had. He was lying with his head on her lap, dreamy as usual, and she was running her fingers idly through his hair when, out of the blue, Aparupa had asked if his parents would approve of her.

Ghatakarpara spied a movement away to his left. Turning, he observed with surprise a bullock cart parked in the middle of the stream, the water barely submerging the hooves of the two oxen in yoke. The stream was a patchy affair of small trickles and puddles that filled out only in the rains; during dry spells like this one, it served no purpose, so hardly anyone came this way. The seclusion was tailored for their meetings, but today, it looked like they would end up sharing the spot with the two men in the stream, assiduously washing cart and oxen.

While one part of Ghatakarpara wondered if washing a bullock cart in such shallow water was worth the effort, the other part went back to Aparupa from two days ago. Her question had knocked him flat — because the prospect she had suggested hadn't once crossed his mind. Ghatakarpara had just lain there, blinking up at the girl, trying to work out a satisfactory answer, when her next words picked him up and threw him down all over again.

"I don't suppose my father would approve of a common soldier as his son-in-law," she had said, plucking a blade of grass and chewing on it. "To top it, the son of a weaver? No," she shook her head firmly. "That would be well beneath his status. But we don't have to bother about him. If he doesn't accept you, I am willing to leave everything and come with you."

It had taken the prince an entire night of sleeplessness to comprehend the enormity of Aparupa's trust in him. And knowing that her trust was built on an elaborate framework of falsehood that he had erected around them had left him ashamed and conscience-stricken. That night, in the midst of all that shame and remorse, Ghatakarpara also discovered that he loved Aparupa more deeply than he had imagined possible.

The young prince reached into his shawl and extracted a bangle made of seasoned bamboo. It was intricately carved, two snakes twisting around each other and swallowing one another's tails in an infinite loop. With a small knife, Ghatakarpara made tiny holes for the snakes' eyes, and filed the bamboo smooth, carefully blowing away any rough splinters and shavings. The bangle was the second of a pair he had made; he had already gifted the first to Aparupa a few days ago.

Glancing downstream, the prince got the impression that the cart had drawn closer. Dismissing the notion, he went back to carving the bangle and honing his thoughts. He obviously had to reveal his true identity; no passing off as Ghataraja, a silk weaver's son, any longer. But he feared the knowledge of his subterfuge would only incite Aparupa, prompting her to leave him despite his honesty.

I could break it to her gently, he reasoned, examining the bangle against the light of the setting sun to check for irregularities. I could tell her in a week, maybe, once I have

gained her trust some more and shown how much I love her.
He dropped his hand in frustration, knowing he was only
fooling himself. The longer he hid his identity, the more he
delayed in exposing the lie, the harder it would get being
upfront with the girl. And the tougher it would be for her to
pardon him later.

Sighing inwardly at his dilemma, Ghatakarpara looked in
the direction from where Aparupa would approach. Nothing
there. She was later than usual, and for a frantic moment, the
fear that she had discovered his duplicity and was punishing
him for it flared in his chest. No, she couldn't learn about him
from elsewhere; *he* had to be the one to look her in the eye
and tell her.

That was one thing. There was another. What if she heard
him out, understood his reasons for being dishonest with her
and accepted his apology? Then, what if in the new light of
things, she posed her question again — would his parents
approve of her?

Would they? He was of royal lineage, a scion of Avanti's
powerful Aditya dynasty. One of his uncles was King
Chandravardhan of Vatsa. The other was Samrat Vikramaditya,
overlord of Sindhuvarta. Would the courts of Avanti and
Vatsa welcome Aparupa, daughter of a millet merchant from
faraway Udaypuri, into the royal household? Ghatakarpara
dredged a memory of his mother's cold, disapproving glare
and shook his head in dejection.

And what had Aparupa said — she would leave everything
and come with him if her father, Aatreya, didn't give them his
blessings. Would *he*, Prince Ghatakarpara, forsake the palaces
of Ujjayini and Kausambi for Aparupa? Could he surrender
the councilorship of Avanti, and the pride and authority
that came with it, for the sake of a provincial girl? If he did,
would he be forgiven by everyone who had showered so
much time, attention and affection on him — the Acharya,

Vararuchi, Amara Simha? And wouldn't he be letting his uncle Vikramaditya, who had such high hopes of him, down?

Aparupa, he understood, had already placed her wholehearted faith in the love she had for him. Did he have as much faith in his love for her? Running his fingers along the edges of the sun-crest medallion he had hidden under his *angavastram*, Ghatakarpara realized he was scared of finding out the answer. He knew it would entail making tough choices and demand hard sacrifices that could never be undone.

The clatter of a pebble kicked loose on gravel got Ghatakarpara to turn expectantly to the bend in the path, but Aparupa didn't put in an appearance. It took the prince a moment to realize that the sound had come from somewhere behind the boulder — and his face brightened in a playful smile. The girl had taken the long route around so she could sneak up on him and startle him. Well, he could turn the tables on her, make her the victim of the prank instead, he chuckled under his breath.

Leaping lightly to his feet, Ghatakarpara crouched and crept forward, grinning, ready to pounce at the first sight of the girl. He noticed her shadow, long on the ground, hugging the boulder, her head bobbing. Drawing his breath in, he took a long stride around the boulder, all set to go "ho" and scare her —

— but he drew up short, staring in surprise at the figure hiding behind the rock.

Figures, not figure. For there were three of them. All men, all three armed with short swords and ironwood quarterstaffs.

The men were as taken aback as the prince was. They stared wide-eyed from his face to his hands, which were thrust forward, the fingers hooked like talons, as if meaning to reach out and grab them. Whatever they had been up to, Ghatakarpara had caught them unawares, so they just stood there blinking uncertainly at him.

"Oh," Ghatakarpara said, letting his hands drop to his sides, trying to act nonchalant. "Who... are you?"

The men, who were attired like farmers but bore weapons like soldiers, exchanged quick glances. They didn't, however, offer a reply. The one closest to Ghatakarpara, a tall man with a rough, swarthy complexion, took a hesitant step forward. Immediately, the other two spread out behind their leader, as if barring an exit route.

"I see," the prince said, his expression clearing. "You must be members of the local militia. Very good, the way you are helping the Imperial Army and the Frontier Guard."

The men didn't respond. They kept staring at him with watchful eyes.

"What?" Ghatakarpara cocked an eyebrow. "Oh, you think I am...?" he nodded. "That's it. You don't know who I am. I am Ghatakarpara, prince and councilor of..."

The rush was so sudden and unexpected, Ghatakarpara almost had no time to react. The leader charged, swinging his quarterstaff at the prince's head, and it was only instinct and years of training that made Ghatakarpara raise his arm swiftly to block the blow. As the quarterstaff deflected off his forearm, the prince stepped in, again by reflex, and rammed his right elbow hard into his attacker's chest, just below the breast bone. The leader grunted and doubled, his head dropping, and Ghatakarpara instantly smashed his left fist into the man's cheek, dislocating his jaw. The man went down with a painful howl, and the prince stepped past him, his hands raised and balled into fists.

"I told you I am Councilor Ghatakarpara," he spoke loudly, so the two men standing uncertainly before him would be in no doubt. "Wait, if you don't believe me, look..." He slipped a hand into his *angavastram* and extracted the councilor's medallion, hanging on its chain. "See? I am not an enemy of Avanti, so do not attack, please. If you..."

The net was thrown expertly, landing on the prince from behind, swaddling him from head to toe in one swooping motion. Before he could gather his wits, the strong mesh began drawing tight around Ghatakarpara, bundling him in. As he swatted and flailed, trying to break out of captivity, the men in front of him jumped in to help the two who had cast the net. Squinting through the mesh, the prince identified the newcomers as the men who had been washing the bullock cart.

"What is the meaning of this?" he snarled and thrashed and kicked up a turbulence that marred the tranquility of eventide. "Do you have any idea of what you are inviting upon yourselves? I am the Samrat's nephew, fools. He will have your heads for this. Let me go!"

The blow dealt to the back of Ghatakarpara's head was so loud that its crack rang out over the little stream, causing a pair of greenish warblers to take hurried flight. The blow was so strong that it brought a flood of darkness to Ghatakarpara's eyes. He swayed for a moment, giddy, then went down on his knees.

One of his assailants spoke in the local tongue, a dialect of Avanti, and though the prince did not follow what was said word to word, he understood that the speaker was worried the blow would cause their prisoner's death.

"No", another voice mumbled, and as Ghatakarpara fell over on his side, he saw the group's leader staring balefully down at him, his quarterstaff in one hand, the other hand nursing his broken jaw.

"The swine will be fine — though I'd very much like to kill him," the leader muttered through a grimace.

Another wave of darkness came crashing over Ghatakarpara. His head felt as if it had split into halves, and a humming, throbbing pain was pushing its way from the back to the front of his head, growing louder and more insistent and strident with each passing moment. He closed his eyes.

"They won't pay if he's dead. They want him alive."

The prince wondered if Aparupa was alright. He was happy she hadn't shown up after all. All this would have been so much more complicated had she been around. Or had she come and had these men harmed her as well?

"He is alive, so shut up and fetch the bullock cart."

He really wished nothing had happened to her. He wanted to ask the men, maybe even plead with them to let her go if they had taken her captive. He tried opening his mouth to speak, to form words, but he realized he couldn't. It was as if the link between his mind and his muscles — his vocal cords, his tongue, his jaw — had snapped.

"Search the place thoroughly while there is still light. Look behind the boulder where he was sitting. If you find anything, bring it here. Nothing of his should be found when they come looking for him."

Darkness settled over Ghatakarpara like a giant bird on wings. It felt like hands were lifting him off the ground, carrying him, but he was certain it was the same dark bird, bearing him away in its clutches into a dark, bottomless abyss.

* * *

Night had woven a tight cloak around the palace, smudging the contours of its rising domes, balconies and terraces, so to Dhanavantri's travel-weary eye, it was difficult to tell where the night ended and the palace began. Even the lights dotting the palace windows seemed to shrink and withdraw in deference to the darkness, while the torches lighting the causeway were pale halos of uncertainty, their reflections undulating like ghosts in the lake below. Peering through the carriage window, the physician was struck by how fragile and insubstantial the palace appeared in the dark.

The carriage rolled onto the causeway, and Dhanavantri

realized with some relief that it was the mist rising from the lake that was playing tricks on the eye, causing structures to lose form and appear indeterminate. Yet, when the carriage drew to a halt at the palace gates, Dhanavantri sensed a heavy, brooding silence pinning the palace to the ground, a silence that reaffirmed everything he had heard during the last leg of his journey back to Ujjayini.

"Greetings, councilor," a captain of the Palace Guards bowed as the physician stepped to the ground.

"Greetings, captain." Looking up, Dhanavantri noticed that the old gate — the one that had been smashed open by the giant, blue-skinned rakshasa the night the palace was attacked — had been replaced in his absence by a new one, built of black iron and fortified with brass.

"Is the Samrat still awake?" he asked, slipping through a smaller door set in the gates.

"I am not sure, your honour. I can get someone to check and…"

"No, no," Dhanavantri waved a hand. "It's fine. Don't bother the king. I am here to check on Queen Vishakha. Is someone with her?"

"I can get someone…"

"It's alright. I know the way." The physician gave the captain a curt nod. "You can head back to your post."

Dhanavantri had crossed the hallway and was almost at the foot of the stairway leading to the levels above when another voice hailed him in greeting. Turning, the physician recognized Vismaya, a senior and well-respected captain of the City Watch. But in place of a captain's bronze medallion, the man wore the silver medallion of the chief of the Palace Guards around his neck.

"Greetings," Dhanavantri's eyebrows rose as he stared at the silver medallion. "When did this happen?"

"A couple of days back, your honour." Vismaya was

short, the same height as Dhanavantri. He had a disfigured nose over a short, well-groomed, grey beard. "When did you return from Kausambi?"

"Some two hours ago. I heard about the queen, so I came to have a look at her."

"Let me not keep you then," Vismaya bowed.

Dhanavantri began mounting the stairs. After three steps, he paused and spoke over his shoulder. "My congratulations, commander. You richly deserve the medallion you have on."

"Thank you, councilor. I hope I get the chance to repay the palace's trust in me."

Climbing the stairway, the physician's mind was drawn to the whole host of changes that had occurred in Ujjayini in his short absence. The palace had a new gate and a new chief of the Palace Guards; these were probably the only two *good* pieces of news in a landslide of depressing reports that had greeted him and his company of escorts as they had made their way home.

It had begun the previous afternoon, when he and his men had stopped at a horse station to refresh their mounts. One of the guards had got into conversation with a drunk honey vendor, who painted a florid picture of half of Ujjayini being destroyed by a serpent that spat venom from the sky. Dhanavantri and his men ascribed the story to an excess of firewater and dismissed it, but later that night, as they had set up camp in a fallow field, they were joined around the fire by a family of metalworkers fleeing Ujjayini. From them, the physician learned of the destruction wrought by the giant serpent, and how it had finally been vanquished by the combined courage and extraordinary powers of Kshapanaka, Amara Simha and Shanku. The metalworkers also made a mention of the Healer's unexpected departure from Ujjayini — all they knew was it had to do with the dagger given to the samrat by the Omniscient One.

The night passed fitfully, and morning brought more bad news. Dhanavantri and his men encountered another scared family coming from Ujjayini, and this lot confirmed much of what the metalworkers had said. In addition, they gave an alarming but disjointed account of Vishakha being attacked by some creature and slipping back into a vegetative state. The shock of this hadn't yet fully sunk in, when a few hours down the road, they met a small contingent of the Imperial Army, from whom Dhanavantri heard about the bitterly entwined past of Kalidasa and Vararuchi, and of the *samsaptaka*'s refusal to serve Avanti and its throne any longer.

It was with sheer disbelief that Dhanavantri had entered the gates of Ujjayini, but on arriving home, Madari, his wife, had confirmed every piece of news he had heard along the way. She told him about Ahi and the defence of Ujjayini, and about the miraculous powers that the councilors had discovered they possessed. She told him about the shapeshifting yaksha's attack on Vishakha that had led to her relapse and to the unmasking of Shukracharya. And he listened in despair about Kalidasa finally remembering his Huna ancestry — and recalling the coldblooded killing of his family by Vararuchi.

A light knock on the door to the queen's chamber, and the physician was let inside by one of Vishakha's two maids. The chamber was lit by a pair of lamps, and in their light, Dhanavantri saw the elderly matron and the second maid, who was waving a fan made of cane and peacock feathers over Vishakha's recumbent form. One look at the queen's blank and fixed stare was sufficient for Dhanavantri to surmise that everything he had been told about her relapse was true.

"Has she been eating enough?" he asked, nodding in response to the matron's bow. "Enough water?" He took Vishakha's wrist and felt her pulse, soft but steady. Her hand was too thin and too pale, though, as was her face.

"Your honour, we try our best to feed her as we can," the

matron replied. "Councilor Kshapanaka makes sure she eats something."

The door opened to admit one of the apprentice physicians in the palace. He had obviously been alerted by Vismaya, and he came hurrying into the room, bowing to Dhanavantri. "Greetings, councilor." The young man stopped, suddenly unsure of himself. "I am... should... should I summon Kunjala vaidyanath, your honour?"

"No," Dhanavantri shook his head as he pulled Vishakha's eyelids up to study her pupils. "I shall talk to him in the morning. Can you tell me what medications are being administered to the queen?"

Eager to impress the royal physician, the apprentice launched into a detailed and enthusiastic report of all the liniments, *kashayams* and sundry preparations that Kunjala had prescribed for Vishakha. The report was exhaustive and to Dhanavantri's satisfaction. He was nodding his approval when the door opened once again and in walked Vikramaditya and Upashruti.

"Greetings, Queen Mother," the physician offered Upashruti a *pranaam*.

"We were told you were here." There was a note of surprise in the samrat's tone. "When did you get back to Ujjayini?"

"A little while ago." The physician noticed another recent change in the palace — a fine beard with a sprinkling of grey hair now covered the samrat's cheeks and jaw. "I heard about this from Madari and had to come."

"It could have waited until the morning," the king said. "The journey must have left you quite fatigued."

Dhanavantri shrugged so his neck disappeared into his fat shoulders. "I wanted to take a look. It's my duty as the court physician... and as your friend and councilor."

Vikramaditya inclined his head as he moved to Vishakha's side and looked down at her face, wan and expressionless.

A curtain of gloom seemed to fall over the samrat, and Dhanavantri couldn't bear to see his dejection.

"What do you think?" Upashruti gestured towards the bed. "Is she... Will she...?"

"I honestly can't say, Queen Mother. We have to observe her, try different things... as before..." The physician sensed the samrat and his mother's resignation from the sudden slump of their shoulders. "We mustn't lose hope, of course. I mean... she *did* recover, so there *is* hope... and I'll do everything I can."

A little while later, the samrat and the physician were walking down a gallery. Even though the hour was late, the palace was quieter than Dhanavantri ever remembered it being at night; it appeared to him as if the very walls and pillars were in silent mourning.

"I can't bear to see her like this." The words escaped the king's lips in an anguished rush, a compulsive baring of the heart that made Dhanavantri look at his friend's face. The firelight from the torches lighting the gallery shone in the tears in Vikramaditya's eyes, tears held back by sheer force of will.

Not knowing what to say, the physician kept silent. They walked past the turn that led to the samrat's chambers, and Dhanavantri realized Vikramaditya wanted to talk. The gallery opened onto a curved, partially walled terrace, with stone benches arranged along the wall. The samrat sank onto a bench and Dhanavantri sat down by his side.

"She remembered me," Vikramaditya turned to the physician with a small smile, and Dhanavantri saw that behind the sadness, there was joy that the memory had brought. "She remembered me as Vikrama, from when we were both younger. And she made the connection."

"I know. Madari told me."

"And then it was over." If the samrat had heard Dhanavantri, he didn't show any sign of it. "Gone again."

The physician placed a hand over the king's hand. "Why didn't you let the Healer take one look at her? It might have helped."

"Then I would have been obliged to him. And then, what if he had asked for the dagger?" Vikramaditya shook his head. "I will do nothing that can jeopardize my promise to Mahadeva."

They lapsed into silence once again, and once again, it was the king who broke it.

"I owe you an apology." Seeing Dhanavantri look at him sharply, the samrat nodded. "I was charmed by the Healer's words, blinded by his assurances, taken in by his obvious talents. I wanted to see Vishakha cured, and that obsession and the Healer's successes made me forget everything you had done. I ignored you, I gave the Healer the importance that I should have reserved for you. I am sorry. Forgive me if you can."

"Ah, what is this…" The physician took Vikramaditya's hand between both of his and gave it a reassuring squeeze. "I understand, my friend. There is nothing to seek forgiveness for, there is nothing to forgive. Don't bring this up again, please."

King and physician were making their way back down the gallery when the latter shook his head in disbelief. "Such a lot has come to pass in so little time," he remarked, looking up at Vikramaditya. "What… what's happened to us? Why are we suffering like this, what sins are we paying for?"

Glancing at his friend, the samrat shrugged. "You do recall the Mother Oracle talking of an eclipse devouring Avanti's sun, don't you?" Seeing Dhanavantri nod, the king added, "I wish the oracle had been wrong on this one, but I suspect she isn't."

"Let's hope this eclipse passes us soon then."

"It will inevitably pass." They had reached the fork where they had to part for the night. Vikramaditya looked down the gallery, then surveyed the palace. "I just don't know what its sweeping shadow will take with it; what will remain, and what will be lost forever."

* * *

The pool was in the middle of the herbarium, wide, placid and shallow, carefully concealed by an assortment of broad-leaved plants and dense, trailing creepers that fell in curtains from the branches of nearby trees. With the intoxicating scents of arcane herbs tickling her senses and welcoming her in, Holika swept aside the creepers and emerged by the pool's side to see Hiranyaksha submerged in the water up to his chest. The asura lord's eyes were closed as he soaked in the silence, flush with tropical fragrances. The water itself was clear, so the fish that slipped between the round, black stones at the pool's bottom were in plain view.

Holika stood quiet for a moment, drinking in the sight of Hiranyaksha, muscular, broad-shouldered and naked in the water, the curling ram horns majestic on his forehead, his face hard, hairless and handsome. Her skin tingled at the thought of the little ripples that lapped the asura's body, desire coursing through her quicker than lightning, causing her to catch her breath sharply.

"Holika?"

The Witch Queen of Patala looked at the asura in surprise, noting that the eyes were still closed. A small, playful smile danced on his lips.

"How did you know it was me?" she asked.

The smile broadened and Hiranyaksha opened his eyes, golden like sunshine. "Who else but you would come here in search of me at this time of the night?"

The asura stretched out an arm in invitation, but Holika

ignored it. Turning around, she moved towards a moss-covered stone bench set to one side and sat on it.

"I was told that you were back from Devaloka," she appraised Hiranyaksha with her cold, blue eyes.

"Yes, the mahaguru suggested I should come back and prepare for our brother's return."

"Hiranyakashipu is returning from his penance?" Holika sat up, her face alight with anticipation. "When?"

"The mahaguru didn't say, but the bones have told him that brother will be with us before long."

A short silence followed, during which Holika deduced that Hiranyaksha had returned alone.

"The mahaguru didn't accompany you back?" Seeing the asura lord shake his head, Holika asked, "What's keeping him in Devaloka? Hasn't he succeeded in convincing Indra about the need to cooperate in defeating the human king?"

"Oh, Indra came around to the idea of working with us very quickly." Hiranyaksha splashed water idly as he spoke. "He may be stubborn, but he's not stupid. No, the mahaguru has stayed back because he says he has some unfinished business."

"Unfinished business?"

The asura lord nodded, then shrugged.

Holika let the matter rest. "What of the grand plan that the mahaguru had spoken of, the one designed to break the human king?" She leaned forward in excitement. "Have we made any progress there?"

"Of course," Hiranyaksha said with a chuckle. "According to the mahaguru, an irreparable divide has already occurred between the king and one of his councilors. So, the powers that the Nine Pearls exert have begun eroding. But that's only the beginning. The real blow to the human king will come from the deva Gandharvasena."

"Gandharvasena?" Holika tried to place the name. With a frown, she added, "Not a name I am familiar with. Who is he?"

With a few powerful strokes, the asura lord swam over to the bench. Staying in the water, he explained who Gandharvasena was and the influence the deva would exert over the course of events. Fascinated by Shukracharya's cunning, the Witch Queen listened with interest, her red lips parting in wonder at the devastation that had been planned for Vikramaditya.

"Has Gandharvasena departed for the human kingdom?" she asked in an awed whisper, once the asura had completed his narration.

"He and Indra are supposed to leave soon."

"And what happens after that... after Gandharvasena?"

"After that, the human king and his Nine Pearls will be of no consequence."

"And the Halahala?" There was sudden alarm in Holika's voice. "Indra will be in the human kingdom. He could somehow get..."

Hiranyaksha reached out and took Holika's hand between his. Stroking it, he spoke soothingly. "Nothing will happen to Veeshada's dagger. The devas know nothing of its whereabouts. The mahaguru knows it is safe where it is, at least for now."

"How much longer will it be safe where it is?" Holika had slid down the bench and was kneeling by the pool.

"I don't know," the asura lord replied, tugging Holika gently by the hand. The Witch Queen responded by shrugging the light shawl off her shoulders and slipping into the water. "Which is why the mahaguru has instructed that besides preparing to welcome our brother, we should also prepare for battle."

"Whom do we go to battle against?" Holika's voice shivered, though she couldn't say if it was because of the cold water or the sudden hardness of Hiranyaksha against her.

"It could be the human king, if there's any fight left in him. It could be the devas." The asura put his arm around the Witch Queen's waist, drawing her close, and she responded by latching herself tightly around his neck. His golden eyes bored into hers, as if looking into her soul. "Who knows, we might even end up fighting them both."

Holika stood on tiptoe and pulled the asura's head down to her. Their lips and limbs locked in feverish haste, hardness and softness creating delirious spaces for one another, and the heady aroma of their lust blossomed and fused with the exotic scents around them.

* * *

"Salutations, my lord."

Indra, his elbows planted on the parapet he was leaning on, looked over his shoulder at the door connecting his bedchamber to the balcony, where a figure stood in silhouette, lit from behind by torches in the bedchamber, yet hidden in the shadows of the door, out of the pale moonlight illuminating the balcony.

"Matali."

"Yes, my lord."

As Indra pushed himself upright, the figure stepped onto the balcony. The moonlight showed a deva, stocky in build and swathed in a dark shawl that imparted him an air of secretiveness. A stylishly scruffy beard, iron grey in colour, adorned his chin, and he had a broad forehead with a high, receding hairline. He wore small but heavy earrings. His eyes were large but retained a sleepy appearance on account of heavy, drooping eyelids.

"I am all set to leave for Sindhuvarta, lord," the deva announced.

"You know what to do once you reach the kingdom of Vikramaditya."

It wasn't a question. Matali inclined his head silently.

With a nod of satisfaction, Indra said, "Gandharvasena and I will be there shortly."

"Then I shall depart tonight itself, my lord. I shall await your arrival."

"I don't need to remind you that the human king is smart and..." Indra paused briefly, before forcing himself to continue, his mouth twisting as he spat out the word, "... brave. You know how the Ashvins and the Maruts fared. Whatever you do, be very careful."

"I will, my lord. You can trust me."

The lord of the devas nodded with finality. Taking his cue, Matali bowed and stepped back. In what appeared as a deceptive shifting of shapes and shadows, the deva slipped and melted and oozed across the balcony and the bedchamber until he dissolved from sight altogether. For a moment, Indra blinked and stared at the spaces that Matali had occupied and vacated in rapid succession, before turning back to gaze over Amaravati.

The balcony jutted out from one of the highest spires in the palace, offering a sweeping view of the city that shimmered under a light veil of mist the same colour as the moonlight. It felt as if the light had been poured from the heavens and lay congealing amid the city's parks and woodlands. Closer to the palace, the mist sent fumbling fingers around the high rocks and cliffs, but stayed firmly away from the abyss, as if in dread of what might be lying in wait in its depths. The night air was still as the palace and Amaravati slept.

But Indra himself was without sleep.

When Shukracharya had first told him what Gandharvasena was capable of achieving, the deva's jubilation had known no bounds. All that hatred for Vikramaditya piling up inside him, all the shame he felt thinking of the Ashvins and the Maruts returning humbled and humiliated, the deep yearning to settle scores that accompanied him everywhere — Gandharvasena was the answer to all of that. The desire to crush the human king burned so bright that he had wholeheartedly followed every one of Shukracharya's suggestions, and now they were on the verge of journeying to Avanti.

However, with the calming influence of time, it had dawned on Indra that this alliance of theirs was temporary, that the devas and asuras were no more friends than they had been before. With Vikramaditya out of the way, the tussle for Veeshada's dagger would once again take precedence. He would be a fool to believe that the asuras had set aside their quest for the dagger in good faith, and if Shukracharya was in the hunt, it was imperative that the devas learned of the Halahala's whereabouts first.

Which was where Matali came in.

Indra thought he spied movement somewhere beneath, and he dropped his eyes to the broad palace courtyards way down below. The courtyards were lit by torches, and in their light, he thought he saw a shadow flit and weave past. He followed the shadow as it slid onto the southern drawbridge, but within moments, it was gone, swallowed by the darkness of the yawning abyss.

You can trust me, Matali had said. Indra knew he could. A loner and a survivor, Matali had served him well in the past. The deva had a way of burrowing under obstacles. And he wasn't afraid of getting his hands — or his conscience — dirty.

Matali would find out where the human had hidden the dagger. Matali would figure a way of finding out.

Ransom

The door to the council chamber was straight up ahead, dark, heavy and uncompromising, barring Shanku's path like an old adversary. Experiencing a nip of hesitation at its sight, the young councilor dropped her pace a fraction, and for one fickle moment, she was overcome by the urge to turn back and slip away.

The moment passed and Shanku approached the door, conscious of the time she had last been on the other side of that great bulk of carved wood — it was the day after the serpent-dragon had attacked Ujjayini and the yaksha had tried to kill Vishakha in the meadow. They had all been in that room with the samrat, discussing the looming iron crisis precipitated by Shoorasena's capture of the iron mines at Dandakabhukti. To offset the shortage of ore, the council had agreed that the Acharya would lead a diplomatic mission to Queen Abhirami's court, to try and convince Odra to trade iron with Avanti.

It felt as if that day was eons ago. Not surprising, Shanku reflected as she pushed at the door; so much had transpired in the palace since. That day, both Vetala Bhatta and Kalidasa had been present in the council, and Vararuchi had not yet returned from the battle to save Dvarka; whereas now, the raj-guru was headed for Uttara Tosali with an intent to strengthen Avanti, while Kalidasa had picked an unbelievable quarrel with Vararuchi and Avanti and left the palace, never to return...

Shaking thoughts of Kalidasa aside — and wondering if things would have turned out differently had the Acharya been present when the madness bore fruit — the girl stepped inside the council chamber, nodding her greetings to the councilors still present in Ujjayini. Amara Simha sat to the left of Vikramaditya's high chair; beside him was Dhanavantri, who, she guessed, had returned late the previous day. Kshapanaka and Varahamihira sat across the table, to the samrat's right. Vararuchi, she knew, was not in the palace; he had left to visit his mother Ushantha three days ago. The samrat himself stood leaning over a small table set by an open window, browsing through a scroll.

"Shankubala," he exclaimed, looking up from the scroll. "Sit. I shall join you in a moment."

Dhanavantri smiled and patted the seat next to him, and Shanku sidled into it. A quick survey of everyone's expressions confirmed that she wasn't the only one feeling subdued. Amara Simha, Kshapanaka and Varahamihira were also circumspect and absorbed in their own worlds, it seemed.

"Do you still need to knock and enter through doors?" A small smile played on the corners of Dhanavantri's puffy lips, and Shanku realized his attempt was to enliven the atmosphere a little. "Can't you just..." he waved his hands around vaguely, "...appear here... next to me, or... wherever?"

The girl smiled shyly and shook her head. With her new talent — her *gift*, as the Mother Oracle put it — she knew she could if she wanted to. She was practising every day, discreetly, and getting better at it, wielding her talent with greater confidence and precision. But that hadn't been the point of the physician's question. Dhanavantri had only tried infusing some levity — though going by the response it fetched, he needn't have bothered. Amara Simha offered a perfunctory smile and went back to studying the chamber's high ceiling. Opposite them, Varahamihira pretended not to have heard and continued biting and examining his fingernails. Kshapanaka, consumed by her own thoughts, exchanged looks with Shanku before darting a glance at the samrat. No one was inclined to say anything, and Dhanavantri joined in the indifference by placing his hands over his big paunch and gazing placidly at nothing in particular.

The ensuing silence was awkward, bloated and self-conscious. Shanku wondered if she should be polite and ask the physician when he had returned, but mercifully, the hush was broken by the rustling of the palm scroll that the king was reading. Five pairs of eyes turned to Vikramaditya in guarded anticipation as he approached the council table.

"It has been a while since we all assembled here and exchanged notes." The samrat dropped into his chair at the head of the table and placed the scroll at his elbow. "I have a few things that I wish to discuss with you, but first, do any of you have anything that *you* would like to bring to the council's notice?"

The king's question got the councilors looking at one another, not really knowing what to say, expecting someone else to speak first. At long last, Varahamihira propped himself up in his chair and cleared his throat.

"I don't have anything specific, but... yes, there is a lot of fear among the townsfolk. Of course, you all know that. Also," he paused, as if making his mind up, "I sense some resentment building."

Shanku observed a pained expression pass over

Vikramaditya's face, but he blinked and made a brave attempt to conceal it. The new beard suited the samrat, she thought; it added to his charisma but also made him look sadder, more solemn.

"I understand the fear, but resentment?" he looked perplexed. "Over what?"

"It stems from fear, I guess," Varahamihira shrugged. "And loss."

"The people think I shouldn't have accepted the responsibility of keeping Veeshada's dagger," the samrat nodded, his brooding eyes on the motif of the sun-crest emblazoned on the table. "That is the root of our troubles, and *I* brought it on Avanti. But what was I to do —" he looked at the faces around him in helplessness, "refuse to honour Shiva's trust in me? In *us*?"

"Not everyone blames you for that decision, Samrat," Amara Simha rushed in to offer comfort. "I can wager that those who do are an insignificantly small minority, and," he gave a contemptuous snort, "are complete fools."

"Sending the Healer — I mean, Shukracharya — off has also hurt," said Varahamihira. He winced and sneaked an apologetic glance at Dhanavantri, but the physician stared back in stoic silence. "The people had got accustomed to his miraculous cures."

"And, of course, they hold me responsible for that as well," Vikramaditya's voice had a bitter, gravelly edge.

"Again, a small minority," Amara Simha said emphatically. "The people of Avanti are in pain and fear, but they are proud of their king. Take it from me."

"Then why is there resentment, and why is it rising?" asked the samrat.

"It's actually…" Catching Amara Simha's eye, the lame inventor hesitated. He gave Shanku a brief, sidelong glance, then drew his breath in. "Well, some of our subjects aren't happy with us letting Kalidasa leave Ujjayini. They... they believe he is a threat to the kingdom's security."

The chamber seemed to shrink and grow claustrophobic. The councilors sat quietly, avoiding each other's gaze; the curtains hung unobtrusively, trying not to draw attention to themselves; even the early morning sunlight coming in through the long windows faded and folded and retreated into shadowy corners, as if pushed there by Varahamihira's words.

Sensing the carefully averted gazes of her fellow councilors, it struck Shanku that this was what she had feared when she had neared the chamber's door. She had known that mention of Kalidasa was inevitable, especially in context to Avanti's safety, and she had prepared herself to deal with it without letting her emotions betray her. But she wasn't ready for people feeling sorry for her — it worried her to think that their sympathy would break her defences down.

"Some of our subjects?" Vikramaditya raised a quizzical eyebrow at Varahamihira. There was an undercurrent of irritation in his tone. "With so many troubles to keep them occupied, I didn't know our subjects had the time or wherewithal to worry about Kalidasa as well. If I may ask, who *are* these subjects?"

Varahamihira shifted in his chair. It was Kshapanaka who answered.

"There is fear among soldiers that sooner or later, Kalidasa will be a threat to us. The feeling is strongest in sections of the Imperial Army."

"The soldiers know what he is capable of in battle, Vikrama." Seeing how distressing this was to the king, Varahamihira spoke soothingly, inadvertently addressing him by name. "Their fear is real. There have been sightings of him, and in every instance, he has been seen heading west. Everyone knows what lies to the west."

"We have to acknowledge that the soldiers might be right," said Kshapanaka.

"We will acknowledge things once we have irrefutable evidence of their existence," the samrat replied heavily. As if to signal the matter closed, he turned to Dhanavantri. "The council is keen to hear about your visit to Vatsa. Would you be kind enough to oblige us with an account?"

Starting with his arrival in Kausambi, the physician detailed all that had transpired in the palace of King Chandravardhan — his struggle to talk about the real purpose behind his visit, his treatment of Chandravardhan, the dramatic improvement in the king's condition, his final broaching of the topic of Princess Rukma's marriage and Chandravardhan acceding to declare Prince Shashivardhan the next king of Vatsa.

"So Harihara gets what he wanted — a king for a son-in-law." Amara Simha scowled, his elbows on the table, interlocked fingers grappling with one another in displeasure. "The fool had better behave now and stop trying to make friends with Shoorasena."

"We must send a messenger to Heheya promptly, informing King Harihara of King Chandravardhan's decision to name Shashivardhan his successor," said Vikramaditya.

"There is no need," said Dhanavantri. "Messengers from Kausambi have already been dispatched to King Harihara's court, letting him know of the succession and accepting Princess Rukma as the future queen of Vatsa."

"So, the alliance of Sindhuvarta's kingdoms stays intact," Varahamihira sighed. "One piece of good news we've heard lately. Well, two actually…" With a small smile, he looked across at the physician. "This curing of Chandravardhan — sounds like you discovered a magical touch yourself."

"Indeed, despite your rather limited talents, you seem to have come good at last." His tone cheery and playful like old, Amara Simha turned to Dhanavantri, poking the physician in the ribs. Laughter bubbled around the room, as this time, the humour caught and spread. Even the shadows seemed to unravel and scatter. "Hell," Amara Simha grinned, "without even trying, we may have found a replacement for the Healer. But seriously, how did you do it?"

"I don't know if I played a part at all," Dhanavantri shucked his fat shoulders, sobering up. "Chandravardhan's physicians had been treating him ever since he fell ill, so it's quite possible it is *their* efforts that brought about his recovery. I might have just been there at the right time."

"Stop it," Amara Simha admonished. "Humility doesn't suit you one bit."

"I'm not being humble," the physician protested earnestly as laughter again rolled around the room. "I really don't know if I've acquired a healing touch or something."

Varahamihira nodded his head sagely. "We'll see, we'll see."

"I presume you met Councilor Yashobhavi in Kausambi?"

The samrat's tone, coupled with the sudden change of subject, caught the councilors' attention.

"I did," answered Dhanavantri.

"What was your impression of him? Did anything — his behaviour, or something he said — strike you as... *strange*? Anything to do with Shashivardhan?"

"*Strange?*" The physician let the word roll in his mouth, savouring it. At last he shook his head. "Not that I can recall. But why, Samrat?"

Observing the five faces turned towards him expectantly, Vikramaditya took a deep breath. "Because, if my dear sister is to be believed, Yashobhavi is of the opinion that Ghatakarpara, and not Shashivardhan, should be crowned the next king of Vatsa."

For a few moments, the silence in the chamber was absolute.

"Pralupi told you this in as many words?" Amara Simha shook his head in disbelief.

Vikramaditya nodded. Composing his thoughts, the samrat detailed Pralupi's obsession with having her son succeed to Vatsa's throne. He revealed his encounter with Pralupi after the *rajasuya yajna*, when she had first urged him to arm-twist Chandravardhan into making Ghatakarpara the next king.

"I told her I wouldn't do it, and I thought that was the end of it. But she was back some days ago — the morning Kalidasa left us, incidentally — and she wouldn't take no for an answer. She insisted Shashivardhan was unfit to rule Vatsa and argued that King Chandravardhan's council was of the same opinion. I was quite taken aback and asked her for names of these so-called councilors. I assumed she was bluffing, but she named Yashobhavi."

"Only him?" asked Amara Simha.

The samrat nodded. "For now. Maybe there are others, though."

"What do we make of this?" asked Varahamihira, looking at the physician.

"I don't know," Dhanavantri replied, trying to remember everything he could from his trip to Kausambi. "Yashobhavi was angry at Harihara for trying to dictate the terms of Rukma's marriage to Vatsa, but that's natural, given his loyalty to Chandravardhan. In fact, Yashobhavi's loyalty has always been exemplary, so I find it hard to believe Pralupi."

"As do I," Amara Simha agreed.

"In which case, was Pralupi bluffing? She is quite capable of it..." the king pondered, stroking his newly grown beard. "But somehow, I got the sense she wasn't."

"Is she still in Ujjayini?" The physician looked at the samrat, who nodded. "Perhaps, then, you could probe a bit more..."

"I am in no mind to bring the subject of Ghatakarpara and Vatsa's throne up with Pralupi and get her started again," the king passed a weary hand over his face. "I have enough to deal with without adding to my troubles." Shaking his head and pushing the matter aside, he picked up the scroll instead.

"There is one more thing I have been meaning to share with you — this." He rapped the scroll lightly on the table. "It is really the Mother Oracle's idea." In a few short strokes, Vikramaditya outlined the oracle's suggestion that they reach out to the danavas of the Dandaka Forest for assistance.

"The danavas exist?" Amara Simha looked around dubiously. "And assuming they do, would they even help us?"

"The Mother Oracle says they exist. Whether they would help us — we won't know unless we ask them."

"How are we going to find them?" Kshapanaka wondered.

"With this, I'm hoping," the king waved the scroll, then placed it in Amara Simha's outstretched hand. "This will go to all the governors of our provinces. It is an announcement that town criers will carry all over Avanti — to every little village, every tiny hamlet, every garrison and every outpost. The palace is offering a reward and full amnesty to anyone who can prove that he or she escaped from the Forest of the Exiles and returned to Sindhuvarta. The palace is also offering a reward to anyone who can provide reliable information on convicts who escaped the Dandaka Forest and are now residing in Sindhuvarta."

"A hundred gold coins as reward?" Amara Simha exclaimed, reading from the scroll. "People would lie for that sort of money. How can we verify the claims once they start coming in?"

"You haven't read the whole thing."

The brawny councilor looked back at the scroll. "Ah, yes. It says here... any person or persons found guilty of providing false information to the palace will straightaway be exiled to the Dandaka Forest." He grinned with satisfaction. "That should keep anyone from lying."

"And if we find the person we are looking for, we will get

him or her to lead us into the Dandaka, in search of the danava capital of Janasthana," Varahamihira smiled at the ingenuity of the plan. "Of course, we make no mention of that in this announcement."

"That might keep them from telling the *truth*," Dhanavantri chuckled. Pushing himself away from the table, he looked around. "If there is nothing else of import, I would like to be excused. I wish to see the people of Ujjayini with Kunjala. I might be able to bring them some relief."

The councilors all rose from their seats, but Vikramaditya motioned Shanku to stay back. When they were alone, the king considered Shanku for a moment. "I didn't get an opportunity to speak to you earlier, but... didn't he ask you to go with him?"

Shanku looked down at her hands clenched in her lap. Looking back up, she nodded.

"I would have been surprised if he hadn't." The samrat gazed thoughtfully out of the window. "At least there was something of Avanti that still held a place in his heart."

Rising from his chair, Vikramaditya came around to Shanku, who got to her feet. The king stared into the girl's face, his eyes gentle yet weighed down with care. "You and I suffer more," he said, "because *we* have lost more. We have lost a part of ourselves that we loved. As a consequence, it falls on us to protect everyone else from what we have loved and lost. We have to be braver than the others should the need arise. We have to be crueller — on ourselves and on what we loved."

Shanku nodded, swallowing the lump that had mysteriously formed in her throat, not trusting herself to speak.

"I want you to ask the Mother Oracle to read every sign coming from the Great Desert. I want her to follow Kalidasa if she can; watch him, decipher every movement of his. Most importantly, I want her to let us know the moment she gets a hint that Kalidasa is on the move..."

The samrat paused, then completed his words.

"...marching with the Huna army against Avanti."

* * *

King Harihara rolled up the scroll and cast it down on the table, where it landed with a muffled clatter and unrolled partially. Some of its contents were revealed again, as if mocking his predicament, and the king leaned back in his chair and considered the scroll with distaste, his left cheek cupped in his left palm.

How quickly things switched from good to bad, he thought morosely. When he had retired to bed the previous night, he had been in high spirits, ecstatic at having received a courtier from Vatsa bearing a message from King Chandravardhan, seeking Rukma's hand for the king-in-waiting, Prince Shashivardhan. Vetala Bhatta had been true to his word and had brokered the deal, and before long, Rukma would be queen of Vatsa. The prospect had happily interfered with his sleep, and Harihara had been up before daybreak, walking the palace orchards, admiring the marigolds and sniffing at the jasmine, when a guard had announced the return of his messengers from Girivraja.

"A reply from King Shoorasena, your honour," one of the messengers had said, extending a scroll as the first rays of the sun set the tops of the orchard's tallest trees on fire.

Propping himself up wearily, Harihara drew the scroll to him and unfurled it. He knew nothing could have changed in its contents, yet a part of him wanted to believe he had misinterpreted Shoorasena's missive, and that re-reading it would somehow alter the meaning of things.

The scroll was the one he had originally sent Shoorasena, with his submission to accept Rukma as his wife. The submission, richly worded and exquisitely calligraphed, occupied most of the space on the piece of canvas, but Shoorasena had found enough space at the bottom to scrawl a terse reply: 'The wisdom of your choice is appreciated. I accept.' Stamped below was the royal seal of Magadha, a hawk in flight, the upward sweep of its wings ending in flames. Harihara couldn't help noticing the flames, a recent addition to Magadha's old hawk ensign, obviously put in after Shoorasena's coronation and in keeping with the kingdom's newly acquired martial attitude.

I accept. There was no ambiguity in Shoorasena's words.

It was not as if Harihara had not feared that things would come to such a pass. Even as he had savoured Chandravardhan's invitation seeking Rukma as his daughter-in-law, the shadow of Shoorasena had hovered nearby. Yet, the king had been in denial, irrationally convincing himself he had no cause for worry — Shoorasena would be busy in Vanga and the message would somehow get lost and fail to reach him until it was too late; Shoorasena would simply ignore his offer; Shoorasena would decline to accept Rukma's hand... All perfectly honourable exits, but the doors had been slammed on them with just two words.

I accept.

Harihara rubbed a hand over his tired eyes. Shoorasena had accepted. Chandravardhan had also accepted. As an outcome, he was stuck between Vikramaditya and Shoorasena, two powerful kings. One, the established samrat of Sindhuvarta. The other, a challenger, an emerging champion with burning ambitions. Both men who could crush him and Heheya into the dust. He would have to choose between them now.

Avanti was an immediate neighbour, thus a more direct threat. Avanti could hurt him with brute military force as well as through all sorts of economic sanctions and embargoes. Yet, Vikramaditya was a just and considerate man, and there were limits to the misery he would inflict on Heheya's innocent subjects. Moreover, Vikramaditya had other headaches at this time. Magadha, on the other hand, was far away, but all evidence suggested that Shoorasena was ruthless and vindictive, definitely not someone to be crossed. Siddhasena had already paid the price, and if he could kill his own father... Harihara shuddered. Moreover, Magadha was on the rise, and who was to say what the equation of power in Sindhuvarta would be in a few years? Avanti was being hammered by the devas and asuras; it was anybody's guess how long Vikramaditya could withstand the onslaught before caving in. Whereas Shoorasena was already expanding his borders and Magadha might cease to be all that distant from Heheya. What would a slighted king nursing a deep grudge do then? Harihara had no illusions about how far Shoorasena would go to exact revenge upon an enemy — he would raze Mahishmati to the ground at the first available opportunity.

Avanti or Magadha. It was a tough call. And there was no point in seeking his wife's counsel; Sumayanti had made her choice clear the day she had secretly sent her messenger to Vikramaditya's court. But for her interference, matters would never have come to such a head, Harihara thought bitterly. He dared not mention it to her, of course. Sumayanti would only scoff at him for having invited the crisis through his foolish act of sending messengers to Girivraja...

With a push that sent the scroll sliding halfway across the table, Harihara leaned an elbow on the table and clutched his forehead in anxiety.

* * *

King Bhoomipala had summoned only three of his most trusted courtiers to the private meeting, and it was to these three that he now turned, crossing his arms across his chest and leaning against the window that offered an unobstructed view of the Ajiravati, flowing sedately less than half a mile away. The king assessed the three men — the most seasoned veterans of war and diplomacy in Kosala, behind only Pallavan in calibre and experience — and couldn't help thinking that one of them would definitely stand to gain in rank and esteem if Pallavan failed to make it back from Girivraja alive.

Wondering if similar thoughts had crossed the three courtiers' minds, Bhoomipala raised his eyebrows at them. "You have heard the terms set forth by Magadha for Pallavan's release. What, in your opinions, should we do?"

"Whatever we do, we cannot let any harm befall Councilor Pallavan," said Kadru, the youngest of the three, a slightly built man with ears that stood out sharply from both sides of his head.

Bhoomipala watched the other two courtiers nodding their agreement. Stroking his salt-and-pepper beard, he said, "That drastically narrows down our options to one — giving into Shoorasena's demand and handing Gajaketu over to him." The idea seemed to make him uncomfortable, and he turned to look out of the window. In the streets below, he could see the citizens of Sravasti going about their business, blissfully unaware of the crisis brewing in the palace. "How are we ever going to explain this to our allies?" he sighed hopelessly.

"We could explore a way of helping Pallavan escape."

The king didn't need to turn around to know who had spoken – Adheepa, the oldest of the lot, a gruff general with Kosala's army. "We can send in a small, undercover team of soldiers to plan and execute the breakout. Of course, we will need assistance from within Magadha as well, but that is never hard to come by if the bribe offered is large enough."

"What if the plan fails?" Bhoomipala swung back to face the courtiers. "What if we find no one willing to be bribed out of fear or loyalty to Shoorasena? What if the persons we approach double-cross and expose us? What if our soldiers are able to break into wherever they have confined Pallavan, but are unable to reach him and are instead caught by Magadhan troops? What would happen to Pallavan then?"

The barrage of questions took the general aback. "We... but it can also work if planned out in meticulous detail," he mumbled defensively.

"How long would this meticulous planning take?" the king asked. "The scouting out of the prison that holds Pallavan, the recruitment of Magadhans willing to accept our bribe in return of favours, all of it?"

"Twenty days... maybe a month," Adheepa replied, suddenly unsure of himself.

"We don't have that kind of time," Bhoomipala threw his hands wide open in despair. "Shoorasena has set an ultimatum of four days for the exchange. There is an envoy from Magadha waiting downstairs. The envoy will leave this evening, and we have to have our answer ready by then."

The four men settled into a glum silence as they contemplated the extremely slender set of choices at their disposal. "A full-scale armed conflict with Magadha is out of the question, isn't it?" asked the third councilor, Kirtana, a thickset man with a broken nose.

"Absolutely," the king said. "We are severely short on troops, and we have already lent the cream of our warriors to Matsya. We can't look to Vatsa for help either — most of their men are guarding the frontier as well." He gave a rueful shake of his head. "It would be foolhardy to wage war with a full-strength Magadhan army. Our troops will be beaten senseless before they can free their swords from their scabbards."

"If we can buy time from Magadha, we can plan the breakout," said the general, displaying an uncharacteristic oafishness that irked Bhoomipala.

"We can't buy time because Shoorasena is clever enough to see it as a delaying tactic," he snapped.

"And even if we do succeed in springing Pallavan from prison, he and our men will still be in the heart of Magadha, miles away from the border," reasoned Kadru. "The probability of them being caught again is very high. It's not a risk worth taking."

Bhoomipala's face took on a faraway, contemplative expression as he heard the courtier out. For a full minute, he stood immersed in thought, plotting the way forward. Finally, with a sigh and a slow shake of his head, he turned to the courtiers, who were looking to him for a verdict.

"We don't have much choice," he shrugged. Addressing Kadru, he said, "Will you ask one of the guards outside to bring the Magadhan envoy to us?"

Not more than a couple of minutes had passed before the door opened and the guard ushered the envoy in. The envoy bowed to Bhoomipala and stood quietly, waiting for the king to speak.

"We have a message for your king," Bhoomipala said, drawing up his short, stocky frame to muster as much authority as he could. "We are prepared to trade the musician Gajaketu for Councilor Pallavan's freedom. We also accept the terms of the exchange as laid out by Magadha. Four days from now, we will hand Gajaketu over to you. You will simultaneously release our councilor, unharmed. The exchange will happen at the same time — one hand gives, the other hand takes. It will be a fair exchange — neither party will resort to any force or intimidation, and both sides will honour their word." The king paused to assess the messenger. "Have we both understood the terms correctly?"

"Yes, your honour," the envoy gave another stiff bow. "We have."

* * *

"What do you mean he is not to be found?"

Commander Atulyateja's glare switched between the three soldiers of the Frontier Guard lined up in front of him, before finally settling on the young lieutenant standing in the middle.

"He is the prince of Avanti," the garrison commander's tone was flat, as if weary of stating the obvious. "People recognize him. Somebody is bound to have seen him. *Somebody* would know where he is."

The lieutenant shifted on his feet and gave a small shrug. "We asked," he said, looking at the men flanking him. Both soldiers nodded vehemently. "No one has seen the prince since morning. Actually," he hesitated, "since... yesterday afternoon."

"Wha—"Atulyateja stared at the lieutenant in bewilderment. "And... you tell me *now*?" His voice exploded in the narrow confines of his office inside the garrison. "If I hadn't sent word asking to meet him, I wouldn't even have known, right? Forget about me, even *you* wouldn't have known!"

The lieutenant dropped his eyes. "We didn't... realize..."

"You didn't realize *what*?" Atulyateja thundered. "Are you or are you not in charge of the prince's security detail, lieutenant?"

"I... we... we always go with the prince when he visits the command centres and outposts along the frontier, sir," the lieutenant mumbled. "Here, inside the garrison... we didn't think it was necessary..."

As the soldier trailed off lamely, Atulyateja took a deep breath to keep himself from snapping at the man. The lieutenant was right, he realized. There was no compelling reason to offer Ghatakarpara security — or have someone with him at all times — as long as he was in Udaypuri. What could happen to the prince inside a well-guarded garrison in a well-populated garrison town? Yet, his friend was nowhere to be found.

"When was the last time anyone saw him?"

"The prince led an inspection of a regiment of Frontier Guardsmen yesterday afternoon," one of the soldiers offered. Looking out of the window to estimate the time of day, he added, "About this time, or maybe an hour later."

"Where is the soldier who was appointed to take care of the prince's needs?" Atulyateja asked, suddenly remembering. "He should have realized something was amiss. Why didn't he report the matter to someone?"

"He was taken off that duty on the prince's orders, commander." Seeing Atulyateja's eyebrows rise, the lieutenant added, "The prince insisted he didn't want any soldiers being in his attendance all the time. He said the garrison and the kingdom would be better served by having all soldiers focus on training for battle instead."

The garrison commander puffed his cheeks and blew a stream of air in exasperation. Running his fingers through his hair, he looked out of the window and thought of Ghatakarpara with pride. Deciding to embrace the life of a soldier at the frontier, the prince had dispensed with all the trappings of comfort that palace life provided. It showed remarkable commitment on Ghatakarpara's part, and under different circumstances, Atulyateja would have been overjoyed at his friend's transformation. Now, however, the prince's decision would prove to be a hindrance in finding him.

"The prince was last seen inspecting the Frontier Guard around this time, right?" he asked, making sure.

"Actually, he was last seen leaving the garrison by the sentry at the gate, commander," the other soldier replied. "This was after the inspection, much later in the afternoon."

"On horseback?" asked Atulyateja.

"No, on foot."

The garrison commander's eyes narrowed shrewdly. "Any idea where he was going?"

"No, sir. But he often goes out in the evenings. Probably for a walk. He always returns a little after sunset."

"And he wasn't seen coming back yesterday? That should have alerted the sentry."

"There was a change of guard at sunset yesterday, earlier than usual," the lieutenant said. "Therefore, no one picked up on the fact that the prince hadn't returned."

"And we learn all this now, almost a day after the prince has disappeared?" Atulyateja stared at the three guardsmen, who hung their heads. "No one needed the prince for anything all morning? No one was curious about his absence? It struck no one to check whether the prince was here or not?"

The soldiers shifted uncomfortably.

"We're absolutely certain he isn't in the garrison?" When the men nodded, Atulyateja pulled himself erect. "You may go, but keep yourselves handy. I might need you once I have seen the governor."

The young commander literally hurtled down the dark, twisting stairway and jogged across the garrison ground to get to the governor's office at the other end of the fort. His head was full of misgivings for having agreed to go north to Madhyamika, leaving Ghatakarpara all by himself in Udaypuri, so he hardly noticed his men staring after him in surprise. Reaching Satyaveda's room, he almost cannoned into the governor who was on the verge of leaving.

"Whoa, commander! Watch where you're going." Satyaveda's hooked nose wrinkled in disapproval as he stared down at Atulyateja.

"My deepest apologies, Governor," Atulyateja smoothed his tunic and ran a finger over his clipped moustache. "But there is something urgent you need to know."

"Can't it wait until tomorrow morning?" the governor asked, adjusting the official turban on his head. "And when did you come from Madhyamika?"

"Around noon. The thing is Prince Ghatakarpara is missing."

Seated across the governor's table, the garrison commander updated Satyaveda on all that he had learned about the young councilor's disappearance. Satyaveda drummed his fingers on the edge of the table as he listened, his eyes thoughtful, his right leg shaking anxiously under the table.

"He left on foot, which means he didn't intend going very far," Atulyateja pointed out in conclusion. "Without a mount, he couldn't have gone far, even if he intended to. And anyway, he always returns to the garrison around sundown, which shows he doesn't go far."

"You are right," the governor agreed in his high, nasal voice. "But if he didn't go far, where has he vanished?"

"That is why I have come to you."

"Eh?" Satyaveda jerked backwards, blinking in alarm. "Me? Why me?"

"I intend to launch a full-fledged search for the prince, Governor," Atulyateja said in a patient tone. "For that, I need to marshal men from the Frontier Guard as well as the local militia. I need your permission to pull troops and press them into the search."

"Of course, of course, of course," Satyaveda rocked back and forth, and Atulyateja got the impression the man was secretly relieved about something. "Of course, yes."

"Do I have your permission?" the commander enquired again.

"Permission... yes, mmm..." Satyaveda tapped his fingertips, looking thoughtful. He then leaned forward with a frown. "You know, I am not so sure..."

"Sure about what, Governor?" Atulyateja looked irritably across the table. "Whether the prince is missing, or whether we should launch a search?"

"*Both*, actually."

As the garrison commander blinked in disbelief, Satyaveda leaned his forearms on the table, clasped his hands and bent forward.

"You mentioned the fact that he goes out often." The governor's voice almost dropped to a conspiratorial whisper. "Perhaps he has found a reason to go out often."

"What reason?"

"He is a young man, used to the luxuries of the palace, commander. There are hungers that are easily and discreetly satisfied in the palace, but here... not so easily or discreetly. Maybe he has found a place hereabouts that gives him what he craves."

"Pardon me, Governor, but I don't understand a word of what you're saying," the younger man struggled to keep the heat and irritation from his voice.

"Women, my friend, women."

"Oh," said Atulyateja, finally getting it. "No, I know Ghatakarpara. He is not like that."

"Please," Satyaveda gave the commander a pitying look. "You and I, *commoners*, we can't even pretend to understand what members of a palace household are like." Leaning even closer, he said, "Look at it reasonably. He goes on foot. Why? Because he doesn't want the horse to be seen and identified as one belonging to him. He goes almost every day, but returns at sundown. Why? He's courting this woman, that's all. Then, one night they decide..." Satyaveda sat back and rubbed his hands in glee.

Atulyateja knew this didn't sound like his friend, but as the governor had pointed out, who was to say — "But... why hasn't he returned so far?"

"Sometimes, you go to satisfy a craving only to realize your appetite has redoubled. Some women are like that. My point is, while we are assuming the prince is missing, perhaps he just doesn't want to be found."

Atulyateja frowned, a storm of indecision brewing and eddying in his head. "But what if... he is in some danger? Every moment of delay can have irreparable consequences. We are dealing with Avanti's royalty here, a scion of the Aditya dynasty."

"I agree with you. But what if *I* am right, and we launch a search and he is found under questionable circumstances, in a tryst with a woman of questionable character? Think of the scandal that will ensue. It's the king's own nephew we're talking about. It would stink all the way from here to Ujjayini, no?"

Atulyateja heaved a huge sigh. In both instances, the outcome would be terrible, he realized. "So, what do we *do*?" he asked. "We can't just sit here..."

"I'll tell you," Satyaveda pressed the air in front of him down with his palms, urging calm. "Let us wait until tomorrow morning. If he doesn't show up by then, you have my permission to rope in men from the Frontier Guard and the militia to start a search. Happy?"

The garrison commander thought about it for a moment, then nodded. He had resigned himself to waiting, but no, he was not happy.

Ga'ur Thra'aKha

The marble steps underfoot were cool to the touch and in sharp contrast to the sun-scorched stones of the open courtyard that Ushantha had hobbled across to get to the other wing of the house. She now laboured up the stairs, one hand supporting her arthritic knee, wincing mildly with every step, her ears tuned to the melancholic strains of the *rudra veena* coming from above. Not stopping to catch her breath on the landing, she followed the music to a broad and shady verandah, where Vararuchi sat on a straw mat, plucking at the *veena*'s strings.

The sight of her son seated with his eyes closed, enraptured by the beauty of his own creation, brought a sad smile to Ushantha's kindly face. Leaning against the jamb, she watched quietly as Vararuchi's fingers skimmed along the frets, coaxing melody out of bamboo, wood, brass and string, and for a moment, she found it hard to believe that there was a mighty storm enclosed in his chest — one that he had kept hidden from her for the three days he had been here. Even now, he seemed at peace, and Ushantha realized she would never have got an inkling of Vararuchi's distress had her maid's husband not returned from his weekly visit to Ujjayini's cattle market with an account that had rattled her and caused her to miss her afternoon siesta.

He ordered the killing of Councilor Kalidasa's father and sister.

"What is the matter, mother?"

Ushantha blinked and realized that the music had stopped. Her eyes focused on her son's concerned face.

"Why aren't you resting, mother?" Vararuchi set the *rudra veena* aside and stood up.

"I wanted to see you," Ushantha replied, limping onto the verandah.

"You should have sent for me." Vararuchi hurried over, took her hand and led her gently to a low seat. "You mustn't strain your joints by climbing stairs, mother."

"I know."

Vararuchi nodded — then, perceiving a difference in her tone, he looked at her in puzzlement. "What?"

"I know," Ushantha repeated. The pause stretched for three heartbeats. "About what happened so many years ago... the reason you are here."

"Mother..."

The word escaped her son's lips in a choked, anguished cry. Ushantha reached out, and Vararuchi grabbed her hand like a drowning man, clutching it tight. The resilience of so many days gave way to a sparkle of hot tears that splashed down his cheeks.

"I didn't know how to tell you, mother," he mumbled, as Ushantha drew him down and sat him beside her. He instantly put his arms around her, placed his head on her shoulder and wept.

"It is alright, my son," Ushantha patted Vararuchi's head.

She heard her own voice waver with grief and shock. "I don't judge you for what happened."

The sun had dropped halfway to the horizon when mother and son descended the stairs and made their way to a broad, wooden swing that occupied the centre of a portico situated to the east. Sitting side by side in the shadow thrown by the house, they gazed at the paddy fields, where ribbons of the wind cut rippling paths in many shades of green, and gaunt egrets hunted for morsels on stiff, twiggy legs. A cooling breeze helped dry the tears on their cheeks and revived conversation.

"Were you ashamed of what you had done? Is that why you hesitated to tell me?" Ushantha asked.

"No..." Vararuchi pondered the question a while and shook his head with certainty. "No. I am not ashamed. It was war, mother. The demands of war may look unreasonable in times of peace, but the willingness to meet those demands determines whether one ends up victorious or vanquished."

"Then why didn't you say something? You spoke of Ahi, you told me about the defence of Dvarka against the Huna warships... but not *one* mention of this."

"I wanted to keep you from the hurt, mother. I didn't want it to touch you, I didn't want it sullying the beauty of this place."

"Hurt?" Ushantha peered into her son's face. "I don't understand."

"The hurt of rejection, mother. Of being misunderstood by your very own, of realizing that no matter how selfless your motivations are, your decisions will be questioned and your actions will be judged. The pariah's hurt."

Hearing the bitterness creep slowly into Vararuchi's voice, Ushantha paled. "Who has misunderstood you, son?"

There was no immediate response from Vararuchi. Instead, he stared across the fields with flinty eyes, as if seeking to pierce the gathering curtains of haze and darkness

to the east and narrow the distance, so that he could see all
the way to Ujjayini. Without taking his eyes off the faraway
horizon, he let out a sigh that sounded to Ushantha like the
dying of hope.

"You know that I hated the palace, didn't you?" Vararuchi
glanced sideways at his mother. "And that the palace hated me
back with equal vehemence?"

"I guessed it was difficult for you there because you were
my son," Ushantha gave a sad shrug.

"It was more than difficult. I cannot put the Queen
Mother's dislike for me in words. There wasn't much she could
do because father wished me to be around, but she missed no
opportunity to snub me, put me in my place. And Pralupi... I
never even existed for her." Vararuchi chuckled mirthlessly. "I
can't remember her ever saying more than two sentences to me
at a stretch. It was utter misery, being with the two of them.
Thankfully, Pralupi married Himavardhan and went away to
Kausambi, but no such luck with the Queen Mother."

Ushantha's face crinkled with dismay. She put a comforting
hand on Vararuchi's arm. "You never told me it was so bad."

"Father wanted me in the palace and there was no
escaping that, and telling you would only have upset you,"
Vararuchi shrugged.

"You could have at least told your father."

"You forget that the barbarians had arrived, mother. Father
was hardly ever there. He was either fighting off the invaders
or was away building alliances." Vararuchi paused to gather
his thoughts. "The Queen Mother's hatred for me got worse
after father's death. I think she worried that I wouldn't give up
the throne for Vikrama. That's why I volunteered to lead the
campaigns to drive out the barbarians — anything to keep me
from the palace and that woman. Fortunately, Vikramaditya
lived up to his promise and grew into a fine young man. He
was the reason I returned to the palace and agreed to become a

councilor. He treated me with the love and respect I had never had before. He brought light to a place I always associated with darkness."

Despite the shadows of dusk falling on him, Ushantha saw her son's face turn sour.

"I gave Vikramaditya everything I had in return — my love, my loyalty, even my life. Yet, he now sides with Kalidasa, accusing me of committing atrocities on the Hunas and claiming innocent lives. I..." his voice shook with emotion. "*I*, who fought to free Avanti and Sindhuvarta from the brutality of the barbarians, am being told that *I* was wrong in killing them, that I should have shown mercy to the merciless. Kalidasa proclaims himself a Huna and walks out after issuing a challenge to Avanti, and he is allowed to go free. Whereas *I*, who have stood by Avanti in its darkest hour, am expected to feel sorry for what I did to liberate my kingdom from Huna occupation. Where is the justice in this, mother?"

"Is it true that Kalidasa has left Avanti to join the Hunas?"

"Riders and soldiers of the Imperial Army have spotted him heading west. Where else could he be going but back to his blood brothers? It is plain as daylight, yet the instructions are clear that he should not be stopped. Why? Because, apparently, *he* is the wronged one here."

In his agitation, Vararuchi stood up and started pacing the portico. The darkness made it hard for Ushantha to discern his features, but the quiver in his voice revealed his mental turmoil.

"This is insanity! If Kalidasa crosses over to the Hunas, they will have all the information they need to strike and cripple us. That man is a threat to us, but tears are shed for him while I am being made to feel guilty. *That* is what hurts, mother. This blind love of Vikramaditya's for Kalidasa — and his blind disregard of all that I, his own blood, have done for him and Avanti."

He stopped pacing abruptly and faced his mother. "Am I right in my thinking?" he asked.

"I understand how you feel about this," Ushantha spoke slowly, piecing her thoughts together. "Your sense of betrayal is natural, especially after all that you have done for Avanti. Yet, I also understand Vikrama's predicament. Those who died that day were the kin of his dearest friend, killed by a representative of the throne. If you are driven by a deep sense of loyalty, Vikrama is compelled by an overriding desire for fairness."

"Are you saying what I did twenty years ago was unfair to Kalidasa, and he is justified in carrying the grudge?" Vararuchi's tone was challenging.

Ushantha rose and took the two intervening steps to her son. Taking his right hand, she clasped it and brought it to her lips, kissing it gently. A housemaid emerged from a distant doorway bearing a lamp, and its glow fell on mother and son, holding hands and looking deep into one another's eyes.

"What is justified and what isn't are points of view. You did what you thought was right and justifiable, and no matter how much we debate it, what happened cannot be undone now. Kalidasa is a consequence of what happened that day, and he cannot be undone either. What we need to remember is this, son," Ushantha nodded sagely. "If we sow seeds of blood, we must be prepared to reap a harvest of swords. Kalidasa is the bitter harvest that Avanti must now be prepared to reap."

* * *

His breath catching in his throat, his fleshy bosom heaving with anxiety and the effort of walking quickly, Aatreya shuffled and stumbled through the thick stalks of corn. Big corn leaves scraped and clutched at him, their rustling loud in his ears, and he worried the sound would carry back to the house and someone — a servant or his wife or even Aparupa — would come looking. And they would discover...

Blanking the thought from his mind, the fat merchant pushed on towards the back gate of the small plantation that was an extension of the kitchen garden. He had never been able to fathom why his wife insisted on a corn patch when she could have grown anything there, but right now, he was grateful for it as it gave him much-needed cover.

Meet me at the back gate of your house after sunset.

Scrawled on a scrap of palm leaf, the message had been handed earlier that evening to one of the bullock-cart drivers in his employ, along with strict instructions that it be given to Aatreya without delay. Thankfully, the cartman couldn't read, nor did he recognize the person who had given him the palm leaf. But Aatreya had known instantly, and he had been cursing ever since, hating the fact that the meeting was so close to his home.

Reaching the back gate, the merchant looked right and left but saw no one. He pushed the gate open and stepped into the small backroad that led to the faraway millet fields, but the road was vacant. But for the chirping of crickets, the night was silent. Deciding that the meeting must have been cancelled — and thankful for it — Aatreya was about to turn back when a figure stepped out from behind a *salmali* tree.

Aatreya didn't need light to tell that it was Chirayu, the governor's lackey.

"I have made it clear that I don't want to meet anywhere near the house," he hissed at the lackey, even as he threw a stealthy glance over his shoulder. "Why this then? A meeting with the governor is scheduled for tomorrow — couldn't this have waited?"

"I had the choice of meeting you here, now, or at your shop in the market, earlier in the evening," Chirayu's tone was mocking, bullying. "More people would have seen us together there. Would you have wanted that?"

"What do you want?" Aatreya asked petulantly.

"They have discovered the prince is missing."

"So?" the merchant shrugged. "They would have, sooner or later."

"They are launching a hunt for him tomorrow morning. The governor has managed to buy time until daybreak, but he cannot stall after that without attracting suspicion."

Chirayu took a step closer, so that he was just a hand's breadth away from Aatreya.

"Tell your friends from across the mountains to move fast. They only have tonight to take the prince as far away from Udaypuri as possible."

"What do you mean *your* friends?" Aatreya sounded resentful at the lackey's apparent lack of courtesy. "They aren't just *my* friends. They are *your* friends too... *and* friends with the man you serve so loyally. Let's not forget that."

Chirayu was silent for a moment. When he spoke, it was as if he hadn't heard the merchant at all. "Commander Atulyateja is the prince's friend. He will look behind every tree and under every rock. Tell your friends they have tonight to take the prince into the mountains — ideally, *over* the mountains and into the Marusthali."

The lackey spun on his heel and walked off, darkness swallowing him like a ravenous beast. Aatreya stood in the middle of the road, suddenly feeling all alone.

* * *

I have convinced the Samrat to take me to the meadow. We ride there in the morning.

Kshapanaka remembered the eagerness in Vishakha's voice, her eyes sparkling in triumph as she had looked up from the pillow that night before her fall — the *second* one. Kshapanaka had dropped by to see how her sister was faring, and the queen had spoken of little else in her excitement at revisiting the meadow. And, despite her deep reservations, Kshapanaka had smiled in encouragement, knowing how desperate Vishakha was to recollect her past — especially the bits linked to Vikramaditya.

But now, seeing her sister lying listlessly on the same pillow, eyes dead to everything around her, Kshapanaka felt a familiar swell of anger at herself. *Why, why, why*, a voice in her head screamed critically, *why didn't you dissuade her that night, tell her that going back there was a terrible idea? Why didn't you put a stop to the foolishness when you knew no good would come of it?*

Leaning forward, the young councilor ran her palm over Vishakha's brow and stroked her head, patting down a stray strand of hair. The day had barely dawned, but the queen had already been bathed and attended to by the matron and the maids in whose care she had been placed again. Both maids were still hovering close by — one was dicing mangoes and papaya for Vishakha's first meal of the day, the other was preparing to file the queen's nails — and it was to keep them from noticing the tears that Kshapanaka bent and kissed her sister's forehead.

Why, why, why, the voice in her head suddenly — irrationally — trained its rant at the samrat. *Why did* you *have to listen to her and take her to the meadow? You* could have *refused. You are the king, after all. Why did you indulge her?*

"Do you wish to feed the Queen, your honour?"

Kshapanaka blinked and discreetly brushed a tear clinging to her eyelashes. Sitting erect, she accepted the bowl of fruit from the maid.

Vishakha's dramatic recovery under the Healer's supervision had ushered a period of relief and joy, the likes of which

Kshapanaka had not experienced for a very long time. One by one, the sisters had rediscovered the bonds that had held them close since their childhood in Nishada, and these bonds had been reinforced in the course of umpteen conversations as Vishakha pieced together her past. They had almost come all the way, closed nearly every gap in Vishakha's memory... and then, suddenly...

Why, the voice demanded, strident, accusing, *why did you stop the Healer from taking a look at her? What harm would it have done? It's not as if you had asked a favour of him — it was the Healer who offered. The Healer might have been able to revive her — but no, you wouldn't have it. Adamant. Stubborn. Insisting it would be incorrect...*

Conscious that her hands were shaking uncontrollably, Kshapanaka set the bowl aside. Clearing her throat, she addressed the maid, "I just remembered something. I have to go." Rising abruptly, she was halfway to the door when she looked back. "Make sure the Queen eats well."

Striding down the palace galleries, the councilor reached her room, where she stopped just long enough to grab her bow and quiver, which held three stout arrows. Slinging the quiver onto her back and retracing her steps, Kshapanaka felt the hot flush of anger on her cheeks and realized she was helpless to it. Sorrow, rage and frustration had been brewing in her for days now, and the concoction was finally on a boil, refusing to yield to reason, refusing to be placated, an amalgamation of emotions that felt like the sizzling of a rebellion in her veins.

...adamant, stubborn, and blinded by your goodness. Insisting on letting him *go, when he should have been restrained and put in the dungeons. He said he was the son of Zho E'rami, chief of the x'sa line of Hunas. He rejected the name Kalidasa for his Huna name. He said he wouldn't serve the throne of Avanti any longer. Yet you let him go, the son of a murdering Huna...*

Kshapanaka traversed the palace causeway and turned in the direction of the royal stables. A bead of sweat trickled past her temple and ran down her cheek, but she hardly noticed it. Not a leaf stirred in the still morning air, and the day promised to be hot and oppressive.

An image of the council chamber formed in her mind's eye as she walked, and she saw the king frown and say, *we will acknowledge things once we have irrefutable evidence of their existence.*

Irrefutable evidence, the voice in her head retorted scornfully. *We will get that when he shows up at the frontier at the head of the barbarian army. His token of gratitude for letting him leave Avanti unharmed.*

"How can I help you, councilor?"

Kshapanaka stared at the young stable boy bowing to her, then glanced around the stable. The place was more or less empty at this hour, and even Keeri, the Warden of the Stables, was nowhere to be seen. The councilor thought that was just as well. She was in no mood to answer any questions that the Warden might have had.

"Saddle my horse," she replied. "The old one."

"The old one, councilor?" The boy scratched his nose in confusion, eyeing the bow held combatively in the woman's grasp with mild concern. "I don't think I know…"

"Follow me."

Kshapanaka brushed past the groom and walked deeper into the stables, past stalls filled with horses on both sides of the aisle. Snorts and whinnies filled the air as she took a twisting route almost to the very end, where she pointed at a big, grey stallion occupying a large, empty stall.

"No one rides that horse, your honour," the boy's tone was uneasy. "I'm told it has quite a reputation."

"It definitely has a reputation," Kshapanaka answered

tersely. The boy was obviously unfamiliar with the stallion's history. "Saddle him up."

In almost no time, Kshapanaka was galloping along Ujjayini's main streets. The day was young, the traffic on the streets thin, so the councilor was able to push her old mount hard. Though the beast had not been ridden much in the two years since Vishakha's first fall, it had been well exercised — and on account of either that or old, unforgotten instincts, it responded well to Kshapanaka's subtle commands. In a few minutes, they had slipped past the shadow of the city's south gate and were on the high road to Mahishmati.

Zho E'rami was leader of the x'sa — the x'sa who murdered your wife's father and mother, Samrat, my father and mother... shrill and furious, the voice in her head rose in pitch, drowning out the smaller, softer whispers cautioning her, urging restraint. *But you turned a blind eye to that and let an offspring of the x'sa leave the palace because he was your friend. Your love for your wife is a lie, Samrat Vikramaditya. Else, you would have allowed the Healer to cure her fully...*

You and I, we must make a visit to Nishada, Vishakha had said one evening, making plans as they had walked along the promenade around the palace lake. It made no difference to her that there was hardly anyone left in the province of Nishada who was related to their father, King Vallabha, or to anyone else in Vallabha's court. The Hunas may have wiped out every member of the royal household, but to Vishakha, a return to Nishada was a return to the childhood she remembered fondly.

Of course, remembering was once again no longer possible for Vishakha...

...and you are responsible for it, the voice was back to censuring her. *For not stopping her from going back to the meadow, for letting her ride your horse...*

Kshapanaka reined in sharply, yanking at the bridle. She had come to a halt on a quiet patch of the road, a small rise with the highway falling away on both sides. A few *kimshuka* trees dotted the rise, while farmland lay to the left and right. The stretch of road was deserted as far as her eyes could see. Dismounting, the councilor strode two dozen paces in the direction of Ujjayini, before turning to survey the horse grimly. The stallion's black eyes were on her, watching her with hopelessness and remorse.

Lifting the bow, the councilor drew an arrow out of her quiver and nocked it in place. Pulling the string slowly back, she sighted down the sturdy shaft, fixing her aim on the horse's silvery coat, at the point just above the beast's forelegs. The horse's heart lay just under the spot she was targeting.

You threw her down in the meadow, the voice directed its ire at the horse. *You, to whom she caused no harm, but to whom you were most unkind. But for you, none of this would have come to pass. You should have been put down that very day, but the Samrat's mercy saved you. No more kindness for you, though, bringer of darkness. Today, you shall pay.*

Kshapanaka pulled the bowstring back, past her right eye, past her temple, past her ear. The bow bent and quivered in her left hand under the strain, the wood creaking in protest.

He didn't ask me to ride on his back. It was my decision, so how can this poor beast be faulted for what happened?

Vishakha's words, addressed to the Warden of the Stables the morning they had both gone to see the stallion, came back to Kshapanaka. She stared down the arrow at the stallion, which was still looking at her regretfully. She wanted justice, but more than that, she wanted revenge. She wanted to settle scores with something, with *anything*. She wanted to kill the horse, but her sister wouldn't let her. And that enraged her and brought fresh tears to her eyes.

With a cry of frustration, she let the arrow fly.

A split-second earlier though, she had shifted her aim in a small arc, so the arrow whizzed past the stallion, burying itself deep in the trunk of one of the *kimshuka* trees growing by the roadside.

Her shoulders drooping, Kshapanaka trudged back to the horse. As she drew near, the beast, as if sensing its life had just been spared, stretched its head and nuzzled her. Throwing her arms around the horse's neck, the councilor buried her face in its yellowing mane and let the pent-up anguish and rage run down her cheeks in torrents.

Because her face was to the horse's coat, Kshapanaka missed the coal-black smear that had appeared on the *kimshuka* where her arrow had struck. She didn't see the stain spread rapidly like an inkblot over the tree's bark, nor did she observe the tree's leaves shrivel, burn and blow away in a sudden gust of wind. The ground around the tree's roots turned dry and collapsed a little, pulling the desiccated trunk down. The tree stood, gnarled, agonized and lopsided, its spindly branches entreating the sky for mercy.

* * *

They had been observing the rider from the moment he had appeared as a discernible speck on the shimmering desert landscape. Of course, as a speck in the distance, there was nothing to tell it was a rider — or that the rider was male — but as the speck had drawn closer and taken form, the details had become plain to the seven horsemen. Judging from where he was coming — east, where the faraway mountains were no more than ghostly outlines in the haze — and the way he drooped on the saddle, it was evident to the horsemen that his ride had been long and exhausting. Even the horse, otherwise a hardy specimen, shambled along, its last drink of water many miles behind it.

"*Gwa'ake?*" Cocking an eyebrow, one of the watchers surveyed his companions.

The men, who had the *hriiz* etched on their foreheads, exchanged uncertain glances even as they watched the approaching rider, their eyes narrowed against the glare. The youngest of the lot, a rough, shaggy-haired boy still in his teens, answered harshly.

"*Iga uzz thra'akh*," he said, his right hand going to the quiver hanging by his saddle, fingers hovering over the feathered arrows. 'Let's kill him.'

The others in the group turned to the horseman who sat at their centre, square and upright on his horse. He sported a straggly, grey beard and looked to be their leader.

"*Eb'a*," the man said, raising his hand to stay the boy.

The Huna patrol waited. Around them, erratic pockets of hot wind kicked up small puffs of dust that collapsed to the desert floor almost immediately. The wind plucked at the cotton shawls that the men had draped over their heads and around their shoulders, making the cloth flap and billow. Their shadows were short and stubby behind them, growing stubbier as noon ascended. Besides the seven horses — eight, if one included the stranger's — not an animal, bird or insect was in sight.

When the rider was within earshot, the leader of the group hailed him. "*Eb'a zuh!*" Then, as if to make himself clear, he switched to slow and heavily accented Avanti. "Stop you!"

Slumped low on the horse's neck, the rider seemed oblivious to the command. The beast kept up its plodding gait, coming nearer and nearer to the Hunas ranged in front, blocking its path.

"*Eb'a zuh*," the leader shouted again, louder. He drew his sword to match tone with action, and the other six men did likewise, unsheathing swords and nocking arrows into bows.

This time, the order registered, and horse and rider came to a fumbling halt. With a degree of effort, the new arrival propped himself up on his saddle, and that was when the

Hunas first sensed the gigantic bulk of the man. Under the linen shawl he wore to shield himself from the sun, the stranger's shoulders were broad and massive, his thick, muscular neck rising to a dark face where a scruffy beard, matted with sweat and grime, pointed to a considerable time spent on the road. The rider's long hair was pulled back in a high ponytail, accentuating his martial stance. The Hunas instinctively gripped their swords tighter, while bows were steadied and bowstrings were drawn back.

"*Z'ah hriiz*," one of the horsemen muttered under his breath. 'No hriiz'.

The leader nodded. When he spoke, his voice was colder, more challenging. "*Zuh te'i go?*" Then, in Avanti, "Who you?"

The stranger considered the patrol with tired eyes. Licking his sore and cracked lips, he spoke in halting words, his voice a gravelly croak, "*Ma... rek'e tcha.*" He raised a thumb to his lips, miming the act of drinking, and when the horsemen didn't respond, he pointed to the sheepskin flask hanging by the leader's saddle. "*Tcha,*" he repeated.

The Huna looked at the flask thoughtfully. Reaching down, he lifted it up, uncorked it and brought it to his lips. After swallowing a few measured gulps of the water, he carefully put the stopper back in, wiped his lips and beard with the back of his hand and appraised the rider with taunting eyes. "*Zuh nukhi zuh te'i go,*" he said, letting the flask drop back by the saddle. 'You didn't say who you are.'

The stranger stared back for a moment before speaking. "*Zuh te'i ba'dor. Bun unnu zuh'i shy'or.*" 'You are impolite. Lead me to your chief.'

The horsemen exchanged looks, and a snigger caught and leaped from one to another like wildfire. With mocking grins, they prodded their steeds forward, opening up and spreading to both sides simultaneously, first flanking the rider, then surrounding him. The leader rode up until just ten paces separated him from the stranger.

"*Ma'a khi shy'or, ur zuh ki'slat,*" he said, scratching his beard and grinning. 'I am the chief, unluckily for you.'

The rider did not respond, his eyes on the sheepskin flask. Just then, one of the Hunas pointed and shouted, "*Urug ha, sho gwede'r.*" 'Watch out, he has a sword.'

Instantly, the horsemen raised their weapons, swords and arrows pointed at the rider, eyes wary and watchful. The newcomer appeared unperturbed, studying the ring around him before swinging his leg over the saddle and dismounting stiffly. He took three weary steps towards the leader, unsheathing his scimitar as he walked, and the horsemen promptly edged their mounts forward, drawing close and tight, their blades and arrowheads now steady, aimed purposefully at the man's head and torso.

The stranger, whose head easily reached the top of all eight horses' heads, stopped and planted the tip of his scimitar into the baking soil at his feet. Looking up at the leader, he repeated in a calm but hoarse voice, "*Bun unnu zuh'i shy'or.*"

"*Ma nukhi zuh ma'a khi shy'or?*" The leader's eyes flashed angrily at the rider. 'Didn't I tell you I am the chief?'

Without warning, like a stone plummeting heavily and fast, the stranger dropped to a crouch. The two Huna archers released their arrows on reflex, but instead of striking their target, the missiles sailed over his head, one striking the horse positioned opposite in the chest, the other whistling harmlessly into the desert. As the struck horse neighed and reared in pain, the stranger swept his scimitar upwards and hard in a scything arc, striking the swords pointed at him in a fierce rattle of metal, unbalancing the Huna riders.

Displaying none of the fatigue that had seemingly gripped him moments ago, and moving at a speed that the patrol could never have anticipated from a thirsty, beat-up traveller, the stranger flung himself at the first Huna archer, the boy with the shaggy hair. The scimitar's blunt edge struck the boy on the chest, unseating him before he could fit a second arrow in his bow. Even as the boy landed on his rump, his foot tangling clumsily with his bow, the stranger brushed aside the swords coming at him to reach the second archer, who had nocked a fresh arrow and was drawing the string back. Another furious lunge, another swing of the scimitar, and the bow snapped into two before the arrow could be shot. Whirling around, the rider ducked and weaved past thrusting swords, parrying cuts and stabs, while grabbing the surprised horsemen by their wrists and ankles and yanking them off their saddles as he passed them. With a final drop and roll under the forelegs of a rearing horse, he rose and leaped astride the steed that bore the group's leader, the only Huna still on horseback.

"*Eb'a*," the stranger roared, slipping a massive arm around the leader's neck, locking him in a tight, choking stranglehold. "*Eb'a*."

As the horse struggled to bear the combined weight of the two men, the stranger swung his scimitar in wide arcs at the warriors he had brought down, pushing them back before pressing the sword's point against their leader's ribs.

"I could have killed any of your men," he hissed into the leader's ear. Flexing his forearm, the giant tightened his grip around the Huna's neck, squeezing hard. The Huna gasped for air and clawed at the heavy, constricting forearm in desperation, his eyes rolling.

"I can kill you right now, if I want," the stranger added. "But I have spared them, and I am sparing you."

Releasing his hold of the Huna's neck, the giant swung off the horse's back. As the leader of the band doubled over on his saddle, coughing, drawing in air and rubbing his throat in relief, the grateful mount whinnied and shied away from the stranger, who slipped his scimitar back into its sheath.

"I have spared you because I come as a friend," he said in an imperious tone, loud enough for everyone to hear. "But friend or foe, never again deny a thirsty man water." Pointing to the sheepskin flask, motioning with his fingers, he demanded, "*Ma rek'e tcha.*"

Still coughing and panting, his eyes watering freely, the Huna grabbed the flask and thrust it at the giant. As he tossed his head back and drank deep, satisfying gulps, the rest of the Huna warriors, sore and disgraced, stared with a mixture of wonder, suspicion, fear and dislike at the man who had ridden into their midst and hammered them into submission.

"*Zuh te'i go?*" the young archer asked in a tone that was sulky yet awed, wincing and feeling his chest gingerly where the blunt edge of the scimitar had rapped him.

The stranger nearly emptied the water in the flask, slaking a burning thirst, before looking at the archer and then at the other faces around him. "*Ma'a…*" he said, catching his breath, "*…ma'a Ga'ur Thra'akha. Duz'ur Zho E'rami. Oi bun unnu zuh'i shy'or.*"

'I am Ga'ur Thra'akha, son of Zho E'rami. Now lead me to your chief.'

Lost

Shukracharya and Jayanta ran into one another on the path that led to the stately pavilion at the centre of the large, overgrown garden. The pathway was narrow, twisting through dense clusters of fragrant *parijata* and *ketaki*, so the high priest and the young deva were hidden from each other's view until they were face to face, almost bumping chests. Jayanta mumbled an apology and tried edging past the stranger, but Shukracharya blocked the way, staring at the boy with one beady eye.

"I didn't realize there was anyone else in this garden," the guru of the asuras observed in surprise. Looking mildly flummoxed, he added, "This place is a bit of a maze. Could you be my guide, if you don't mind?"

Jayanta opened his mouth to remonstrate and beg off, but as he groped for an excuse, Shukracharya took advantage of the deva's confusion and held him by the shoulder.

"I am tired," he wheezed and coughed, his head drooping for good effect. "Is there someplace I can sit for a moment, please?"

Left without choice, Jayanta escorted Shukracharya to the open pavilion, its dome held aloft by a dozen fine marble columns. Broad marble steps were laid around an ingeniously designed waterfall that cascaded quietly into a pool where shoals of rainbow-coloured fish darted about. Ferns and creepers were in abundance, swaying in the cool breeze, while overhead, a family of white-throated munias flitted in and out of the recesses in the vaulted ceiling where they nested. On a raised platform to one side of the pool was a *jal-yantra* — eight small bronze bowls filled with water, placed in a tight semicircle.

"Ah, sweet relief," said Shukracharya, sinking onto the steps. He watched keenly as the deva left his side and headed for the platform that held the bronze bowls.

Stepping onto the platform, Jayanta sat before the bowls, crossed his legs and picked up a pair of thin wooden sticks, a foot in length. With one, he struck the rim of one of the bowls to produce a clear, liquid note. Then, striking the sticks on the bowls in a rapid sequence, his hands moving with practised ease, the deva created a rhapsody of gently ringing notes and lilting melody that was deeply soothing to the soul. Finishing with a flourish, he looked over to Shukracharya, who was nodding his appreciation.

"Impressive. Who trained you to play so well?"

"Nobody," the deva shrugged, striking up a fresh set of notes. "I learned it by myself."

Indeed, Shukracharya thought to himself. You've taught yourself lots of clever little things, deva. Like learning how to play the *jal-yantra*... or awakening Ahi. He smiled benignly at Jayanta, who hadn't the foggiest idea that this had been a meticulously plotted meeting and not a chance encounter between strangers. The high priest had been stalking the deva — in person, and with the aid of the bones and the mandala — for days now, studying his schedule, probing his weaknesses and devising ways of making contact. With Indra finally departing for Avanti earlier that morning, Shukracharya had decided it was time to move in on the young prince.

"Are you by any chance... Jayanta?" he frowned suddenly. "Heir to Devaloka?"

"Yes." Jayanta stopped playing and looked up. "How did you guess?"

"I see a bit of Indra in you," Shukracharya lied. "The Indra of old, the handsome one. In fact, I would say you're better than he was at your age."

Seeing Jayanta blush and his chest swell in pleasure, the high priest realized he had done well in appealing to the young deva's vanity.

"And you... how do you know my father?"

"Ah, look at me, I haven't even introduced myself. I am Shukracharya."

The hands holding the sticks over the bronze bowls tensed. "Guru Shukracharya, guru to the asuras?" Jayanta looked warily at the high priest, his tone awed.

"The same. You must have heard that I am a guest of your father's."

Jayanta gave his head a doubtful shake.

"Not just me, the asura lord Hiranyaksha was also here until two days ago." The high priest smiled at Jayanta's confusion. "We came to discuss matters of peace and mutual interest."

The deva didn't know what to say, so he kept mum, wondering whether to continue playing or get up and leave.

"You play the *jal-yantra* so well, you're young and handsome — I'm sure you must be good with the sword too. The apsaras must find you quite irresistible," Shukracharya grinned and winked at Jayanta. "They must be falling over one another for your attention, poor things. And the one who catches your eye... she must know how incredibly lucky she is." The high priest watched the deva. "Is there such a one?"

The prince did not answer straightaway. He sat looking morose, and the silence grew and wrapped around them like a constricting vine. At last, seeing that the high priest was still waiting for a response, Jayanta offered a half-hearted nod.

"Just as I thought," Shukracharya clapped his hands in triumph. He walked down the steps to sit by Jayanta. His manner oozing friendliness, he asked, "This apsara... does she realize she is special? Have you told her?"

Jayanta opened his mouth, then shut it, plainly caught in two minds.

"You can tell me," Shukracharya's tone was offhand but reassuring. "I'm only a visitor to Devaloka. I have nothing here and won't be around for long anyway. Once I am gone, what you tell me is also gone for good."

The deva prince considered this for a moment. "She... she is my father's mistress."

"Really?" The bones had already told Shukracharya much of what he needed to know, so he had to work hard at looking suitably scandalized. "You mean... Urvashi?"

Jayanta glanced at the high priest in sudden apprehension, and Shukracharya instantly threw his hands up.

"It's none of my business. I won't tell anyone, so don't worry." Shukracharya's voice changed and a sly smile spread across his face. "But it is so obvious — the most desirable of apsaras falling head over heels for a handsome deva like you. How does she even stay with Indra when you're around?"

"She says she doesn't love me. She ignores me; she despises me."

Jayanta's admission surprised the high priest. He hadn't been expecting such candour from the deva, but it was good; it showed Jayanta was dropping his defences, opening up to him.

"Look at her, going off without even bidding me goodbye," the prince's face twisted in rage, sorrow and self-pity. "I didn't even know she wasn't in the palace until I overheard some apsaras saying she's gone off somewhere with father."

Shukracharya had been caught off guard too when he had learned that Urvashi was accompanying Indra and Gandharvasena to Avanti. Gandharvasena's going made sense — *he* was meant to break the back of the human king's resistance. But taking an apsara along had never been discussed. The high priest suspected Urvashi had been included on Indra's impulse, solely to cater to his entertainment.

There was a definite upside to Urvashi's absence, though. Jayanta was at his lowest ebb, pining away with no one to turn to for support. Shukracharya believed the deva would be susceptible to influence, as long as he could be convinced that he would eventually have the apsara to himself.

"What choice does she have, Prince? She is your father's mistress. Her job is to obey his wishes and commands. She can't be caught professing her love to you, can she? She knows your love for each other will incur Indra's anger; she is protecting you and herself from that anger."

"You mean she is lying about her feelings for me?"

Shukracharya saw excitement and hope flare in the deva's eyes. "Isn't that obvious?"

"I didn't... she..." Jayanta gazed down at the *jal-yantra*, grappling with the idea the high priest had planted. "She has been protecting me, and I..." he looked up, a slight smile on his lips. "You're right. She does love me."

Satisfied with the progress made, Shukracharya decided to press his advantage. "But you must get her to admit her love for you. Otherwise, how will the two of you ever embrace, how will you make love," the high priest's tone changed, "unless you're quite happy seeing her from afar with your father..."

"No," Jayanta snapped in frustration. "I want us to be together. But..." he turned to Shukracharya. "How do I convince Urvashi to express her love for me? How can we share our love when father is around?"

The high priest stared thoughtfully at the fish swimming in the pool at their feet. "Give me some time," he said at last. "I will help you — on one condition. There is something you will have to part with in exchange. Do you agree?"

"What is it you want from me?"

Shukracharya smiled mysteriously as he got to his feet. "There is no point in telling you now, because I have nothing to offer you in return. I will let you know what I want once I have a solution to your problem."

Watching him climb the stairs and exit the pavilion, the prince was struck by the fact that the guru of the asuras looked neither tired nor at a loss to find his way out of the garden.

* * *

"We are lost, raj-guru."

Instead of replying, Vetala Bhatta continued gazing over the Aanupa, which lay below and around them. His face was tired but otherwise inscrutable as he fiddled with the vine that was knotted around his waist, binding him to the nine surviving men who comprised his escort to Odra.

Though panoramic in scale, the Ghost Marsh was a study in monotony. It sprawled in every direction from the foot of the hill where the councilor and his guards now stood, a drab and limitless landscape wreathed in drifting curtains of mist with clumps of mossy forest and pools of shimmering swamp visible in the gaps in the mist. The marsh dwindled into a rising steam of haze, and haze and yellow-grey clouds merged such that it was impossible to say where the earth ended and the sky began. Colour had leeched from everywhere, leaving behind lifeless greys and splotches of dull green. The air was humid and still, yet puffs of chill wind that didn't quite stir the leaves of trees set the travellers from Avanti shivering. Nothing moved in or over the marsh.

"We are truly lost," the soldier standing at the Acharya's right elbow repeated with a resigned sigh. He was Kedara, the captain in charge of the escort, a reliable enough soldier whose nerve had deserted him over the course of the last two days.

"Not permanently," the chief councilor shook his head and pointed towards the horizon. "That's the sun there, see?"

Vetala Bhatta sensed his escort gather around him, voices exclaiming, fingers pointing at the watery halo of light that had somehow speared through the haze. The light gradually assumed the form of a limpid, pale yellow disc, gaining a modicum of strength to shine a hand's breadth above where the horizon should be.

"That way is west," said one of the soldiers, gesturing in the direction of the sun.

"Which means this way to the east," the Acharya jerked a thumb over his shoulder. "Uttara Tosali lies behind us. Come, let us make some headway before sundown."

The urgency in the raj-guru's words did not translate into action as his escort trudged downhill with the enthusiasm of men bearing the dead to their pyres. The councilor knew the cause of their lethargy — the men had no reason to think that a path would miraculously emerge at the bottom of the hill to lead them out of the Aanupa. They had been stumbling around the marsh for nearly two days now, but still had no clue how far they were from the place where they had first lost their bearings, or from their destination. Yet, he couldn't afford to let their morale sink.

Trouble had arrived in the form of a thunderstorm when they were still on the other side of the Riksha Mountains, in the open plains. Except for the minor inconvenience of damp clothes, they had thought little of the storm, but by the next evening, as they trekked across the mountain ridges, their guide — a small trader familiar with the route — had contracted a burning fever. He slipped rapidly into a delirium, and the Acharya sensibly called for a break to give him rest. In two days, the guide had recovered adequately for them to resume travel, but as they had come down the southern slopes of the range, weakness triggered a relapse, and in a few hours, he had parted their company for good.

Faced with the choice of returning to Avanti or continuing without a guide, the chief councilor figured that having come three-quarters of the way to Odra, scrapping the mission was a ridiculous idea. So, they had stayed the course, keeping to the shadows of the Riksha range so they would be safe from the grasp of the Aanupa. But the following morning brought a dense mist, and before anyone knew it, the group had unknowingly drifted from the mountains and blundered into the marsh. Worse, in a bid to find a way out, three of the men had strayed from the group and were swallowed by the mist, not to be seen again. The others had wisely bound themselves with a chain of vines, so that more of them wouldn't be lost to the mist and the hungry swamp hiding in its folds.

Feeling the rough vine on his palm and on his waist as they tugged one another along, single file, Vetala Bhatta worried about the group's predicament. The delay caused by the guide's illness had already taken a chunk out of their food reserves, and this wandering about the marsh was a further strain on resources. While they were running through their rations, there was little in the Aanupa to compensate for the depletion — they had seen no edible plants, nor any bird or animal. The horses and pack mules had nothing to nibble either, and as a consequence, were weakening rapidly.

The marsh's maze-like quality rattled the chief councilor the most. At ground level, the mist played constant tricks, weaving this way and that, opening paths and closing them at random, so it was a perpetual challenge to discern where one was going. The topography of moss-covered trees and stagnant reed pools was dismally unvarying, offering no distinguishable landmarks for the eye and the mind to remember. To top it all, the sun was almost always blotted by clouds, so telling the direction was, at best, guesswork. Lastly, the marsh occupied a huge area; the Acharya realized with a sinking feeling that the group was staring at the horrifying prospect of going around in circles looking for a way out, all of them wearing themselves down and dying of starvation — if insanity didn't first drive them to take their own or each other's lives.

It was not without reason that the Aanupa was called the Ghost Marsh.

Vetala Bhatta was lost in these morbid thoughts when one of the guards in front shouted.

"There, a house! Like the one yesterday."

Heads turned in that direction, and the councilor observed a hut — once probably a hunter's, but long since abandoned — made of bamboo and thatch, nestling under a copse of trees with low, drooping branches. The copse was in the middle of a swamp, so the only way of accessing the house was over a rickety bridge made of crudely tied logs and planks.

"Isn't this the one where we spent last night?" asked another of the men.

The question was met with an ominous silence as each man weighed its implications. Vetala Bhatta assessed the ramshackle structure anew and was rewarded with the uncomfortable feeling that the man was right. Finally, the captain spoke.

"Hard to say. Let us take a closer look."

One after another, still in single file, still tied together by vine, the group traversed the slippery wooden bridge, watching the hut and its environs keenly for signs that would tell them this was a different hut. There was hope in their faces but also the fear of being disappointed. By the time the Acharya, who was bringing up the rear, set foot on the wet soil in front of the hut, Kedara and a couple of soldiers had already entered the hut.

"I don't think this is the same one," said a soldier, surveying the hut's surroundings. "I don't remember…"

He stopped on seeing Kedara emerge from inside the hut. Everyone turned to look at the captain, and the anguish in his eyes told them what they didn't want to know.

"It is the same hut. The place where we lit the fire to prepare yesterday's dinner is the same. Even the ashes are still warm. We have been walking in a circle."

The captain's eyes came around to meet those of the councilor. "We are lost, raj-guru. We are hopelessly lost."

* * *

The Mother Oracle was not in her room, and Shanku had to look in a couple of places before finding her on a terrace that overlooked the southeastern corner of the palace lake. The oracle was leaning against a parapet, her gaze switching between a pair of peacocks prancing on the bough of a nearby tree and the lake's wooded eastern shore, which was swiftly turning dark as twilight fell over the land. Overhead, the first stars were twinkling into view and a cool breeze blew from the south, stirring the lake and sending small, silvery ripples towards the palace.

Her grandmother had not noticed her, so Shanku stood for a moment, observing the slight form bent with age. The old woman looked forlorn as she stared out of the palace, heart and soul yearning for the wilderness that had been her lifelong companion. The city and the palace, Shanku realized, were slowly choking the oracle out of existence, and it crossed the girl's mind that she should, perhaps, just take her grandmother back to the Wandering Tribe, so that she could live out her days in peace.

"Why are you standing there, my child? Come here."

Something must have given her presence away, Shanku thought as she joined her grandmother with a smile. The oracle took Shanku's hand, and they stood, side by side, watching the night gradually smother the day in its dark embrace.

"Have you learned anything of Kalidasa?" Shanku finally broke the silence.

The oracle studied the girl for a moment. "Who wants to know? You or the king?"

Shanku did not reply. Instead, she freed her hand and faced away, watching the lake's shore melt and recede into darkness. After the passage of what seemed like many minutes, the oracle shook her head.

"I haven't learned anything so far."

The girl gave a swift nod. Her grandmother glanced at her out of the corner of her eye, then turned to face her.

"Why didn't you ever tell one another what you felt — what you *both* felt?"

Shanku thought about this for a while. "Maybe because we're both reserved by nature." She shrugged. "Maybe because we always assumed the other would understand, without us needing to say anything."

"And between the reluctance to say and the hesitation to understand, the moment was lost. You realize that, don't you?" The Mother Oracle's sigh was heavy with lament. "Why do we struggle to put into words what we express so easily with our eyes? And why do we seek assurances in words when the eyes speak so eloquently, so honestly?"

For a while, neither spoke.

"Perhaps it is best this way," Shanku said wistfully. "It makes the parting more bearable."

"Would you have parted if you had been together, child?"

"He would still be a Huna, and I would still be loyal to the Samrat. He would have wanted to go; I would have insisted on staying. We can never quite overcome who we are."

Shanku paused and looked at her grandmother. "You sent word that you had something to share." Her tone and the change in topic implied she didn't want to discuss Kalidasa any more.

"Yes," the oracle's voice turned weary. Stalling for time, she added, "Can we go in? It is turning chilly here."

Back in the oracle's room, Shanku lit the two lamps to push the darkness back, while her grandmother unrolled and spread a mat on the floor. A house lizard watched them warily from high up on a wall.

"Tell me," said Shanku, once they had settled down. Her tone was less brusque, her eyes kinder as they appraised the oracle.

"Yes, yes…" The Mother Oracle seemed troubled and at a loss on how to begin. "Remember the other night we spoke… the day I had fallen unwell?"

The girl nodded. "The night you told me about the Huna ships sailing for Dvarka, the black butterflies on the Dark River."

"Yes, yes… *that* night. You may recall that I also told you I had read a message for you in the spider webs in the Labyrinth."

"You said that there was a desire for atonement in the dungeons," Shanku's face was closed, unreadable. "You were speaking of father, I gather."

"Yes," the oracle sighed. "I have read more signs that say the same thing, child. Your father wishes you to forgive him. I understand that he has been entreating you to meet him?"

The girl studied the back of her hand. "He sent a message through the guards a few days ago," she said heavily. "He wanted to meet."

"And?"

"And nothing, grandmother. I do not want to meet that man. One cannot expect to be forgiven just because one is suddenly repentant. That would be too convenient. There is a price to pay, and part of the punishment is not knowing when... *if* one will be pardoned. That is the price my father has to pay for betraying the king and for robbing me of mother's love."

* * *

The samrat's dinner was underway when Vismaya received the rider, who had ridden nearly half the distance from the garrison of Lava with a message for the king. The message had originated at Udaypuri earlier that afternoon, relayed east via *suryayantras* until nightfall, after which it had fallen on the rider to deliver it to the palace in person. No sooner had the chief of the Palace Guards heard the gist of the message than, understanding its urgency, he ushered the rider into the privacy of the king's dining chamber.

"My apologies, Samrat," Vismaya said, pushing the curtains aside discreetly and bowing. "There is a rider here with a message for you from Commander Atulyateja."

Vikramaditya looked up from his meal, but before he could say a word, another voice addressed Vismaya in mild annoyance.

"Can't the rider wait until the Samrat has finished his dinner?"

Drawing the curtain wider, the chief of the Palace Guards peeked to the right to see Queen Upashruti regarding him sternly. He hadn't expected to see her in the samrat's company, and now he hesitated.

"It is... I'm sorry, Queen Mother, but it... I thought..."

"It's alright," the king interrupted. He looked past Vismaya, brows raised in enquiry at the rider. "What does Atulyateja have to say?"

The rider and Vismaya looked at one another before the chief of the guards shot an uncertain glance at Queen Upashruti. From the way he stood blocking the rider, preventing him from entering the room and addressing the king, it was evident that the chief had reservations about who should hear the rider's message.

"You may speak," said Vikramaditya to the rider, correctly interpreting Vismaya's indecision. "There are no secrets to be kept from the Queen Mother."

The two men standing at the door once again exchanged glances, but this time, the chief of the guards offered a minute shrug. Stepping into the room, he made way for the rider to pass him, yet he didn't seem satisfied with the situation. The rider too looked uncomfortably at Upashruti as he cleared his throat to speak.

"Your honour, I bring..." he stopped, then started again. "Commander Atulyateja wants you to know that Prince Ghatakarpara has been missing from the garrison."

For a fraction of a second, there was complete silence in the dining chamber as the samrat and his mother stared at the rider in incomprehension.

"What do you mean, missing?" the king blinked in bewilderment.

"My apologies for not being clear, your honour," the rider shook his head, gathering himself. "What I meant was that the prince has not been seen in Udaypuri for the last two days. They have launched a search for him, but no trace of him has been found."

"Oh heavens!" Queen Upashruti's hand flew to her mouth in horror, her eyes wide with concern for her grandson. She took two unsure steps towards the rider. "What's happened to him?"

The rider began shaking his head, but Vikramaditya, who now saw why Vismaya had been reluctant to let the rider speak in front of the Queen Mother, rose from the low table, his half-eaten meal forgotten. "I'm sure he is fine, mother. It must be a misunderstanding. He must have just gone off somewhere without letting anyone know..."

"But he says it has been *two days*..." Upashruti looked at the king, pointing a trembling finger at the rider.

"Mother, we will look into it. He *will* be found..." Putting an arm around her, the samrat gently drew his mother away and manoeuvred her towards a divan. "Please sit down and don't worry. I am here; I will take care of things."

As Queen Upashruti sank into the divan's soft cushions, her eyes brimming with tears as she imagined the worst, Vikramaditya motioned to one of the palace hands, asking her to take charge of the Queen Mother. At the same time, he looked over his shoulder at the rider and Vismaya. "Meet me in the council chamber. And inform the entire council to assemble there as quickly as possible."

Not more than twenty minutes had passed before Amara Simha, Kshapanaka, Shanku and Dhanavantri had joined the samrat and the rider in the council chamber. All four councilors had been brought up to date on Atulyateja's message, and they now sat around the table looking at one another in disbelief.

"I should never have left him back there alone," Amara Simha shook his head and said irrationally. "I should have waited for his return from Dvarka and brought him back with me."

"Don't be silly," Dhanavantri reprimanded him gently, "This has nothing to do with you."

"Indeed," said Vikramaditya. "This is no fault of yours."

"But you did send him to the frontier under my care," Amara Simha countered.

"I did, but the idea was for him to grow out of your shadow

and become independent. And that is exactly what happened when he volunteered to go to Dvarka with news of the Huna invasion by sea. If I had wanted him to stay under your care, wouldn't I have asked you to bring him back when I asked for your return to Ujjayini?"

Seeing the samrat's point, Amara Simha nodded, but he still looked miserable. Meanwhile, Kshapanaka addressed the council.

"Atulyateja speaks of Ghatakarpara taking charge of the frontier south of Udaypuri. Maybe he is visiting one of the remote outposts on inspection..." she trailed off as that possibility sounded unlikely even to her own ears.

"The message says they have checked," said Dhanavantri.

"They couldn't have checked *every* outpost," Amara Simha offered, more in hope than with any real conviction.

"Yes, but the command centres would still know if he was visiting any of the outposts, wouldn't they?" the physician argued.

"We are forgetting the fact that he left the garrison without his horse," Vikramaditya interrupted, looking at the rider briefly for confirmation. "And that he seemed to have made it a habit to leave the garrison every evening and return around nightfall. He followed this routine even on the evening he was last seen. Ghatakarpara didn't go anywhere on inspection. That much is clear."

"Where could he be then?" Kshapanaka looked at her co-councilors in mystification.

"What we have to ascertain is whether there was more to Ghatakarpara's..." the king paused as the door to the council chamber opened to admit Varahamihira. From his expression, it was plain the councilor had already been briefed about the purpose of this sudden meeting. Gesturing at Vikramaditya to continue, he limped to the closest available seat.

"I was saying we have to find out more about Ghatakarpara's

routine in Udaypuri, especially his penchant for leaving the garrison every evening," said the samrat. "This habit of going for walks all by himself — I think it has something to do with his disappearance."

"Why wasn't his security detail with him when he went out of the garrison?" Varahamihira interjected. "Soldiers *were* appointed to escort him, weren't they?" The lame councilor looked around the table, seeking affirmation.

"There were, but he took them along only when he went out of town," Kshapanaka explained. "Atulyateja's message says so."

"More proof that Ghatakarpara did not intend leaving Udaypuri," the samrat shrugged.

A silence simmering with uncertainty and apprehension fell over the room as the king and his council pondered over what they had learned. Amara Simha finally looked up at Vikramaditya and spoke.

"I think I will go." Seeing the confusion on the faces around him, he said quickly, "To Udaypuri."

"What for?" the physician looked at his friend in surprise.

"To help look for Ghatakarpara." As the others gave him dubious looks, he added, "I know this sounds stupid, but I feel I am somehow responsible for this."

"You are *not*," Dhanavantri said in exasperation, even as the others began to protest. But before anyone could add to what the physician had said, Amara Simha raised a hand, demanding silence.

"I know, but still," he said, strongly, adamantly. "Also, as the Samrat said, we have to find out more about what happened there — where Ghatakarpara used to go, whom he met and befriended... We need to press in more men in the search; we need someone there making quick decisions."

"Why can't Commander Atulyateja do all that?" asked Varahamihira.

"Because we have that idiot, Satyaveda, sitting in Udaypuri," Amara Simha scowled. "That man loves wielding his authority to cause hindrances and make people's lives miserable. He revels in his pettiness." Seeing heads nod, he went on, "If we intend making any headway in this affair, someone will need to overrule Satyaveda's authority, and I doubt Atulyateja would be able to do that the way *I* can. Also, in all honesty, Atulyateja can't be expected to man the frontier *and* oversee the hunt for Ghatakarpara. In a more peaceful time, maybe…"

The king and the councilors looked at one another, knowing Amara Simha was right. Yet, the king looked troubled by the suggestion.

"I see your point, but… I don't know whether we can afford to send you away from Ujjayini," he confessed at last. "You were at the frontier, but we called you back for a reason." The samrat looked around the table. "That reason, that threat, still looms over Avanti. We need you here — I need all of you here — when the devas or asuras come next for the Halahala. Ujjayini can't let you go, councilor."

"What about Ghatakarpara then? Can we affo…"

Before Amara Simha could say more, the door to the chamber swung violently open and Pralupi stormed into the room, her eyes wild with anger and apprehension.

"What is this I am hearing — is it true?" she screeched. The seriousness in the faces of those seated around the table gave her the answer she sought, and she pinned a furious glare on her brother. "I *told* you. I told you a hundred times not to send my son to the frontier. Did you listen? *No.* I begged you, I pleaded with you, I beseeched you to let him come back to Ujjayini. Did you listen? *No.* You did whatever pleased you, and now look where it has landed me and my son. *He is missing*," she wailed theatrically. "Not to be found anywhere for two days. Do you know that, Vikrama? *Do you*?"

"Sister, I know how you feel about this…"

"*No, you don't,*" Pralupi cut in sharply, approaching the samrat. "You are sitting here playing games, while my poor son is somewhere at the horrible frontier, all alone..."

"Sister, *please* listen to me," Vikramaditya struggled to stay calm as his voice strained in the effort to remain gentle and assuring. "Please... you must have more faith in your son, even if you have none in me. He is trained to become a soldier, trained by none less than the Acharya and Amara Simha and Kal..." The samrat checked himself a tad too late. "He is a fighter and a survivor. Nothing will happen to him, I assure you. And no, sister, we are not playing *games* here — we are working on a plan of action to find Ghatakarpara."

"Really?" Pralupi railed implacably. "And what plan have you devised?"

Before the king could say anything, Amara Simha piped in. "I will be leaving for Udaypuri to look for your son, Pralupi," he said. "We took the decision just before you came in."

Even as the king and the rest of the council stared at Amara Simha, Pralupi turned to the brawny councilor. "You will find my son, won't you?" she asked, mollified. "You will bring him back to me safe?"

"Of course, I will. Don't worry."

"When are you going then?" No thank you, no sign of gratitude from the king's sister.

Pralupi was remarkably ungrateful, and shamelessly selfish and pushy, the samrat thought to himself as he looked at Amara Simha, wondering if the man had saved him from more censure and criticism with his glib lies, or whether he had simply taken advantage of a tricky situation to cement his plan to travel to Udaypuri. Either way, Vikramaditya couldn't keep a small smile from playing on his lips.

"I..." Amara Simha looked stumped for a moment. "Tomorrow. I depart at daybreak."

"You can leave even now," Pralupi pointed out unreasonably.

Dhanavantri rolled his eyes and looked at the samrat, who pulled a wry face and shrugged.

"Yes, in fact, I intend to, as soon as I can," Amara Simha replied sportingly, as he rose to usher the woman out of the chamber. Vikramaditya couldn't say if he had imagined the smirk of exasperation concealed behind the councilor's big, red beard.

Once Amara Simha and Pralupi had left, Varahamihira considered Vikramaditya. "Well, it looks like we had one decision made for us," he said with a grin. "Two birds with one stone. Clever of Amara Simha."

As the councilors nodded their admiration, Vikramaditya looked at the rider. "I will have a message ready for dispatch in the morning. You may leave and get some rest."

They were all rising from the table, preparing to disband, when Dhanavantri approached the king. "With Amara Simha going off, we should call Vararuchi back," he said. With a meaningful pause, he added, "Just in case something comes up."

The samrat pondered the suggestion. "No, let's not," he shook his head. "Brother spends so much time working for the palace that he rarely goes to meet *badi-maa*. It's unfortunate on both of them, but I guess it can't be helped. Now that he has made time for her, let us not force the needs of the palace between mother and son — at least for as long as we can help it."

* * *

A deep sense of dissatisfaction afflicted Shukracharya as he crouched on his haunches and drew a mandala with rice flour. Unlike charcoal, rice flour was easily swept and washed away, and left no detectable stains on the white marble floor of the palatial summerhouse that the devas had put at his and

Hiranyaksha's disposal. Even though the devas had left him free and unsupervised for the most part, the high priest had closed all the windows of his chamber as a precaution against prying eyes.

Settling down before the mandala, Shukracharya muttered his mantras and cast the six pieces of human vertebrae, asking the question that he always asked first of the bones these days. 'Where is Veeshada's dagger?'

It is in the banyan that holds up the field of endless pyres.

Though tediously repetitive, the answer was reassuring in its familiarity — at least no one else had got to the dagger first. This was a status quo the high priest was happy with until he cracked the enigma of the Halahala's whereabouts. He asked his next question, one that he had also started asking often of late: 'Where are the mantras to awaken the serpent-dragon Ahi?'

The bones dutifully told him that the mantras were secure in Brihaspati's possession.

Grimacing at Jayanta's foolishness that had inspired him to hand the mantras over to Brihaspati willingly, Shukracharya posed a few more questions to the bones. Once he had an update on everything of concern to him, he cleared the floor of all traces of the mandala before stepping out onto the balcony that abutted his chamber. Outside, the night was cool and quiet and filled with the scent of *devadaru*. A sedate mist rolled down the face of Mount Meru, plunging the valley in a diaphanous shimmer of moonlight. Far to the right were the lights of Amaravati, reflected off a misty sky.

His eyes on the diffused glow on the horizon, Shukracharya reflected, not for the first time, that since his arrival in Devaloka, he had achieved practically nothing of significance. Yes, the human king had lost his friend and most trusted councilor, but that had been inevitable and was not entirely his doing. Yes, his *next* move was a masterstroke that would put a permanent end to Vikramaditya, but it was up to Indra and Gandharvasena to deliver that blow — and they were both still some distance away from achieving that objective. What had he done beyond that?

He had hoped to lay his hands on the mantras to raise Ahi, but Jayanta had already stupidly parted with them. He had flirted with the prospect of sneaking into the palace of Amaravati to retrieve the mantras, but as he didn't really fancy his chances of dodging an army of alert devas, he had to rely on Jayanta stealing it back from Brihaspati, something the wayward prince would do only with the right kind of incentive — such as a method to win Urvashi's affection. Shukracharya knew Urvashi well enough to realize that Indra's wimp of a son stood no chance of attracting the apsara, yet he had to contrive a way to make that happen. Failing which, he would have to hoodwink Jayanta with a plausible-sounding plan to seduce the apsara, so the fool would nick and trade the mantras. All very shaky, the high priest thought.

Then there was the Halahala itself, still mysteriously hidden in the banyan outside Ujjayini. For now, its secret was safe with the asuras, but who was to say the devas wouldn't learn of it? What if they did, and Indra beat him to it? Indra would be in Avanti — what if the human king inadvertently gave away the dagger's hiding place? And even if the devas didn't get wind of it, what would happen once Vikramaditya had been broken? This truce wouldn't hold. Who would first take the human kingdom apart in the quest of the dagger — the asuras or the devas? The answer to that was self-evident; the asuras had to have a head start in this race. That was the reason he had sent Hiranyaksha back to Patala, to prepare the asuras for war. But when would it be right to attack Vikramaditya, and what would be the ideal strategy to hold off the devas?

Even as he fretted over these uncertainties, something

completely different occupied one corner of the high priest's mind, nagging him incessantly. It was something he had seen in the human councilor Vetala Bhatta's mind the morning the councilor had tried reading *his* mind near the bath. He had seen the human king in the chief councilor's mind, he had seen Narada, he had seen the young girl speak of him as the Healer... He had also seen a flash of something hidden in dense, white fog...

That vision had stayed with him ever since, and came back to him often when he was least expecting it. A curtain of white fog drifting past something huge and shadowy — something that seemed to suggest gigantic proportions. Something surrounded by fog, concealed by fog. Something vaguely familiar, reminiscent of... *what?*

Shukracharya had tried pushing his way through the fog to get a better view, but every time, he had been thwarted. Still, some instinct told him this was important.

An instinct that kept insisting this elusive thing in the fog was the key to everything.

Frontier

Daybreak was still a few hours away when the moon finally tore free of the black, scudding clouds and shone down on the little ship making its solitary progress over the dark, undulating expanse of sea. The upward sweep of the ship's prow pointed straight at the pale half-disc, which had made an appearance for the first time since the vessel had set sail from the estuary east of Tamralipti a couple of days earlier. The silence about the ship was complete, except for the occasional flap of the single, large sail, braced against the brisk, freshening breeze.

After two days of being battered by rain and gale-force winds, the calm of the moon-bathed night should have come as a relief to Chancellor Sudasan, but the chief of Vanga's erstwhile Grand Assembly shifted nervously from one foot to the other as he stood on the ship's deck in the company of a small knot of men. The group of seven stood in a tight huddle, the moonlight on their faces betraying the anxiety that they kept relaying back and forth and round and round through an exchange of uncertain glances.

"I wish the moon would go back into the clouds," one of

the men muttered, throwing a fearful glance over his shoulder, his eyes sweeping the dark recesses of the sea in the ship's wake. "It is too bright and we run the risk of being sighted."

"This is a very large sea, brother, and anyway, we are too far south of the coast to be seen," answered another. "I don't think we have anything to fear." For all his confidence, the speaker cast a wary eye around the ship.

"But we have everything to fear," retorted a third man with a thin, squeaky voice. "Have you already forgotten the market square of Tamralipti?"

The reminder of the market square ushered a discomfiting silence over the group. It had happened the day after the army of Magadha, led by Prince Kapila and General Daipayana, had marched into Tamralipti. The General Assembly of Vanga had taken a near-unanimous decision to fight the advancing army — near unanimous because three chiefs of the republic's eighteen principalities had abandoned the Assembly and sought Magadha's amnesty by means of surrender. The battle for Tamralipti had barely lasted half a day. Magadha's forces had broken Vanga's brittle defence, sending the members of the Grand Assembly into hiding. In a matter of hours, seventeen members of the Assembly — including the chiefs of four principalities — had been apprehended, and the next morning, seventeen bodies hung in Tamralipti's market square as a gruesome reminder to those who dared challenge Magadha.

"I have forgotten nothing," the man who had tried to allay everyone's fears snapped in response. Nerves were fraying on account of the tension, suspense and uncertainty they had endured. "All I am saying is that at this rate, we will end up being afraid of our own shadows."

"That is different from saying we have nothing to fear," the third speaker shrilled. "Look at us. From eighteen, we are now down to just six chiefs. Seven, if we include the chancellor. This is all that is left of the Grand Assembly of Vanga. Our homes have been taken by Magadha, and we have nowhere to go. Still you say we have nothing to fear?"

The old man's voice rose hysterically before quavering and breaking into sobs. Sudasan put a comforting arm around the man's shoulders.

"We are already on our way to reclaiming our homes. Do not worry, for we shall take back from Magadha all that was ours." The chancellor gently turned the man in the direction of the ship's stern. "Why don't you get some sleep?"

Three of the chiefs escorted the man away, leaving the others on deck to contemplate the quiet sea. Once it was clear that Tamralipti had been overrun, Sudasan and the fifteen chiefs had fled the city and sought refuge in the surrounding countryside. After the capture and public hanging of four of them, Sudasan had continued eastward, with Magadha's soldiers hot on his trail. The chancellor had finally given his pursuers the slip in the dense, tiger-infested mangrove swamps that formed a broad belt around the delta of the Yamuna and the Lauhitya, and it was here that the surviving chiefs of Vanga had regrouped.

Although the mangroves offered excellent cover from detection, staying indefinitely in the malarial swamp was not an option; venturing west towards Tamralipti wasn't one either. So Sudasan and the chiefs were faced with the option of crossing the estuary and making a long trek north to Pragjyotishpura, or sailing to the distant shores of Sribhoja and Srivijaya.

The third choice facing them was to seek asylum in the court of Abhirami or that of her brother Veerayanka.

"Do you think we will be welcomed with open arms?" the chief who stood to Sudasan's right asked.

The chancellor shrugged. The question had plagued them as they had sat inside the huts hidden among the mangroves, sheltering from the rain and the coming storm. They had asked themselves over and over again if it was worth approaching Queen Abhirami and King Veerayanka, but had found no satisfactory answer.

The fact was that Pragjyotishpura, being too remote and far removed from the rest of Sindhuvarta, had never really interacted with Vanga — all contact between the northern kingdom and the republic was limited to the initiative of small, unorganized traders. Therefore, there was no real basis to believe that Pragjyotishpura would entertain them. With Sribhoja and Srivijaya, the prospects dimmed even further, as the two kingdoms depended extensively on trade with the port of Tamralipti. The rulers of Sribhoja and Srivijaya knew Sudasan and were likely to be moved by Vanga's plight. However, it was uncertain whether they would risk antagonizing Tamralipti's new rulers by extending support to Vanga's fugitive chiefs.

That only left the mountain-bound kingdoms of Odra and Kalinga. Unfortunately, as with Pragjyotishpura, neither kingdom had made efforts to establish relations with the other kingdoms of Sindhuvarta — and all efforts at building friendship with them had been quietly rebuffed. For as long as anyone could remember, Kalinga and Odra had existed in splendid isolation, protected by the Riksha Mountains to the north, the Aanupa or the Ghost Marsh to the west and the Dandaka Forest to the south.

Deadlocked between three discouraging alternatives, Sudasan and his chiefs were at their wits' end when one of their informers brought a stray piece of news from Tamralipti — Magadha was apparently drawing up elaborate plans to march its army against Odra.

Sensing the slenderest of opportunities in this development, Sudasan had chosen the ragtag group's destiny. Two small ships had been smuggled into the delta, and taking advantage of the brewing storm, they had set sail, steering far south to put distance between them and the coast, before veering west. The gamble seemed to have paid off as they had escaped the notice of Magadhan ships and vessels, but it had also exacted a heavy price. The terrifying storm had claimed one of the ships along with its entire burden, which included five of the fleeing Vanga chiefs.

"We bear news that is of importance to Odra," the chancellor said. "We can only hope that would be adequate to get us an audience with Queen Abhirami. After that, our fate is in her hands."

The moon chose that moment to hide behind a bank of clouds. The wind picked up, sending a whispering chill across the ship's deck. Sudasan felt goosebumps crawl up his exposed forearms. With a shiver, he gazed into the western horizon, in the direction of Uttara Tosali.

* * *

After half a night spent tossing and turning, the Mother Oracle finally gave up on trying to sleep. She stared at the blank wall in front of her for a while, before deciding that since she was awake, she might as well look at something a little more pleasant. Such as the yellowing half-moon that hung outside her window like a lantern.

Sleep had eluded her a lot recently — in fact, within a day or so of her arrival at the palace on the samrat's request. She had always had grave doubts about coping in such a large and cluttered city as Ujjayini; unfortunately, her worst fears were coming true. Every day she felt less inclined to eat, her digestion was troubling her, and she was constantly fatigued because she didn't eat well and couldn't sleep. After her bout of illness, when the members of her tribe had come to look her up, she had been tempted to leave the palace with them. It was only her word to the king, and the thought of disappointing

Shanku by not aiding the throne at its time of need, that had held the oracle back.

Blinking what little sleep there was out of her eyes, she now watched the moon, her mind on the conversation with her granddaughter earlier that evening. The girl was heartbroken by Kalidasa's departure, though she did an excellent job of keeping her feelings to herself. Yet, for all her loss, she was too proud of her king and too loyal to the throne (and too stubborn for her own good, the oracle's mind interjected) to let her love for Kalidasa colour her decisions. And for the very same reasons, the Mother Oracle realized, Shanku would never forgive Brichcha, who was pining for a pardon in the palace dungeons.

Though her own hatred for the man — who had caused her daughter to take her own life — was fierce, the oracle worried for Shanku. The girl was already an introvert, and without a shoulder to lean on, the oracle believed Shanku would end up even more lonely and embittered. Whatever his faults, Brichcha was her father and a repentant one; in his old age, he could give her the emotional support that he had never provided her as a child. She wished the girl would stop running away from her past and come to terms with —

The Mother Oracle blinked and stared. Then, raising her head a little, she refocused her eyes and stared, fully alert, out of the window, at the small, stray patches of clouds floating across the face of the moon.

Yes, something was there, she was certain.

Scrambling up as best as her advanced years would allow her to, the oracle hobbled over to the window and peered up at the sky. There were more clouds coming from the west. As they slipped past the moon, she read a pattern in their tattered bodies and ragged tails. Sketchy, veiled, but a pattern nonetheless.

She read a message in the clouds, a message coming from the west, from the direction of the Great Desert.

* * *

Dawn was a faint blush on the horizon as Amara Simha and his escort, a group of eight soldiers, rode out of Ujjayini's northern gate. The councilor had promised the king's sister that he would leave for the frontier by dawn and he had kept his word, not because Pralupi would hold him to it if he didn't, but because he was in as much of a hurry to get to Udaypuri. Despite everyone else's assurances to the contrary — and despite knowing they were correct — Amara Simha still felt indirectly responsible for having left Ghatakarpara behind at the frontier. He intended to find the boy and return him to the palace if it was the last thing he did.

The sun was still not free of the horizon and they had ridden not more than a couple of miles, when one of the soldiers at the rear of the escort heard the high-pitched bleat of a horn coming from somewhere far away and behind them, from the direction of Ujjayini. Looking over his shoulder, the soldier saw a horseman riding hard in pursuit, so he passed the word along and the company drew to a halt, waiting for the rider to catch up. When the rider arrived, he rode straight up to Amara Simha and bowed.

"Greetings, councilor. The Samrat has asked me to escort you back to the palace."

"But I just left the palace," replied Amara Simha, frowning.

"I have orders to bring you back, your honour," the rider looked apologetic. "I was told it is of utmost urgency."

Thoroughly mystified, the brawny councilor addressed his escort. "I have no idea how long this will take, so you might as well return with me." Then, wheeling his horse around to face the city, he spurred it to a gallop. To the rider, he said over his shoulder, "You've done your job. You're free to go now."

When he strode into the council chamber, Amara Simha saw the samrat's face lighten with relief upon seeing him, although his jaw was set, firm and grim. At the same time, he felt the tension pressing down on the shoulders of those in the room — his fellow councilors and the Mother Oracle, all looking grim and deprived of sleep.

"What's the matter?" he asked, studying the faces around the table. He reserved a lingering look for the oracle, intuitively knowing she had something to do with all of this. "Why did you call me back?"

"The Mother Oracle just brought something to our notice," said the king. Addressing the old woman, he added, "Could you repeat what you saw, mother?"

The oracle nodded and turned to face the councilors. "I wasn't able to sleep well — I haven't been able to for many nights now," she added pointedly. "But never mind that. I was lying staring out of the window at the moon and the clouds drifting by. The wind had borne the clouds from the west, and I saw a sign in them, a message."

"What did the message say?" prodded Dhanavantri.

"The clouds spoke of three things. One was an account of a young man being beaten unconscious by a stream outside a city."

"Which city?" Kshapanaka interjected.

"The clouds didn't say," the oracle shrugged. "The second thing they spoke of was a young man being carried over the mountains, towards the Great Desert. The man was dead or unconscious."

"Or drugged," said Vikramaditya, a little too hastily.

The oracle inclined her head at the possibility, but she didn't speak.

"And the third thing?" asked Amara Simha.

The oracle looked at him before turning her head to look at each councilor, turn by turn. "The third thing they spoke about was the golden sun that accompanied the man who was being carried over the mountains."

"Who was carrying this man?" asked Kshapanaka with a puzzled shake of her head.

"Again, the clouds didn't say." The Mother Oracle suddenly looked tired and irritable. "I can't ask questions. I only overhear and read sense in what the signs are saying."

"And for that, we are eternally grateful to you, mother," said the samrat, mollifying her. "But..." he turned to Kshapanaka, and then to the other councilors, "who is carrying this man is not the point. That we can infer. The question is *who* is this man. I say it is Ghatakarpara."

"Really?" asked Amara Simha, combing his beard with his fingers thoughtfully.

"Yes, and so does Shanku," said Vikramaditya, pointing to the girl who sat, as usual, quietly to one side. "She brought what the Mother Oracle told her to my notice."

"I went to see whether the oracle needed anything, and she told me what she had read in the clouds," Shanku explained. "I couldn't think of it being anyone other than the prince."

"What makes you so sure?" Varahamihira leaned across to peer at the girl.

"It is logical," she replied. "A man is beaten unconscious outside a city. The city could be Udaypuri, though it need not be. Then, a man is carried over the mountains towards the Great Desert, and he is dead or unconscious. If he's dead, there's no reason why he's being carried into the Great Desert. So, it's likely that he's unconscious. One man beaten unconscious, another unconscious man being carried — they're probably the same person. Now, the man being carried over the mountains is accompanied by a golden sun. That doesn't make sense, unless the clouds meant the councilor's golden sun-crest medallion. So, the man has to be Ghatakarpara."

"And he's being taken into the Great Desert, into Huna-Saka territory," Amara Simha smacked a meaty fist into his palm in a spurt of rage. "He's been *kidnapped*."

The word cracked and echoed like a whip, its ominous import swelling and filling the room, accentuating the hushed silence that inevitably followed.

"That is why I called you back." Vikramaditya's expression was solemn, his eyes fevered and volatile. "We have to formulate a new plan of action."

"The Hunas kidnapped him from Udaypuri?" Dhanavantri looked shocked and disbelieving. "They were so deep inside Sindhuvarta?"

"They had local help," said the samrat, his voice full of suppressed rage. "Someone provided the Hunas information on Ghatakarpara — his presence in Udaypuri, his movements, his whereabouts. They couldn't have figured it all out by themselves. They couldn't have taken him without local assistance. There are traitors in our midst along the frontier."

"Possibly the same people who were responsible for the death of the Huna scout at the Sristhali command centre," Amara Simha remarked.

"Possibly, but this time, they have dared to touch someone from the palace, a member of my own council, *my own dear nephew*." The words came out in a low, vengeful snarl. "In crossing my path, they have sealed their fates. I will make them rue the day they decided to trade their loyalty using Ghatakarpara as their currency."

"We will, Vikrama, but we must first figure out a way of freeing Ghatakarpara," Varahamihira gently but firmly brought the conversation back on course. "The Hunas will want to ransom him..."

"Ransom?" Amara Simha roared, his voice crashing

against the chamber's walls like the dashing of a mighty wave on a rocky coastline. "We will not wait for those savages to come back with a demand in exchange of Ghatakarpara's life or his liberty. *No* — we will go into the Great Desert and free him. This kidnapping is an act of war. Let us give them a war they won't forget."

The other councilors and the samrat exchanged glances, knowing instinctively that Amara Simha's words might well have been snatched from their own hearts and minds. This was war all over again, with one small difference. This time, Avanti would take war into the barbarians' homeland. This time, the dust of the Marusthali would know the flavour of blood.

"In which case, who will lead..." Varahamihira had barely let the words form when Amara Simha interrupted him a second time.

"I will," he snapped. His tone made it clear that he was past discussing and debating this. "I was heading for Udaypuri anyway. I know Atulyateja at the garrison. I also know Brihatsa, who is in charge of the command centre at Madhyamika. And during my last visit, I met Dattaka, who heads the Sristhali command centre. Between them, I will coordinate an attack on the Hunas."

"Very well, but even though they need to be suitably prepared, I recommend we don't update Atulyateja, Brihatsa and Dattaka on what we suspect has happened to Ghatakarpara," Varahamihira cautioned.

"Absolutely not," Vikramaditya shook his head with vehemence. "There is evidence of traitors on the frontier. Let us not tip them off about what we know and what we intend to do. The savages shouldn't learn of any of our plans."

"But Atulyateja will be expecting a reply from the palace," said Dhanavantri. "Our not responding could raise a red flag."

"We will send him a message, asking him to intensify the search and press in more men. We will behave as if we think

Ghatakarpara can be found inside Avanti's borders by looking harder everywhere. We will not mention Councilor Amara Simha at all," the samrat replied.

"But we'll tell him to stay put in Udaypuri, so he's there when I arrive," the brawny councilor clarified.

"In my opinion, one of us should come with you," said Kshapanaka. Looking around the table, she took in Shanku, Dhanavantri and Varahamihira. She knew that with Vishakha in need of attention, Dhanavantri couldn't be spared. Varahamihira on a crutch would be of little value in battle, while Shanku was needed in Ujjayini to take care of and interpret the Mother Oracle. "I will come," she said.

"No, you should stay here," Amara Simha said with a shake of his head. "The city will need protection when the devas or asuras come next. And don't worry…" a wolfish smile of anticipation lit his face, "I am more than enough to give the Hunas a taste of hell."

"Amara Simha is right," said Vikramaditya. "Still…" the samrat turned to Amara Simha, "you must take some more seasoned and reliable warriors with you, especially as you are taking the fight into the Great Desert. I suggest you take Angamitra and a sizeable force of *samsaptakas*."

"That is a good idea," said Dhanavantri. He looked at Amara Simha. "Don't say no. There are enough Hunas out there for everyone to share and still have some left over."

"Where do you think they've taken Ghatakarpara?" Kshapanaka asked suddenly.

The rest of the councilors and the king looked at one another. In all of this, they had overlooked the fact that none of them had ever set foot in the Marusthali. The Huna stronghold was completely alien to all of them.

"Yes, unless we know where to look, you will be running around in circles with only frustration to show for your efforts," said Varahamihira.

A glum silence engulfed the chamber. Outside, the sun was blazing down, laying the foundations for a torrid, sweaty day. Vikramaditya raised his head and looked across at the oracle hopefully.

"Can you or anyone else in the Wandering Tribe help, mother?"

The Mother Oracle shook her head. "I am afraid not, king. We might be nomadic, but the desert is an accursed place. We know of the Dark River because it exists in our stories of old, but that is all. We don't know the Great Desert; we never want to know it."

Everyone looked disheartened, staring in front of them as the prospect of rescuing Ghatakarpara waned and vanished. Amara Simha looked the most disappointed, his face morose and angry at having been thus thwarted by ignorance. Then, all of a sudden, his eyes twinkled and he flashed a triumphant grin around.

"I've got it," he exulted, clenching his fists in delight. "I know how to find the savages' hideouts in the desert."

"How?" asked the physician. Excitement rekindled in the room.

"The Huna scout," said Amara Simha. "The one I brought back from Sristhali, who told us about the Huna plan to attack Dvarka."

"The one languishing in the city garrison, of course," Varahamihira clapped his hands. "Wonderful! The fellow obviously knows the Great Desert well. He'll know where the oases are, where the barbarian cities and forts are located."

"But can he be trusted not to double-cross you at the first opportunity he gets?" Kshapanaka asked.

"I suspect I've put enough of a scare in him, so he doesn't entertain the idea," Amara Simha answered with a small chuckle. "But I'll take an interpreter along, just to make sure the fellow behaves. Now, if you will allow me, I must make all these arrangements. I wish to leave without delay."

"Yes," said the samrat, rising from his high chair. "I shall have Angamitra and his *samsaptakas* report to you." He came around the table to stand in front of Amara Simha. The councilor reached no further than the king's chest, but he was twice the king's size in bulk. The two men stared gravely into one another's eyes.

"I entrust you with a very big responsibility," said Vikramaditya. "I may not show my affection for him, but Ghatakarpara is very dear to me. And to mother and Vararuchi… and, of course, to Pralupi. I would never be able to forgive myself should anything happen to him. Please bring him back safe — the Aditya dynasty will be in your debt."

"I taught the little fellow how to hold a sword when he didn't know how to tie his own *dhoti*, Vikrama," the bearded councilor reached up and gripped the king's shoulder. "I am going over the Arbuda Mountains to bring him back for myself. But thank you for believing I am capable of the job. Allow me to go, so I can repay your faith in me."

* * *

The pungent aroma of freshly pressed mustard oil greeted Yashobhavi's nostrils when he brushed past the curtains to Chandravardhan's private bath chamber. The morning sun, pushing through the slats in the high windows, fell in bars on the king's back and shoulders, which were golden yellow and slick with oil. The king sat on a low stool, his legs stretched out in front of him, naked except for a plain linen *dhoti* that covered him from hip to thigh. To his right and left, a pair of masseurs worked oil into his ageing joints and muscles, while a third squatted by his feet, rubbing oil along the king's right leg. A palace *vaidya* hovered nearby, overseeing the ministrations with a critical eye. Chandravardhan himself looked healthy and at ease, his head lolling mildly due to massage-induced relaxation.

"A pity I couldn't meet the king as I was away."

Hearing Shashivardhan's voice, Yashobhavi tensed and stopped mid-stride. He hadn't expected the prince to be with his father this early, and from where he stood near the door, Shashivardhan was hidden from view, standing by the window that overlooked the Yamuna.

"Yes... you... were in Prayaga... I was told." Chandravardhan still laboured a little in putting words and sentences together, a grim reminder of the paralytic stroke from which he had just recovered. "Boat ac... accident... yes."

Undecided whether to walk into the chamber or leave, Yashobhavi stood by the doorway. The decision was made for him when one of the masseurs noticed him and murmured into the king's ear. Chandravardhan turned a stiff neck and their eyes met, killing the possibility of his beating a quiet retreat.

"Yash... shobhavi... come," the king motioned with his head.

The councilor bowed in greeting and stepped forward, minding his step to avoid skidding on any accidentally spilled oil. The masseurs and the physician bowed to him as Shashivardhan's tall and willowy frame came into sight.

"Greetings, councilor," said Shashivardhan, flicking a strand of his long brown hair back from his face.

"Greetings, my... *Prince*."

Yashobhavi wondered if anyone else in the room had been alert to his hesitation. For just a fraction of a moment, he had considered addressing Shashivardhan as 'king' — a formal announcement to that effect was due in a couple of days anyway. Yet, he had refused to do so, taking refuge in the technicality that Shashivardhan was still only the prince of Vatsa. He wished there were a few more handy technicalities around to stop Chandravardhan from making the announcement.

"Good... you went," said Chandravardhan. It took the councilor a moment to realize the king had resumed his conversation with Shashivardhan. "Go... to your people... when... when they are in trouble. People respect... a king who... cares. Y-you don't rule... by occupying... throne. You rule by... occupying a place in your... your people's hearts."

"I will remember that, father." Shashivardhan turned to Yashobhavi. "We were discussing King Baanahasta's visit here when father was unwell. You must have heard that there was a rider from Matsya last night?"

The councilor nodded, his face turning grave. "I understand the situation is rather bleak at the frontier. The Saka horsemen are getting bolder and are making deeper forays into Matsya, raiding at will and harrying Sindhuvarta's troops."

"A Hu.. Huna... fleet in Dvarka," Chandravardhan gasped, looking distraught. "Sakas along... M-Matsya's border. It... it is all hap... happening again."

"Father, it is alright." Shashivardhan took two steps towards Chandravardhan and crouched beside him. Placing a reassuring hand on his father's oily shoulder, he bent to look Chandravardhan in the eye. "We know what happened in Dvarka. The Huna fleet was wiped out. Led by Vararuchi, the soldiers of Sindhuvarta fought like lions."

"But... but something came out of... the sea to help us."

"It doesn't matter, father. What counts is that the Hunas have been dealt a severe setback. Who knows what kind of losses they have suffered? It is going to take them time to regroup. That is good news for us."

"That can also spell bad news."

Father and son turned to Yashobhavi with apprehension.

"If the Hunas have been put out of action for a while, we can count on the Sakas to build pressure along the frontier," the councilor explained. "The barbarians know they can't afford to be seen on the back foot."

"The councilor... is right," Chandravardhan nodded at his son. "And... and if so m-many troops are in... Dvarka, the fro-frontier is weaker."

"Can't we send some more of our troops to Matsya?" Shashivardhan looked from the king to Yashobhavi.

"I don't think we can spare more than a thousand men — archers, infantrymen and cavalry, all put together," said the councilor. "Maybe a thousand five hundred at the most. We need soldiers in the kingdom too... should the need ever arise."

Should the Saka hordes break through the frontier and sweep down the river plain into the heart of Sindhuvarta, is what the councilor meant.

"We can s-send troops. But what the frontier needs is lea... leaders." Chandravardhan sighed and slouched, so that a masseur could slather more oil on his back. "In Dvarka, Vara... Vararuchi turned the... fight against the... Hu... Hunas. We need someone... like that. Someone to ins-inspire the men... and... l-lead by example."

For a long moment, silence reigned over the bath chamber. Shashivardhan stood up and walked to the window to stare out over the Yamuna, where trails of mist still hung over the water and clung to the reedy riverbanks. The only sounds were those of the masseurs' hands slapping and kneading Chandravardhan's back, and the faraway call of crows. Yashobhavi finally cleared his throat to speak, but he was beaten to it by the prince.

"Permit me to go to the frontier, father."

All heads in the room turned to look at Shashivardhan, who stood framed in the light, a slight breeze ruffling his soft, shoulder-length hair. His bearded face was in shadow, but there was earnestness in his posture as he appealed to his father.

"I... don't know, son." Chandravardhan looked from the prince to Yashobhavi in confusion. The masseurs resumed their work, while the physician tried not to eavesdrop.

"Why, father? I want to go."

The king waved his hand at the masseurs, making it plain that they were to leave. The men bowed, picked up their bowls of oil and their hand towels, and bowed again. The *vaidya*, taking the cue, also bowed and prepared to exit. Chandravardhan waited patiently for the room to clear before turning his full attention on Shashivardhan.

"Why... now? In som-some days... you will be n-named... king. Plans... are made."

"All the more reason I should go, father," the prince approached and crouched beside Chandravardhan again. "If men have to be led into battle, would they rather be led by a prince or a king? And if I am going to be named king, wouldn't I be wasting that authority by sitting here in the palace? Shouldn't I, instead, be putting that authority to use at the frontier, where it could help inspire the men fighting for Sindhuvarta?"

Shooting another glance at Yashobhavi, Chandravardhan gave a troubled sigh. He shook his head indecisively, casting around for an argument to counter the prince. "The frontier... is hard. You... you are not accustomed to it..."

"Father, Sindhuvarta is in trouble. More critically, Matsya is in trouble. Haven't you always said that King Baanahasta is like a brother to you? He was the only one to come enquiring when you were unwell. He *needs* us now, father. We can't let him face the Sakas alone. Please," he took the king's hand into his own and entreated, "let me go."

Chandravardhan nodded, his eyes suddenly a little moist. Observing his king's eyes well up, Yashobhavi wondered if the emotion was the outcome of a rush of pride in a son from whom there were no expectations left, or the fear that his offspring was heading to a place from where the chances of a safe return were limited. The councilor suspected a combination of both factors. He, for one, hadn't expected Shashivardhan to volunteer for the harsh frontier. And though it was surprising and commendable on Shashivardhan's part, the councilor wasn't impressed. Intimate knowledge of the prince's nature told him the young man wasn't capable of matching his zealous words with action. If he were a betting man, Yashobhavi wouldn't have placed his money on the prince coming back to Kausambi, no matter what the odds were.

Shashivardhan was about to say something when a soft voice spoke from the doorway. "Where iss Plalupi?"

All three men turned to see Himavardhan at the door, holding the curtains and staring at them with his big, childlike eyes. Seeing the men looking at him, Himavardhan raised the edge of a curtain to his mouth and bit it self-consciously. "Where iss Plalupi?" he asked again, looking around the room. Pouting, he said, "I want to play with Plalupi."

"Of course, you can play with Pralupi," Shashivardhan clapped his hands and walked over to his uncle. There was playfulness in his tone and his eyes shone with excitement. "But first, don't you want to go for a boat ride?"

"Yess." Himavardhan grinned at the prince, all thoughts of Pralupi forgotten. Letting go of the curtain, he took Shashivardhan's hand and turned around. Together, uncle and nephew left the bath chamber.

"He is s-so loving to...wards Himavardhan," the king said, staring fondly at the empty doorway. "When Shashi leaves... for the f-frontier, how... how will my little brother cope? Pralupi... ha-hardly cares about him. Isn't sh-she back from... Av-vanti yet?"

When the councilor didn't reply, Chandravardhan turned to him. "He volunteered to... go to the frontier," he said, admiration in his voice. "He was always a g-good boy at heart... I... I think he has finally become res... responsible as well. I can see the makings of a good... k-king in him. And you know... I d-didn't smell *soma* on his breath this morning."

"That's nice, your honour," Yashobhavi nodded curtly. His eyes were expressionless.

"Yes... yes." The king suddenly looked anxious, and his words were directed more to himself than at the councilor. "He's getting... better. More responsible. No-nothing should happen to him... at the frontier. We must make sure... guards... he needs a good s-set of guards to... to protect him." Then, as if suddenly remembering that Yashobhavi was still with him, he looked up. "W-what brought you here so early?"

"A delegation of traders and farmers has come to meet you from the principalities of Karusha and Dasarna, your honour. They claim the recent floods have destroyed their crops, and they are seeking waivers in taxes. They say they are being harassed by our tax collectors."

Chandravardhan picked up a small brass bell that was kept to one side and rang it. A shrill tinkling issued, and almost immediately, the masseurs who had withdrawn came right back in.

"I shall see the... the delegation once I have b-bathed and breakfasted," said the king. "T-tell the royal Master of... of Records and Accounts to also at-tend the meeting."

"Your honour," Yashobhavi bowed and left the room, heading to where the delegation awaited an audience with their king. But the councilor's mind was elsewhere, closer to the rugged, inhospitable frontier where Shashivardhan was going.

The councilor's mind was already formulating a plan.

Search

Guided by the lucid notes of the *jal-yantra*, Shukracharya approached the marble pavilion over one of the overgrown paths that crisscrossed the garden, his step surer than it had been on the morning he had made Jayanta's acquaintance. That day, he had been cautious, circling his prey; today, he was intent on luring it into his trap.

This did not imply that he had hit upon a tactic to make Urvashi pliant towards Jayanta. If anything, the guru of the asuras was conscious of the hollowness of his suggestions to win the apsara's affections, and he feared Jayanta would call his bluff. Still, time was running out, and he had to make a play for the mantras to awaken Ahi before Indra and the human king met. So, he had waited for the prince and followed him unobtrusively into the garden, his gamble hinging on the hope that the deva's desire for Urvashi was ultimately greater than his capacity for common sense.

Climbing the steps to the pavilion and ducking into its welcoming shade, the high priest sought out the platform located by the side of the pool, where, he knew, the *jal-yantra*

and its player would be found. He was rewarded by the sight
of the young prince seated with his back to him, striking the
bronze bowls rhythmically and swaying his head, lost to the
music; for a moment, the high priest let himself be drawn
into its rapture as well. Then, forcing himself to concentrate
on the task that had brought him here, Shukracharya began
descending the steps leading to the pool and the platform.

Halfway down the broad marble steps and closing in on
his quarry, the high priest was assailed by the sensation that
something was amiss. For one, he got the feeling that he was
being watched. And as his vision adjusted to the shadows
inside the pavilion, it occurred to him that the player seated
before the *jal-yantra* was a bit too bulky for Indra's son.
Shukracharya froze where he stood, but before he could react
any further, a familiar voice addressed him.

"I don't recall you ever having cultivated such a consuming
interest in music. Is this a recent passion?"

Turning slowly, Shukracharya looked over his shoulder
to where Brihaspati had made an appearance from behind a
column. The portly chamberlain had a cunning and superior
smile on his smooth face, and his manner was condescending
as he waddled down the steps on his bowlegs. Shukracharya
waited for his old opponent to draw close, so that their
eyes were level.

"One tries to learn whatever one can, which is more than
can be said of others, who are happy to let old habits and older
stupidities define who they are."

"Indeed, indeed," said Brihaspati, smoothening the ring of
white hair on his scalp with one hand. "In that case, I suspect
you have applied yourself very poorly to your lessons. Else,
you would have been able to tell that *he*," pointing at the
player, who, Shukracharya realized, had stopped playing,
"is nowhere as talented as Prince Jayanta. And if you had

managed telling that difference, you wouldn't have walked into this little trap I had set for you."

"Jayanta? Trap?" The high priest scratched his beard in puzzlement in a brave attempt to save face. "Are you in your senses, good friend?"

Brihaspati's smile was thin and without mirth. "Surely, even *you* are not foolish enough to assume you would be allowed to roam around Devaloka unsupervised, and that your attempts to befriend the prince would go unnoticed and unreported?"

"Pardon me, but I didn't know that spying on guests was the latest in deva etiquette."

"Etiquette, like respect, is conferred on those deserving of it. One can't abuse the privileges of being a guest and expect etiquette in return."

"Talking to the prince is an abuse of privilege now?" Shukracharya snorted in mock merriment. "I was craving company; the prince was alone. We bumped into each other, so I stopped to chat. There was nothing more to that."

"Two things," the chamberlain held up two fingers. "If you are craving company, why are you still here? Hiranyaksha left for Patala a few days ago. You could have gone with him. Nobody's asked you to stay on, so what's holding you back? The way I…"

"I'm a guest of your master Indra," Shukracharya interrupted hotly, an accent on the 'master' to show Brihaspati his place. "I don't need to explain why I'm still in Devaloka to anyone other than your master. But as you've asked, let me tell you that I had told Indra that I would wait for his return, so we can decide on the next course of action together."

"Fair enough. But… *but*… coming back to Jayanta, let me tell you why your chats with the prince aren't as innocent as you make them out to be," Brihaspati retorted. "You know that Jayanta has the mantras needed to raise Ahi; you're also aware that only offspring born out of a deva and asura union can control the serpent-dragon. When I look for those who can command Ahi, other than Jayanta, only two names suggest themselves — Chandasura and Amarka. Your sons, half-bloods. Now if only *they* had the mantras…"

"Nonsense," the high priest smirked and shook his head dismissively, even though he knew he wasn't fooling Brihaspati. "You read too much on account of your paranoia."

"To test my theory, I devised this little trap," the chamberlain continued as if Shukracharya hadn't spoken. He pointed to the deva who now stood by the pool in respectful silence. "I got him to dress up like Jayanta, walk into this garden and play the *jal-yantra*. And look at what came in after him…" Brihaspati grinned and looked Shukracharya up and down, "like a swarm of bees attracted to a pot of honey."

"You really think way too much, and I've already wasted a lot of my time on you." Seeing that he was at a disadvantage and needed to beat a retreat, the high priest turned and began mounting the steps back out of the pavilion. "I might want company now and then, but if the choice is between you and loneliness, I would settle for the latter every single time."

Shukracharya had just about reached the archway that led out into the sunny garden when the guru of the devas called after him.

"You'll be pleased to know that loneliness is what you can expect for the rest of your stay in Devaloka. Because you'll definitely not be running into Jayanta, that much I can tell you. I have instructed the guards at the palace to ensure that such opportunities do not arise hereafter."

* * *

The hunt was not going well at all, at least from Shoorasena's point of view. Yes, they had cornered and brought down a majestic specimen of *barasingha*, besides which they had also slaughtered four spotted deer and snared a handful of *teetar*, the carcasses piled high in the carts accompanying the hunting party. But the tigers and leopards had proved elusive, and despite doing their best, the royal trackers and drum beaters had failed to flush the big cats into the open. Some days were like this, Shoorasena knew, yet it hurt his pride that his first hunt as king of Magadha had given him no ferocious trophies to bear home. If he were a superstitious man, he would have read an omen in this, but not being one, he just cursed and kept pushing on in the hope that a predator would finally show itself.

Having been on the trail since daybreak, fatigued and in poor spirits, the party had broken for rest and repast around midday, when a rider arrived with news of King Bhoomipala having agreed to trade the musician Gajaketu for their diplomat Pallavan.

"Wonderful," Shoorasena exclaimed, slapping his leg and sitting up on the divan on which he had been reclining. He beamed at Kapila and General Daipayana, who were sharing the tent that had been pitched for him. "Exactly as I hoped and expected."

"Indeed, your honour," Daipayana grinned through his stained and uneven teeth. "Very clever of you to have predicted how Bhoomipala would behave, and tricking him in his own game of espionage and manipulation. You deserve a salute, your honour." Swaying drunkenly, he took the pitcher of firewater and splashed some of the spirit into his cup, which he then raised in a toast. "A salute to the king of Magadha."

"What do you propose to do with this musician once we've brought him to Girivraja, brother?" asked Kapila.

"He will never set foot in Girivraja," Shoorasena answered, getting to his feet. "It is too dangerous. He knows too much. I don't want anyone learning what he knows, even by accident."

The king pushed the flap of the tent aside to look out at the forest, where a light drizzle was coming down. "No, we'll kill him and bury him as soon as the exchange is complete."

Whether it was the news of Bhoomipala's meek surrender or the cooling rain, Shoorasena's mood lifted, and he turned to face his brother and his general with a satisfied smile. "First, King Harihara offers me his daughter's hand, and now, Bhoomipala agrees to our demands like a dog with its tailed tucked between its legs. These are powerful kingdoms of Sindhuvarta, remember. Heheya and Kosala. They see us for who we are... Magadha, a land of promise, power, prestige. One day, not far in the future, we will hold them chained at our feet. Each one of them, including Avanti."

"In a way, we already have them chained and held hostage, brother," said Kapila. "From what I hear, our restrictions on the trade of iron out of Dandakabhukti have already started hitting the other kingdoms of Sindhuvarta hard. The price of iron has doubled, and still there's practically nothing in the market. Everyone is bound to get desperate soon."

"Right now, it is iron," the king chuckled as he poured himself some firewater. "Wait until we start imposing duties on all goods that pass west through Magadha. Teak and bamboo and spices from the valleys of Pragjyotishpura, the fine and fragrant rice from Vanga, silk and dyes and pearls from Sribhoja and Srivijaya... Our neighbours will pay more for everything they need, unless they accede to certain demands of ours. Tributes that will earn them trade concessions, but give us greater power and leverage over them, military alliances that will be favourable to us... Just wait and watch."

"Yes, your honour, but in order to strangulate the kingdoms of Sindhuvarta, we must act quickly against Odra and Kalinga first," Daipayana pointed out. "There is no point in controlling Tamralipti if goods can still flow uninterrupted through the ports of Tosali and Uttara Tosali. And let's not forget about the iron mines in Odra. The deposits may not be as abundant as those in Dandakabhukti, but the quality of the ore is impressive. We must block off all supply from there as well."

"Undoubtedly, general." Shoorasena took a long pull of firewater. "The moment this affair over the musician is settled, I intend turning all our focus back on Kalinga and Odra. In fact," he turned his gaze to Kapila, "I want you to proceed to Tamralipti immediately."

Kapila nodded once, silently.

"When you get there, meet Bhadraka and the rest of the Vanga chiefs who swore their loyalty to Magadha and get them abreast of our plan to attack Uttara Tosali."

"Would that be wise, your honour?" asked Daipayana. "Trusting them so soon?"

"What choice do we have, general?" asked the king, stroking his manicured beard. "If we have to take Tosali and Uttara Tosali, it will have to be by sea. We need ships, and we need men who can control those ships and navigate the sea. I don't know if such men exist in Magadha, but they certainly do in Vanga. We need the assistance of Vanga's chiefs to take Odra and Kalinga."

"I see what you mean, brother, but the general has a point." Kapila leaned forward. "Can the Vanga chiefs be trusted not to send warnings to the courts of Queen Abhirami and King Veerayanka? They swore their loyalty to us, but are they loyal enough yet? For them, we are still invaders who have forcibly taken their land — and their right to rule their land."

"You are right. Which is why, it is time to let them know that we are not really taking their land, nor their right to rule it." Shoorasena paused and looked from his brother to his general, who exchanged puzzled glances. "When you get to Tamralipti, you will make an official declaration on my behalf, appointing Bhadraka as Chief Governor of Vanga. He will be the administrative head of all the principalities and the official representative of the kingdom of Magadha."

"Bhadraka," said Daipayana in surprise, but there was also slow comprehension in his eyes. "A clever move, your honour."

"The most sensible and ambitious of Vanga's chiefs. He was quick to see there was no point in standing against us, so he switched sides early. And he got the other chiefs to come over as well. A bit of an opportunist, which suits us fine. He'll love our gesture, and he'll ensure the others comply with our wishes."

"I shall leave for Tamralipti tonight, brother," said Kapila.

A troubled frown creased Daipayana's forehead and Shoorasena was quick to notice it. "Something the matter, general?" the king asked.

"Just wondering, your honour... We are making Bhadraka Chief Governor of Vanga. But we have already promised that post to the courtier Asmabindu. If you recall, that was the deal he had negotiated with us to expose Uttama, Diganta and Bhaskara, and turn them and Pallavan over to us."

"Hmm." Shoorasena's eyes were suddenly angry and unhappy over this complication.

"How do we sort this out, your honour?"

Shoorasena rose and went to stand at the door to the tent, gazing out into the green forest. Overhead, the light rain pattered on the leaves and drops drummed on the heavy fabric of the tent.

"It is too bad that Asmabindu also wants the post," the king said finally with a helpless shrug of his broad shoulders. "He cannot have it. Not just yet, at least. Maybe after Bhadraka has served his purpose. Bhadraka as governor will have far greater value for us than Asmabindu. So no... Bhadraka it will be." He turned to face Daipayana. "Find some other way to compensate Asmabindu. Make him chief of... something. Or... maybe give him money. Just do what is needed." Shoorasena dismissed the matter with a wave of his hand. "I think it is time to return to Girivraja. We must prepare for Pallavan's exchange, and it is getting late…"

At just that moment, a soldier arrived at the tent. "Your honour," he said with a bow, "the trackers have sighted a tiger further down the valley. A mile to the south."

"Really? That close?" Shoorasena turned to Kapila and Daipayana with bright eyes. "Get your bows. Let's go."

"I thought you just said it was getting late and…"

"Of course, it is getting late and all that, brother," the king cut Kapila off with a smile. "But you heard him. The tiger is just a mile away. If what you want badly is within arm's reach and you do not go after it — that is foolishness. Whether it is a tiger or a crown or an empire the size of Sindhuvarta, if it is there to be taken, you must take it."

* * *

"They have taken him hostage. Do you realize that? *Hostage*!"

Pralupi's high-pitched rant ended in a ragged shriek, and Shanku immediately slowed down, then stopped a few feet from the door to the terrace adjoining the samrat's chambers.

"I realize that, sister," Vikramaditya's tone was patient but tired. "Which is why I had the message sent to you, letting you know what we have learned about Ghatakarpara."

"So?"

"So…?" The king repeated, not knowing how to interpret Pralupi's question.

"So, will you just stand here, doing nothing?"

"Amara Simha has already left for the frontier with a force of *samsaptakas*. Didn't the messenger deliver my full message?" The samrat sounded exasperated. "The councilor is going into the Great Desert to look for Ghatakarpara."

"I know that," Pralupi snapped back. "But why has Amara

Simha gone alone? Why haven't more councilors gone with him? What can he do all by himself, where all can he search?"

"He is not alone. He has an army there to help him."

"Pshaw!" Pralupi said in a dismissive tone. "*You* should have gone. You *should* go. You can go even *now*."

Shanku wondered if she should go away and return in a while. She didn't like the idea of eavesdropping on the king's conversation, but the palace hand had insisted that the king wanted to see her urgently.

"I can't go, sister, because Ujjayini needs me. For the same reason, I can't send more councilors with Amara Simha. The city needs protection from the devas and asuras."

"The city and its people are more important to you than my son?" Pralupi sneered. "Humph, to think that this is the city and throne my son wants to serve."

"The city and its people are *as important* to me as Ghatakarpara," Vikramaditya corrected in a steely tone. "I think your son understands this far better than you do."

"So that's it — you won't go yourself, nor will you send more councilors to rescue my son?" Pralupi's voice rose in challenge, hard and uncompromising. "What about your brother, Vararuchi? I don't see him anywhere *protecting the city*." Shanku winced at the sarcasm in the last three words. "Send him to find my son."

"Vararuchi is *our* brother, whether you like it or not. And no, no one else goes, leaving the city at the mercy of what Indra and Shukracharya have in mind next."

"Do as you wish, but you are not worthy of being uncle to my son," Pralupi's voice broke in anger and frustration, and Shanku had a sense that the woman was moving towards the exit, towards her. "I have never seen a more heartless and uncaring man. What did I do to get *you* as a brother?"

Pralupi emerged from the terrace in a storm, teary-eyed and tormented, and Shanku had to step hurriedly back and out of the way to prevent a collision. Their eyes met, but if Pralupi recognized Shanku, it didn't show on her face as she swept past and down the gallery, a tempest on the move. Shanku watched her for a moment before turning and stepping through the door.

"Shankubala, you're here," the samrat said wearily, but with some relief as well. "Lucky you didn't get blown away by that whirlwind." His eyes crinkled in humour.

"I am sorry, but I couldn't help overhearing some of it," the girl replied with a small smile.

"The way she was going on, I wouldn't be surprised if half of Ujjayini knows what was said," the king grinned, and Shanku couldn't help laughing.

"You wanted to see me?"

"Yes."

Vikramaditya turned and walked over to the parapet. Leaning his hands on the stone railing, he looked out over the lake, which was shimmering in the early afternoon sun. Shanku took a few steps in and stopped under an archway that trailed creepers. She waited for the king to speak. At last, Vikramaditya turned to appraise her.

"I take it that you've received a message from your father recently?"

The girl's expression hardened instantly. "Yes, Samrat. Did you hear that from the Mother Oracle?"

"Why would your grandmother tell me that? No," Vikramaditya shook his head. "I heard it from him."

"Him?" Shanku blinked at the samrat. "From my father?"

Vikramaditya nodded. "He sent me a message through one of the guards an hour ago. The message said that he has been trying to meet you."

"He sent me a message through a guard as well," the girl confirmed. "Some days back."

"You know he wants you to forgive him."

It wasn't a question, so Shanku didn't reply. Instead, she dropped her head and studied the patterns on the marble floor.

"You know what is interesting? In his message to me, your father never once asked me to pardon him. But he tells me that he seeks *your* forgiveness."

"That's too bad for him," Shanku replied tightly and shook her head.

The samrat drew a deep breath and looked away towards the far shore of the lake. "Can you guess why he sent me a message? What his message was about?"

Shanku studied the king's face, not knowing what was coming next.

Vikramaditya let the suspense draw out for a few extra moments before returning his gaze to the girl. "He claims he knows someone who escaped from the Dandaka Forest, and he says he can help us with that person's whereabouts."

"Who is this person and where is he?"

The king shrugged. "Your father is not telling. He is not telling *anyone* that. He insists he will share that information with only one person."

Shanku's eyes widened in comprehension, then quickly narrowed again. "He is doing it for the gold coins."

"He made no mention of the reward, if that helps."

"It is just a trick to try and meet me," the girl said adamantly. "He knows nothing."

Vikramaditya pushed himself off the railing he was leaning against and walked up to Shanku. "You may be right, Shankubala. But what if he is telling us the truth? What if he *does* know someone who escaped from the Forest of the Exiles, someone who can take us back in?"

The girl did not reply. Seeing her stand silent and sullen, staring away at nothing, the samrat stepped up and placed his hands on her shoulders. "I cannot ask you to go and meet him…"

"You can," Shanku mumbled. "You are my king."

"I *will not* ask you to go and meet him against your wishes," Vikramaditya corrected himself. "Brichcha may or may not be lying, but if you think this is an elaborate ruse to bait you into meeting him, we will not allow it. I am sorry I brought this up."

Shanku looked up at the samrat's face. In his eyes, she saw hope ebbing away, and disappointment and helplessness creeping in. The samrat let his hands slip from her shoulders and drop to his sides.

"You may go," he gave a brisk nod, forcing a smile that didn't quite reach his eyes. Then, as a new thought struck him, he stayed the girl. "Kindly do me a favour. I need a rider to go to *badi-maa*'s house with a message for Vararuchi. He needs to know about Ghatakarpara's kidnapping. Also, with Amara Simha no longer here, it would be good if we had Vararuchi back protecting Ujjayini. See to it that the rider is dispatched promptly."

Shanku inclined her head. Turning around, she left the terrace without a word.

* * *

The gate that gave into the garrison command of Udaypuri was broad and imposing, constructed from heavy ironwood and reinforced with thick bands of black iron. Its high archway, which housed armoured stockades on both sides for archers to shoot from, compulsively drew the observer's eye, and together with the surrounding stone-and-mortar wall, it dwarfed the adjacent town buildings into insignificance. The gate was thrown open at the moment, offering a view into portions of the wide courtyard and fort within. Soldiers flitted beneath the arch, in and out, in small, frantic rushes. Judging by the hive-like activity, Aparupa surmised that something of import was afoot.

"You don't see him anywhere, do you?" she asked, turning her head halfway towards the man standing to her left, her gaze still fixed on the gate. A troubled frown appeared to have taken permanent possession of her face.

Dveeja, the son of Aparupa's maid, blinked stupidly at the gate a couple of times, then let his eye trail the wall. "Aai... ai..." he said with a single shake of his head that could have meant anything, but which Aparupa seemed to understand.

"I can't see him either," she said with a short sigh. Craning her neck, she looked past a gaggle of Frontier Guardsmen who had stopped to converse with the sentries. "Let's wait for some more time."

In truth, the girl had been standing under the tree opposite the garrison gate half the morning, and had returned to the spot with Dveeja as soon as lunch was complete. As the day progressed into afternoon and the shadows crawled and lengthened along the ground, she had grown increasingly anxious, fighting to keep the rising tide of desperation in check. It had been four days since she had last seen the soldier — and three since she had heard from him.

Three mornings ago, as she had lounged in her bed twirling the snake bangle he had gifted her and smiling happy thoughts, a palm leaf tied to a weighted stub of bamboo had sailed in through the open window. The leaf bore a short message from the soldier, telling her that he had been detained on some work and would not be able to meet her later that evening. Disappointed though she had been, Aparupa had accepted it. The next day went by without any word from him, and when the next — yesterday — brought nothing either, she had gone to their chosen meeting spot in the hope that he would show up like he always did. She had sat on the grass by the big boulder, watching dusk fall, listening for his footsteps over the soft gurgle of the stream, but he hadn't come. It was almost dark when she finally rose to return home, confused over his absence, heavy with sorrow, sick with longing.

And now, almost all of today had gone by, and there was still no news from him, no indication of his whereabouts.

"I am sure there were no messages from him other than the first one," she said, half to Dveeja, half to herself. Instinctively, she touched the bamboo bangle she was wearing on her right hand. "I looked everywhere... there was nothing."

The sound of approaching drumbeats came from away to their left. Aparupa and Dveeja turned to see two men with drums around their necks emerge from a side street and turn away from the fort, heading towards the town's centre. They were followed by a small rabble of children, all noisy and excited about the drummers. Dveeja was taken in by the sight as well and gaped after the little procession, but the girl was back to watching the gate. The town criers had been about since morning, beating their drums and making some announcement about people who had escaped from the Forest of the Exiles, and there being a big reward from the palace in exchange for information. Reward or no reward, Aparupa couldn't be less bothered about runaways from the Dandaka. All she cared about for the moment was finding the man she loved.

Suddenly, as if making up her mind, she grabbed her maid's son by the hand. "Come."

Pulling Dveeja along behind her, Aparupa impulsively crossed over to the gate, where there was a momentary break in the comings and goings. Once on the other side of the road, however, she hesitated, overcome with uncertainty.

"Yes?" One of the sentries looked at the two of them with raised eyebrows. "What do you want?"

Aparupa approached the gate tentatively, conscious of three pairs of eyes on her. "I am... there is a soldier I am looking for," she managed.

"There are many soldiers here," the sentry replied. "It's a big garrison."

"His name is Ghataraja."

The sentry shook his head; the name meant nothing to him. He looked across at the other two sentries, who had heard the exchange. Both shrugged and shook their heads, signalling their ignorance.

"I *have* to find him," her tone took on a pleading edge. "Can you help me, please?"

The sentries looked at one another before the one doing the talking shrugged helplessly. "We're on duty. And we don't know this soldier you speak of."

"Is there some place I can go and ask, or *someone* who would know?" Aparupa's voice strained and cracked in desperation.

"I... don't know..." The sentry was moved enough by the girl's plight to want to help, but he was at a loss how to. "Maybe you should..."

He was interrupted by the clatter of hooves from inside the garrison, and moments later, a posse of four cavalrymen veered into view. Aparupa and Dveeja were bang in their way, and the horsemen had to rein in quickly to stop the horses from running over the two of them.

"What is this?" thundered one of the riders, a man with a pink face and a huge, grey moustache. Turning to the sentry, he chided, "Why are these two standing in front of the gate? They would have got themselves killed and we would probably have suffered worse. Move them aside."

"My apologies, captain," the sentry mumbled and bowed. Then, as a thought struck him, he said, "Captain, they are looking for a soldier. A soldier named..." he looked at Aparupa enquiringly, urging her to speak up.

"Ghataraja," the girl said quickly.

"So?" The captain looked from the guard to Aparupa to Dveeja, who quailed at the horseman's glare and ducked behind Aparupa with a small whimper. "So what?" the captain demanded again.

"This is the Second Captain of the garrison of Udaypuri," the sentry gave Aparupa a nod loaded with meaning.

"Ghataraja... *sir*," the girl repeated, catching on quickly. "I am looking for a soldier by that name, sir."

Mollified just a little, the captain looked at his three companions. The name didn't strike any of them as familiar, though.

"What is he a soldier of, girl?" the captain asked. Seeing her blank expression, he added, "Is he a soldier of the Frontier Guard or the Imperial Army?"

"I don't know, sir. I just know he is a soldier of this garrison. That's what he told me."

Two of the horsemen exchanged glances and shook their heads at the girl's naiveté. The captain, meanwhile, frowned.

"That doesn't help," he said. "This garrison houses Frontier Guardsmen, soldiers of the Imperial Army and even members of the local militia who're not from Udaypuri." He paused, then snorted, "Hell, we even have soldiers from the Anartas and Heheya here, girl. This soldier of yours could be any of these."

"Sir, he is from Avanti, sir. A silk weaver's son," the words tumbled out of Aparupa.

"Unfortunately, we don't categorize soldiers by their father's professions. If you don't know which division he serves in, finding him will be impossible."

"Sir, I first met him near the village of Balipura, along the frontier," Aparupa was literally wringing her hands, beseeching the captain. "I met him again here recently, and he was here until *four* days ago. He was..."

"Listen, girl," the captain interrupted firmly. "This is a garrison headquarters. Soldiers from all over the place come here, and they are transferred to command centres and outposts along the frontier. This is routine even during peacetime — and now we are dealing with a potential Huna-Saka invasion." He nudged his horse forward, trying to edge past Aparupa and Dveeja. "Your soldier can be anywhere right now, and I cannot waste my time…"

"Sir, please, somebody would know. There must be some records of where…"

"Listen, girl. *Listen* to me." The captain raised his voice sharply, his patience wearing thin. When he was certain he had the girl's attention, he continued, "I have bigger headaches to deal with right now. A prince of this kingdom has gone missing, the Samrat's nephew, no less. Gone from this very garrison, without a trace. If I have to look for someone, I would rather spend my time looking for the prince than for this soldier of yours, understand? Now move aside and let us pass."

The posse nosed past them and was away in a quick gallop. Their departure coincided with another discharge of a platoon of soldiers of the Imperial Army, led by a captain with a tough, no-nonsense attitude. Aparupa's shoulders slumped in defeat, and as she turned away, she saw the sentry look at her with sympathy. Somehow, that look hurt even more than the Second Captain's apathy.

"Come, Dveeja, let's go home," she said. As they walked away, heads down in defeat, she added bitterly, "Of course they will look for the prince and not Ghataraja. What do they understand about the importance of my love, what do they care?"

"Aaai…" Dveeja pressed Aparupa's hand. He knew she was upset, and his own lips turned down at the corners. "Aauuu…"

"It's okay." The girl felt the crushing weight of hopelessness in her chest, and she struggled to keep her voice steady. "We will keep looking for him. Nobody can stop us."

The road ahead became a watery blur, as long-suppressed tears finally rose in revolt.

Revelation

The man staring out from between the heavy iron bars of the cell had piercing black eyes that reflected the light from the torches in flickering orange specks. His gaze was fixed in what appeared to be a cross between wonder and disbelief, and he gripped the cell's bars tightly to keep himself from sagging to the ground, for his legs were quivering, threatening to give under him any moment. Without warning, tears sprang to his eyes, and letting go of the bars, he slowly backed away from the door, withdrawing into the deeper shadows of the cell.

Shanku stood rooted to the spot, ten paces outside the cell's door, caught in two minds about the wisdom of coming here. One part of her mind assured her that she had made the right choice; the other told her she still had time to reverse her decision and leave the dungeons behind her. Realizing that she was holding her breath — and that the figure in the cell was no more than a silhouette in the darkness within — she exhaled and stepped closer to the door.

"Unlock it, please," she said to the guard accompanying

her, aware that her throat felt strangely dry, making her voice
crack a little.

The door swung open on poorly oiled hinges, a whining,
grating protest of metal on metal. Taking a torch from a
nearby wall bracket, the councilor entered the cell. The
torchlight illuminated the modest space, and Shanku saw
that the man had backed into the farthest wall and had slid
down to sit on his haunches, his face buried in his hands,
his shoulders shaking as he wept silently, uncontrollably.
The councilor took a couple of paces towards the man, then
stopped and glanced at the guard, who had followed her
inside. Meeting her eyes, the guard inclined his head in respect
and slipped out of the cell.

Turning back, Shanku walked the few remaining paces to
stand in front of the huddled figure. Holding the torch up to
see him clearly, she spoke, striving to keep her tone even and
matter of fact.

"You wanted to see me."

The man raised his head and looked up at the councilor,
his eyes still streaming tears. "You came," he said, the words
coming out in a wet croak of relief.

"Yes," Shanku breathed in deep to steady herself. "You
insisted that I come."

The man nodded, then wiped his eyes with his palms, using
his forearms to dry his cheeks. For a moment he sat quietly,
looking away to one side.

"I know you've come for the king's sake and not mine," he
sniffled once. "I should have been more like you, putting the
king ahead of anyone else. But I wasn't. I should have made
you proud. But I didn't. I am sorry I failed you, Shankubala."

The councilor opened her mouth to speak, but found that
the words had caught in her throat, struggling to get past the
painful lump that had suddenly formed there. She swallowed
and looked down at the bowed head of Brichcha.

Shanku had very little recollection of the man from her childhood — she had been all of eight when Brichcha's treachery was discovered and he was removed from the post of Warden of the Imperial Stables. The only thing she remembered vividly was him putting her on a saddle and taking her on rides around the palace grounds, wind whipping her hair as they laughed together in abandonment. She didn't even recall much from Brichcha being sentenced to be exiled into the Dandaka, her mother committing suicide out of shame and Vikramaditya sparing Brichcha from exile and consigning him to the dungeons out of pity for her, Shanku. She had gathered all that in little pieces much later, as she had grown up in the palace under Vetala Bhatta's tutelage. But with that gathering and understanding had come anger and revulsion for the man who had deprived her of so much. Slowly, her visits to the dungeons had dropped in frequency until one day, five years ago, she had determined never to look at the man's face again.

Five years ago, Brichcha had still been tall, with a haughty, unrepentant air about him. But the figure squatting at her feet was frail and bent, the black of his hair and beard replaced by a dull shade of yellow-white. His shoulders had narrowed and his cheeks had sunk in, and Shanku realized that she would barely have recognized the man had she met him outside his cell. It came as a shock to her that Brichcha had not been done in by age — he had been broken by her neglect of him. Her vengeance on the man had worked like a charm, she realized to her horror.

"You think that I seek pardon, so I may be set free of the dungeons," the man looked up at her with a sad smile and shook his head. "No, I am happy here in this cell, my home for the last ten or more years. No, Shankubala, *this* is not my prison. I am a prisoner of my guilt, my shame at what I have done — to myself, to your mother, but mostly to you. *That* is the prison I seek escape from. And only you can grant that to me. I beg your forgiveness, Shanku. Rid me of my guilt and shame."

A fresh burst of sorrow brought a fresh flood of tears, and Brichcha hid his face in his forearms. Crouching down before the man, Shanku reached out a trembling hand and touched Brichcha's shoulder.

"Father," she said, fighting to keep the tremor out of her voice and failing. "Father."

Raising his head, Brichcha looked gratefully at the councilor. Then, taking her hand gently from his shoulder, he placed it between his own and brought it up to his bowed head.

"Forgive me, Shankubala, forgive me," he mumbled through his tears, pressing his daughter's hand to his forehead.

"I do, father," the girl heard herself say, through the rush of sobs that broke from the very core of her being. She wasn't entirely certain whether she had only thought the words or had said them out loud, so she repeated them as she wrapped her arms around Brichcha's shoulders, drawing him close, tears running down her face. "I forgive you, father."

Father and daughter held each other in a quivering embrace that neither dared to break. It was almost as if they were holding together their futures in the span of their arms, and that by letting each other go, they feared all they had achieved would come apart and fall away around them. It was only when the fear and the tears subsided that they slowly unclasped from their embrace, looking at one another with new eyes.

"Promise me you will visit me more often," said Brichcha, still holding Shanku's hand. "Once in ten days, once in fifteen... even once a month if you..."

"I will come every week," Shanku placed a finger on her father's lips, silencing him.

"You promise?"

As Shanku nodded, Brichcha looked at his daughter closely, taking in her features. "You have grown in the last five years. No more a child. I have been hearing about you," his voice took on a note of pride. "They told me about how you led a charge against the horsemen from Devaloka, how you forced them to come into the range of our archers. My daughter, so brave. They also told me about how you can... disappear."

"You've heard about all this?" The councilor looked surprised.

"Of course. Gossip is all we do here. We have all the time. But with you, there was active interest — I have earned a reputation for pestering the guards to bring me news of you. I have tried my best to keep abreast of what is happening in your life."

Shanku dropped her head, suddenly feeling guilty for having ignored her father for so many years. But Brichcha himself didn't seem bothered, now that he had her pardon. "You do this appearing and disappearing thing... now it will be easier for you to come and go from the dungeons," he smiled at her. "You won't need to climb up and down the stairs. So come every week, okay? Just like that," he flicked his fingers.

The girl smiled, then looked at her father. "You sent the Samrat a message saying you know someone, an exile..."

"...who escaped successfully from the Dandaka Forest," Brichcha completed for her. "Yes. I don't know if he's still alive, but he was, when I was Warden of the Stables."

"Oh, that was a long time ago," Shanku's face fell.

"Yes, but there's no harm in looking for him."

"Who is he and where can we find him?"

"He was the leader of a gang of highwaymen who operated along the road between Lava and Viratapuri some twenty years ago. The gang had earned quite a reputation for looting in those days, skulking in the forests and plundering trade caravans plying between Matsya, Avanti and the Anartas. They successfully eluded capture for a long time, I remember. But then they committed a blunder that the law could *not* turn a blind eye to, and that led to their undoing."

"Meaning?" Shanku asked with childlike curiosity. For that moment, they were father and daughter, narrating stories until sleep got the better of them. "What happened?"

"I suspect the gang stayed beyond the reach of the law for so long because they kept the law enforcers in that area happy with gifts."

"Bribes, you mean?"

"Bribes, a share of the spoils, call it what you may," said Brichcha. "The forest there is dense — it was even denser back then — so those entrusted with upholding the law had a handy excuse for failing to nab gang members. And since the gang's crimes were limited to robbing wealthy merchants, many of these merchants were happy to cough up protection money instead of incurring the gang's displeasure. Thus, no one cared enough to bring them to justice, and the outlaws more or less operated with impunity. Then one day, the band attacked a wedding procession. They took the money and jewellery, of course, but three gang members also abducted the bride. Her body was found in a roadside ditch the next day. She had been molested, killed and left for wild animals."

"And that brought the full wrath of Avanti upon the gang," said Shanku. "How come I have never heard this tale before?"

"Not Avanti. Nishada. This was just before the savages from the Marusthali arrived." Brichcha scratched his head self-consciously at the mention of the Hunas and the Sakas. "Back then, Nishada was an independent kingdom. Anyway, yes, a crime so severe was impossible to overlook. Nishada launched a hunt for the gang, and the whole lot of them — eleven in all — were apprehended. No amounts of bribes could save them this time. They were all tried and exiled to the Dandaka. Their leader, of course, pleaded mercy, insisting that only the three who had abducted the bride should pay the harsh penalty of Dandaka, but all eleven of them were sent there, to be made examples of for other gangs of highwaymen in Sindhuvarta."

"How do you know he escaped the Forest of the Exiles?"

"He told me so himself. I met him in a tavern here by the Kshipra. We hit it off, and we talked deep into the night. He got drunk on firewater and told me everything."

"If you knew he had escaped from the Dandaka, why didn't you bring him to the notice of the City Watch?" Shanku looked more surprised than outraged.

"Well..." the old man hesitated before offering an apologetic shrug, "...back then I didn't care. My loyalties were not with the throne anyway, so..."

The councilor nodded. "How can you be sure the man you met was who he claimed to be, and wasn't making it all up, stringing you along with a fancy tale? He was drunk, after all."

"He was drunk, but he was also scared while talking about the Dandaka. Drink makes you brave, not scared, and he was terrified. He said he survived four years in the Dandaka, living by his wits and pure luck, before getting out. He said he had watched his friends die one by one, and in the end, just two of them were left. He was the only one to make it out alive, he said. Beyond that, who knows..." Brichcha shrugged expansively.

"So where is this highwayman now? Don't tell me he's right here in Ujjayini?" The girl's voice rang with a note of anticipation.

"No, he was only passing through Ujjayini, on his way back to the village he said he hails from. A place called Bhiwaha, north of Lava, on the road to Madhyamika. I reckon he thought it was safe to return as the place was overrun with barbarians, and no one in Nishada could be bothered with a convict who had fled from the Dandaka."

"Bhiwaha, on the Lava-Madhyamika road," Shanku repeated. "You are certain about this? Good. You still haven't told me his name, though."

"Greeshma," said Brichcha. "As a highwayman, he was Greeshma the Wild."

"Thank you for this, father," Shanku began getting to her feet. "I hope what you have told me comes in use."

"You aren't leaving, are you?" Brichcha caught his daughter's hand, pleading. "Stay a while longer. It's been so many years since I saw you."

"I have to go, father. This news about Greeshma is important for us. I have to convey it to the Samrat, so we can send troops to Lava to look for him." The girl disengaged her hand gently. "But I will come back soon. I have promised, haven't I?"

"Okay, I understand." The old man's face dropped, but still he smiled. "Bless you."

Shanku smiled at him and rose to leave the cell, but Brichcha addressed her again.

"Once you've found Greeshma, and the palace is satisfied that I haven't lied about him, I would want the reward the palace has offered... the hundred gold coins."

The councilor turned and looked at her father. Her tone was a little frosty when she spoke. "You shared this information because you wanted the reward?"

"No, but as there is a reward attached, I would like to claim it," Brichcha answered. "Not for myself, though. I would want the palace to divert my hundred gold coins into building the ironmongers' houses, the ones destroyed by that snake thing. Better still, the money could be given to the present Warden of the Stables, so he can buy the best horses for the kingdom. I am told there will be a need for horses in the days to come."

Shanku flashed a big smile of relief at her father. "I shall convey your wish to the Samrat."

"One last thing. I know the Mother Oracle is in the palace. When you meet her next, tell her I feel terrible for what I did to her daughter."

"I will," said the girl. "But I think grandmother already knows you are sorry."

* * *

Night was falling around the small garrison of Musili as Vararuchi stood atop the garrison's old, central tower and gazed over the wooden palisades in the direction of Ujjayini, an hour's ride to the southeast. The gathering darkness made it hard to discern the councilor's features, but the two soldiers of the Imperial Army who stood flanking him — Sharamana, the garrison's commander, and Pulyama, a young captain — could tell that Vararuchi's face was set in a grim frown, one that had nearly frozen into place since that afternoon.

"And the *samsaptakas*, your honour. Can they be trusted?" the garrison commander spoke in a soft but troubled voice. "Having taken the Death Oath, they share a close bond. And most of them are heavily inspired by Kalidasa, which is why they volunteered to take the Death Oath in the first place. When the time comes, will they swear allegiance to Avanti and stand against their erstwhile commander and hero?"

Vararuchi's head turned to consider Sharamana, though practically nothing could be seen of his expression. After a moment spent in what appeared to be careful thought, he turned back, saying nothing.

"And what is the message we are giving those soldiers who have joined us from Heheya and Vatsa and the Anartas —" this came from the captain, Pulyama, "— that we are willing to let anyone cross the frontier and join the enemy, no questions asked?"

"Pulyama is right, your honour," Sharamana stressed fervently. "There is talk among the men that we are becoming a bit of a joke among the soldiers from the rest of Sindhuvarta. They can see what is happening, and they are bound to ask questions. But we have no satisfactory answers." The commander's tone took a rough edge. "Avanti's Imperial Army cannot be reduced to a joke, your honour."

"I know how you feel about this, commander," Vararuchi growled in reply.

Sharamana waited for the councilor to add to this in some concrete way, but when he was met with silence, he decided to force the issue. "We must do something, your honour. Perhaps you could put the Samrat abreast of the situation. We must clear the air for *our* soldiers as well as those of our allies."

"If the air were cleared, would it make everyone more comfortable facing Kalidasa in battle?" Vararuchi once again looked at the garrison commander. From his tone, it was clear he was being caustic, and the silence from the two soldiers was more telling than any words could have been. "I thought not," the councilor snorted. "But I shall have a word with the Samrat. Ask someone to fetch me my horse."

It was fully dark by the time Vararuchi left the garrison, but this portion of the road connecting Ujjayini to Sristhali was straight and well paved, so the councilor didn't need to depend on the starlight to guide him. And as his horse was familiar with the path, he let his mind wander over everything that had brought him to this dark and lonely road to Ujjayini.

The rider sent by Sharamana, an old loyalist of his from the days they had last fought the invaders from the Marusthali, had arrived immediately after lunch, bringing with him a report of a sighting of Kalidasa from two days ago — the giant had been nearing the Arbuda Mountains and was unerringly making for the frontier. That hadn't come as a surprise; what *had* was the rider's passing remark of Amara Simha and Angamitra leading a force of *samsaptakas* to Udaypuri to find Ghatakarpara, who had apparently gone missing.

Shocked into action by this news, Vararuchi had taken quick leave of Ushantha, but instead of returning straight to the palace, he had taken a detour to the garrison of Musili — one of the oldest in Avanti, no longer strategic and nowadays used only to house soldiers who couldn't be accommodated in the newer city garrison — which was under Sharamana's command. From Sharamana and the young Pulyama, Vararuchi had learned the full story of his nephew having been kidnapped by the Hunas for ransom. He also heard for the first time about the hunt for escapees from the Forest of the Exiles...

...and was assailed by the unhappy realization that he was no longer a priority for the palace.

With it, came a simmering anger at the palace's callousness and disrespect for all that he had done for it in so many years of selfless service.

It had all started with Kalidasa accusing him of having murdered his family in cold blood all those years ago near Lava. He, Vararuchi, had admitted to putting the entire Huna garrison to the sword as revenge for the atrocities that the Hunas had been committing on Sindhuvarta's hapless subjects, but the throne had unashamedly — and unfairly — sided with Kalidasa, ignoring what he had to say in his defence, and holding him guilty of taking the lives of innocents. Rubbing salt into his wounds, the palace had gone on to offer Kalidasa an apology, which the graceless Huna had rejected before severing ties with Avanti and going west to join his tribe — with, as was obvious to everyone, the blessings of the palace.

Naturally, unease was spreading within the Imperial Army; not only was Kalidasa a fearsome foe in battle, he carried with him all of Avanti's military secrets, which would now inevitably land in his new Huna friends' hands. The throne's decision to let Kalidasa do as he wished was not only terrible for the morale of Avanti's troops, but it also sent conflicting signals to Avanti's allies who had thrown their weight behind Avanti to keep the Hunas and Sakas out of Sindhuvarta. This, Vararuchi reflected bitterly, was what the palace had come to — falling over itself to win back a traitor's confidence, while a loyal shoulder that had propped up the throne was ridiculed and sidelined. This was how the palace was squandering the legacy of his father, the proud king Mahendraditya.

If the special treatment being meted out to Kalidasa had hurt, the fact that the palace had not considered him worthy of being informed of Ghatakarpara's kidnapping — *his own nephew's kidnapping* — was like a slap on the face. From what he had understood, the news of the prince's disappearance had arrived in the palace the previous evening, and even a full day later, the palace hadn't bothered to let him know. It was as if the palace had chosen to disassociate itself from him, cut him adrift, in the hope that *that* would somehow mollify the traitorous Kalidasa into returning to Avanti's service.

Smarting with anger, but also afflicted by a deep sense of alienation and hopelessness, Vararuchi pondered his next move as he neared the Kshipra. One part of him wanted to turn back and return to the comforting arms of his mother, the one person who did not judge him poorly for what had happened in Lava years ago. If the palace did not want him, he did not need the palace either, and it was entirely the palace's loss, he told himself. But a more belligerent part of him screamed to be heard, indignant at being treated so shabbily, demanding answers, asking for justice and refusing to give up what was his by birthright — a place at the council table and an uncle's right to know about his nephew's well-being.

It was this part of Vararuchi that held sway, pushing and propelling him to take the boat across the Kshipra, ride through Ujjayini's western gate into the city and cross the palace causeway to confront his brother for answers.

Entering the palace, Vararuchi traversed the hallway and began mounting the stairs, anger, sorrow and regret pulling him in different directions. Reaching the top, he turned into the gallery leading to Vikramaditya's chambers when, most unexpectedly, he ran into Upashruti and Pralupi, who were both coming from the opposite direction. Standing within an arm's length of one another, the three of them stared, not knowing what to say, yet unable to dodge and pretend they hadn't seen each other. Vararuchi could almost see the hostile vibes coming at him from the Queen Mother.

"Greetings, mother," he mumbled, bowing his head, suddenly unsure of himself.

"Greetings indeed," Upashruti arched an eyebrow, her voice dripping sarcasm. "I see you have found the time to attend to the needs of the palace. We should all be grateful, I presume."

"I am always available for the palace, mother," Vararuchi said, regretting his choice of words almost immediately. He was saying the right things, the servile things, and not giving voice to the words of rebellion brewing and boiling in his chest. He hated himself for that.

"Of course," the Queen Mother smirked and rolled her eyes. "Your nephew has been kidnapped by the Hunas, Amara Simha is halfway to the frontier and you just show up saying *I'm always available for the palace.*" Upashruti mimicked the words in a crude impersonation of a male voice. "Sure, I believe you."

"I di…" Vararuchi began saying, but he stopped on seeing the two women brush past him and walk away. He stared into Pralupi's face and saw his half-sister stare back at him, her eyes dull and half-closed in studied insolence. Pralupi turned away with a dismissive toss of her head, and mother and daughter departed, not sparing a glance for Vararuchi.

They will not listen to you. They don't want to listen to you. Don't you see, they've already made up their minds about you.

Staring at the retreating figures, the samrat's brother felt the hot surge of rage wash all over him, burning his cheeks, warming his innards. Clenching his hands into tight fists to control the sudden tremor in them, he swallowed hard once, then a second time, forcing down the bile that was rising up his throat like venom. Tears of outrage stung in his eyes, and blinking them away, he turned and walked off — in a direction opposite to the one that would have taken him to Samrat Vikramaditya.

* * *

Dattaka leaned back in his chair and frowned at the palm-leaf scroll lying on the table before him. The frown had been there all afternoon, like a fever under his skin, ever since the scroll had arrived in the official dispatch from Udaypuri. But with so many pressing duties to attend to, Dattaka had been compelled to keep the scroll off his mind. Now with the day's drills complete, the Guardsmen units out on patrol and the command centre hunkering down for the night, its commander finally had the capacity to return to the bothersome piece of palm leaf.

There was nothing earth-shattering in the contents of the scroll. It was a simple roster of the names of soldiers serving at the Sristhali command centre who had been picked for promotion. Since he was the head of the command centre, the list had been submitted to him per procedure, notifying him about the promotions. On the face of it, there was nothing out of line in any of this. But seeing the names on the scroll, Dattaka had felt mildly unsettled — he intuitively knew something was amiss, yet he wasn't being able to put a finger on it.

Pulling the scroll closer, the commander looked at the three names again. All familiar names, all three unremarkable men, soldiers who could be banked upon to follow orders, but from whom resourcefulness and clever thinking could never be expected. Which was alright; every army was full of such men, and it could be argued that armies needed men who followed orders and did not think much for themselves or asked too many questions. Still, Dattaka couldn't see why these three had been chosen for promotion when there were other deserving candidates around. He himself had recommended half a dozen soldiers the last time the garrison headquarters had asked for suitable names, but none of them had been picked. Instead, *these three...*

Scratching his chin, Dattaka studied the governor's seal at the bottom of the scroll; it explained why none of the men he had recommended had received their promotions yet. This list hadn't come from the garrison. It had originated in the governor's office.

And that, the commander understood, was what was really troubling him.

It was highly uncommon for the governor's office to recommend soldiers for rewards or promotions, and whenever distinctions were made, the chosen soldier's service was so meritorious, his achievement so striking that the governor's recommendation was more an added stamp of honour, a gilt-edged acknowledgement of duty to the throne. But there was nothing remotely spectacular or meritorious in the way these three men had dispensed their duties. They were average soldiers who definitely weren't deserving of a governor's recommendation.

As he sat scrutinizing the names, it occurred to Dattaka

that there was a pattern about them, something vaguely familiar. The more he thought about it, the more certain he became, but the pattern itself remained tantalizingly out of reach. Three names that he was familiar with, three soldiers he knew, three men...

Heaving an exasperated sigh of defeat, the commander stretched his tired arms, unlocking the kinks in the muscles along his hands, back and shoulders. Then, with a tired yawn, he picked up the scroll and put it away with the rest of the communication that had come from Udaypuri. Within a few minutes, he had extinguished the lamp and was lying on his bed, preparing to slide into restful sleep.

Three names that he was familiar with, three soldiers he knew, three men... Like a stubborn child that refuses to leave its playthings alone, his mind went over the problem in a loop. Three names that he was familiar with, three soldiers, three names written on a palm leaf...

Three names written on a palm leaf.

Dattaka sat up, his eyes wide in the dark, his heart beating in excitement. He had it. He had solved the puzzle that had been gnawing at him ever since he had set eyes on the contents of that scroll. He knew why the three names had been bothering him so much.

Those were three of the six names in the list of suspects that he and Councilor Amara Simha had written down on a piece of palm leaf, once it had been discovered that the Huna scout they had captured had died of a mysterious snakebite. They were three of the six guards on duty the night the Huna scout had died.

Three names written on a palm leaf. That was the pattern his mind had noticed.

Although he knew he was clutching at a half-chance, Dattaka lay back on his pillow with a sense of achievement. Councilor Amara Simha had entrusted him with the investigation of the scout's death, and this was the closest he had got to a real lead. Three guards on duty when the scout had died. Three very ordinary soldiers. Yet, the same men get a promotion on the governor's recommendation — *and the governor had been at the command centre the night the scout had died.*

The shock of what had just crossed his mind made the commander gasp. A shiver ran through him, and he realized he would have to interview the three soldiers again to see if he could get them to confess what had happened to the Huna scout that night.

* * *

Burning up in shame and anger and incapable of summoning sleep, Shukracharya snatched up his ironwood *danda* and slung an *angavastram* over his shoulder before stepping out into the night. The sky was black and clear, stars running amok everywhere except around the spot where the moon shone near the summit of Mount Meru. The wooded valley was full of wafting breezes that bore the scent of *devadaru* and gentle banks of cool, white mist in alternating tides. Away to the right, as always, the horizon was awash with the glow of Amaravati's lights.

Directing a particularly bitter glare at the capital's lights — seeing them as mocking him in their profusion, revelling in his disgrace — the head priest turned his back to them and set out in the direction of Meru, using his staff and his intuition to find his way through the dense groves of *devadaru*, where even moonlight struggled to enter.

He had been in torment ever since his return from the calamitous mission to the garden, smarting from the systematic humiliation that Brihaspati, his oldest nemesis, had dealt him. The evening had passed in a blur of rage and self-flagellation, where he had switched between swearing revenge on Brihaspati and cursing his reckless pursuit of Jayanta, which had severely affected the asuras' chances of ever acquiring the mantras. But clearly, what grated most was the chamberlain's self-congratulatory smugness at having outfoxed him, Shukracharya, in his own game of cunning.

I got him to dress up like Jayanta and walk into this garden and play the jal-yantra. Brihaspati's gloating face swam to the surface of the high priest's mind. *And look at what came in after him like a swarm of bees attracted to a pot of honey.*

Walking through the forest where fallen pine needles cushioned the soles of his feet, the high priest was aware that in his eagerness to befriend Jayanta, he had dropped his guard, and that, in turn, had handed Brihaspati the perfect opportunity to make a complete fool of him.

You'll definitely not be running into Jayanta. I have instructed the guards at the palace to ensure that such opportunities do not arise hereafter.

Not for the first time, it occurred to Shukracharya that he had no reason left to extend his stay in Devaloka, but the knowledge that he would leave empty-handed, having gambled and lost to the one he hated losing to the most, was galling. How could he, mahaguru of the asuras, leave like this, jeered by the devas, his dignity in shreds? This alone was enough for him to consider slipping out of Devaloka under cover of dark, but he equally loathed the idea of being branded as a coward who fled into the night. Yet, the notion of staying back without any purpose, and giving Brihaspati the satisfaction of seeing him squirming and helpless, held no appeal either.

So, Shukracharya did what little he could under the circumstances. He walked where his feet took him, unmindful of the mist, the darkness and the uneven ground. He vented his anger in dire warnings of revenge on the devas, and swore to humble Brihaspati's hubris by somehow, *somehow*, taking away the mantras to raise Ahi.

He was so lost in his misery and recriminations that he failed to notice the bank of mist forming around him. Deeper and deeper he walked into its folds, and it wrapped itself tighter around him. Yet, the high priest kept walking — until a sudden burst of moonlight made him aware of his surroundings. He stopped to look around him, and straight ahead, through the parting skeins of mist, he observed the huge trunk of a tree.

He realized that he would have blundered straight into the tree had the moon not shed its light at the right time.

Shukracharya was about to correct his path when he stopped short and stared at the tree blocking his way, his pulse quickening. He looked at the drifting mist, like curtains being drawn aside, and he watched the tree trunk emerge and take form.

The scene playing out in front of his one good eye reminded him of something else that he had seen somewhere. Mist. And something hidden inside it. Something large.

Not mist. *Fog*.

Dense, white fog. And something large and shadowy inside it. Something gigantic.

A tree. A gigantic tree.

The high priest almost ceased breathing. That was what he had seen in Vetala Bhatta's mind that morning by the bath — a gigantic tree, hidden in fog. And in a stunning flash, Shukracharya realized why that particular scene had seemed so familiar and had stuck with him all this while.

His subconscious had recognized what it had seen.

The banyan that holds up the field of endless pyres.

Borderworld.

Gandharvasena

Warmed by a bright sun, the morning mist was rising off the palace lake as Vismaya ushered King Harihara onto a sheltered terrace, away from the day's heat and glare. The terrace faced west and was landscaped with flowering creepers and trailing vines, swishing and rustling and billowing in the breeze blowing from across the Kshipra.

"I hope the bathing arrangements were to your liking, your honour," said the chief of the Palace Guards.

"Yes? Oh yes… very much," Harihara answered, blinking and looking distracted.

A palace hand had trailed the two men to the terrace, bearing a tray on which a tall brass tumbler was set. The chief of the Palace Guards took the tumbler and offered it to the king.

"Buttermilk, your honour," he said with a bow. "With very few curry leaves, as you had instructed."

The king took a sip of the cool, spicy drink and nodded appreciatively. In a moment, he asked, "Where is Queen Upashruti? I don't see her about…"

"The Queen Mother and Princess Pralupi have gone to pay obeisance at the Kali temple by the holy Kshipra, your honour. They left at daybreak, before your arrival, and haven't yet returned."

"Ah, I see." Harihara sipped his buttermilk and lapsed into silence.

"Are you certain you wouldn't care for a bit of rest?" Vismaya asked. "Travelling all through the night must have been quite fatiguing."

"The bath was sufficiently refreshing. I'm quite alright," Harihara waved away the offer, then looked searchingly at the palace. "Does the Samrat know of my arrival?"

"Most definitely. I had him informed the moment I learned you were at the palace gate. I would have let the Samrat know even sooner had a messenger come in advance." Then, gauging the intent behind the king's question correctly, he quickly added, "The Samrat is visiting Queen Vishakha's chamber; he should be with you any moment."

"Oh, is the queen better?" Harihara looked at the palace official in surprise. "I mean, is she recovering... from..."

"I'm afraid not, your honour," Vismaya gave his head a sad shake.

"Oh," Harihara said again.

Reconciling to a wait, the king took another sip of the buttermilk and strolled over to watch the swans glide gracefully about the lake, while kingfishers dived into the water in search of food. Hearing Vismaya excuse himself, Harihara nodded over his shoulder in acknowledgement, but his mind was back on what had brought him to Ujjayini in such a rush so early in the day, that too unannounced.

Three days earlier, the first reports of the fallout between Kalidasa and Vikramaditya had filtered into Mahishmati, borne by travelling tradesmen and soldiers returning from the frontier. The news came in unreliable snatches, and as it was hard to tell facts from loose talk, Harihara had directed one of his most dependable hands to piece the truth together. The officer had done a commendable job, his picture of the situation in Avanti compelling Harihara to reconsider the politics of Sindhuvarta in the days to come.

While leaving the services of Avanti, Kalidasa had made it plain that he was severing all old ties, and his ride west implied he was intent on forging an alliance with the barbarians. But what did this switching of loyalties really portend? For one, it made the Huna army even more formidable; the savages now not only had one of the most fearsome warriors on their side, but all the information the warrior had on Avanti and its allies was also theirs to exploit. Then, the fact that Kalidasa would naturally view Avanti's allies as extensions of Avanti meant that none of the allies would be exempt from the heat of his anger. This, to Harihara, was worrying.

These were the obvious and expected outcomes of Kalidasa changing sides. Harihara was more occupied with fathoming Vikramaditya's response to the challenge Kalidasa had set down, and the course of action that the samrat would pick when Kalidasa returned at the head of a Huna legion. Because that, Harihara realized, would determine how the war for Sindhuvarta would pan out.

He needed to get a sense of how that war would go before deciding whom to offer Rukma's hand in marriage to — Shashivardhan or Shoorasena.

Or now to Kalidasa.

So far, Vikramaditya's approach towards Kalidasa appeared needlessly conciliatory; he had literally granted his old friend the liberty of picking sides in the battle to come. Harihara found the samrat's decisions irrational, and wondered who among Chandravardhan, Baanahasta, Bhoomipala and the Anarta chieftain Yugandhara would appreciate Vikramaditya for allowing Kalidasa to cross over to the Huna camp. He suspected none of them would, which meant their alliance was already under threat of coming unstuck the moment Kalidasa arrived at the frontier. And what about the rest of Vikramaditya's council — how were they reacting to all of this?

Watching a kingfisher plunge into the lake and emerge with a fish trapped in its beak, Harihara decided that if the alliance between the kingdoms of Sindhuvarta wasn't going to hold, it was best to give Rukma to Shoorasena. In the absence of a strong alliance, Vatsa — even Avanti, but definitely Vatsa, of that Harihara was certain — would be overrun by the barbarians, and Shashivardhan would end up dead. So, Shoorasena it would have to be. But what if the Hunas didn't stop at Vatsa and swept all the way to Magadha and defeated Shoorasena as well? Would Rukma be safe then? Very unlikely. So, instead, what if he cleverly distanced himself from the whole alliance and made it clear to the Hunas that, as far as he was concerned, they were welcome to settle in Sindhuvarta? Would they believe him and spare Heheya? Quite possibly... if he offered Rukma as a token of good faith and friendship to Kalidasa.

But then, what if the alliance survived under Vikramaditya, and what if the Hunas were routed and sent packing? Those who had stood by Avanti would be rewarded, and Shashivardhan might end up becoming one of the most important men in Sindhuvarta. Harihara gritted his teeth in exasperation, not knowing what to do, knowing it was almost impossible to make a correct prediction. But yes, if he knew what was in Vikramaditya's mind and how he intended acting once war commenced, it would help him...

"Your honour, the Samrat wishes you to join him for breakfast."

Harihara turned to see Vismaya behind him. Seeing the small smile on his face, the king got the absurd idea that the officer had read his thoughts and knew why he was here.

"Sure," he coughed and covered his mouth self-consciously. "Delighted."

Harihara had scarcely moved when a short but shrill blast of sound fell on his ears. It came from somewhere far to his left, borne over the rooftops of Ujjayini by the wind, but there was no doubting its intensity. It was like the blare of a trumpet, harsh and warlike, making the hairs on his neck stand up. Alarmed, he shot a glance at Vismaya, who was staring away to the north, head to one side, listening. When the sound didn't repeat itself, the palace officer turned to his guest. The raising of Harihara's eyebrows was met with a faint shrug.

"This way, your honour," Vismaya said, bowing. As he straightened, his gaze went towards the north of the city, where it lingered, his expression hard to decipher.

When Harihara was ushered onto the terrace where breakfast had been served on a low table, Vikramaditya stepped forward, his hands joined in a *pranaam*.

"My sincere apologies for keeping you waiting," he said. "Come and have a seat."

"I heard about Ghatakarpara on the way. Taken hostage by the barbarians," Harihara shook his head in dismay. "Terrible news."

"Yes," the samrat's face turned grave. "But Amara Simha has left for the frontier with a band of *samsaptakas*. I'm certain the prince will be rescued and brought back safely to us."

"The barbarians are becoming more and more brazen every day," said Harihara, studying the younger king's face closely.

Vikramaditya nodded, but in reply, he merely gestured to the seat placed for Harihara. The two men sat down and waited as a pair of maids served them a simple repast of freshly cut melons, rice pancakes dipped in honey and millet *rotis* with spicy coriander chutney. Once the maids had withdrawn, Vikramaditya took a bite out of his *roti* and looked across at Harihara.

"If I may ask, what brings you here? Your visit is welcome but most unexpected."

Harihara took a sip of cumin-flavoured water before answering. "It has been a while since I came. Much has transpired — Vishakha, the serpent monster... *Kalidasa*. So, I thought... I'm told Vishakha is still... not..." he groped for words, "alright."

"She isn't, but I'm grateful for the consideration you have shown. Thank you."

A brief silence ensued as the kings chewed their food.

"This whole affair around Kalidasa is sad," Harihara said finally.

The samrat looked at his guest, but didn't say anything.

"I mean... the way he went away."

Vikramaditya was about to speak when there was a sudden flurry of activity outside — voices called out with a ring of urgency, a horse snorted and galloped past below, while a door banged and feet pounded up a pathway. The samrat paused to listen, his eyes sharp, but the sounds receded. He turned his attention back to his guest.

"You were speaking about Kalidasa..." the samrat nodded and shrugged. "Indeed, it is sad, but it couldn't be helped."

"You didn't stop him?"

"No."

"And what if he comes back? You know he will."

"What of it?"

Harihara looked at the face opposite him, the deep black eyes, the high forehead, the beard with streaks of grey. "Will you stop him?"

"That depends on how he comes back," Vikramaditya brushed back the hair that was falling over his face. "If he comes as a friend, why would I stop him?"

"It doesn't look as if he has left to return as a friend," Harihara shifted uncomfortably.

"Then he will be met like a foe in battle. With respect but without mercy."

"You will tell your troops to fight him? Our allies also? Is that the message you will send them?" Harihara looked keenly at the samrat. "You wouldn't hold back because he was a friend once?"

Vikramaditya looked back at the king shrewdly. He opened his mouth to speak, but changed his mind and continued looking at Harihara, who squirmed under the needle-sharp scrutiny. Finally, the samrat nodded.

"If it is to protect Sindhuvarta, then yes. There will be no holding back."

"And the rest of your council?"

"What about them?" Vikramaditya asked with a puzzled frown, reaching for the bowl of chutney.

Before Harihara could explain himself, footsteps approached the terrace in a rush. As the two kings turned towards the door, Vismaya pushed aside the curtains and bowed.

"My deepest apologies for the intrusion, Samrat." He appeared uncharacteristically hassled, even overawed.

"What is it?" asked Vikramaditya, the mild frown still on his brow.

"Your honour, there are… you have visitors, your honour."

"Who?" The frown deepened a little, the voice hardening in suspicion.

"Samrat…" the chief of the guards hesitated and stopped, then began again. "Samrat, the message from the City Watch says the visitors are led by Indra, lord of the devas."

The terrace fell silent. Nothing but the bubbling of a fountain was audible. Far away, someone issued what to Harihara's ears sounded like a hurried set of commands.

"At which gate are they waiting?" the samrat asked in a flat voice.

"They came by way of the north gate, your honour... but they are not *waiting* there. They forced the guards aside and barged their way into Ujjayini. They are inside the city and are headed for the palace, Samrat."

There was a sudden snapping, cracking noise, and Harihara stared in wonderment at the wooden chutney ladle that Vikramaditya had been holding to serve himself. The ladle had broken into two, its bowl lying on the table where it had fallen amid a splatter of chutney, its handle still gripped in Vikramaditya's fist, his knuckles waxy white with pressure. Harihara's gaze rose from the broken shaft to the samrat's face, which was impassive, except for the eyes, where anger flared without restraint.

"How many of them?"

"Other than Indra himself, there is a chariot and a lone horseman, Samrat." Seeing the surprise on his king's face, Vismaya licked his lips nervously. "It is Indra's elephant, your honour. They are saying it is too intimidating. No one wants to come in its path."

"Inform the council immediately and secure the palace." Dropping the broken ladle, the samrat leaped to his feet. Outside, the first of the city's alarm bells began pealing. As if to rival the bells, the strident, trumpeting blast that Harihara had heard on the terrace sounded again, more menacing and much closer. "Tell the councilors to be fully prepared to defend Ujjayini, and let them know I am riding out to stop Indra."

* * *

Drawing his chair close to the table, Dattaka sat down and smiled at the elderly soldier seated across him. An amiable, non-threatening smile, the commander reckoned, though he had to modify his opinion when the soldier stared back anxiously.

"I wanted to let you know that you have been awarded a promotion," Dattaka said, closely observing the man opposite him. No brightening of the face at the suddenness of the news, no surprise, no sign of joy. It seemed as if the man already knew he was being promoted but was deeply unhappy about it, as if the promotion was too heavy a burden to bear. Or maybe he was just apprehensive, feeling the constriction of the small room like a noose tightening around him. "Congratulations."

"Thank you, sir," the soldier mumbled.

"Recommended by the governor himself," Dattaka looked awed. "Big honour."

The man blinked and glanced around the room nervously, as if seeking out exits.

"You must have left the governor terribly impressed for him to do what he's done."

"Thank you, sir."

"What did you do for him that's made him such a big fan? Tell me," the commander grinned, "so that I can try and do something similar to earn a garrison command in the next round of promotions."

The soldier gave a weak smile and shifted in his seat, eyes still darting to all sides.

"You seem a little uncomfortable. What's the matter? Is it the heat?"

"I'm fine, sir."

"No, there *is* something. Tell me. What's bothering you?"

"Nothing, sir." Beads of perspiration flecked the soldier's brow, and he licked his lips.

"Okay." Dattaka nodded. Realizing that he wasn't making any headway, he dropped the affable tone and stared at the man with a serious face. "Tell me what you did for the governor that made him decide you were worthy of a promotion."

"I don't know, sir."

"We both know these recommendations are rare. We also know that you would never have got a recommendation under normal circumstances. So, you might as well tell me what that remarkable circumstance was that won you this recommendation."

The soldier tilted his head to wipe a trickle of sweat on his shoulder, and shook his head in reply. "Only the respected governor would know, sir."

"Clever." Pushing back his chair, Dattaka got to his feet. "You know I would never dare question the governor." He started pacing the tight space, four steps this way, five steps that, his hands clasped behind him. The soldier's eyes followed him, worried yet calculating.

"I forgot to add that we both also know I have only my suspicions to go on, that I have no evidence. If I had any evidence, I would have slapped your face with it by now, you're thinking. So, if you say nothing, admit to nothing, I can do nothing and you are safe. Right?"

"I don't know what you mean, sir."

"Nice idea, this feigning of innocence." The commander quit pacing and bent over the soldier, placing one hand on the man's bony shoulder. "I really can do nothing to you. Except..."

Dattaka paused and peered into the thin, bearded face staring back at him in sudden doubt. "Except that, you may recall, there were three of you that night."

"I don't... I'm sorry, which night do you mean, sir?"

"There were three of you that night, and *all three* have received recommendations for promotion from the governor's office. Proves nothing, I know. But if you notice, I have put the three of you in three separate rooms, so you can't meet each other. Any guesses why?"

The soldier blinked in response.

"I'll tell you why." Dattaka sat on the edge of the table, by the man's elbow. "We both agree that I can do nothing to any of you, if none of you says anything about what happened that night to the Huna scout we had captured. You say nothing to me; I have nothing to prove my suspicions; all three of you get your promotions and are happy. Correct? But here's the deal. There are three of you, and I will talk to each of you individually, asking the same questions. Now, if any *one* of you tells me what happened that night, that person gets lucky — he gets to keep his promotion, *and* he walks away unpunished."

The commander paused and looked down at the soldier, who was leaning forward, straining to catch every word. "But what happens to the two who didn't confess?" Dattaka asked theatrically, enjoying himself. "I shall have to report them to the garrison and to the palace, and then I shall put them at the very front of the line that will meet the charge of the Huna and Saka hordes. *At... the... very... front.* If, by some divine stroke of luck, they survive that, I will petition our Samrat to have them sent to the Forest of the Exiles for conspiring against Avanti and its king. Thus, the one who confesses gets away scot-free, but the others..." The commander shook his head and pulled a sad face.

"What if two people confess...?"

"If their confessions match, they get promoted, while the one who *didn't* confess will be sent to the frontline to stop the barbarians," Dattaka replied in a snap, moving past the soldier's defences, closing in for the kill.

"And if all three confess, all three keep their promotions and walk away free?" There was the gleam of unexpected opportunity in the old man's eyes.

"Do I look like an idiot to you?" asked the commander. "If all three of you confess, none of you gets a promotion — *ever again* in your lives as soldiers of Avanti. And no, you do not walk away free. You serve in the Frontier Army and fight the savages. But you will *not* be sent to the frontline, and you will *not* go to the Dandaka, that much I promise. The frontline and the Dandaka are for those who don't confess."

A long silence followed, punctured only by the shallow breathing of the old soldier as he tried to wrestle his options and priorities into a disciplined line. Somewhere outside on the parade ground, commands were being issued, and the drumming of soldiers' feet came from the direction of the bridge leading into Sristhali's civilian districts.

"None of you confess, no problem for any of you," Dattaka did a helpful recap. "One or two of you confess, good for them, but a big problem for those who don't confess. All three of you confess, all three get punished, but to a much lesser degree than if you don't tell the truth. Think about it."

"What if I tell you more than what the others tell you?" asked the soldier, fixing his greedy eyes on the commander, hardly making an effort to mask the tremor in his voice that showed how close he was to breaking. "As a reward, will I be excused from fighting against the barbarians?"

Dattaka slid off the table and went around to his chair. Sitting down, he pulled the chair close to the table, then jostled and adjusted it as if trying to find a comfortable position, delaying deliberately, letting the soldier stew in suspense. When at last he looked up, the old man was pleading with his eyes.

"A reward... mmm..." Dattaka seemed to consider the idea. "That depends entirely on how unique and useful that additional bit of information is. But there is only one way of finding out." He planted his elbows on the table and leaned towards the soldier. "Stick to the truth and tell me what happened to the Huna scout that night..."

* * *

The ground trembled under the pounding of horse hooves, and the resulting roar felt like thunder to Harihara's ears as he clung to his saddle and gripped the reins of his mount in fright. He desperately wished to be elsewhere, but there was no escape — he was smack in the middle of a crowd of two dozen riders of the City Walk and the Palace Guards, pressed in on both sides and from behind, so he had only one way to go, which was forward. He rode the torrent of hooves and windblown manes, a hapless branch snared in river currents, sweeping away towards its destruction.

Muttering curses, he looked at Vikramaditya, who was leading the pack, leaping over ditches, careening around corners, and driving his steed down vacant side streets with the aim of intercepting Indra. Once Vismaya had left the terrace, the samrat had turned to Harihara and asked if he had brought his sword along. Harihara didn't know what had prompted him to say yes, but he guessed that even if he had lied, a weapon would have been procured for him, and he would still have ended up here, riding to his death at the hands of Indra or his infernal elephant, whose intermittent trumpeting sent shivers down his spine.

It is Indra's elephant, Vismaya had said. *No one wants to come in its path.* And here Vikramaditya was hell-bent on putting him straight in the path of peril.

The city's alarm bells could still be heard over the beat of the hooves, but there was a listlessness about them, as though the ringers were unsure of what they were meant to achieve. Yet, the bells had served their purpose — the morning traffic had scattered and Ujjayini's streets had emptied, its citizenry hiding indoors, eyes pressed to the cracks in doors and shutters in dread and anticipation. Harihara supposed the recent spate of attacks had made the people adept at responding to danger.

Now more than ever, Harihara understood this desire for self-preservation, but he was powerless to act on it, buffeted as he was this way and that, down one alley and then the next, by the swarm of Ujjayini's riders. He didn't even have an idea of where they were dashing off to — these side streets were alien to him, and all he had understood was that in order to minimize the loss of innocent lives, they were taking shortcuts to stop Indra's advance before the deva turned into one of Ujjayini's residential districts.

The alley they were in opened quite unexpectedly onto a wide, arterial avenue. The samrat didn't seem to have any doubts over which way to go, and like a flock of birds flying in unison, the rest of the group flowed out of the alley and turned right, swiftly and intuitively following their leader. Harihara allowed his horse to be led by the other mounts, not resisting, yielding to whatever lay in store for him down the road.

A moment later, the thing that was in store for him revealed itself.

It appeared from one of the side roads bisecting the avenue, and at first sight, Harihara was so thrown by its bulk that his mind failed to make sense of what he was looking at. It wasn't until the beast turned to face the wave of riders that Harihara realized they were hurtling towards a gigantic, white, woolly mammoth. The animal was so large that it towered over its surroundings, its big ears blotting out the view down the street. But for the fact that it had been concealed behind a pair of tall, three-storey buildings, they would surely have got a glimpse of it sooner.

Responding to some mysterious, atavistic instinct, the horses pulled to a dead halt, rearing up and whinnying in distress, forelegs kicking, nostrils flared, eyes wild with fear. Everyone fought to get their mounts under control while keeping an eye on the mammoth that stood in the middle of the street, massive legs splayed and braced to charge, its head and trunk swaying threateningly to a rhythm only it could hear. Six huge tusks the size of tree trunks sprouted from the mammoth's upper jaw, each capped with iron and sharpened to a point, curling dangerously into the air as the beast tossed its head. Harihara gaped as the animal raised its trunk and trumpeted a bestial call that mauled the morning, its echoes sending roosting pigeons into spirals of panic.

As the elephant lowered its trunk, Harihara, for the first time, took note of the hulking figure seated atop the beast. Broad shouldered and heavily muscled, the figure had a luxuriant crop of golden hair and a luscious golden beard that came down to his chest. Harihara could almost imagine the radiance of authority forming a nimbus around the figure, who he rightly guessed to be Indra.

Vikramaditya's mount, which had been ahead of all the others, was not immune to the mammoth's terror, but Harihara saw the samrat whisper into the horse's ear and stroke its neck, soothing it and bringing it under control. It still nickered and danced around a bit, but Vikramaditya was able to urge it forward gently, narrowing the distance between himself and the mammoth ever so slowly. Harihara held his breath on seeing the samrat cross his arms and draw the swords that hung at his waist, the weapons coming free of their scabbards with the sibilant *seeng* of metal scraping against metal.

Kshapanaka and Shanku instantly nudged their mounts after their king, flanking him on both sides, Shanku with a *chakram* in her hand, poised for a throw, Kshapanaka with her bow drawn, arrow in place, ready to let fly at any sign of trouble. Emboldened, a few riders of the Palace Guards and City Watch also pushed forward, weapons drawn and ready. Harihara didn't move, his eyes transfixed on the blades in Vikramaditya's hands, which seemed to turn red hot under the sweltering sun. Moments later, small blue-green flames began dancing in loopy patterns along the swords' edges and surfaces.

The wind died down and the street fell deathly silent, as

time stood motionless in dreadful anticipation. Ujjayini's bells tolled mournfully in the distance as Vikramaditya drew closer and closer to the mammoth, until he was in the beast's shadow. The beast loomed over him, its sinuous trunk twisting and coiling, ears flapping as it watched him intently. The samrat and Indra were locked in a relentless stare, and Harihara realized he was quaking in fear, his heart hammering in his chest, as if seeking to break free of the ribcage and flee from the spot.

Indra rose on the elephant's back and put one foot on the beast's head. Arms akimbo, his broad chest thrust out, head thrown back haughtily, he surveyed the samrat with a smile that only turned the corners of his lips.

"We meet at last," he said. His gaze dropped to the swords in Vikramaditya's hands. "The Wielder of the Hellfires. Very impressive!"

The samrat stared up at the deva lord, his face set in stone.

"Turn back, deva. You are not welcome in my kingdom."

Harihara winced at Vikramaditya's lack of nuance, and when the mammoth curled its trunk upwards and over the samrat's head, Harihara cringed and let out a gasp, expecting the worst. The councilors and soldiers tensed as well, ready to spring to their king's defence, but the samrat stayed firm on his saddle, watchful as Indra stepped forward and balanced himself expertly on the raised trunk so the elephant could lower him to the street, in front of the samrat.

"I said you are not welcome here," the samrat repeated in an icy tone.

"But I am here in peace." Indra's smile became more genial, and he spread his hands wide, turning a full circle where he stood. "I carry no weapons, see? And there is no army hiding anywhere, awaiting a signal to attack. I give you my word. We are here in peace."

A murmur broke out among the soldiers, and though the

surprise and relief showed in the way bunched up shoulders and tense muscles relaxed, no one dropped their guard. Vikramaditya inclined his head to look around Indra and the elephant, and Harihara did likewise to notice the chariot partly concealed behind the bulk of the mammoth. The chariot was drawn by a pair of white horses, and Harihara could tell that it was a fine specimen of workmanship, crafted from sturdy wood and tastefully decorated with carvings. Curtains of sheer lace fell from its canopy, veiling the chariot's box, so it was hard to determine anything about the shadowy figure seated within. A splendid horse stood beside the chariot, but the horseman's face was concealed from view by a cotton shawl draped loosely over his head.

"You are still not welcome," Vikramaditya strained to keep his hostility in check. The flames on the Hellfires were bright, long licks of fire on old iron. "You brought death and destruction to my people for no fault of theirs. You sent your minions to force me to yield to your will. The misery they inflicted on my people was on *your* behalf, so I hold *you* responsible for what they did. Then you sent the yaksha to attack my beloved wife, and break me…"

"I regret what happened, but I *did not* send the yaksha after your wife," Indra butted in, all earnestness. "Believe me, I only asked the yakshas to take what you loved the most, what you would protect until your last breath. I had *no* inkling how precious your wife was to you. Had I known…"

"Stop right there."

In his eagerness to convince Vikramaditya, Indra had taken a couple of steps forward, but the samrat checked the advance by pointing a sword at the deva. "Stop."

Harihara observed Indra frown in exasperation, and as Vikramaditya dismounted, for a fleeting moment, the mask of amiability slipped, and Harihara saw the calculative ruthlessness in Indra's eyes. The next instant it was gone, and as the samrat approached him, burning swords in each hand, the deva smiled, barely moving to defend himself against a possible attack. Behind Indra, the mammoth watched the showdown with its small, pink, primitive eyes. With hardly any distance separating them now, Harihara saw that the deva was a little taller than the samrat, who himself was no small man.

"How do you even *dare* to pretend you care?" Vikramaditya stepped closer and stared fiercely into the deva's bearded face, his voice a growl that barely carried to Harihara and the circle of soldiers. "Had you known it was Vishakha the yaksha would come after, would it have made any difference? No. Because my wife means nothing to you. *Nothing.* Keep your lies to yourself, deva — especially those that pertain to my wife. I want none of your deviousness to taint my Vishakha. Do I make myself clear?"

Harihara would never wager on it, but he imagined he saw Indra back away from the samrat in a tacit concession of authority. Vikramaditya, though, was not done yet.

"You do realize that the only thing holding me back is this city, which has already suffered enough on account of war," he said. "But that doesn't mean you can test my patience infinitely." Taking a deep breath to keep a hold on himself, he spat out in a hoarse, strangulated voice, "Leave my city *now.* I will not *ask* you again."

Sensing the tautness in the atmosphere, the elephant tossed its head and trumpeted, rocking back and forth while it waited for a command from its master. Harihara could see the citizens of Ujjayini hanging around the fringes of the street, half out of sight, curious and terrified at the same time, keen to learn what was happening, yet ready to bolt at the slightest hint of danger.

"You don't understand. I am here to make amends, right all the wrongs."

The samrat studied Indra with narrowed eyes. "Amends? You?" Seeing the deva nod, the king cocked one eyebrow. "How?"

"By acknowledging you as my blood, and accepting you as one of my very own."

The lord of the devas had been loud enough for everyone to hear, and there was a split-second delay before people got the significance of what had been said. The astonished gasps that followed sounded like the very earth letting out a stifled groan, followed by a silence deeper than the night, deeper than death itself. People leaned in and inched closer, straining to stay quiet, so they wouldn't miss what came next.

"What do you mean, deva?" Vikramaditya hissed under his breath, his eyes boring into Indra's. "What new trickery is this?"

"No trickery, none whatsoever." Placing a hand on the samrat's shoulder, Indra bent his head and spoke in solemn tones. "It is the absolute truth. Deva blood runs in your veins. You are a deva by birth, Vikramaditya."

The samrat shrugged Indra's hand roughly off his shoulder and took a step back. "I am no deva," he snarled. "I am a human and proud of being one."

Indra sighed and gave his head a patronizing shake. "You cannot deny being a deva just because you wish it so," he said. "These swords of yours, these Hellfires... Where do you think you get the powers to wield them? In the hands of humans, they are entirely ineffective. But look at you. *You* are deva blood, and the Hellfires can tell that. These Hellfires show who you really are — son to my son. *My grandson.*"

There was an intake of breath all around, sharper and louder than before.

"Son to *your* son? Are you saying... father was a deva?" The samrat stared at Indra in confusion.

"Not was. *Is*. Your father *is* a deva." Indra turned and gestured, and Harihara's gaze darted to the chariot where the shadowy figure waited.

Vikramaditya too looked at the chariot before his eyes travelled back to assess Indra. Conscious of what the deva seemed to be implying, he shook his head. "My father is no more. He died in battle with the Sakas…"

"No, no," the deva lord shook his head with vehemence. "Mahendraditya might have been a brave king, but he was never your father. *That* is your father."

Every soul present craned its neck in the direction of the chariot, where the breeze lightly ruffled the drawn lace curtains. Looking over a rider's shoulder for a better view, Harihara too watched the chariot, waiting for the figure inside to alight. However, it was the horseman who responded, spurring his mount forward, hooves clinking loudly against the stone-paved road. The breeze tugged at his shawl, but his face remained hidden until he had almost drawn up to Indra's side. Swinging a leg over the saddle, he dismounted, and Harihara saw that the mysterious rider was tall and graceful. As the horseman took the last few steps to join Indra and Vikramaditya, he reached up and slipped the shawl off his head. Harihara was immediately struck by his sharp, handsome features and his soulful eyes the colour of honey.

Once the newcomer had drawn up by his side, Indra put an arm around his shoulders and pulled him a little closer to both himself and Vikramaditya. A smile lit up the deva lord's face, but more than joy, there was an element of triumph, a gloating, a subtle glint of vindictiveness that reflected in Indra's eyes. The samrat, meanwhile, scrutinized the new arrival, his eyes thin slits of suspicion, disbelief and shock. He began shaking his head adamantly, but Indra, who guessed what was coming, nodded.

"This is my son Gandharvasena, and *he* is your father."

"No. No. These are all your lies. *Lies.* My father is Mahendraditya. I recognize no one else as my father. Enough of your lies, deva. *Enough.*" The Hellfires blazed in the samrat's hands, the flames like fingers, seeking out things to burn. "For the last time, leave my city before I..."

"You do not believe me, fine," Indra virtually roared to make himself heard over the king's voice. Vikramaditya paused, and when Indra saw he had the samrat's attention, he said, "I can see why you won't believe me. But a son would believe his mother, wouldn't he? Tell me, will you or will you not?"

Vikramaditya stood glowering up at Indra, the Hellfires hanging limp by his sides as he was finally confronted by the reality of what the deva was saying.

"Let us both agree that your mother's word will be final," said Indra, his voice ringing in the hushed silence of the street. "Let us ask Queen Mother Upashruti who your father is — her dead husband King Mahendraditya, as you claim, or my son Gandharvasena, as I insist."

* * *

When they had set out from Avanti, there had been fourteen of them, including the guide. Now they were down to seven. Six any time soon, Vetala Bhatta knew, when the old soldier — the oldest in the bunch, almost as old as the Acharya himself — would finally give in to weakness and the fever that was radiating off his skin, burning him from inside. The Ghost Marsh is toying with us, Vetala Bhatta thought, looking at the straggling line of survivors behind him, all still tied to one another by a vine, the veteran helped along by two others who themselves weren't far from exhaustion. The marsh is stalking us like a predator, picking out the weakest, one by one...

Stop. I must stop this. I must be careful. I must think

*positive thoughts. For my sake. And theirs. I can't let the men
see what I fear...*

The mood had turned despondent once it had been
established beyond doubt that the party was lost and clueless
about how to get out of the marsh. Sourness and grumbling
had set in, first over the hopelessness of their situation and the
rationing of food, then over little things. As hunger, fear and
fatigue began gnawing at them, tempers frayed over the silliest
of reasons and arguments broke out every now and again. The
raj-guru invariably ended up playing peacemaker, and they
had carried on roaming the marsh, searching for a way out.

Then, the lights had begun to appear.

The first one had taken all of them by surprise, a smoky,
little, yellow-white globe, the size of a man's fist, floating a
little above the swamp and at the very edges of the mist. They
had gone to investigate it, only to find that it drew away as
they approached. Then, some of them thought the light had
disappeared, while the others argued it was still there, leading
them on, perhaps even showing them a way out. They fought
over this adamantly until the light somehow vanished from
everyone's sight, leaving them all surly and angry with each
other. But it appeared intermittently through the day, showing
itself to a few of them but not the others, then revealing itself
to those who hadn't seen it the first time while staying hidden
from those who had. On one occasion, three soldiers insisted
the light was glowing over the swamp to their right, two others
maintained it was straight ahead on their path, while the rest,
the Acharya included, saw nothing anywhere. The lights began
pulsing in and out of sight with greater frequency, tugging
everyone in different directions, gradually tearing the party's
sanity — and its unity — apart.

Realizing there was something hallucinatory about the
lights — and possibly something more sinister at play from
the way the lights were dividing the group — the Acharya

had laid down the rule that none of them would follow the lights unless every member in the party saw the same light in the same place. This had restored a semblance of order and normalcy, but the raj-guru sensed the men were being drawn to the lights in strange and uncontrollable ways; even he had to force himself to stop being mesmerized whenever one of the lights pulsed into his sphere of vision. The men were soon constantly haunted, their eyes scouring the mist and the marsh for a glimpse of the lights, and in no time, all they were talking about was the lights, obsessed by them, held utterly in their thrall.

There was no way to tell if the lights had played a role in the loss of the first soldier, for no one knew exactly what had happened to him. With no real need to set a watch, they had all gone to sleep, and on waking, they had discovered that one of them had cut himself free of the vine and walked into the dark of the night. After regrouping, they had resumed their futile wandering of the marsh when, unexpectedly, a vicious fight broke out between two soldiers. Before anyone could even intervene, one of them stabbed the other in the chest repeatedly with his knife, killing him on the spot. The killer was overpowered with some difficulty, and when questioned, he kept raving that the man he had killed had denied seeing the light the previous day, and this had infuriated him. On Vetala Bhatta's orders, he was trussed in vines for everyone's safety.

That night, the killer also disappeared, much like the soldier the night before.

The Acharya had found the second soldier's vanishing strange, as a watch had been set that night to prevent precisely such an occurrence. The two men who had been on watch apologized for what had happened, saying they had both been overcome with sleep and had dozed off, each assuming the other was awake. Convincing though it sounded, the raj-guru was still suspicious. So, that afternoon, as they had rested after a meagre lunch, he had surreptitiously reached into the minds of his escorts — the first time he had attempted this since that morning by the palace bath, when he had read the Healer.

What he discovered had shocked him. Sometime during the previous day, the men had all conspired against the killer, and after nightfall, when the Acharya had gone to sleep, they had untied the man and forced him into the misty darkness, condemning him to a lonely and dreadful death. Vetala Bhatta understood that the need for crude justice might have fuelled the punishment, but the men had also acted to preserve themselves from a lunatic who could potentially harm them.

Vetala Bhatta also saw abject fear and despair in the men's minds. Fear of the eerie Aanupa, and despair at the slowly solidifying certainty that they would all die in the marsh. An hour later, the old soldier, the one burning up with fever now, had thrown himself into a swamp with the intention of committing suicide and sparing himself an agonizing, drawn-out death brought on by starvation. He had been rescued, but by nightfall the fever had set in, and seeing him shiver and sweat in turns, the raj-guru had wondered if it would have been best to let him drown.

Upon sensing the men's deep dejection and weakening spirit, Vetala Bhatta had decided to try and influence their thoughts. Working hard to stay unobtrusive, he had reached into the men's minds, planting hope where despair grew, masking dark fears with a sense of determination, infusing positivity wherever he could. He had no idea whether this would work at all, but as the day progressed, he found the men more cheerful and saw distinct streaks of optimism. Ever since, he had been working on the men's minds almost non-stop, instilling in them the belief that they could leave the Ghost Marsh alive — while keeping their attention diverted from the lights that still accompanied them everywhere, trying to distract and tantalize.

"I am fairly certain we are moving eastwards, your honour," said Kedara, the captain of the escort, coming to the Acharya's side. There was a slight buoyancy in his step and he smiled at the raj-guru, not knowing that he owed his optimism and the thoughts he had just verbalized to the man he was escorting to the court of Queen Abhirami. "If we stay the course, we should eventually enter Odra."

"I agree," said Vetala Bhatta, pushing his spear subtly out of sight, so that the captain wouldn't notice the skulls near its tip glowing red from within. "I agree," he repeated, running his palm over his face in weariness.

He wanted to say more, assure Kedara that he was right in his thinking and was doing a fine job of leading the men, but the words died on his tongue as he failed to gather the energy to speak. It was good for everyone's sake that he was manipulating the soldiers' thoughts, propping their flagging spirits, keeping them focused and upbeat, but it was a challenging task, sapping him of his strength. He had to constantly monitor the minds around him, looking for traces of depression creeping in and quickly countering it before moving to the next mind. Added to that, he had to keep his own sense of reality — and the gloom it engendered — in check, so that *that* didn't accidentally tinge the minds he was influencing. The whole exercise was so taxing that the raj-guru had started feeling weak in the legs and his vision wheeled and spun now and then, as if suddenly on an independent axis.

"Is something bothering you, raj-guru?" Kedara peered in sudden alarm.

"No, not at all." The Acharya shook his head so vehemently that the swamp swung and veered for a moment. "Absolutely fine," he said, avoiding the ball of light that had showed up to his left. He sent his mind out to the men, trying to gauge who else had noticed the light. Just one of them had, but he was keeping what he had seen to himself.

"When should we stop for breakfast?" Kedara asked. "The men don't look hungry."

Another successful attempt at implanting thoughts on Vetala Bhatta's part — he had got the men to believe they weren't as hungry as they were, so they would think less about food and consume even less of the depleting rations.

"We can break in another hour or so, I suppose. Breakfast and lunch together." Out of sheer habit, Vetala Bhatta looked up at the sky, realizing even as he did so that he wouldn't be able to locate the sun, which was hidden, as usual, somewhere above the stacks of impenetrable yellow-grey clouds.

"What's the matter, raj-guru?" the captain's voice was edged with panic. "Are you alright?"

The Acharya's vision swam violently as he lowered his head. The clouds seemed to descend with his gaze, and for some reason, the swamp suddenly lurched, lopsided, then rose to meet the clouds in a churn. He observed his escort run towards him as he felt a sudden, painful jarring sensation in his knees, as if they had struck something hard.

"Raj-guru! Men, come quickly! Help me lift the raj-guru."

Vetala Bhatta felt something grab him by the shoulders, propping him up, but his head still lolled. The men were running, and behind them, the mist was closing in, dark and heavy. A few balls of light rose and danced, coming in with the mist, and then, for the first time, the Acharya saw shadowy figures approaching him and his men through the mist.

Figures draped in shrouds. Tall and thin and gaunt. Like skeletons. Drawing around them from all sides. Coming with the mist. Like minions of death.

The raj-guru closed his eyes. He was too tired to fight any longer. It was easier to let the darkness win.

* * *

A giant of a man with a fierce black beard, a laugh that burst out from somewhere deep in his gut, and a long, powerful stride that forced him, Vikramaditya, to run along, so that he could keep up on his short, stubby legs. These were the things the samrat remembered most about Mahendraditya.

There were other specific memories from his childhood as well. Mahendraditya lifting him onto the saddle of his horse, and the two of them riding slowly around Ujjayini's countryside, Mahendraditya pointing out spotted deer and *teetar* and migratory cranes as the late afternoon sun slanted through the leaves. And the nights they camped in a forest or an open meadow, Mahendraditya showing him the constellations and the *akashganga*, while all Vikramaditya had been keen on was sitting by the fire and listening to the ghost story where the kind, old man is swallowed by his own shadow.

On one occasion, Mahendraditya had gifted him a finely carved wooden play sword, and Vikramaditya had a vivid recollection of showing it off proudly to everyone, until he discovered that Mahendraditya had given Vararuchi a sword made of *real* steel, which could actually cut things. This blatant act of deception had left Vikramaditya so inconsolable that Mahendraditya had taken him to the foundry the next day and instructed the royal smith to make Vikramaditya a steel sword, but with rounded edges. One night, not many years later, a grievously wounded Mahendraditya had summoned the brothers to his bedside and pressed his two swords into their hands, one for each of them, saying the swords were now theirs, and it was on *them* to protect Avanti and its people. Vikramaditya recalled standing by Mahendraditya's pyre, Vararuchi at his side, the hide-bound hilt of his new sword smooth under his palm, his eyes smarting from the smoke — and from anger at fate, for having taken his father away from him.

"So, are you sending word to the Queen Mother to join us, or do we go to her?"

Vikramaditya blinked and refocused his vision on Indra and Gandharvasena. The samrat observed an amused smile play on Indra's lips, one with the shadow of a supercilious smirk, as if those lips were savouring a hard-fought victory. He realized that the city's bells had ceased ringing, though their echoes seemed to linger like a stale reminder of ever-lurking danger. Other than the stray jingle of a harness and the snorting of a restless horse, the street around him was silent. Vikramaditya became acutely aware that his people were watching how he responded to the deva's shocking revelation.

"No."

"No? What do you mean, no?" Indra asked, taken aback. "Unless you are ready to take my word for it, how are we to establish the truth without your mother telling…"

"No," the samrat repeated, squaring his shoulders and meeting Indra's eye. "I will not have anyone disturb the Queen Mother."

Indra's eyebrows rose in minute movements, and when he spoke, his words had a sly texture. "Could it be that you are afraid of learning the truth about your real father?"

Every shadow in the street was immobile, every soul hanging on to every word that was being traded at the centre of this tense tableau.

"I don't fear confronting the truth, deva," came Vikramaditya's reply, his voice sharp, clear and emphatic for the benefit of everyone present. "But I will not insult my mother by having her character put to test just because someone comes along questioning my paternity. I will not allow you to humiliate my mother in front of her people. I don't know how you treat your women in Devaloka, but in Avanti, the dignity and honour of our women is sacrosanct.

No, deva," the samrat glanced from Indra to Gandharvasena hotly, "*my mother is not answerable to the two of you.*"

Indra looked at Vikramaditya with his cold blue eyes, and the samrat saw uncertainty thrashing about in their depths. The deva had clearly not anticipated such stubborn resistance. "Whether you want to involve the Queen Mother or not is your decision, but you cannot run away from the fact that you are a deva," he said. "Do you realize what it means to be a deva? There is so much…"

A sudden stir and a murmur of voices arose to Vikramaditya's left, interrupting Indra. The commotion came from one of the side streets, and the samrat noticed those gathered along that street parting way for someone. The crowd's manner was awed and respectful, and as more onlookers made room and the heads blocking his view moved aside, Vikramaditya saw a familiar face ploughing its way through the throng.

Pralupi.

His eyes had barely widened in surprise at his sister's unexpected appearance when a few more heads in the crowd shifted to give Vikramaditya a glimpse of the person coming behind Pralupi.

Queen Upashruti.

Even as the shock registered and alarm raised a white-hot flare in his mind, the samrat remembered why his sister and mother were in this section of Ujjayini. The previous evening, over dinner, he had overheard them planning a visit to the Kali temple near the city's western gate. In his hurry to confront Indra, he had forgotten all about their planned trip, and now they were both on their way back to the palace, their route taking them past the exact spot where he had forced Indra to stop.

"Mother," he exclaimed, wondering why they were out when the city's bells had been ringing, and why they weren't under the escort of the Palace Guards.

Pralupi and Upashruti nudged past the crowd and stepped into full view. The samrat saw the wicker baskets they were carrying, filled with flowers, coconuts and other offerings brought back from the temple. Pralupi, who was in the lead, noticed the samrat, but switched her attention to the elephant, her jaw falling open at the size of the beast. Upashruti also looked at the mammoth once in astonishment, but her gaze drew back to Vikramaditya.

"Guards," the samrat shouted, staring wildly about him. "Your Queen Mother is unprotected. Get to her side, quick. Take her and Princess Pralupi away. Go, go!"

Shanku, who was to Vikramaditya's left, instinctively spurred her mount towards the two women. The king's commands galvanized the Palace Guards and the soldiers of the City Watch, and there was a scrabble of feet and hooves as men rushed to shield Upashruti and Pralupi. The queen stared at Vikramaditya, her eyes wide with confusion, and the samrat waved his hand, motioning her to step back.

But Upashruti either didn't see him or didn't comprehend his gesture. Instead, her gaze swept over the scene in front of her, moving curiously from Vikramaditya back to the imposing elephant, and from there to Indra to —

The samrat was looking straight at his mother when he saw her eyes move to the deva standing beside Indra. Vikramaditya saw Upashruti's eyes widen in surprise, her face turning pale and then freezing in bewilderment and horror, as her gaze was riveted to the deva. Suddenly finding it hard to breathe, Vikramaditya jerked his head around to Gandharvasena, who was staring at Upashruti, his deep, soulful eyes glowing with the unmistakable light of recognition.

The galloping of hooves was loud in Vikramaditya's ears; his hands felt numb, the Hellfires heavy in his grip; he had trouble lifting his head to look back in his mother's direction. By the time his gaze went to where she was standing, the

Palace Guards had formed a cordon around her and Pralupi, obscuring them from view, and Shanku was driving a wedge through the crowds, pushing the onlookers back and clearing a path, so that the guards could swiftly take their Queen Mother and her daughter away from danger. Vikramaditya stood on tiptoe to catch a glimpse of his mother, and as he watched her retreating form, she turned once, throwing a glance over her shoulder, her frightened eyes seeking out the face that she had encountered so unexpectedly.

With the queen and the princess safely away, the hubbub in the street died down as quickly as it had started, and Indra and the samrat once again became the focus of undivided attention. The deva lord understood that Vikramaditya had escaped the embarrassment of Upashruti and Gandharvasena coming face to face by the slenderest of margins, but seeing the samrat's discomposure, a superior smile spread across his face, and he gave Gandharvasena a nod of satisfaction. The younger deva was shaken, though, and his gaze kept straying to where the Palace Guards had taken Upashruti.

"What was I saying?" Indra looked at the samrat for a moment. "Yes... being a deva..."

"You said something about me being afraid of learning the truth about my real father," Vikramaditya cut in. He had gained full control of his emotions, and his eyes were calm but cold as they assessed Indra and Gandharvasena. "In all honesty, it matters little to me who my real father is. I have always thought of myself as Mahendraditya's son, and it makes no difference to me if he is or isn't my father. I am still his son."

Gandharvasena turned to the samrat and took a step forward. "Son, I wish you..."

"Stop," Vikramaditya snapped, his voice crackling like wildfire. "Do *not* call me that. The only one who had that right was King Mahendraditya, who showered me with love and affection and taught me everything I know. From him, I learned the worth of a friend, the value of a promise and the price of loyalty. He gave me a sword, so I could put my strength and courage to good use; he offered me wisdom, so I knew when to keep the sword sheathed. He told me stories of war but sang me songs of compassion. He was all the father a son could ever want. You — even assuming what you say is true — *you* don't count. Father is King Mahendraditya. *No one else.*"

Gandharvasena stepped back, thrown by the force of the samrat's words. He turned to Indra in distress, seeking guidance, and Vikramaditya saw the deva was but a tool in Indra's hands, helpless to think and act for himself. Indra, for his part, seemed in two minds, not entirely pleased at the turn of events but not wholly unhappy either.

"It saddens me no end to see you turn away from your father's embrace." Indra gave his head a morose shake. Despite his words, to the samrat it felt as if the deva was satisfied with the way things had unravelled, which was worrying. "As your grandfather, I had hoped to give you everything befitting a deva," Indra went on. "Why, I wanted to set right all the troubles this city and its people have had to suffer recently, but..."

"The troubles that *you* brought upon my city and its people." Disregarding the flash of anger in Indra's eyes, the samrat continued, "And for all that you say you can give me, why do I think *you* are the one with the greater sense of loss when I refuse to accept any so-called deva lineage? Wait... let me guess. Were you hoping that I would cry in joy and hand Veeshada's dagger to you?" Vikramaditya's tone turned sarcastic.

"You are a deva, Vikramaditya. You owe allegiance to Devaloka, and it is your duty to uphold the glory of the devas." In one final bid to sway him, Indra stepped close to the samrat and took him by the shoulders. "Veeshada's dagger will ensure that the asuras never get the better of us, *ever*. Give it to me, Vikramaditya. For the sake of the blood that courses through your veins."

The samrat looked at the two massive hands resting on his shoulders, then turned to stare into Indra's blue eyes, cold and calculating, but also full of hope and expectation. Keeping his gaze locked on Indra, Vikramaditya sheathed his swords very carefully. Then, taking Indra's hands by the wrists, he lifted them off his shoulders one by one and dropped them, freeing himself of the deva's hold. Instead of stepping away, the king narrowed the distance between him and Indra by another inch, and when he spoke, his cold tone had a heavy finality.

"To your credit, your intentions have always been unwavering and crystal clear," he said. "You may not realize it, but that makes two of us, deva. I have promised to protect the Halahala. No matter what you do or say, no matter who I am or who my father might be, you will never get Veeshada's dagger from me. My suggestion to you is to leave my city in peace."

Scrutinizing the samrat with eyes narrowed in displeasure, Indra drew in a deep breath and offered a smile that curled his lips, giving it the semblance of a snarl. Without a word, he nodded once and turned back towards the beast towering over the street. It wasn't until he was seated on the elephant and Gandharvasena was back on his saddle that the lord of the devas spoke.

"You think you are very brave, Vikramaditya," he sounded like the faraway rumbling of thunder. "Knowing it is my blood coursing through your veins, you probably are. But you make a mistake. You are only part deva. The other half of you is human, which makes you weak and vulnerable. That is the part I will crush when I return next." He turned to look down at the faces of Ujjayini's citizenry, staring nervously up at him. He directed his words as much at them as at the samrat, working on their anxiety, nudging them slowly towards the precipice of abject fear. "Promise or no promise, grandson or no grandson, nothing will stop me from taking the Halahala. I will be back soon. That is my promise to you — it is also my warning."

Promise

Hey," he shouted. Then louder, "*Hey you... can you hear me?*"

His head almost didn't hurt when he was sitting still, his back pressed to the rough stone wall of his cell. When he moved, it throbbed with a dull, insistent pain that he had somehow learned to ignore. But the effort of shouting brought an explosion of agony, a shower of pain that sent shards down his neck and caused his world to tilt precariously. Still he shouted, doing what he could to attract the attention of whoever was outside.

"Hey, I know you can hear me, you idiots. Let me out." He shook his manacled fists vigorously, partly in frustration, partly with the idea of getting the heavy chain and bracket tethering him to the wall to rattle loudly enough for the sound to carry outside. The metal links chinked against one another dully, and the chain clattered and sank to the cold stone floor in an abrupt little collapse. "*Heyy!*"

Fighting the giddy spin of the room and the accompanying wave of pain that cascaded down his neck and shoulders, he paused, ear cocked in the direction of the broad, wooden door, waiting to hear the sound of approaching footsteps.

Nothing.

He turned his attention to the small window set high in one wall, impossible to reach because there was nothing to stand on, and impossible to breach because of the thick mesh of iron bars stretched across its opening. Outside, whoever had been pounding grain had gone silent, and for a moment, it seemed his cries were going to be answered. But the next instant, the rhythmic beat of a mortar striking a wooden pestle resumed, and he felt the despair rise to his mouth, bitter like bile.

"*Hey*," he half-shouted, half-snarled, flinching as the pain triggered a kaleidoscope of sparks under his eyelids. "Let me out of here, you... you retards. You don't know who I am. I am Ghatakarpara, nephew of Samrat Vikramaditya. Release me now and I will make sure you are treated with mercy. Release me. *Hey*."

The prince had no idea where he was or how many days had passed since the evening he had been waylaid by the little stream. He had surfaced to consciousness slowly — it had felt like rising out of a river, submerging again, then coming back up for air, sinking, then up again — and he couldn't say for certain how long he had been drifting in and out. He had a vague recollection of people carrying him on a litter made of cane, a strip of blue sky with high, rugged mountain ridges on both sides slipping past over his head. Another time, he lay on hard ground, a fire was burning nearby while the sky overhead was full of stars, and he could hear someone playing a drum. Maybe these were just dreams, though the more he thought of them, the more he knew they weren't.

Because always, *always*, there had been that splitting pain in his head. *Inside* his head.

Ghatakarpara touched the back of his head gingerly,

feeling around the spot where he had been struck with the quarterstaff. Probing through the rag that had been tied there, his fingers encountered something soft and lumpy under the crude bandage — a dressing for the wound, he guessed. He withdrew his hand and sniffed his fingers; the pleasing scent of turmeric mixed with some other herb filled his nostrils.

He had regained full consciousness just that morning — at least he thought it had been morning from the quality of the light entering the cell — to find a meal of fire-baked *rotis* and yoghurt laid out for him. Utterly famished, he had attacked the food, washing it down with a small pitcher of lukewarm water. His hunger partly sated, Ghatakarpara had assessed his situation and concluded that although he was at the mercy of his captors — who, like common thieves, had swiftly rid him of his councilor's gold medallion — they had attended to his injury and fed him, which meant they posed no immediate risk to his life. However, this said nothing about their identity or their intentions behind taking him hostage, and that greatly bothered the prince.

Except for the earthenware utensils he had used and the rough goat-hair blankets that had covered him as he had slept, the cell was bare and gave no hint of culture or geography. Failing to ascertain where he was, Ghatakarpara had been on the verge of dozing off when the noise of a mortar pounding grain close by had caught his attention. He had been yelling ever since but to no avail, and now all that shouting had left his throat hoarse and scratchy.

"Hey, please, I want some water."

The pounding continued. The prince wondered whether they could hear him at all, and if they could, whether their act of ignoring him was part of a torture method meant to break him. Another part of him — one whose opinion he didn't want to consider — told him that the pounding was nowhere but in his imagination.

"Please…" this time his voice cracked harshly, "some water, please."

The pounding ceased.

Ghatakarpara held his breath, waiting to see if it resumed as it had earlier. Moments passed and there was nothing to fill the emptiness inside and outside the cell. The square patch of light from the window laboured across the floor, as if carrying the full weight of the sun on its gossamer shoulders.

Footsteps outside the door.

Using the wall for support, so he wouldn't collapse from dizziness, the prince got to his feet. He took one, then two, then three faltering steps towards the door, seeing if he could rush the person coming in, but after the fourth step, he was yanked back by the chain clasped to his wrists. Looking at the taut chain extending from the wall bracket, Ghatakarpara realized he was not even halfway to the door and let out a sigh of disappointment.

A key rattled in the lock and the door swung open to admit a figure smothered in shawls.

Ghatakarpara stared at the figure in surprise. He had been expecting a male guard, a big loutish character or a battle-scarred brute, someone who fitted everyone's popular notion of a minder. Instead, the person who entered the cell was a woman of indeterminate age; from the strands of grey hair that had escaped her headdress, he judged her to be in her forties or early fifties. She had a pair of stern grey eyes, which she now turned on him, the corners of her lips turning down in a disapproving frown. In her hand was another earthenware pitcher, larger than the one that he'd been served water in.

As he stood staring at her, the woman plonked the pitcher rudely down on the floor. Then, without a word, she whirled around and headed for the door. She had crossed the threshold and was swinging the door shut when Ghatakarpara finally found his voice.

"Where am I?"

For an instant, the woman looked at him with her piercing gaze. Then, heaving the heavy door on its hinges, she slammed it shut and slid the bolts in place. The prince heard the lock click and the woman's footsteps recede. A minute later, the pounding of the mortar picked up once again.

Ghatakarpara sighed, feeling deeply dejected with life. Whoever his captors were, they had left him with an elderly woman as his jailor. *A woman*. Not even a warrior. Just an *ordinary woman* who did mundane chores like pounding grain, for whom getting her grain pounded was of higher priority to slaking her prisoner's thirst. It showed how little a threat his captors thought him to be, how insignificant he was in their scheme of things.

Leaving the pitcher of water untouched, Ghatakarpara returned to the comfort of the wall. Leaning against it, he slid to the ground, weary and depressed, and sat hugging his knees with thoughts of Aparupa flooding his mind, cramming everything else out.

* * *

The sword hung on the wall to the right of Vikramaditya's seat at the council table, flanked on one side by an ancient map of Sindhuvarta — gold-thread embroidery on faded red silk and dating back to the reign of the early Adityas — and on the other by the javelin that Dharmaditya, Mahendraditya's father, had used to bring down the twin man-eating tigers that had once terrorized the locality of Bhojapuri, when Bhojapuri was no more than a sleepy little village. The sword was long, with a great curved blade of old steel, its weight so considerable that not everyone found it handy in battle. It — and its twin, for they were a pair — had been designed with Mahendraditya's bulk in mind, and all through his warring life, the king had used only those two in combat. Its hide-bound hilt was scuffed from long use, the knuckle guard crisscrossed with nicks and scratches from umpteen other swords and axes met in years of conflict.

It is a strong sword and it will keep you safe. But remember, son, a sword is only as strong as the courage of the hand that wields it.

Staring distractedly at the sword, thoughts of Mahendraditya running through his mind like snatches of echo, the samrat remembered the first time he had taken it to battle — the night they had freed Betaal from captivity in the cremation ground. The fury and terror of that battle was still fresh in his mind — he remembered running through the fire and smoke, cutting and hacking his way through the Huna defence to get to the banyan where Betaal was imprisoned. The sword had mutilated and killed dozens of barbarians that night; that had been new to him, but was routine for the sword. Over the years, it had carved a bloody path wherever he went, leading his army against the retreating savages. He had used the sword until the last of the Hunas and Sakas had crossed back into the Great Desert, and Vikramaditya realized that were it not for the Hellfires, he would probably still be using it. He wondered where its twin — the one given to Vararuchi — was; Vararuchi had fought with that sword until his expedition to the Southern Kingdoms introduced him to the *urumi* and the *katari*, which had since become his favourite weapons.

"Where is Vararuchi?" the samrat frowned and turned his attention from the sword to those seated around the council table.

The abruptness of the question took the depleted council by surprise, and five pairs of eyes stared back at Vikramaditya in mild incomprehension. Kshapanaka, Varahamihira and Shanku sat to his right, while Dhanavantri was to his left, with

King Harihara for company. Harihara, by virtue of being a royal guest, had been invited to join everyone in the council chamber, but he was quite out of his depth as he listened to the consultations.

"Do we know why he isn't back yet?" Vikramaditya's gaze travelled over the council before coming to rest on Shanku. "You did send a rider yesterday, as I had asked..."

"I did. Right after we spoke about..." the girl checked herself. "The rider should have delivered your message; had he failed for some reason, he would have surely returned and told me. Still, I shall check with him, just to be sure."

"I'm sure the rider must have done his job," the samrat nodded, but the frown didn't go away. "But it is strange of Vararuchi not to have returned to the palace — especially after hearing what has befallen Ghatakarpara. It is so unlike him. I hope *badi-maa* is alright..."

"If that were the case, Vararuchi would have sent for Dhanavantri or Kunjala," Varahamihira pointed out.

"I shall speak with the rider, Samrat," said Shanku, trying to reassure her king.

"Why don't we just send another rider to Ushantha's place?" Dhanavantri suggested.

"Let's not panic," said Varahamihira in response. "Something must have held him up, but it can't be anything critical, otherwise he would have informed us. He must be on his way — for all we know, he'll walk in through that door before we're done, or later in the day."

"I agree," said the samrat. "Let's give him until tonight. If we don't hear from him by tomorrow morning, we'll send another rider."

With that settled, a momentary hush fell over the small gathering. "What were we discussing just before this?" Vikramaditya asked. "I'm afraid I got a little distracted. We were talking..."

"I was asking how we are to take Indra's threat to Ujjayini."

"Very seriously," Kshapanaka butted in. "His intent was clear. He wanted to strike fear in the hearts of the people, scare them, put them in a place where they can see nothing good coming of our fight with the devas. I would say that Indra's little speech was aimed at turning popular opinion against the palace."

As an uncomfortable silence took hold of the chamber, Vikramaditya looked at his councilors and asked, "What exactly is the popular opinion in Ujjayini these days?"

"Well," Varahamihira shifted in his seat, "It's more or less divided like before. There are those who support us in our stand against the devas and asuras, and there are those who are unhappy, mostly people who have suffered much. But yes, after today…" the councilor exhaled deeply and shrugged.

"What of today?" the samrat watched the elderly councilor closely.

Varahamihira didn't reply immediately. A lot had transpired today. He stared back at the king, waiting to see if Vikramaditya clarified the question, so that he could tailor his answer accordingly. The samrat, however, was equally dogged, not expanding on his question, and the stalemate dragged on for a few awkward moments.

"Well, you see, the people have seen Indra," the councilor spoke at last. "They have seen *the lord of the devas*. They have seen his elephant. They have heard his threats. They know what they are up against. Opinions can change."

"Maybe we should evacuate the city," said Vikramaditya after a short pause, assessing his councilors. "Tell those who can leave the city — those who have other places to go to — to leave. And find safe and secure places for those who have nowhere else to go. That way, we reduce the risks a little."

"Formalize the exodus that has been happening ever since

the Ashvins attacked us?" Dhanavantri raised a doubtful eyebrow.

Seeing the samrat nod, the heads around the table tilted in contemplation of the idea.

"What would be the impact of such a decree on the power of the throne, Samrat?" Varahamihira countered. "Would it not send a wrong signal to the people who are already scared — that the palace cannot assure their safety, so it wants them to leave? That the palace is incapable of protecting its own people?"

"Varahamihira is right," Harihara made his way into the conversation at last. "Your image as king can take a serious beating. Your image as Samrat of Sindhuvarta would also suffer."

"You make a fair point," Vikramaditya considered Harihara and Varahamihira. "But I am not here to protect *my image*. I am here to protect *my people* from harm, and if that entails falling in their esteem, it is a sacrifice I am willing to make every day, all the time. The subjects of Ujjayini will not suffer if I can help it."

"I understand, Samrat," said Varahamihira, a faint smile of pride playing on his lips. "It is a sacrifice we will all make as your councilors."

The samrat nodded. "It is not fear for my citizens alone that prompts me to suggest an evacuation; there are less sentimental reasons as well. When the fighting begins, I want the Imperial Army, the Frontier Guard, the City Watch and the militia to focus on the *fighting*. I don't want our soldiers distracted and running around protecting innocent civilian lives. I also don't want the city's resources stretched — when fighting erupts, everything Ujjayini has to offer should be available to our soldiers. The more civilians we have in this city, the more constraints we lay on our soldiers. Now is the time to free their arms so they can draw their bows back further, swing their swords higher and faster."

"I get it," said Varahamihira, and all the heads around the table nodded in consent.

"When do we start the evacuation?" asked Kshapanaka.

"Let us hold that decision until Vararuchi is back," the samrat replied. "I would like to hear his thoughts as well."

"Very well," said Varahamihira. "Meanwhile, let us take stock of the troops available to us in Ujjayini. Should the devas launch a sudden..."

Before the councilor could complete his thought, the door to the council chamber opened and a palace hand stepped in.

"I apologize for intruding, your honour," he said, bowing deeply. "But the Queen Mother seeks an audience."

The image of Upashruti being hustled away, but turning and stealing a dazed glance over the heads of the milling crowd, flashed before the samrat's eyes.

"With me?"

"Yes, your honour."

"She is outside?" Vikramaditya's voice rose in surprise.

"No, your honour. She wishes to see you in her chambers."

Vikramaditya was quick to sense a distinct uneasiness in the way his councilors and his guest from Heheya avoided looking at him. Everyone sat in their chairs, wooden and circumspect, afraid of doing or saying anything that could fracture an already fragile situation. The samrat realized that Indra had opened a door that could prove impossible to shut again.

"Let her know that I am with the council. I shall see her once we are done."

The samrat turned back to Varahamihira, but out of the corner of his eye, he observed that the palace hand hadn't moved. The man stood by the door, shifting and shuffling.

When Vikramaditya looked at him, he paled visibly, but stayed where he was.

"Is there something else you wish to tell me?" the samrat asked.

"No, your honour. Just that the Queen Mother instructed me to tell you she wants to see you."

"Why don't you go along and see the Queen Mother?" Dhanavantri said to the samrat, interpreting the hand's words correctly. Glancing at the others, he added, "We will stay back and see what needs to be done next."

Seeing the other three councilors nod in agreement, Vikramaditya pushed back his chair, and as he rose, he addressed Harihara. "Pardon me, but I have barely spent any time with you." Even as the older king began waving off the apology, the samrat continued, "I may not be able to join you for lunch, but I presume you would be staying with us overnight?"

"I suppose so," Harihara said uncertainly.

"Wonderful. I look forward to meeting you at dinner. Now, if you will excuse me."

Nodding to his guest and his councilors, Vikramaditya stepped out of the council chamber, closing the door softly behind him. The walk to the Queen Mother's chambers wasn't a long one, but the samrat felt his feet drag all the way, a weight pressing down on his shoulders and chest as he drew closer to the turn that led to her door. Even as he stood at the threshold of the chamber, the door half-open in invitation — and half-shut, as if to give him one final chance of going away unseen — he wondered what good would come of this encounter.

Upashruti was seated on a small stool, her hands on her lap, staring vacantly out of the window. As the door swung open, she turned and looked at Vikramaditya. Her eyes sought out his, searching his face for some sign that would tell her where she stood in her son's esteem.

"You wished to see me?"

"Come inside, Vikrama."

Upashruti did not rise, but followed her son with her eyes as he approached. The samrat stopped well short of her, however, and stood diffidently to one side, avoiding eye contact. Neither of them spoke, each waiting for the other to make the first move.

"You wished to see me." This time, tactically, the words were not framed as a question.

"Don't you want to know the truth?" asked Upashruti, staring into her son's face.

Vikramaditya looked away, steeling himself before replying. "I think I already know the truth."

The Queen Mother rose and took a step towards the samrat. When he turned to her, she said, "Don't you want to hear the truth from your mother's lips?"

* * *

The faces lining the sides of the road grew gradually in number as the little cavalcade neared the settlement of Mun'h. Curious faces, suspicious faces, some openly hostile. Faces that were tired and worn out and scoured by the harshness of the land around them. Men's faces, women's faces, even children, one or two with shy smiles. All upturned, all watching Kalidasa, their eyes trailing him until the riders were blotted out by the dust kicked up by the departing horses.

The first onlookers had turned up as early as the day before, as Kalidasa was escorted by the Huna patrol past frugal farms irrigated by the morning dew in place of water. Poor farmers scraping an existence out of the hard, unyielding

earth, and shepherds tending to emaciated goats and sheep
that nibbled on almost nothing, had stopped to observe the
parade as news of the arrival of Zho E'rami's son had spread to
the sparse Huna hamlets scattered over the desert. Later, when
they had halted at a shallow well to replenish their sheepskin
flasks, the women who were there to fetch water had nudged
and whispered and tittered among themselves, ogling the giant
brazenly while being coy and secretive about it, getting the
leader of the patrol to give Kalidasa a lewd grin.

"I don't know about the *shy'or*, but the women seem
more than happy to welcome you," he had said with a
chuckle and a wink.

The men escorting him had all thawed towards Kalidasa
over the course of the journey, the beating he had dealt them
definitely not forgotten, but accepted with grace. They weren't
exactly friendly yet, but accorded him sufficient respect, having
understood that they were dealing with someone above them
in talent, ability and authority.

Now with Mun'h a dark and growing smudge on the
northern horizon, and the road leading to it full of people
drawn there just to have a look at the stranger who claimed
to be Zho E'rami's son, the patrol had fallen silent and grown
formal, knowing that fraternizing with the stranger could
land them in trouble with the *shy'or*. Kalidasa welcomed this
silence, for it provided him with the perfect opportunity to size
up the town and its people before he met its chief.

Mun'h, he had understood from his escorts' conversations,
was one of the four significant Huna settlements in the Great
Desert, second in size only to its sister town of Se'shyi, which
was situated further west on the banks of the Dark River.
As there were no trade routes nearby, it wasn't clear why
Mun'h had come up where it had, though Kalidasa suspected
that the small hill on which the town was built might have

played a part in its early formation, probably as a defensive bastion. The town itself was a hodge-podge of leather tents and mudbrick hutments nestling to a larger stone structure on the hill's crest, reminding Kalidasa of a fat sow with a brood of piglets suckling at it. From the midst of the stone building, a flag thrust out, fluttering on a flagpole like a beacon, announcing the town's location to troops and travellers alike, and once they drew closer, Kalidasa noticed the faded sigil of the desert scorpion embroidered on it. Judging by the number of Huna warriors milling around — many now joining in the staring — he guessed Mun'h served as a garrison command, and the stone building was the fortified garrison and abode of the Huna *shy'or*.

The patrol was still some distance from Mun'h when a posse of a dozen fully armed riders came out from the town to meet them. The posse was led by a Huna of superior rank, and he took charge of Kalidasa, dismissing the patrol and gesturing to Kalidasa, respectfully but firmly, to accompany him and his men back into Mun'h. Resuming his ride, Kalidasa looked over his shoulder once at the leader of the patrol that had intercepted him and then brought him this far. Their eyes met, and the Huna bowed his head and lightly touched the *hriiz* on his forehead with his forefinger — a token of respect and friendship among the Hunas. Kalidasa nodded and turned to face Mun'h.

They entered the town through a wooden archway festooned with blue, yellow and red buntings, and these decorations continued along the one main, paved street that constituted the town's thoroughfare. On both sides were shops — an ironmonger's smithy, a bakery where men were baking dough balls on a metal dome inverted over a dung fire, a woman churning butter, a basket weaver — and here too people pressed and jostled against one another to catch a glimpse of Kalidasa. The Huna leading them had to routinely swing the switch he carried to force the townsfolk back from the road.

By the time they arrived at the small stone fort and dismounted in its open courtyard, the sun was well on its westward course. The Huna officer gestured to Kalidasa, and the two men entered the fort, which was spare and martial, and lacked the comforts generally associated with dwellings of those wielding great influence. Kalidasa was taken to a medium-sized hall overlooking one portion of the desert, where he was told to wait. Again, fully expecting the *shy'or* not to hurry things along, Kalidasa settled down by one of the windows to bide his time when he heard a footfall by the door, and a voice that was rich with authority and accustomed to obedience addressed him.

"Zuh te'i duz'ur Zho E'rami?"

Kalidasa turned to find two men inside the door. The one who had spoken stood in front and was of average height and build, clothed in coarse cottons and wools. He could easily have passed off as an ordinary Huna peasant, but for the nobility and animal magnetism reflected in his eyes. Seeing the set of the man's shoulders and the firm thrust of his chin, Kalidasa understood he was dealing with the *shy'or*.

"Ma'a," he nodded once. Then, looking the Huna up and down, he said, *"Zuh te'i barr shy'or?"*

The Huna gave a small smile that wasn't entirely cordial and shrugged. When he replied, it was in slow but grammatically proper Avanti. "You ask if I am the biggest chief. Let us first make sure *you* are who you say you are, shall we? Let me ask the questions, alright?"

Kalidasa observed the Huna standing behind take a step forward. The man was huge, nearly as tall as Kalidasa himself, with a girth that was twice that of Kalidasa's. To the untrained eye he could have looked obese, but Kalidasa knew there was hard muscle concealed under those rolls of fat. Kalidasa nodded at the smaller Huna.

"You say you are the son of Zho E'rami. Why should I believe you?"

"I can tell you exactly what happened the day father was killed... the *entire garrison* was killed."

"I know, I know. The rider dispatched by the patrol said you have the full story on Zho's death, that you were the only survivor that day, that you witnessed the whole thing. My question is, how can I believe *that* is how things happened that day? There is no one else alive to contradict you, offer a different version of events, is there?"

"You can ask me what you want about my father," Kalidasa said gruffly.

"I can." The Huna stepped closer and into the light angling in from the windows, and for the first time, Kalidasa saw the great scars that crisscrossed the man's cheeks, the one on the right coming straight down from cheekbone to jawline, the one on the left curving from just under the temple to the upper lip. The man's skin was dark, leathery and deeply lined; together with the scars and the black *hriiz* etched on his forehead, his face appeared to be at perpetual war with itself.

"I can," he said again, looking thoughtfully at Kalidasa. "But the stories about Zho E'rami are a part of legends. Anybody could know about Zho. And what you don't know you could pass off as having forgotten. After all, you were no more than a child when Zho was killed, right?"

Not knowing what to say, Kalidasa stared at the Huna defiantly. The Huna stared back unperturbed.

"You mean to say you would not accept my word?"

"Why would I? *You* came to me claiming to be Zho's son. The onus is on *you* to prove it." He shrugged expansively. "You could be a spy from Avanti, for all we know. You don't even wear the *hriiz*, and you expect me to…"

"I don't have the *hriiz* because everyone was killed before…"

"I have heard that," the Huna raised his hand and his voice. He was not accustomed to being interrupted.

As Kalidasa looked at the man, his brow knotted in frustration, the Huna chief clasped his hands behind his back and walked to one of the windows to gaze into the desert, where the shadow of the fort was slowly creeping eastward. At last, he turned to face Kalidasa.

"Tell me, who else was with Zho when he was killed? I mean the rest of his family."

Kalidasa blinked and jerked his head back as the picture of the four manacled figures being prodded and shoved into the granary sprang to his mind. It felt as if the image was lined with sharp, cutting edges, yet he forced himself to look at it, reliving the scene of the smoke-filled valley, the three wailing women and the haughty, unbending man.

And closer to him, the man on horseback, facing the granary, giving the soldiers the signal to set it and the captives it held alight…

"Other than father, I lost my elder sister Ei'hi, aunt Nei and her daughter Pli'isa that day," Kalidasa muttered, slamming the windows shut on the scene in his mind.

The answer seemed to please the Huna, but he looked at Kalidasa sharply. "What of your mother then? Wasn't she there that day?"

"My mother died while giving birth to me," Kalidasa replied. "That was why my father named me Ga'ur Thra'akha. Death came for my mother, but even as it took her, it left me behind as a gift for father. Ga'ur Thra'akha — the Gift of Death."

With a nod, the Huna turned to face Kalidasa. "I admit that you seem to know things not many others do, which suggests that you speak the truth. But I need to be certain, so we shall have to wait a little."

"For what?"

"For our *droiba*. The spells he casts will prove if you are Zho's son or not."

Droiba. Kalidasa turned the word around in his mind, remembering when he had last heard it used. It was years ago, the night he and Vikramaditya had stormed the Huna encampment at Ujjayini's cremation ground. It had been a new moon night, and their job was to find and rescue Betaal, who had been taken captive by the Huna *droiba*...

"Why do we have to wait for the *droiba*?" Kalidasa asked.

"Because he isn't here. He is out in the desert with the *yah'bre*." The Huna didn't expand on that, so Kalidasa tried to figure out what that could mean. *Yah'bre*. Dust-souls. That didn't help.

"You wanted to know if I was the biggest chief," the Huna looked up at his guest. "I am *shy'or* Khash'i Dur, chief of the *b'wo* line of Hunas. We are related to the *x'sa* Hunas by marriage, which makes me a distant relation of Zho E'rami. I have had the honour of meeting him a couple of times. A most remarkable man and warrior. Now, to answer your question, yes, I am one of the biggest *shy'ors* you will meet in the wide expanse of this desert. It is under my command that the great Huna army will cross the mountains and conquer Sindhuvarta."

* * *

He had been a guest at the palace for almost a week before she chanced upon him one evening, quite by accident. She had been taking a walk along the shore of the palace lake when she observed him, sitting under an *amlika* tree, painting the palace as a flock of cranes skimmed over the dark water. It was from her handmaidens that she later learned that he was a gifted artist and musician from the foothills of the Riksha Mountains, and that he had been welcomed by King Mahendraditya himself, who was in admiration of the man's skill with brush and *vamsi*.

Their paths crossed just once during that first visit of his to Ujjayini. One evening, a recital was organized in court in honour of her and Mahendraditya, where the artist had to share the spotlight with two other travelling balladeers who were the king's guests. But such was his talent that he effortlessly outshone the other two musicians, his performance leaving Mahendraditya so deeply impressed that the king singled him out for an endowment and invited him to dine with him and his queen. That was how Upashruti and Gandharvasena met formally for the first time.

The same evening, while partaking dinner, Mahendraditya extended Gandharvasena the added privilege of staying at the palace as his guest whenever he was passing through Ujjayini. The artist accepted the offer with customary gratitude, but took leave of the king and queen the very next morning. He was not seen or heard of for over a year, and the palace had all but forgotten him when, one rainy evening, when Mahendraditya was visiting faraway Nishada, a guard announced that the artist was at the palace door, seeking shelter for the night. Aware of her husband's promise of hospitality, Upashruti welcomed Gandharvasena and saw to it that he was looked after by the palace hands.

The rain only intensified the next morning, and by afternoon, the Kshipra was rising and the streets of Ujjayini were flooded, making travel inadvisable. Upashruti pressed Gandharvasena against venturing out, assuring him that he was welcome to stay in the palace until the waters subsided; in return, the artist offered to paint a portrait of her. The painting was stunning in its tribute to her beauty, astonishing Upashruti, and as day progressed into evening, Gandharvasena kept her entertained by playing the *vamsi*, raga after melodious raga. And somewhere between rapturous ragas, she — increasingly lonely in the palace as Mahendraditya travelled the breadth of Sindhuvarta, rallying an alliance against the invaders — melted under Gandharvasena's hypnotic gaze. That night, as the moon broke through the clouds and the world glistened wet in its soft, limpid light, Upashruti draped her arms around the artist's shoulders and pulled him down to her breast, quivering and gasping with love.

"I had..." she broke the silence between her and Vikramaditya, but then stopped. She looked out of the window with unseeing eyes, gazing inwards rather than at the world outside. "I... thought about telling your father... *the king*..." she corrected herself quickly. "I wanted to tell him everything. But he had so much on his mind those days that I didn't have the heart to burden him further. Moreover," her eyes dropped to her fingernails, bitten crudely in anxiety, "I could never summon the courage. How could I? He was so loving. He..." her voice choked as old memories stirred, "...he doted on me."

She wasn't sure if Vikramaditya had flinched at her words, but he said nothing.

It had only been that one night of transgression. The rain having let up, the artist left the palace the next morning without ceremony or courtesy; Upashruti learned of his departure only through the palace hands, and she had never laid eyes on him again — until that morning, bang in the middle of the streets of Ujjayini.

In all the time that he had been in the palace, he had given no indication of being a deva. Was he really a deva, she wondered, really Indra's son? The lord of the devas had been there with his elephant, so perhaps he was, after all. The shock of seeing him, handsome and virile, after so many years, came back to Upashruti. He hadn't aged at all. He looked the same as he had that day, playing the *vamsi* as the rain beat down on Ujjayini. He had to be a deva.

"I thought, over time, I would be able to break it slowly to your... *the king*," she said. She turned to Vikramaditya, standing before her, silent, emotionless. "But once you were born he adored you so much that..." Upashruti's voice shook with remorse, and she violently twisted and knotted the tassels of the light shawl she wore. "Then... one day he was no longer with us."

"I didn't seek any answers, so why admit to all of this now?" Vikramaditya's tone was flat.

"Because I have always wanted to," the words came out in almost a wail. "You have no idea what it is like to carry guilt in your chest. The weight can crush you."

"Yet, in all these years, you never said a word. It took Indra to bring it into the open."

Vikramaditya's tone was calm, but hidden in its folds, Upashruti felt the raw edge of accusation. She didn't blame her son; she knew he was right. The guilt had remained even after Mahendraditya's death, but she had expected time to set everything right. And it had. Until now. Now, all that she had once dreaded would resurface. All the shame, the outrage, the insults. Everything.

"I expected you to come here without being called."

The samrat didn't answer.

"I thought you would want an explanation."

"It is not for me to ask for an explanation, mother. I do not need one. But what explanation can you offer that will put everything back the way it was for *you* this morning?"

Looking up at Vikramaditya's face, patient and full of pain, Upashruti realized with a shock that her son's words had followed her own train of thought. She was the one with needs — the need to confess, the need to be forgiven, the need for redemption.

"Are you angry? Are you ashamed of me? You have a right to be."

Vikramaditya thought this over for a moment before shaking his head. "I am not angry with you. Why should I be? You are the same person with the same secrets that you were this morning, before Indra's arrival. You are still my mother. I have nothing to be ashamed of either. My father is Mahendraditya, the only father I care to have. Nothing can change that. I do feel a little cheated at having been told a lie all these years, but I think the only one who has a right to feel cheated is father, and he is no longer with us."

"You forgive me then?"

"There is nothing I can forgive you for, mother. It is father who was wronged, not me. I can only accept..."

"Don't you realize people are bound to talk now, ask questions?" Upashruti cut in apprehensively. "You will have to listen to the whispers, deal with the gossip, Vikrama. *Your* people, talking about *your* father and *your* mother, questioning your paternity, doubting my character. Can't you see how much I have wronged you?"

The samrat met his mother's gaze for the first time.

"I heard how you refused Indra the opportunity to question me in front of everyone." The Queen Mother's eyes were suddenly moist and her voice shook. "You stood up... you saved me the humiliation. But now, you will have to do that again and again..."

"What questions will people raise? Who my father is?" The samrat stuck his jaw out. "I have made it clear there is only one father I acknowledge — King Mahendraditya. I don't care if people harbour any doubts beyond that."

"And you would shield me from them the way you did with Indra?"

Vikramaditya took a moment to collect his thoughts.

"I will shield you, mother," he nodded. "Because you *are* my mother and nothing can ever change that. And also, because father would have wanted it no other way. It's a promise I made him when he gave me his sword — to uphold your dignity to my last breath. You are right. He loved you very much, mother. I will not break my promise to him."

Vararuchi

The glow from the dying sun illuminated Vararuchi's face, turning his features golden and setting the red *tilaka* on his forehead on fire. His eyes, in contrast, were grim and glacial, gazing away into the distance as Sharamana, the commander of the garrison of Musili, recounted the standoff between Indra and Vikramaditya. Propelled by Indra's scandalous claim, reports of the confrontation had spread everywhere, but it had taken Sharamana and his deputy Pulyama the better part of the afternoon to sift fact from fiction and distil the whole into a coherent narrative. The councilor listened without interruption, and when Sharamana was done, he stayed sunk in thought for a while. At last, he turned away from the window to look at the commander and Pulyama, who stood in the deeper shadows of the room.

"The Samrat refused to call the Queen Mother to counter Indra's assertions, is it?" With the sun now behind him, Vararuchi's face was in silhouette, making it hard for Sharamana to judge his expression. His voice, lacking any intonation, was inscrutable.

"Yes," said Sharamana. "He flatly refused to involve the Queen Mother in any way."

"But the Queen Mother did happen to come there, quite by chance. Correct?"

"Yes, your honour."

"And...?" The councilor paused, then, "Didn't Indra seize the opportunity?"

"From what we gather, there was a lot of confusion all around," Pulyama answered. "There were crowds everywhere, as well as soldiers of the palace and the City Watch. The Samrat was quick to order them to take the Queen Mother and Princess Pralupi away. It seems Councilor Shankubala herself escorted them to safety. We don't think Indra got the slightest chance."

"Interesting."

Vararuchi glanced out of the window again, where the sun was losing hold of the day and fast slipping towards the purple of the horizon. Then, as a new thought struck him, he turned back to the two men, whom he had come to trust more and more over the past few days.

"This deva who came with Indra... what did he look like?"

"The rumour is that he was very handsome, your honour."

"Ah, no... that's not what I meant." Vararuchi hesitated, almost as if he was ashamed of what he had in mind. "I mean... did anyone think he looked like... any mention of a resemblance to the Samrat?"

Even though it was too dark to see, Sharamana and Pulyama looked at one another searchingly. They both shook their heads.

"Not that we know of."

"What about the Queen Mother?"

"I don't understand," said Sharamana in confusion.

"Following what happened, has she made an official announcement denying Indra's allegations?"

"We don't know, your honour."

"And she and this deva… they never came face to face?"

"Your honour… you don't think Indra's claims are true, do you?" The commander peered at the councilor, his tone a mix of doubt and apprehension. "It can't be…"

"I am trying to ascertain if they are, that's all," Vararuchi snapped. Instantly regretting his tone, he smiled and softened his voice. "You have both done well. Thank you."

Once again turning his back to the two men, he watched the last of the sun disappear, leaving a pink-red stain in its wake. A flock of birds, too far away to be identifiable, flew across this splash of light and colour, while down below, in the garrison's courtyard, two bullock carts bearing rations for the men trundled in through the gate. After his brief but bitter encounter with Upashruti the previous night, Vararuchi had stormed out of the palace, bent on putting distance between himself and his stepmother. Instead of returning to his mother's mansion, he had ridden straight back to Musili, where he was welcomed by Sharamana, Pulyama and a bunch of his old, faithful friends from the Imperial Army. He had passed the night between pitchers of firewater and vague nightmares, and on waking around midday, groggy and bleary-eyed, his mind was made up to ride to Udaypuri and join Amara Simha in the hunt for Ghatakarpara. He had decided to set out right after lunch, but when he returned from his bath, the first rumours of the happenings at Ujjayini had filtered in, causing a change in his plans.

Gandharvasena.

Turning the name around on his tongue, Vararuchi cast his mind back to the time he was six or seven, and tried to think of a person he'd known by that name. Of course, he failed — it was almost impossible to remember that far back into one's childhood. Back then, he had spent much of his time in the isolation of his mother's mansion and not in the palace, which he visited only when Mahendraditya was around. Later, of course, he had moved into the palace to train under the Acharya, but that was a year or so after Vikramaditya's birth.

Gandharvasena.

How he had hated living in the palace, deprived of the love that Ushantha lavished upon him, and Mahendraditya hardly around to shield him from Upashruti's jibes and barbs, which grew harsher by the day. He remembered once having dashed into her while rounding a corner. She had grabbed his arm in a fierce, vice-like grip.

Who do you think you are, silly boy, she had asked, shaking him, breathing fire into his face. *You are never going to be the king of Avanti, so stop treating this palace like it's your own and learn to conduct yourself with the dignity expected from a soldier. If you can't do that, go back to the gutter you came from.*

Afraid, guilty and all alone, he hadn't immediately understood what the Queen Mother had implied, but over the years, he had learned to distinguish Upashruti's unique brand of viciousness; on her part, Upashruti gave him ample scope to learn, rarely missing an opportunity to subtly snub him. She called him names when no one was around to observe them; she was partial against him when she had to decide on his behalf; she made her displeasure clear to him, in private, but without once making it obvious to the rest of the world. The woman had been a creature straight out of hell those first few years he had been in the palace, and she was the reason he began spending more and more time in the training ground, which ultimately moulded him into the superb fighter that he was. Something he owed her, he thought with a wretched little smile.

Your nephew has been kidnapped by the Hunas, Amara Simha is halfway to the frontier and you just show up saying

I'm always available for the palace. *Sure, I believe you.*

Her son, the samrat, hadn't cared to let him know about Ghatakarpara's kidnapping, but Upashruti had made it look like he was at fault. Like the time when the six-year-old Vikramaditya had sneaked into the Labyrinth and couldn't find his way out, and it had taken a platoon of Palace Guards to find and bring the boy back, sobbing and terrified. When asked why he had ventured into the Labyrinth, Vikramaditya had said that he had heard Vararuchi mention the place, so he had decided to explore. Upashruti had summoned Vararuchi and scolded him, blaming him squarely for what had happened.

Why would you talk to a kid about the Labyrinth? she had demanded. *You know the boy could have died of fright in there. Is that what you had in mind, so you could get him out of the way, you devious little cheat?*

Devious little cheat, she had called him.

Gandharvasena.

The way it looked now, someone else had been up to some cheating in the palace. Someone else hadn't known how to conduct themselves with dignity. Someone else had come to the palace from a gutter.

The time had come to put that person in her place. The time had come to repay all the insults.

Vararuchi looked over his shoulder to see if Sharamana and Pulyama were still there. Two dark shadows in the increasing gloom.

"I would like my horse saddled and ready at dawn," he said. "I intend leaving for the palace at first light."

* * *

"Are you asleep yet, grandmother?" Shanku asked softly, poking her head through the old woman's door.

The oracle lay on her side on the straw mat, motionless, a dark shape in the light of the lamp that had burned low. It was impossible to tell whether she was awake, but on hearing her granddaughter, the oracle stirred and raised her head to the door.

"I have nothing for you from the desert, child," she said in a frayed and weary voice. "Neither clouds nor birds nor the breeze have anything of significance to say. Tell your king I am sorry."

"It's alright, grandmother," said Shanku, stepping into the room. If the oracle wanted to be left alone, it wasn't going to happen.

Reaching the oracle's side, the girl kneeled, picked up the old woman's hand and gave it a gentle, reassuring pat. "The king didn't send me here — I came on my own accord. I would have dropped by in the day as well, or at least come earlier in the evening, but there have been so many things to attend to and..."

"Hush, child. How much you talk," the Mother Oracle smiled and squeezed Shanku's hand. The smile drove away some of the exhaustion from the wizened face, but the dark circles from sleep deprivation, visible even in this dim light, hung around the eyes like stubborn spectres.

"No, I know I ought to visit you more regularly, more *often*," the girl protested unhappily. "You are lonely here, the palace is so big, and no one comes..."

"Shhh." The oracle squeezed the girl's hand again. "Come when you can, child. I understand. I know you are busy." The woman's face turned grave. "I heard about this morning... The deva's coming, and all that happened between him and the king."

Shanku looked at her grandmother and nodded. There was nothing to say about that.

"Sit," the old woman said, patting the mat and shuffling to one side to make some place.

Once Shanku had made herself more comfortable, she tenderly took the oracle's hand again. The two women exchanged fond smiles, nurturing the bond between them as they soaked in the calming late-night silence. Shanku's mind skimmed over the day's events, and she couldn't help thinking how beleaguered the samrat suddenly was, pushed and challenged and harried relentlessly from all sides. Downright nothing was going in their favour, and she fervently hoped help would come soon in one form or another.

"I met father," she said, abruptly and self-consciously. "Two days ago. He insisted on a meeting."

The oracle propped herself up on an elbow and eyed her granddaughter closely. "I thought you did, but it's becoming hard to read the signs these days. But I'm glad you did." A slight pause, then, "How is he?"

"Old." Shanku burst into a laugh. The laughter melted what was stubborn and afraid inside her, liberating her in such a way that her eyes smiled at the oracle. "I mean he has aged. Otherwise, he is fine."

"You have forgiven him."

The words were not framed as a question. The Mother Oracle knew, and even if she didn't, she had guessed. The girl nodded all the same. The oracle lay down again.

A comforting silence settled around them. It was as if neither felt the need to say anything more. The oracle looked strangely at peace with herself, a small smile on her lips.

"I am glad you did," she repeated. "Glad for both of you."

This time, it was Shanku who squeezed her grandmother's hand and smiled. "There is relief in forgiveness," she said, her voice choking a little. "It's only after I met him that I realized that I too was a prisoner of that dungeon all these years. I was a prisoner because I was holding him there. He couldn't come out, but neither could I. There was no escape for either of us. But now… now I think we are both free."

The Mother Oracle nodded. "What happens next?" she asked a moment later. "I mean, is the king going to pardon him?"

"I don't know. He didn't seem keen on a pardon — father, I mean. He seemed happy staying in the dungeons as long as I visit him now and then. He didn't even want the gold coins being offered as reward for himself. He said he wanted the money to be given to the Warden of the Stables to purchase more horses. I think he really repents what he did. He told me to tell you that he is sorry for what happened to mother."

The oracle was silent for a long moment, lost in the past. At last, with a sigh and a nod, she said, "When you meet him, tell him I have forgiven him, and he must also forgive himself."

"I will."

"What is this reward that he didn't want?"

"Oh, it's *your* idea." Seeing her grandmother's eyebrows rise in surprise, Shanku said, "Not the reward, but looking for people who can show us a way to Janasthana."

"Ah, the search for those who have escaped from the Forest of the Exiles."

"The palace is offering a hundred gold coins to anyone who can prove he or she has escaped and returned from the Dandaka or to anyone who knows such a fugitive."

"Your father said no to a hundred gold coins?" The Mother Oracle stared at the girl in shock. "He *has* changed. And he knows someone who fled from the Dandaka?"

"So he says."

"Who?"

"A highwayman by the name of Greeshma, who hails from north of Lava. Soldiers have already been sent to find him and bring him to Ujjayini, if possible."

"A highwayman..." the oracle's expression was one of dismay. "Look at the kind of company your father kept."

"I thought you had forgiven him," Shanku said sternly, but her eyes were playful.

"I have," her grandmother said. "I was just remarking…"

"I know," Shanku laughed. "I was joking." Then, as a new thought occurred, she peered at the old woman. "A little while ago, you said it is getting hard for you to read the signs these days. Why is that?"

The Mother Oracle's face crumpled as the levity went out of it. Her expression became strained and the circles around her eyes seemed to widen. "What can I say, child?" she said. "There is… there are just too many confusing signs to read."

"Where?"

"Here, in the palace. There are shadows that shouldn't be here, footsteps that come out of nowhere and go nowhere… even the breeze that blows through the halls and doorways is corrupt and whispers lies." The oracle stopped, then tightened her grip on the girl's hand. Her eyes were uneasy, and her voice held a panicked edge. "Child, there is something bad inside this palace. There are omens everywhere, but I can't read them. And I feel something terrible is about to happen. Something much worse than everything that has happened so far. I am afraid, child — I am afraid for your king."

* * *

Kalidasa was awake and conscious of the approaching footsteps long before those coming for him had even set foot on the landing outside the sparse room he had been given to sleep in. As he blinked in the dark and made an assessment of the number of people — judging by the footfalls, he thought there were three — he took note of the fact that it was still night. His hand instinctively crept to his side, where he always kept his scimitar. But he stopped, realizing the sword would not be there; he had been asked to surrender it before sitting down to dine with Khash'i Dur. The *shy'or* had said parting with the scimitar would be a measure of the trust that he, Kalidasa, placed on his hosts, and that trust would be reciprocated with trust. Khash'i Dur hadn't been lying; no guards had been posted outside his door, which had also stayed unlocked.

However, men coming to his door in the dead of night didn't bode well, so Kalidasa threw off the sheepskin blanket and rose to a crouch. Because he didn't quite know what to expect, he didn't quite know what to do either. He decided it was best to weigh the situation before reacting. He counted the footsteps — definitely three men — until they came to a stop outside his door. Seeing torchlight seep through the gap between the door and the floor, he let his breath out; the torch said they were not here to assault and kill him swiftly in the dark. They were here to fetch him.

That, of course, didn't mean they wouldn't try to kill him wherever they took him.

The door swung on its hinges with a loud squeak and a rattle, reinforcing Kalidasa's assumption about the men's intent — no attempt at masking sounds. Light flared in the room as the man holding the torch entered, followed by the other two. All three stared in surprise at Kalidasa, who was still crouched amid the sheepskins; they had been expecting him to be asleep. All three bore spears, but Kalidasa saw their stance was non-threatening.

"*Gy'e,*" the one with the torch said, motioning with his hand, asking Kalidasa to come with them.

"*Kohor?*" Kalidasa asked. 'Where?'

"*A gy'e,*" the man said, a trifle impatiently. He jerked his spear in the direction of the door and again motioned with his hand.

Deciding there was no point in arguing with the men, Kalidasa rose and accompanied them outside. He noticed that none of them even came up to his shoulders and that they didn't try to herd him, instead allowing him to walk casually with them.

It wasn't until they crossed an open verandah that faced east that Kalidasa realized it wasn't as late in the night as he had imagined it to be. The horizon was a distinct line, with the sky above it a lighter shade of black, hinting that daybreak was not far away. This surprised him — why was he wanted at such an early hour? He was tempted to ask his escorts, but guessing he wouldn't get a very helpful answer, he kept quiet.

He was marched into a hall on the ground floor of the fort, where a sizeable number of Huna warriors were already gathered. Their eyes followed him — the way they had all day, since his arrival in Mun'h — all the way in and stayed on him as he was presented to Khash'i Dur.

"Thra'akha, my friend," the *shy'or* exclaimed, choosing to address him by a shortened name — and choosing Avanti over the Huna tongue once again. "I hope you slept well."

"I had just begun sleeping well when I was woken up," Kalidasa replied.

"Ah," Khash'i Dur made a face and shrugged as if to say he was helpless.

"What is this about?" Kalidasa asked. He cast a glance around and observed that all the warriors gathered there were armed.

"Someone wants to meet you."

"Who?"

"The *droiba*."

"Right at this moment?" Kalidasa looked incredulous. "Couldn't he have waited for a more civilized hour?"

"The *droiba* heard about your arrival and decided to come back right away. He is keen to meet you, so he has been travelling all night."

"Honoured and all that," Kalidasa snorted, "but it could still have waited. It's not like I was running away."

The *shy'or* did not respond to that.

"Where is he?" Kalidasa asked, looking around.

"He is on his way."

"We're going to stand here and wait for him?" Kalidasa's eyebrows shot upwards.

"He sent word to keep you ready."

For the first time, Khash'i Dur frowned. Kalidasa got the sense that the *shy'or* was unhappy with his impatience and didn't understand why he, Kalidasa, found the whole situation absurd.

"Okay," he shrugged.

He tried remembering why the *droiba* was so important for the Hunas, but couldn't glean much from the memories of his own childhood. The Hunas worshipped the *hriiz* or the mythical desert scorpion, though their concept of prayer was nothing like what it was for the people of Sindhuvarta. The *droiba*, from what he recalled, was soothsayer and sorcerer rolled into one, a rare individual vested with great powers. He had heard his father mention a *Wa'a droiba*, supposedly the first *droiba* who helped the desert scorpion create the world. Beyond that he knew nothing and —

It took Kalidasa a moment to register the sudden drop in the murmurs across the hall. As the words and whisperings eased into a hushed silence, he saw that the men stood with their heads bowed, and even Khash'i Dur had bent his head in the direction of the door. Kalidasa turned to see a figure standing just inside the hall, assessing him with shrewd eyes.

One look at the man, and he knew he had to be the *droiba*. He looked like an identical twin of the *droiba* he had killed that night many years ago. A little younger, a little taller...

His eyes fixed on Kalidasa, the shaman walked into the

hall in a strange, awkward gait that reminded Kalidasa of herons in a paddy field. The man wore a headdress made of feathers — vultures' feathers, he remembered — and his face was painted with a blue pigment; the lips were blackened with charcoal, and the whole effect was creepy. It was hard to gauge his age under all that paint, but his skin was smooth, so Kalidasa figured he couldn't be too old. The *droiba* carried a shamanic staff that was fashioned to resemble the barbed tail of a scorpion.

"*I'da duz'ur Zho E'rami?*" he asked in a deep baritone at odds with his personality.

Khash'i Dur gave a respectful nod. "*Ga'ur Thra'akha.*"

The shaman approached Kalidasa. When they were an arm's length from each other, he stopped and peered up into Kalidasa's face.

"*Zuh te'i ge ba'dor,*" he said. "*Zuh'i bor h'yet.*"

'You are without manners. Bow your head.'

"*Seh?*" Kalidasa stared down calmly at the face that barely made it to his chest. "*Ma'a kunu e'rim. Ma ud droiba thra'akh.*"

'Why? I am not afraid. I have killed a *droiba*.'

Even as the shaman reeled back, his eyes flying open in fear, a collective hiss of gasps sprang up all around the room. In his peripheral vision, Kalidasa saw the Huna warriors draw swords and daggers, and though he was tempted to look up and take stock of the situation, Kalidasa kept his eyes on the *droiba*, pinning him in a merciless gaze.

"What are you saying?" Khash'i Dur pushed himself between Kalidasa and the shaman, his voice hoarse, his knife at Kalidasa's throat.

Kalidasa switched his gaze to the *shy'or*, and even as he felt the knife's blade nick his skin — and half-a-dozen other swords press into his back — he kept his voice equable and reasonable.

"I come here as a friend, but I am treated like an enemy. I give up my sword only to have knives put to my throat. Is this how you repay my trust? Is this what the Hunas have come to? No honour, no dignity?"

"You insult our *droiba*," Khash'i Dur snarled softly. "That is not the Huna way. Every Huna knows that, yet you claim to be a Huna. Didn't your father teach you anything?"

"Don't talk about Zho E'rami and what he taught me and what he didn't." There was an edge to the giant's voice, and he seemed unmindful of all the swords sticking into his flesh. "Zho E'rami taught me how to fight like a man, not like a coward, with a room full of armed warriors for help against a weaponless foe."

Khash'i Dur glared up at Kalidasa, and the moment shimmered like the surface of a lake, thin and waiting to erupt and boil over. Day had broken, and the first rays of the sun found their way into the hall, lighting up Khash'i Dur and Kalidasa in a shade of gold stained with blood.

"*Eb'a*." The shaman slowly reached out and touched Khash'i Dur on the shoulder. "*Eb'a*," he repeated. 'Stop.'

The *shy'or* glanced briefly over his shoulder, then inclined his head at the *droiba* and eased the pressure on the knife. He stepped back, and almost in unison, the swords pricking Kalidasa from behind were withdrawn.

Letting his breath out, Kalidasa touched a finger to the spot where the knife had pressed into his throat. It hurt just a little, and when he drew the finger away, he saw a small smear of blood on the fingertip. He suspected there were similar wounds on his back as well.

The *droiba* was whispering something into Khash'i Dur's ear. The *shy'or* listened for a moment, then nodded and looked at Kalidasa.

"You say you have killed a *droiba*. Our *droiba* will find out if what you say is true, and whether you are the son of Zho

E'rami, as you claim. If the *droiba* thinks you are telling the truth, you will live. Otherwise, you die."

* * *

The stillness of the morning carried the drumming of hooves up to the terrace, where Vikramaditya stood twirling a weighted wooden mallet over his head in an elaborate exercise regimen. The samrat paused, and lowering the mallet, he looked at the far shore of the lake, where a horse was in full gallop. The trees grew thick and close on that part of the shore and the early light was still insufficient, so the king failed to make out the rider until he made a turn for the palace causeway. Vikramaditya's eyes brightened on recognizing the horseman, and relief spread over his face in a soft tide.

Placing the mallet on the ground, where it unbalanced and toppled with a clatter, the samrat strode over to a wide stone basin at the centre of which a small fountain gushed, sending boats of bubbles to the basin's rim. He quickly splashed water on his face, neck and arms, rubbing and washing the sweat away, before running his wet palms once over his hair. Blinking and dripping water over the basin, he extended his hand to the boy standing attendance.

"Towel," he said, snapping his fingers a trifle impatiently.

He was still wiping his beard dry when he descended the stairs to the central hallway, and his foot was on the bottom step when a shadow fell across the entrance. Looking up, Vikramaditya saw the rider walk into the palace and smiled.

"Brother," he exclaimed. "It is nice to set eyes on you."

Vararuchi gave a curt nod, his eyes surveying the galleries and passageways on the upper levels. The samrat saw the graveness in his half-brother's eyes and his own expression turned serious.

"What took you so long? Is *badi-maa* alright?" he asked.

"She is," Vararuchi answered a little absent-mindedly. He had paused and was still looking about the hall and the galleries searchingly.

"A lot has happened in the last few days," said the samrat, interpreting Vararuchi's reticence as a reaction to the chain of recent events. He walked towards his brother, closing the gap between them. "You've obviously heard that..."

"I have heard," Vararuchi cut in a trifle harshly, and when Vikramaditya looked at him in surprise, he added, "What does the Queen Mother have to say?"

"What?"

The samrat stopped and peered at his brother in confusion.

"I said, what does the Queen Mother have to say in her defence?" Vararuchi repeated, his eyes fixing on the samrat's.

"The Queen..." Then, finally getting it, "Brother, how does it matter what mother has to say?" He took a couple of steps forward. "I consider father as my..."

"*Which* father — the one who came yesterday or the one whose ashes we scattered in the holy Kshipra?" Vararuchi looked up at Vikramaditya combatively. "Which one?"

"*Brother*," the samrat let out a gasp and froze, his face twisting in agony.

"And how does it *not* matter what the Queen Mother has to say?" Vararuchi went on. "Some stranger comes along claiming to be the *legitimate* father of her son, who is the ruler of Avanti because he happens to be her late husband's *legitimate* son. Isn't it the Queen Mother's duty to clear up the matter and put all doubt to rest?"

"Brother, why are you..." the samrat began, but Vararuchi wasn't done yet.

"Shouldn't the Queen Mother have issued a public statement? *Who* is the legitimate father of her son? Why isn't she saying anything? Why is she hiding behind a wall of silence? Why can't she..."

"*Brother*," Vikramaditya shouted in a sudden fit of temper, his voice echoing from the end of the hall, silencing Vararuchi.

A couple of palace hands who were up and about their business stopped in their tracks and turned to observe the brothers in the middle of the hall. Conscious of the gazes directed at him and Vararuchi, the samrat strived to get a hold on himself. Lowering his tone, he spoke in a slow and measured manner.

"Brother, there is only one man who can be father to me, and that is *our* father, King Mahendraditya. You know he loved me and I loved him, and that is all that matters. Father will be father, always and forever."

Vararuchi stared at the samrat for a moment. "It is not a question of who *can be* father to you, Vikrama. It is a question of who *is*. It is not a question of emotions, but one of facts. Once the Queen Mother..."

"King Mahendraditya is my father," Vikramaditya said heavily, his tone implying he was done arguing. Vararuchi recognized the tone and nodded.

"I believe you." His own tone was stiff and unbending. "But I want to hear the Queen Mother say so as well."

"She will not," Vikramaditya said flatly.

"Why is that?" Vararuchi narrowed his eyes in suspicion.

"Because I won't let her. And because she is not answerable to you either."

Vararuchi's gaze was bleak and bitter as he appraised his half-brother. "You are protecting her, Vikrama."

The samrat inclined his head in a half-shrug. "I have given my word that I will."

"And I thought you said you loved father," Vararuchi said accusingly, his lips twisting in a sneer. "*The man the Queen Mother has wronged.*"

"I still love father, now more than I ever did."

The brothers faced each other like antagonists in an arena,

circling and watchful, their guards up, their growing bad blood fouling the atmosphere around them, hot and stifling. At last, Vararuchi nodded.

"Is this your final decision?" he asked.

"Yes."

Vararuchi nodded again and cast one look up and around him, taking in the galleries that staggered up to the high dome right over their heads.

"Very well," he said. Without another word, he turned on his heel and headed for the door.

"Brother, wait. Hear me out…" The samrat's hand went up to stop Vararuchi, his tone pained and entreating, but seeing that his brother was in no mood to listen to him, the king checked himself and let his hand drop. His face was in turmoil as pieces broke and came apart inside him. But Vararuchi failed to see any of this as he stalked out of the palace, leaving Vikramaditya to stare at the empty doorway.

Letting out an anguished sigh, the samrat retraced his steps, each foot heavy on the stairs, his shoulders stooped under the inexorable weight of endless cares and burdens. The sun broke through a high window and fell on the king, his shadow dragging along behind him, elongated and broken on the steps, like a cripple in mourning.

It wasn't until Vikramaditya had disappeared down one of the passageways — and the palace hands had left, and the hall was deserted once again — that the figure emerged from the shadows of the floor-length drapes drawn across a bank of windows. The figure didn't so much come out from behind the curtains as it *slipped through* them, like a shadow taking form, wavering into existence. The figure looked around to make sure he was alone, then gazed up at the spot where the samrat had gone. Then, slowly, he considered the main entrance, the way Vararuchi had left.

The human king and his half-brother had had a big

disagreement and had parted ways, perhaps even as bitter enemies. This was an important development. He was certain his master would want to know about this too.

Making a mental note to report the confrontation he had just witnessed, the figure slipped into shadow... and immediately out again, this time disguised as a soldier of the Palace Guards, hard to tell apart from the other guards ambling around the palace.

Droiba

The shadows drifted in and out all night — *or was it all day?* — mumbling among themselves in low voices, speaking in a tongue that was alien to Vetala Bhatta. They approached and bent over him before retreating softly. To him, they looked unhappy.

Just once, he imagined a voice speaking in a dialect of Avanti. The royal tutor couldn't remember exactly what had been said, but the memory of the words — the familiar sounds and syllables and intonations — warmed him like the glow from a gentle fire on wintry evenings.

"Wake up, raj-guru."

Yes, he thought. Those had been the words he had heard.

"Please wake up, raj-guru."

The shadows returned, hovering over him from all sides, peering down.

"Raj-guru, you are awake," one of the shadows spoke. The Acharya thought the voice was one that he had heard before. The shadow even looked like someone he knew.

The other shadows clucked in that strange tongue of theirs, but a new shadow pushed through the circle.

"You are back with us, raj-guru," it said in obvious relief. Slowly, the face of Kedara, the captain leading his escort from Avanti, swam into focus.

"Back?" The word lurched out of the Acharya in a thick, wooden stumble. His tongue felt coarse, heavy and leaden in the back of his mouth. "From where?"

"We had lost hope, raj-guru," the captain said. "We thought... we assumed the worst, and somehow..."

Kedara dissolved into shadow again, and the Acharya sank back into the soft pillow of sleep. Nearly an hour passed before he awakened next, and this time, instead of blurry shadows and soft lights, everything was clean lines, sharp angles and clear light. He lay for a moment, inspecting his surroundings, studying the reed-woven thatch that sheltered him from the sky, the mud-plastered bamboo poles that made up the walls and the bright sunlight filtering in through the leaves of the branches just outside the open window. The leaves and branches were so close that Vetala Bhatta understood in a flash that he was inside a treehouse.

"Kedara," he called out, still hoarse. "Captain, are you there?"

It was another half-hour before the five surviving members of the escort sat around the Acharya's bed, updating him on all that had transpired after he had fallen unconscious the previous morning.

"Durra died yesterday evening, raj-guru. Just after sunset," said Kedara, referring to the old soldier who had tried killing himself by jumping into the swamp. "The fever finally took him."

"That's unfortunate, but it seemed inevitable," Vetala Bhatta shook his head sadly, remembering the man shivering with ague. A small woman appeared and thrust a calabash of steaming hot broth into his hands, which he accepted with a grateful nod. "Tell her I said thanks," he said to the interpreter, glad they hadn't lost *him* to the Aanupa.

As the interpreter mumbled to the woman, the Acharya took a delicate sip of the broth and flinched at its spiciness. "Are we still in the Aanupa?" he asked.

"Yes, raj-guru. But by good fortune, we are on the eastern edge of the marsh, not very far from Odra."

"Who are these people?" Vetala Bhatta indicated the retreating woman.

"They are a branch of the swamp tribes, raj-guru," it was the interpreter who answered. "They thrive in the swamps and its neighbouring forests."

"We didn't see a single one in all the time we were lost."

"I understand that they like to keep to themselves."

"How do they survive here in the Aanupa? What do they eat? We found nothing."

"That," the interpreter pointed to the calabash the Acharya was drinking from. "Fish."

"Fish," Vetala Bhatta paused and looked into the bowl suspiciously.

"It is tasty and nutritive, and is found in abundance in some of the marsh pools," the interpreter explained. "The swamp tribes know where to find them."

The councilor nodded and sipped the broth. It was tasty, he had to admit. "How did they find us?"

"They say they saw our footprints going everywhere and realized that we were lost. They found us by following our prints."

"If our footprints were going everywhere, how did they know which set to follow?" asked the Acharya.

"They also use their sense of smell to pick up scents."

"Like animals?" Vetala Bhatta asked, impressed.

"Yes."

"And they are peace-loving?"

"They figured we were too fatigued and too close to death to pose a threat."

"Why are they helping us? I mean, are they?"

"Yes, raj-guru. The moment they learned we are from Samrat Vikramaditya's court, they agreed to help us."

"They know about our Samrat?" The Acharya looked incredulous. "Amazing."

"They have volunteered to lead us out of the marsh and take us to Odra's border."

"That is very good of them. I'm impressed to see that the influence of Avanti extends so far into the depths of the Aanupa."

"I don't think their intention is to help as much as it is to be rid of us, raj-guru."

"Explain yourself, soldier," Vetala Bhatta said, looking stern.

The interpreter checked to see if they were alone before shuffling closer to everyone. "I overheard a couple of them talking last night. I don't follow their language very well, but from what I understood, one was telling the other that they must get rid of us before the evil that taints us taints them as well."

"*Evil* that taints us?" the Acharya repeated. "What evil were they speaking of?"

"I don't know, but the man seemed to think there was an eclipse over Avanti. He said anything touched by its shadow carries evil and can contaminate everything else."

"They spoke of an eclipse?" asked Vetala Bhatta, his mind going back to the morning after the Omniscient One had visited Vikramaditya and given him the Halahala for safekeeping. They had all been in the council chamber, discussing their plans, when Shanku had said that the Mother Oracle had a warning for them.

She asked me to warn you that the sun is on the wane, and that a great eclipse is coming to devour the sun, Shanku had said.

The sun my grandmother was referring to is the royal emblem of the Aditya dynasty, noble councilors. The sun-crest of Avanti...

"Where's my spear?" the Acharya asked, scanning the room. "We must leave for Odra right away." Throwing off the light shawl that covered his feet, he added, "Tell these people that if they want us out of here, we'll go *now* if they can spare a guide to show us the way."

He swung his legs off the crude bed, but Kedara restrained him. "Raj-guru, please... you are weak. You should rest and regain your strength. We can stay here a couple of days..."

"No," the councilor said adamantly. "Avanti is in great trouble, captain. It needs us. Let us finish what we came for and return to Ujjayini as quickly as possible."

* * *

Divided between the mundane task of negotiating the stairs under his feet and pondering what form Indra's threats of the previous day would take, Dhanavantri failed to notice Harihara until the king was almost upon him. The king was coming down the steps from one of the palace's upper galleries and they met halfway up, the physician letting out a small 'uh' of surprise and stopping short to avoid a collision.

"Our dear Dhanavantri, how are you?"

Underneath the forced joviality, Harihara's tone was patronizing, which irked the physician. He still hadn't been able to pinpoint the true purpose behind this unscheduled visit to Ujjayini, but the fact that the king was now prolonging his stay without sufficient reason showed a hidden agenda at play. Dhanavantri suspected that Harihara was sticking around to evaluate the situation in Avanti in the light of the showdown between the samrat and Indra.

"I am well, good king," the councilor answered with a smile. "I trust you had a good night's sleep?"

"Oh yes, yes…" Harihara looked around, as if caught in two minds about something. "Um… is Vararuchi back?" he asked abruptly.

"I don't know," Dhanavantri replied, a little surprised. "If he is, I'm not aware of it."

"Oh, I see." Again, a small hint of indecision. "Actually… I overheard a couple of palace hands saying he was back early this morning…"

"Then it must be true."

"Yes, but I… they also mentioned something about Vararuchi and the Samrat having a disagreement." Harihara looked keenly at the councilor, with a greedy scavenger's expression that Dhanavantri found detestable. "A *loud* argument, they made it seem…"

"I have no idea about any of this, king," the physician said, keeping his face inscrutable while his mind raced to list the causes and implications of what he had just heard. Palace hands gossiping about the king and his brother… "Absolutely no idea."

"I see." Harihara hadn't anticipated that answer, so he didn't know how to react.

Taking advantage of this small window of silence, Dhanavantri waved his hand in the direction of the floors above and climbed a step. "Now if you will excuse me, I have to see the queen. It's a beautiful morning for a walk by the lake, if that's where you're going."

"Yes, yes. Surely." Harihara hurriedly stepped aside, leaning against the handrails to let the physician's girth get past. "Yes, that's where I'm going."

The councilor mounted the remaining steps without

glancing back, lest Harihara try and engage him in conversation again. It was only after turning a corner that he let his breath out and paused to think about what the king had said.

Vararuchi and Vikramaditya in disagreement — that happened, not often, but sometimes. Both were men of strong opinions and both could be stubborn when it suited them. But the two in a loud argument that palace hands could overhear? Never. The brothers shared too much love and respect to ever let the heat of the moment get to them. They also understood decorum, which was the bedrock of the relationship between the samrat and his councilors. Yet, why would the palace hands lie, and why would Harihara lie about what he had overheard?

Turning a corner, this time Dhanavantri almost walked into the chief of the Palace Guards, who was approaching from the direction of Vishakha's chambers. The old soldier appeared preoccupied and was clearly taken aback on seeing the physician.

"Greetings, Vismaya," said Dhanavantri.

"Greetings, councilor."

There was a moment's awkward silence as neither had anything more to say. Pointing over Vismaya's shoulder, the physician asked, "Is the Samrat there?"

It was an unnecessary question, put forth to fill the silly, self-conscious silence with inane words. The samrat was always by Vishakha's bedside every morning, and everyone knew it. The samrat would not start his day without seeing his beloved...

"No, he is not," said Vismaya. Seeing the astonishment on Dhanavantri's face, he pointed to a gallery that was two levels above. "I saw the Samrat heading that way a little while ago, councilor."

The gallery and landing in question led to the council chamber. Dhanavantri paused, unsure of which way to go next — straight on to see Vishakha as planned, or two floors up to the council chamber.

"Are you certain?" he asked the chief.

"Absolutely, councilor."

This was unusual. Very unusual. Dhanavantri turned and took the stairs to the next floor, then the one above it.

When he pushed past the heavy door to the chamber, the physician was treated to a gloom, the source of which he couldn't comprehend at first. It took him a moment to realize that some of the heavy drapes had been let down to keep the morning sunlight out. The windows on the far end were uncovered though, and here Dhanavantri perceived the samrat, standing with his back to the door, hands behind him, gazing broodingly over the palace lake.

"Vikrama," the physician said, as he approached the king. "What are you doing here?"

Looking over his shoulder, the samrat acknowledged Dhanavantri with a small nod, but turned back to the window without a reply. The councilor came and stood beside his king, and for a while, the two of them watched the day unfold and spread itself over the city.

"I heard Vararuchi returned this morning," Dhanavantri sent out a small feeler.

Vikramaditya drew a deep breath and nodded, still staying silent.

"I met King Harihara just now. He said some palace hands were talking about... some sort of a disagreement..." The councilor turned to face the samrat. "Would you care to tell me what's happened, Vikrama?"

A few moments passed before the samrat finally turned to Dhanavantri. "I too am struggling to understand what's happened. I don't know why..." he stopped, looking for the right words, "...why he is suddenly so insistent, so stubborn."

"Stubborn about what?"

Vikramaditya lapsed into silence again, fighting an internal battle. The physician, however, stood his ground, crossing his fat arms, waiting patiently for his king to speak.

"He wants the Queen Mother to make a public declaration, negating the charge that Indra has made," the samrat finally blurted out. "He... I told him what matters is whom *I* consider father, and that Mahendraditya was, is and will always be father to me. But he wants mother to say this."

"And she will not?"

Vikramaditya turned an acidic gaze on Dhanavantri, and the physician immediately nodded and looked away.

"I have given my word that I will not let mother undergo such an indignity."

The two men let the moment idle away as a breeze blew across the lake, ruffling the king's hair and the physician's cotton *angavastram*.

"You do realize that what Vararuchi has demanded today already is — and if not, *will soon be* — on a lot of people's lips, don't you?" Dhanavantri laid a gentle hand on the samrat's shoulder. "People will wonder, and they will ask why the Queen Mother cannot put to rest the doubt that Indra has raised. And when she doesn't, people will speculate. Your own people, Vikrama, subjects of Avanti. And when they ask questions, what will you say to them?"

"I will tell them that I am King Mahendraditya's son," the samrat replied with mulish tenacity. "That is all that matters."

"And they will have to believe you?"

"Why not? If the Queen Mother were to make a declaration, they would be willing to take her word. Why not take mine then?"

Dhanavantri sighed and looked away. When Vikramaditya spoke next, his voice was softer, less combative.

"I know I am sounding adamant," he said. "But what choice do I have, my friend? I have promised mother that

I shall protect her. I promised father on his deathbed that I would never let any harm befall her. Come what may, I cannot break my word."

Dhanavantri gave an understanding nod. "Where is Vararuchi?"

"I don't know. He left the palace. I tried reasoning with him, but..."

"I shall have someone look for him."

"No, don't," said Vikramaditya. Seeing the surprise on the councilor's face, he added, "I think this has come as much as a shock to him as it has to me. He needs to come to terms with it. Accepting is healing, and healing can take time. Let us give him that time. I know brother. I trust him to come back on his own."

The physician wasn't so sure about this, but before he could put across his argument, the chamber's door was pushed open. King and councilor turned to see Pralupi barge into the room.

"I have been looking for you all over the palace, and *here* you are," she said crossly, as if speaking to a child who had disobeyed instructions. For a moment, Dhanavantri did not know whom she was addressing. As she drew closer, he saw that her eyes were trained on the samrat and he sighed in relief.

"Yes, sister?" Vikramaditya asked mildly. "What can I do for you?"

The councilor wondered if there was pointed sarcasm behind the words, but it was impossible to tell from the king's expression.

"For starters, you could tell me how things are going with the rescue of my son," snapped Pralupi. "What progress has been made, if any, and are we any closer to finding him than we were two days ago?"

"As you yourself have pointed out, it has been only two

days since Amara Simha and Angamitra left from here, sister. They wouldn't even have reached Udaypuri yet, leave alone the frontier. Give them time to get there first."

"What about those who're already on the frontier? From what I gather, troops of the Imperial Army and the Frontier Guard are massed all along the frontier, along with soldiers from our vassal states. Why can't someone —"

"They are not our vassal states..." the samrat tried clarifying, but Pralupi pressed on like a thundering chariot drawn by fevered horses.

"— why can't someone lead soldiers into the Great Desert to look for Ghatakarpara? With so many soldiers pressed into the rescue, they can easily find him. Nobody needs to wait for Amara Simha." She paused and looked at her brother skeptically. "Do you need me to tell you what needs to be done?"

"Sister, we cannot simply pull troops out of defensive positions and push them into the desert to find someone," said Vikramaditya in a calm tone that made Dhanavantri marvel at the man's patience in dealing with Pralupi. "None of Sindhuvarta's troops are familiar with the Great Desert — neither its geography, nor its climate. Chances are they will all die of thirst and exhaustion. Secondly, if we pull our troops out of any one place, we give the Hunas an open gate to walk into Sindhuvarta, which is probably what they were hoping for when they got Ghatakarpara kidnapped. The only way to do this is with extreme caution and great skill, which Amara Simha and Angamitra have in plenty. Let them do their job. Trust them, sister."

"I think you should have gone as well. After all, he is your nephew."

"Sister, I told you that Ujjayini and its people need me..."

"Okay, *fine*." Pralupi crossed her arms and looked away in annoyance. Then, turning back to the samrat with a bitterly triumphant smile, she said, "At least now you will admit that I was right in telling you not to send my son to the frontier. You said it was fine; I kept warning you not to, but you wouldn't listen to me. Now who was right?"

Her eyes were challenging Vikramaditya, openly rebuking him for not having yielded to her wishes, but the king said nothing. What could he possibly say, Dhanavantri wondered, feeling sorry for Vikramaditya. Even enemies should never be cursed with such a sibling as Pralupi, he decided.

"Now that we know I am right about these things, what are you going to do about that other issue we spoke of?"

Something in the princess' tone, and the manner in which the samrat stiffened a little, alerted the councilor. He glanced sharply from the king to Pralupi, not knowing if he was even supposed to be here to witness what was about to unfold. He looked at Vikramaditya, hoping to get some sign from him, maybe asking him to leave, but the king looked imperturbable, staring straight at his sister.

"What about it, sister?"

"Well, are you going to make Ghatakarpara king of Vatsa once he has been rescued and brought back?" Pralupi asked in an exasperated tone.

Dhanavantri was aghast at the brazenness with which the demand had been made, but Pralupi didn't seem to care that he was around to hear her speak in such rash and ruthless terms. Niceties were never her strong point, but this was beyond what the physician had imagined even Pralupi to be capable of. It seemed she had discounted his presence altogether as she kept up her badgering. "I have told you my opinion, and as I have been proved right once already, you should listen to me."

"I too have told you my opinion, sister," the samrat replied in a firm and controlled voice. "No matter how many times you bring it up, I am not going to entertain this discussion, so the sooner you forget the whole thing, the better."

"I can't see why you won't do this for your nephew," the princess wailed in barely contained fury. "Why you won't do it for *me*. I have given so much of myself for the sake of Avanti, and what do I get in return? Nothing. I could have been a queen. I *should* have been a queen. *But no*," her voice turned acerbic, "Chandravardhan would not have me because he was already married, but he had to offer father his stupid little brother as an option. And would this stupid little brother ever become king? *No*. But Chandravardhan couldn't care less, and by giving me as wife to Himavardhan, Chandravardhan killed whatever prospects I had of ever becoming queen. He could have accepted me as his second wife; it was easy for him to say yes. If he had, *I* would be queen of Vatsa today, but no. *No, no, no*. I am not queen because he said no, and my son won't be king because *you* say no. How is this fair, Vikrama, how? Where is that which is due to me for having sacrificed so much for Avanti and Vatsa and Sindhuvarta?"

Dhanavantri stared at the king's sister, stunned at the ferocity of her rant, blown away by the bitter disappointments and frustrations she had successfully kept hidden all these years, but which had slowly fermented and curdled inside her, gnawing away at her self-restraint and patience, so that today, it had all come out in a raging flood of anger. He suddenly saw her in a different light, and he realized Avanti had neglected showing Pralupi its appreciation...

Vikramaditya took two steps towards Pralupi. "We never understood you, sister..."

"Stop." The princess raised a palm. "If it is sympathy you are offering, I am not interested. My demand is simple. I want Ghatakarpara to become the next king of Vatsa. Chandravardhan will agree to this because he owes it to Avanti. This time he *will say yes*. All it takes is for the king of Avanti to tell him what to do. You know that is true, Vikrama, so just tell him."

Dhanavantri held his breath and stole a sidelong glance at the samrat. He observed the king look at his sister in a flat but severe stare, and then draw himself up, so he stood with his shoulders squared, his bearded chin jutting out in determination. When Vikramaditya spoke, his words were reasonable, but his tone was hard and jagged as granite.

"If all it takes is for the king of Avanti to tell King Chandravardhan what to do, let me make myself clear for the last and final time, sister. As long as I am king of Avanti, I will not tell King Chandravardhan what to do with his throne and his crown. He is free to do as he pleases."

If looks could kill, Dhanavantri was certain the glare Pralupi offered would have reduced Vikramaditya to cinder. Brother and sister faced each other off, Pralupi's lips lifting in a cold, contemptuous sneer. Spinning around, she headed for the door, but checking herself halfway, she turned back to the samrat.

"Let *me* also make myself clear, brother," she said. "Even without your help, Ghatakarpara *will* become king of Vatsa. I will find a way to make it happen."

* * *

Amara Simha and Varahamihira had barely stormed out of the darkness and into the firelight, screaming and waving their weapons at the savages, when he leaped to his feet and burst from the thicket where he and Vikramaditya were hiding.

"Let's go, Vikrama," he called as he made a dash for the cremation ground, now packed with Huna tents and bristling with fortifications.

He shot a glance over his shoulder and saw his friend emerge from the thicket, King Mahendraditya's old sword gripped tightly in his hand. The thicket spewed Avanti's soldiers by the dozens, and they slipped after him like whispering spectres as he turned to face the ground, where the Hunas and the attackers led by Amara Simha and Varahamihira were already in the snarl of battle.

He wears a headdress made of vultures' feathers. That's what Vikramaditya had said of the *droiba*, whom he was meant to find and kill. And his face is painted blue.

Tightening his hold on his long-handled axe, Kalidasa tried to imagine what the Huna shaman would look like. Absurdly, his mind threw up the hilarious image of a vulture with a blue face, sitting hunched and looking silly on a rock. Dismissing that picture from his head with a chuckle, Kalidasa concentrated on what lay ahead — hundreds upon hundreds of battle-hardened Huna warriors protecting their *droiba*, who had taken the Ghoulmaster prisoner with the purpose of gaining control over Borderworld.

Vikramaditya caught up with him, and they made for the near edge of the cremation ground, crouching low as they drew closer to the ring of firelight but hardly breaking their pace, intent on getting as close as possible before some lookout inevitably noticed them and raised an alarm. Fortunately for them, Amara Simha had led such a blistering foray on the far flank that the barbarians were too busy fending him off to observe Kalidasa and Vikramaditya come up from the rear, and they reached the ground's periphery without incident. Here, they had to split up, one lot going after the shaman, the other attempting Betaal's rescue. With a quick nod, Vikramaditya turned and peeled away to the right, leaving Kalidasa to swerve left and follow the natural curve of the cremation ground.

Despite his gigantic build, Kalidasa was nimble and fleet-footed, and he slunk easily and silently from shadow to shadow, all the while keeping an eye on the Huna camp to his right. All the soldiers behind him laboured to keep up, with one exception — a tall and tough young man nearly the same age as Kalidasa, with a curling moustache and a pointed beard. The soldier almost matched him in speed and came after him like a shadow, his sword nicely balanced in his grasp. Kalidasa circled the encampment, not quite knowing what he was looking for. Spying a break in the trees that allowed him to close in on the Hunas, he turned into the gap, and the big soldier followed him. A moment later, the break funnelled the rest of Avanti's warriors in as well.

Keeping low, the attackers moved in, dodging behind trees and tents, scouting ahead to try and get a fix on the shaman's whereabouts. Off to the other side of the ground, the battle was at its harshest pitch. Already, the scent of blood was in the air, lifted high by the night wind blowing from the Kshipra.

As soon as he caught sight of the thirty-odd Huna warriors ranged around a dense cluster of tents, Kalidasa knew he had found his target. A battle was raging less than half a mile from where they stood, but this set of Hunas displayed no intention of joining that fight — which meant that they had been tasked to stay where they were.

And that could only be because they were guarding something. Or someone. Someone important, who was inside one of those tents. The *droiba*.

Running desperately short of time — Vikramaditya couldn't free the Ghoulmaster while he was under the shaman's influence, and the new moon wouldn't wait for any of them — Kalidasa could think of only one way of taking on the Huna guards. He charged out of the trees screaming at the top of his lungs, and his men came screaming and howling after him. When they crashed into the wall of Huna warriors, the air rang with shouts and the clanging of metal against metal.

Kalidasa cut down four Huna warriors in that first rush, and such was the impact of their charge that the attackers were able to dent the wall, throwing the Huna warriors back.

Kalidasa pushed hard, swinging his axe, mowing through the cordon, and for a moment, it looked as if the defence would wilt under his sustained onslaught. But a fresh crop of savages issued from behind the tents, and before Kalidasa knew it, the tables had turned and he was beset from all sides. He took a slanting blow from a spiked mace on his back, while a sword slashed the outside of his forearm from elbow to wrist, causing the warm blood to run down his fingers and make his grip on the axe slippery.

He cursed and heaved at his assailants, beating them back, but they were too many and they kept coming at him. It crossed his mind that he could have brought a shield along, but then, he needed both hands to wield his axe and inflict maximum damage. The axe was as good as its promise, though, and Huna after Huna buckled from a barrage of withering blows that opened up skulls and ribcages. Another sword dipped past Kalidasa's defence, cutting him in the stomach, and the thought struck that this fight was a lot harder — and could last a lot longer — than he had anticipated.

All his doubts came traipsing out — he might not make it to the *droiba* before the new moon rose; the Ghoulmaster would be sacrificed after all; Borderworld would come under sway of the Hunas; he might die here fighting. The doubts clouded his judgement, and taking advantage of his lapse in concentration, the Hunas moved in, their swords inching closer with every stab, every swipe...

From somewhere to his left, there was a fierce rush, and the savages surrounding him were assailed by someone who fought with both hunger and relish. The Hunas were forced to face this fresh attack, and the press around Kalidasa loosened — which was all he needed to free his arms, swinging his axe high and wide and bringing it down hard. Between him and the soldier who had come to his rescue, the

Huna defence was decimated. When there were no more than five savages left standing, Kalidasa saw that his rescuer was the big man with the curling moustache.

As the last remaining Huna guards were disposed of by Avanti's soldiers, Kalidasa caught the big warrior's eye. "You fight well," he remarked. "What's your name?"

"Udayasanga," the man replied with a smile, leaning on his bloodied sword as he caught his breath.

"We should fight together more often," Kalidasa said.

Before the soldier had a chance to respond, a contingent of Huna reinforcements appeared out of the darkness.

"Men," Udayasanga shouted, drawing the attention of Avanti's troops to the new threat. "To your right, now!"

Turning to face the arriving savages, the big soldier flicked a glance at Kalidasa. "You go ahead," he said, tilting his head at the tents. "We'll take care of this bunch."

Udayasanga strode away to meet the onrush of Huna warriors, his big sword solid as a rock in his strong hands.

Kalidasa turned the other way and made for the tents, but he was challenged by a pair of Huna guards who came at him with their spears, one aimed low at his groin, the other at his face. Kalidasa kicked and flipped a fallen shield into the air, catching it expertly in time to block and deflect the lower spear. Ducking under the second spear, he spun full circle on his heel, and using the momentum gained to his advantage, he drove the axe into the first guard's midriff in a scything blow that almost cut him in two. In the same fluid movement, Kalidasa then hooked the shield's rim into the second guard's face, shattering his cheekbone, nose and front teeth. Dropping both axe and shield, he grabbed the fallen spears and broke both staves on his thigh. Armed with a shortened spear in each hand, he strode to the first tent.

More guards met him as he moved from tent to tent, but he was unstoppable, kicking, stabbing and punching his way forward as he hunted for the shaman. Sweat poured down his body and mixed with the blood from his wounds, and he glistened in the firelight, a golden avenging angel. All doubts and apprehensions had been put to rest, washed clean by the bloodlust that now filled his head; he knew what to do, where to go, how to find the *droiba*. The scent of blood had awakened something predatory in him, and he trusted his instincts to find his prey now.

The *droiba* was in a tent right at the back. When Kalidasa stepped over the bodies of the two guards and pushed aside the tent's flap, the first thing he saw was the shaman wrapped in smoke, swaying and whirling to some inaudible beat. He was mumbling incantations in his desert tongue, eyes closed and ears shut to the sounds of battle, his face streaked in blue paint that had run with the sweat and flowed down his neck in eerie blue rivulets. Kalidasa approached through the smoke, bloodied spears in both hands, but the shaman seemed not to notice, not to care. When he was almost upon him, the *droiba* opened his eyes and looked straight into his... and Kalidasa saw fear lurking there. Yet, the *droiba* swayed and worked his sorcery, fighting the urge to turn and flee, perhaps knowing that flight was futile. He raised a scrawny hand at Kalidasa, as if meaning to stop him or utter some dreadful curse, but Kalidasa brushed past the hand, stepping in close...

Hunched over the low fire, the *droiba* considered him with small, suspicious eyes that reminded Kalidasa strongly of the other one — the one he had killed. There was apprehension in this *droiba*'s eyes too, but here there was wonder as well, possibly at what he was divining. The smoke from the fire curled and twisted around the shaman's lean frame, snakelike and oddly sensuous, hugging him, and Kalidasa marvelled at the man's ability to harness and channel the smoke any way he wanted. Around them, the rest of the warriors and male folk of Mun'h stood in respectful silence, while on a raised platform, Khash'i Dur sat on the Huna chieftain's traditional seat, a low stool made of tanned goatskin and adorned with beads and tassels of horsehair. They were in what passed off as the town hall of Mun'h, a wide and airy chamber within the fort's premises. From time to time, everyone from the *shy'or* downward gave him a disapproving glance.

The *droiba* fanned the fire, and as a wisp of smoke escaped from the burning twigs, the shaman caught it in his fingers and rolled it into a ball, which he then casually flicked at Kalidasa. As the ball exploded on his face, Kalidasa flinched, not bothering to hide his irritation, but the *droiba* had shut his eyes and lapsed into another incantation. Ignoring the cold stares from all around, Kalidasa let his mind wander back to the night of Betaal's rescue.

He thought about Udayasanga, who had come to his assistance, and had later become a friend and joined the *samsaptakas* as one of its best and bravest warriors. Udayasanga was dead now, killed in war against the very people he was sitting with. In another life, he had sworn to avenge his friend's death, but now, old enemies were new friends. He wondered what happened to old promises when enemies became friends.

Sensing a sudden stir, Kalidasa extricated himself from his thoughts to find that the *droiba* was on his feet. Encouraged by a few sharp glances, Kalidasa stood up as well, the tallest man in the room. He watched the shaman go up to Khash'i Dur and whisper in his ear. The *shy'or* kept looking his way every now and then, and finally, he rose and beckoned Kalidasa forward. As Kalidasa took a step towards the platform, Khash'i Dur and the *droiba* got down to meet him halfway. Standing face to face, the chieftain smiled and put his arms around Kalidasa.

"The *droiba* is satisfied that you are who you claim to be, Thra'akha," he said, looking up at the giant. "The *droiba* says you don't lie. Welcome to the house of Dur. Welcome back to your Huna family."

Kalidasa nodded, relieved, suddenly at a loss for words.

A murmur rose and spread through the hall. Even though the *shy'or* had spoken in Avanti, the men around Kalidasa were now smiling at him and at one another; the chieftain's embrace had been understood. Someone even cracked a joke, and laughter flared and crackled. The weight of doubt had been lifted off the men's shoulders.

The *droiba* came up to Kalidasa, and this time Kalidasa bowed his head — even so, he towered over the shaman. Placing a hand on his shoulder, the *droiba* smiled up at him.

"*Oi zuh k'yar hriiz e'te,*" he said. 'You must wear a *hriiz* now.'

"*Ma le'a,*" Kalidasa said softly, with another bow. 'I will.'

His hand still on the giant's shoulder, the shaman pushed to the front and faced the gathering. "*Gha'ar,*" he boomed, banging his staff on the stone floor to get everyone's attention. As the voices dropped in deference and faded into silence, he turned back to Kalidasa. "*Bai'khi zuh si tei'sha,*" he said, his voice carrying to the far end of the hall.

'Tell them why you have come back.'

The hush around the hall was both deafening and demanding, and Kalidasa stiffened as he glanced at the faces turned to him in hope and expectation. Clearing his throat, he stepped forward.

"*Ma'a iti bun zuh te Sindhuvarta,*" he spoke slowly so he could be heard by everyone. "*Te zaa'ri ulla.*"

'I am here to lead you into Sindhuvarta, the land of plenty.'

Bangle

Aaai... aaaaaa... aaaaa..."

"Not now, Dveeja." Shaking her head distractedly, Aparupa pulled her arm free of the man's grasping fingers without even sparing him a glance. "We'll go later."

"Uuu... ai... ai... aaaa..." Dveeja kept up his insistent nagging, now shaking Aparupa by her shoulder, making her frown in mild frustration. "Aaai... uuuuu..."

The girl ignored him, trying her best to focus on the little clay pot she was painting to keep her mind off her missing soldier.

Six days had passed since she had seen him — five since he had last written to her — and despite regular sorties to the garrison and vacant wanderings through the streets of Udaypuri, she had found no sign of him. Hope was already ebbing away, and she was slowly reconciling to the fact that she would never lay eyes on him again. Instead of bringing her relief, that thought only got the hot tears to flow even harder, the weight of grief in her chest threatening to submerge her. The previous night, she had decided she wouldn't go to the garrison any more, and so far, all morning, she had stayed at home, mixing paints over and over again and getting the shades wrong every time. She knew she was very close to setting the pot and paints aside, getting up and going anyway. She was tempted by the irrational belief that he would be there on guard duty, smiling and apologetic; she was scared by the certainty that she wouldn't find him and would return home broken and disappointed.

"Uuuuu… aaaau… aaau… ai…" Dveeja continued shaking her, more forcefully now, and all of a sudden, all the turbulence inside Aparupa erupted in a concentrated stream of anger.

"No," she snapped, her eyes flashing at Dveeja. "No means no, don't you understand? I said later, and I will *not* go now. Wait until the afternoon."

Rattled by this sudden burst of temper, the man shrank back, his eyes wide in alarm. He stared at Aparupa, who stared back at him defiantly for a moment, before turning back to the half-painted pot. Seeing she was no longer looking at him, Dveeja slowly rose and slunk out of the room in his silent, shambling gait.

Almost immediately, Aparupa felt a pang of remorse at having shouted at the man, but she knew she couldn't have helped it. When Dveeja got something into his head, he failed to understand the notion of patience. Last evening, as they had roamed around Udaypuri, he had met and befriended a stray near the old brick kiln on the town's outskirts. Dveeja and the dog had taken to one another instantly, and Aparupa had had a hard time getting Dveeja to return home with her. On waking this morning, he had started pestering her to take him back to the kiln, not willing to listen to her promises to take him later in the day.

Sometimes, Dveeja could be very difficult.

"Aai… aaai… aaaau… uuuu…"

And he was back, barely a minute after being shouted at.

Louder and more stubborn in pitch, not willing to compromise or listen, throwing a tantrum like a child... Aparupa, her own nerves frayed, her patience thinning, put the pot down hard and swung to him with her eyes blazing, her lips peeled back in rage, ready to light into him. She stopped short, staring in surprise at what Dveeja was holding in his outstretched hand.

The bamboo bangle that Ghataraja had gifted her. Yesterday, in a fit of petulance, she had taken it off and put it away in her dresser, never wanting to see it again. For some reason, Dveeja had now gone and rummaged her dresser and brought it back to her.

"Uuuu..." he said, waving the bangle around to show her what this was all about.

"What is it, Dveeja?" Aparupa asked, stretching her hand out for the bangle. She took hold of it, but Dveeja didn't immediately release his grip, holding the bamboo ring delicately between two fingers and thumb.

"Aaaa... aaa... ai..." he said, pointing with his free hand at the bangle, then pointing over his shoulder.

"Who is it?" Aparupa asked, looking behind Dveeja, trying to figure out what was in his mind. "Is someone... outside?"

"Uuuu..." Dveeja nodded vigorously, relieved at having finally been understood.

Even before she realized it, Aparupa's spirits had soared and her face lit up in delight, as the thought of the soldier having come looking for her entered her mind. Maybe he was in the street outside, waiting for her, and that's what Dveeja had been trying to tell her all this while... Checking herself quickly, she looked at Dveeja.

"Who is it?" she asked, trying to keep the excitement in check.

"Aaai... uuuu..." Perhaps he saw her anticipation and understood, perhaps he didn't, but judging from his expression, the girl knew she had been wrong in thinking it was Ghataraja.

Dveeja's face was pained, the strain in his voice telling her something was amiss.

"Aaaaaaaaaa..." he said, finally letting go of the bangle and standing up. He motioned with his hand, urging her to come with him.

The girl put the paintbrush down next to the pot, rose and followed Dveeja out of the room. The man led her through rooms and passageways, down the stairs and into the rear courtyard of the large house. Stopping at the back entrance, he pointed vaguely at something outside.

"Uuuu... aaa... au..." he said to Aparupa in an undertone.

The girl pushed past him and stepped outside. Except for one of the part-time maids who worked at the house, the courtyard was empty all the way to the compound's back gate, which was almost hidden from view by her mother's corn cultivation. The maid was busy winnowing barley on a threshing stone, her back to Aparupa and Dveeja.

"What is it?" Aparupa enquired, looking at the man.

"Uuuuu... aaaiii... aaaa..." Dveeja said, pointing first to the bangle in Aparupa's hand, then to the maid in the courtyard. He then circled his thumb and middle finger around his wrist and twirled his wrist back and forth to signal 'bangle'.

"What about the bangle?" Aparupa asked.

"Aaaaaa..."

Letting out an exasperated grunt, Dveeja took Aparupa by the hand and dragged her across the courtyard until they were next to the maid. The maid looked up at them and smiled, her thin, tired face suddenly attractive as white teeth flashed in the sun.

"Greetings," the maid said, offering a *pranaam*.

"Greetings," Aparupa replied, then looked at Dveeja expectantly.

For a few awkward moments, the three of them just stood there, looking at one another. At last, probably realizing that

Aparupa would never get it, Dveeja stepped forward and pointed at the maid's hand.

Finally, Aparupa saw it.

Resting on the maid's right wrist was a fine bangle crafted in the shape of two twisting snakes, each swallowing the other's tail. The lightweight bangle, made of bamboo, was an exact duplicate of the one the soldier had gifted her.

Her eyes widening in surprise, Aparupa quickly hid the bangle she was holding behind her. She then looked at the maid.

"That is such a lovely bangle you are wearing," she said, allowing her wide eyes to reflect admiration. "It is so rare."

"Isn't it?" asked the maid, basking in the attention being lavished on her. She raised her hand, turning it this way and that, so that Aparupa could see the bangle better. The girl used the opportunity to inspect it closely; it was a double, without a doubt.

"Where did you buy it from?" asked Aparupa.

"I didn't. My husband gifted it to me."

"Your husband?" Aparupa asked, mildly apprehensive. "Who is he, and where did he buy such a beautiful gift for you?"

"He works at one of your father's shops in the market," the maid replied.

"Oh. And where did he buy it from?"

"I don't know. He returned home four nights — no, five nights ago — and he brought this for me. He was drunk on firewater, and he said it was a gift worthy of his queen," she giggled self-consciously at the memory.

"Beautiful!" Aparupa smiled at the maid. "Indeed, it is worthy of his queen. Not every man has an eye for such beauty, so you are doubly lucky to have a husband like... what's his name?"

"Kubja," the maid answered shyly.

"Kubja," Aparupa committed the name to memory. "You are lucky to have a husband like Kubja."

* * *

"A girl has come wanting to see you, commander."

"A girl? To see me?" Vismaya stared at the guard who had brought him the message. The chief of the guards was standing on a small, high terrace located in the northern section of the palace, where a *suryayantra* had been installed. He was overseeing two of his men as they oiled the machine's gears and levers. "Who is she?"

"I don't know, commander," the guard replied. "But she says you are related."

"*I* am related to her?" The chief of the guards looked thoroughly perplexed. Giving his head a dubious shake, he asked, "Where is she?"

"By the entrance to the royal kitchens, commander. It wouldn't have been appropriate to keep her waiting at the palace gate."

"Of course not. Good thinking," Vismaya nodded. He turned to the men servicing the heliotrope. "I need to go, but make sure every part is working smoothly. I don't want someone from the Royal Engineers coming for inspection and saying we're not taking proper care of the *suryayantra*."

The men nodded. Vismaya looked back at the messenger and gestured towards the door leading out of the terrace. "Let's see what this girl wants."

When Vismaya reached the entrance to the kitchens, he spied a young woman in the shade of a small lime tree in a corner of the courtyard. The woman stood modestly to one side, trying not to draw attention, but the fact that she was tall and strikingly attractive didn't make her job easy. Vismaya observed a few guards milling around, talking loudly and trying to catch the woman's eye, while a few male servants appeared to have found lots to do in the kitchen just then. In contrast, the two maids who were around were shooting glances full of envy and venom at the woman.

"Is that her?"

Seeing the messenger nod, the chief of the guards stepped towards the tree. "I'm told you were looking for me. What do you want?"

The woman turned to him, and Vismaya blinked at the beauty in that brown face, with its sparkling black eyes and soft brown hair that escaped in rebellious little twirls from the shawl she had drawn demurely over her head. He guessed she was not more than twenty. He also noticed the knotted bundle by her feet, which told him she had been on the road before coming to the palace.

"Speak up, girl," Vismaya said, finding his voice. The courtyard had gone silent, and he knew that everyone — guards, maids, palace hands, cooks, delivery boys — within earshot would be listening in on the conversation.

"Vismaya… *mama*?" the woman's large eyes assessed him in surprise and wonder. "Is it really you?"

"Yes, I am Vismaya," the chief of the guards replied, conscious of the term she had used to address him. *Mama* — colloquial for uncle in Avanti. "Who are you?"

"Don't you remember me, *mama*?" The woman took a step towards him, a half-smile on her lips. "Mithyamayi?"

Mithyamayi. Vismaya struggled to place the name and finally shook his head.

"Mithyamayi…" the woman said, nodding, "Your niece?"

"*My* niece?" asked Vismaya, frowning. "No girl, you're mistaken. I don't have any brothers or sisters."

The woman's face fell a little, but she took another hesitant step forward. "Your cousin Karunya... you remember her, don't you?" She looked at Vismaya anxiously, even desperately. "Karunya... you grew up together in..."

"Karunya from Viswapuri?" Vismaya's face lit up. "She got married and went there."

"Yes," the woman's face flooded with relief.

"And you are her...?" The chief of the guards peered closely at the woman. "Wait... don't tell me you are Mithi, her daughter."

"Mithyamayi. Mithi," the woman nodded. She had tears of joy in her eyes. "I was afraid you wouldn't remember me, *mama*," she said.

It was Vismaya's turn to take two steps towards the woman. He reached out and held her by her upper arms. "How you have grown, child," he said, looking up at her face. "You were so small when I last saw you. It was years ago, when I visited Viswapuri. You had learned to walk, but you would insist on being carried on my shoulders."

"That's what mother always used to say when we spoke of you, *mama*," Mithyamayi smiled.

"How is Karunya? It has been so..." Vismaya stopped on seeing Mithyamayi bite her lip as her eyes turned sad.

"Mother is dead," she said. "She died last month. That is why I am here."

"Oh." Not sure how to react to this, Vismaya looked around and saw that the guards were still watching and listening. "Don't you have jobs to attend to?" he demanded, his voice carrying across the yard. "I can find something to keep all of you occupied if you have nothing better to do than loaf around the kitchen."

The guards dispersed immediately, and when he turned back to Mithyamayi, Vismaya saw that she was smiling. "My *mama* is a powerful man whom even soldiers listen to," she said with a note of pride. "Wherever she is, mother would be happy to know this."

"Your *mama* is just a soldier," Vismaya smiled. Sobering up, "How did Karunya...?"

"Mother wasn't well for the last few years. After father died, they..."

"Oh, your father is no more?"

Mithyamayi shook her head. "After his death, they drove me and mother out. Father's family. They blamed mother for his death, said she had brought ill luck on the family. We roamed around from village to village, working here, working there..."

"Why didn't Karunya come back to Ujjayini?"

Mithyamayi shrugged. "Perhaps she didn't want us to be a burden on you. You know there is no one else, don't you, *mama*? No other relations, nowhere else to go."

Vismaya nodded. The girl was right. There was no one else.

"Anyway, when it became obvious that her end was near, mother told me to come to you after she was gone. She said you were in the City Watch, and that I was to ask for you. She said you would know what to do with me. So, here I am."

"You have nowhere else to go." It was a simple statement, but there were questions and uncertainties hidden in its folds.

A maid with gentle, motherly looks appeared at Vismaya's side, holding a glass of buttermilk. "Here, child, drink this," she smiled, offering the glass to Mithyamayi.

"My niece," said the chief of guards, as Mithyamayi accepted the buttermilk.

"I know. I heard," the maid replied. "Poor thing. No mother, nowhere to go. Where will she stay?"

Uncle and niece looked at one another.

"She can't stay with me in the palace," Vismaya scratched his grey beard doubtfully. "And I don't have any other home in the city. I don't know..."

"I can't stay here with you, *mama*?" Mithyamayi asked.

"Only those who work in the palace can live here."

"Can't you find me some work at the palace then?" Her eyes were shimmering pools in that beautiful face of hers, designed to melt hearts.

"It's not so easy to find…" Vismaya began, but the old maid interrupted him.

"Oh, look at her, so sweet and helpless. Where will the poor thing go?" She stepped up to Mithyamayi and placed a comforting hand on her arm. "We will do something, don't worry."

Turning to Vismaya, she said, "There must be *some* work available for her here, commander. You are the chief of the Palace Guards. You just have to ask the right people. You know you can do it, commander."

* * *

"I could have sent this to you in the dispatch, but I don't know whom I can trust here, so I figured it was best if I came and met you in person. I couldn't come yesterday as there were two outpost inspections that I couldn't afford to put off. Then there were patrol duties to be allocated for the week. It was almost nightfall by the time it all got done, so I waited until dawn before heading out."

"I understand," said Commander Atulyateja to Dattaka, who was seated across him in his office in the fort of Udaypuri. "And these three… *confessors*?"

"All three are under arrest and under heavy guard, commander."

"You trust the people who are guarding them?"

"I do," replied Dattaka.

"What has the rest of the command centre been told about their arrest?"

"That they are under investigation for stealing firewater from the mess."

"Stealing firewater," Atulyateja chuckled. "That won't make them very popular with the men. Good idea."

"Thank you, commander."

Atulyateja considered Dattaka and couldn't help admiring the man's resourcefulness. He had had nothing but a suspicion to go on, but by cleverly playing on the three soldiers' fears and insecurities, he had extracted the same confession from each of them — that Chirayu, the governor's aide, had paid them five silver coins each and promised all of them promotions if they would let him visit the cell of the captured Huna scout.

"Chirayu," Atulyateja repeated, addressing the third person in the room. "You know him well, I presume, captain."

"I wish I didn't, commander," the man replied, scowling. He was Subha, the Second Captain of the garrison. "He's been here from the day the governor took charge, and he behaves as if he has the governor's authority vested on his shoulders. Slimy fellow. He's always slinking around, spying on everything and reporting back to his master. I hate the man."

"In which case, it should give you pleasure to arrest him."

"We're arresting him?" the Second Captain looked from Dattaka to Atulyateja, his pink face flushed at the prospect, his big, grey moustache quivering in anticipation.

"Why not?" asked Atulyateja. "He will have to pay for his treachery. But we won't arrest him right away. We first need to ask ourselves on whose orders Chirayu was acting, and whether his arrest would tip off whoever he is working for. Chirayu is the puppet. We need to know who is pulling the strings."

"I agree," said Dattaka. "Maybe we can put him under surveillance so that..."

He was interrupted by a sudden uproar from somewhere below. There were shouts from a couple of soldiers, a rush of footsteps up the wooden staircase, and as the three officers exchanged puzzled glances, a woman's voice rang out from the end of the corridor.

"I won't go without seeing him," it said, loud, determined, defiant.

"You can't go there..." a soldier's voice pleaded, but he was cut short.

"Try stopping me."

The next instant, a woman stomped past the half-open door to Atulyateja's room. The garrison commander caught a passing glimpse of her, as at the same time, she peeked in through the gap in the door at him. And then, she was gone.

Atulyateja, Dattaka and Subha were still looking at one another in befuddlement when the door was flung open. Atulyateja turned to find a girl in the doorway, staring wildly into the room. Behind her, a soldier came into view, looking flustered.

"Is this where he is having his meeting?" she was asking. Before anyone could say anything, her eyes alighted on Subha and she cried out. "There you are... *sir*. I have been looking for you everywhere."

The girl stepped into the room, her eyes still on the Second Captain. Atulyateja rose from his chair, vexed at the unfolding drama.

"Stop right there," he said in a voice that carried so much weight that the girl froze and turned to him with big eyes. He saw that she was very young, curvy and heavily built. She wore a gold nose ring and her hair was tied in a long plait.

"What's happening here?" Atulyateja demanded. "What are you doing?"

"I am Aparupa, daughter of the merchant Aatreya," the girl said. Pointing at Subha, she said, "I came looking for him..."

"I don't care who you are, but you cannot walk around the garrison as if it is your father's shop, understand?" Atulyateja snapped. Turning a stern eye on the Second Captain, he said, "Tell the women you are seeing that the garrison is out of bounds. They can't just come in here..."

"No, commander, no," Subha shook his head furiously. "I don't even know her..."

"Of course, you do," the girl butted in angrily. "You saw me that afternoon..."

"*Enough*." Atulyateja rapped his desk hard with his knuckles. "Both of you, leave and sort this out once and for all. And hereafter, don't bring your fights and disagreements into the garrison, captain. Now take her and go."

"Commander, she is nothing to me," the Second Captain entreated. "Look at her. She is only a kid. How could I... I *really* don't know her. All I know is that she was at the garrison gate a few days ago, looking for some soldier. That's all, commander. I swear I don't know why she's here now."

"Because you said..."

"Stop," said Atulyateja, raising his hand. "Stop."

When he was sure the girl had been silenced, he said, "You were looking for a soldier, and you still are." As the girl opened her mouth to speak, he added, "Answer with 'yes' or 'no'."

"Yes."

"And that soldier is *not* the Second Captain here."

"No."

"And this soldier you are looking for has... is not to be found."

"Yes."

"Then why did you come here looking for the Second Captain now?"

"Because I don't know who else to go to." Suddenly, the girl's voice trembled as if she was on the verge of tears. "I thought the Second Captain could help. He asked me the soldier's name, whether he was in the Frontier Guard... I... want..." A tear rolled down her cheek, then another.

Atulyateja heaved a sigh and pointed to the empty chair next to Dattaka. "Sit down." With a small wave of his hand, he dismissed the three soldiers who had come after the girl and were now standing outside the door.

"Will you shut the door, please?" he asked Subha.

Once there were just the four of them in the room, the garrison commander sat down and looked at Aparupa. "Would you like some water?" When the girl shook her head, he said, "Okay, I know this soldier is important to you. What is his name?"

"Ghataraja."

"Interesting name," Atulyateja's eyebrows went up. "Since when has he left... been missing?"

"Five or six days."

"You do understand that this is a garrison headquarters, where lots and lots of soldiers from all over Sindhuvarta come and go."

"The Second Captain said so the other day," the girl sniffled.

"He could have been posted to..."

"No, something has happened to him. Something bad. Because..." she fumbled with the small cloth bag she was carrying and withdrew a circular object. "Because I saw a woman wearing a bangle exactly like this one, and the woman said her husband had got it for her five days ago. Around the same time I last heard from Ghataraja. He made this bangle for me, and he told me he was making me its pair. The two bangles are identical."

Dattaka reached for the bangle and held it up to the light. His expression was skeptical, but Atulyateja was staring at the bangle intently. The garrison commander appeared to have stopped breathing.

"Is that made out of bamboo?" Atulyateja asked slowly.

"Yes, commander," said Dattaka, handing him the

bangle. "Two snakes swallowing each other's tails. Great workmanship. Never seen a design of this sort before."

The long-forgotten face of the old woodcraftsman who had set up his shop next to the taverns by the Kshipra rose to the surface of Atulyateja's memory. The man had come to Ujjayini from god knows where, and he and Ghatakarpara had spent hours inspecting the man's wares, intrigued by the variety on sale — folding fans resembling peacock tails, bamboo and shell wind chimes, boat-shaped lamps that actually floated on water, daggers with hilts fashioned to look like animal heads... They had ended up making friends with the man, who had then started teaching them wood carving. While Atulyateja was quite bad at it, Ghatakarpara had a natural flair for woodcraft, and in a fairly short time, the prince had mastered the art.

One day, the craftsman had set Ghatakarpara the challenge of making a snake bangle, one of the most complex — and therefore, rare — designs to craft. The prince took a month to learn the technique, but when he finally showed the bangle to his teacher, the old man had sighed and patted him proudly. Few made the snake bangle these days, the old man had proclaimed. Of those who did, none made it better than Ghatakarpara, he had insisted. A week later, the man had been found dead in his shop, a happy smile on his face.

Ghataraja.

The garrison commander turned the name over in his mind as he rolled the bangle between his thumb and index finger.

Ghata-raja. *Ghata*-karpara.

"What does this soldier of yours look like?"

"He is young... and very handsome," the girl blushed. "Black eyes, no beard. He looks and behaves as if he is someone very important, like maybe a Second Captain or something."

"Have you seen him wearing something like this?"

Atulyateja pulled out his ceremonial sun-crest medallion from under his tunic and held it up by its chain. "This one is silver, but his would be of gold."

He was conscious of the stares he was getting from Dattaka and Subha, but he ignored them and looked at the girl.

"No," the girl frowned. "He couldn't afford gold, anyway. His father is a weaver."

"Hmm, does he have long hair that keeps falling over his eyes, which he then keeps brushing away like this?" The garrison commander did what he thought was a close enough impersonation of Ghatakarpara sweeping his hair out of his eyes.

"Yes, he is so adorable doing that." The girl's voice broke with relief and she leaned forward in her chair, blinking excitedly at the commander through her tears. "You know him, don't you? Where is he?"

Atulyateja's eyes were hard and sharp as they darted from Dattaka to the Second Captain. He gave them a small, curt nod, which they both interpreted correctly. As they stiffened, Atulyateja addressed Aparupa again.

"This woman who has the other bangle... who is she? Do you know her or her husband?"

"The woman works at our house sometimes. And she told me her husband works at one of my father's shops."

"Here in Udaypuri?" Seeing the girl nod, he asked, "Does this husband have a name?"

"Kubja."

The garrison commander looked at the Second Captain. "Pick this fellow up and bring him here."

The captain had taken two long strides to the door when Atulyateja hailed him. "Bring in the wife as well. And not a word to anyone about why they're being brought here."

Once Subha had left, Atulyateja and Dattaka exchanged glances.

"How long have you known Ghataraja?" Atulyateja asked the girl.

"Not long. We met at the frontier, near my grandparents' house." She paused and looked from one commander to the other. "You will be able to find him, won't you? I know he's only a soldier, but you won't give up looking for him, will you?"

"We won't give up looking for him," Atulyateja answered, amazed at the girl's naiveté — and at the irony of how the only lead they had got so far in their search for Ghatakarpara was one that had walked in through the door, not knowing the value of what she had brought.

* * *

The spot that Shoorasena had picked for the exchange was a narrow, steep-sided valley that funnelled one of the many minor tributaries of the Yamuna. The valley was well inside Magadhan territory, a few miles clear of the border with Kosala, but in a poorly populated region away from the main highways and secondary trade routes between the two kingdoms. The adjoining terrain was rocky and scarred with ravines, the soil unconducive for tilling, so that apart from a few desultory packs of goatherds, people rarely ever ventured into the area.

Which was why, from Shoorasena's point of view, it suited the purpose ideally.

The new king of Magadha squinted down the length of the valley, his eyes on the knot of twenty horsemen assembled at the far end, half a mile away. The riders appeared tense — which was normal under the circumstances — as they waited and watched for a signal from the group of horsemen milling around Shoorasena and General Daipayana. In the midst of the riders from Kosala, a figure sat astride a horse, his hands bound tightly in front of him, his mouth expertly gagged with a thick cloth. The man kept putting up a struggle every now and then, and it was taking two soldiers with drawn swords to keep him quiet.

"That's our man, the musician," said Daipayana. Grinning through betel-stained teeth, he added, "They've definitely gone to great lengths to keep him from talking too much."

"I wonder why," remarked Shoorasena, referring to the gag.

"He would have screamed the sky down by now if they hadn't, my king," the Magadhan general answered. "He knows what's in store for him once he switches hands."

Shoorasena nodded, then leaned backwards and craned his neck to look at Pallavan. The councilor was also trussed in ropes, but there was no gag over his pale, bloodless lips. He was emaciated, his cheekbones jutting out over sallow, sunken cheeks, his face gaunt and drawn. A mild discolouring of his right eye was the sole evidence of the first few beatings he had received in Girivraja's dungeons.

"You must be relieved to see that all those years of loyalty to Bhoomipala were not a complete waste," Shoorasena said with a smirk. As Daipayana and the other Magadhan officers tittered at the jibe, the king thrust his chin in the direction of Kosala's soldiers. "I, for one, would have been gravely disappointed with Bhoomipala had he put a common musician before a trusted minister of the council. No?"

Pallavan sat on his saddle without uttering a word. Apart from sneaking one sideways glance at Shoorasena, he kept his face averted, staring at the team sent to bring him back.

"Not in a chatty mood, are we?" said Shoorasena. "Where are all those magical words with which you charmed Magadha's traitors into plotting against me? Where is that famed gift of the gab that made father want to have a diplomat like you in our royal council?"

The councilor still said nothing, despite a sadistic prod in the ribs from one of the officers nearby.

"The esteemed diplomat appears to have lost his clever little tongue," the general grinned.

"The esteemed diplomat has only one thing on his mind —" Shoorasena transferred his gaze to Daipayana with a mocking smile, "— how to get past the border in one piece."

This time, there was hearty laughter from all around. Their voices must have carried, for the riders from Kosala shifted uncomfortably in their saddles, wondering what was afoot.

Shoorasena waited for the mirth to roll around and subside before raising his hand. "Okay," he said, with a small wave of his fingers. "Let's be done with this."

The four soldiers guarding Pallavan nudged their horses forward. One of them took the diplomat's mount by the reins, and all five horses picked a way down the stony riverbank, riding abreast, two soldiers to each side of Pallavan. Simultaneously, five horses left the other end of the valley, four soldiers escorting the desperate, wriggling musician.

The group from the other side was a third of the way down the valley when Shoorasena turned to a man seated on a horse to his left and a little behind him. The man was old and bent and carried the air of someone accustomed to a life of servitude. Shoorasena raised an eyebrow at the man, who immediately bowed and peered at the approaching horses. At last, he inclined his head.

"You're sure?" Shoorasena asked.

The man peered again before giving an indeterminate nod. "Almost, your honour."

"Yes or no?" The king's voice rose sharply.

"Yes, your honour," came the hurried reply.

Shoorasena turned back to face the horsemen. Everything went still, as those at both ends of the valley held their breath to observe the exchange. A wind blew dry dust down the valley's sides, and the shallow river chattered over the stones. Somewhere, a crow was calling, and the clink of horseshoes on stone carried to Shoorasena.

The two groups of riders met at the halfway mark. For a moment, the four soldiers from Magadha and the four from Kosala eyed one another over a distance of twenty yards, the hostility and tension plain in the stiffness of their postures and the set of their shoulders. Then, at an unseen signal, one of the soldiers from Kosala smacked the musician's mount in the rump. The horse instantly moved towards the Magadhan line. In response, the soldier leading Pallavan's horse let the reins drop and barked a short command. The horse stepped forward to cross over to the other side.

And quick as that, the exchange was complete. Pallavan was being led away down the valley, while the Magadhan soldiers had the bound and gagged musician squirming in their grip.

"What's their big hurry?" Daipayana exclaimed. "They've got what they came for, safe and in one piece as we had promised."

Shoorasena looked past the line of Magadhan soldiers bringing in the musician. The riders from Kosala hadn't even stopped to free their councilor's bonds; they were hustling Pallavan's horse along the uneven, shingle-strewn riverbank at a pace that was potentially hazardous for their steeds. At the end of the valley, the rest of the escort from Kosala was ready to depart, and there was a panicked urgency in the way the horsemen waited for Pallavan and his riders to join them.

"It looks like they want to get away from here quicker than lightning," remarked an officer.

"It is natural," the king trained a lazy eye on the officer. "They are two miles from the safety of the border. I would hope you would be as quick if you were ever two miles inside Kosala."

Shoorasena was about to return to observing the musician's arrival when, out of the corner of his eye, he caught the expression on the old man's face — wide eyes, slack jaw, shock. A quick check told the king that the man was looking at the musician.

"What is it?" he asked in a voice shot with alarm.

"Your honour... I am... It is entirely my mistake..."

"What is it?" Shoorasena roared. "Is it not the musician?"

The man shook his head, terrified. "I am terribly sorry, your honour... My eyes... I am old..."

"Take a good look and tell me, you fool," Shoorasena snarled.

"It is not him, your honour. This man is younger, heavier and fairer. I would recognize the musician anywhere. I served him the night he was at the palace entertaining the good king. This one is not him."

"Fool!" Shoorasena spat the word at the old man and whirled around to look at the prisoner kicking and writhing as his soldiers led him forward. The soldiers from Kosala had gagged him so that he wouldn't shout out the truth, putting everyone on guard, he realized in a flash of rage. "Sound the alarm," he shouted to Daipayana. "We have been tricked into parting with Pallavan."

Within moments, the shrill blast of conch shells filled the valley, a loud bellowing that climbed up its steep sides and spilled over into the adjacent ravines, where it came to life anew in booming, receding echoes. The shells spurred the riders from Kosala to greater urgency — instinct told them their subterfuge had been exposed. Shoorasena watched Pallavan and his escorts stumble and slide over the loose stones in a frantic bid to get to the other end of the valley...

...and he saw the archers rise up from the ridges and warrens along the valley's sides.

This was the second reason why Shoorasena had selected

this location to trade Pallavan. The terms of the exchange —
which he himself had set as a measure of good faith to gain
Bhoomipala's confidence — curtailed the number of soldiers
present to twenty a side. Great from the point of building
trust, but the arrangement had severe limitations. It meant he
couldn't have more men ready for deployment in an emergency
such as this one. Yet, that really was a problem only in flat,
open countryside; the hills and ravines here had nooks and
crannies in plenty, offering ample concealment for extra
Magadhan soldiers.

Through Shoorasena's foresight, these additional troops
now emerged from hiding to rain arrows on the men
from Kosala.

It was a bloodbath. The attack came in waves, and Kosala's
warriors could do nothing to defend themselves, much less
launch a counterattack. Arrows thwacked into heads, necks,
shoulders and torsos, and even some horses were hit. Bodies
tumbled off saddles like sacks of potatoes, and distressed
shouts and neighs filled the air. With the odds stacked so
heavily against them, flight was the only recourse available,
but even so, precise arrows chased and brought the fleeing
riders down, one after another.

Just three soldiers made it out of the valley alive. Only
two crossed the border back into Kosala and lived to tell the
tale. The third, badly wounded in the neck, fell off his mount
a hundred yards inside Magadha, one foot still trapped in a
stirrup, so that his horse ended up dragging his dead body
across the border.

Back in the valley, Shoorasena and Daipayana rode slowly
over the round, slippery rocks to where Pallavan's four escorts
lay, decorated with feathered arrows. At first, they couldn't
see the diplomat anywhere. Then, turning slowly, the general
sighted Pallavan sprawled at the river's edge, face down, arms
thrown wide, his head half in the running water so that his

fine, silvery hair pooled out around his scalp in a ragged, undulating halo.

Two arrows stuck out of the councilor's back. One just beneath his left shoulder, one at his waist, both buried deep in the flesh.

Arrest

May I take a moment of yours please, Princess?"

Pralupi, who was plucking red hibiscuses for the evening prayers, glanced irritably over her shoulder at the elderly soldier in the uniform of the Palace Guards standing some distance away, bowing to her, hands joined in a *pranaam*. He looked familiar, but it was only when she noticed his silver medallion that she placed him as the new chief of the Palace Guards.

"What is it?" she asked, letting the annoyance show in her voice. She didn't want the palace hands to be under the impression that she had time for their idle chitchat.

"Pardon me, Princess, but I have a peculiar problem that I believe only you could solve," the man said with a submissive smile.

The princess said nothing, hoping that her silence would discourage him. It didn't. The man turned and beckoned to someone. Pralupi's gaze went to the rhododendron shrubs the man was looking at, and as she watched, a young woman stepped out from behind the bushes. The woman was tall and shapely, but she kept her head bowed, so Pralupi couldn't see her face too clearly. Even so, the princess could tell she was attractive. Offering Pralupi a small *pranaam*, the woman went to stand beside the chief of the guards.

Smelling a scandal, Pralupi arched one eyebrow at the soldier. Her expression was one-part enquiry, one-part accusation.

"Princess, this is my niece Mithyamayi, newly arrived in Ujjayini from Viswapuri."

"Go on," said Pralupi, her interest piqued.

"She came here just this morning," the man went on. "Her mother, my cousin, is no longer there, so she…"

"No longer where?" Pralupi asked. "Where has her mother gone?"

"Princess, she is… she left us and went." The man looked briefly skywards, his hands rising subtly along with his gaze to make his meaning clear.

"Oh."

"Yes, Princess. As Mithyamayi has nowhere else to go, she has come here to me. Her mother wished it so."

"Okay, but what do you want from me?" Pralupi asked, turning back to start plucking flowers once again. She was losing interest in the soldier and his niece.

"Princess, there is a problem. My quarters are here in the palace, along with those of the other palace guards. Naturally, Mithyamayi can't stay with me. And there is no place of mine in the city where I can accommodate her."

"So?" Pralupi looked back at the soldier. Eyeing the niece once, she said, "What can I do about that?"

"If you could find her some work in the palace, she could stay here with the other maids and servants. Anywhere in the palace would do — the royal kitchen, the palace orchards, fetching water, washing the laundry — any work would do."

"I don't run the palace household," answered Pralupi,

looking around vaguely. "You should speak to mother... the Queen Mother."

"I would most certainly do that, Princess," the man said, bowing. "Excellent suggestion. But it just occurred to me that you don't have a handmaiden of your own here in the palace. Isn't that something you would like rectified?"

Pralupi fixed the soldier with an icy stare. After a while, she switched her gaze to the woman, who quickly lowered her eyes to the ground. The princess looked back at the man, and when she spoke, her voice was cold and measured.

"What is your name, soldier?"

"Vismaya, Princess. And if I have offended you in any way, I offer my deepest..."

"What can your niece do?"

The chief of the guards looked at the princess in a mixture of relief and hope. "I... she can..." he stopped, confused. "I think... she can sing, Princess."

"*Sing?*" Pralupi's lips twisted mockingly. "I don't have much use for that. Can she do any real work..."

"I will do whatever you wish me to do, your honour," the woman spoke for the first time, her eyes still downcast. "If I can't, I will learn. I promise."

Your honour. Pralupi liked that. She really liked that.

"Come here," she said to the woman. "What did you say your name was?"

"Mithyamayi, your honour."

* * *

Striding into the hall of the governor's mansion, Atulyateja was reminded of his last visit to the place, the night Satyaveda had hosted him and Ghatakarpara for dinner. Remembering that night, the garrison commander kicked himself once again for having missed all the little cues that had been telling him that the governor was up to no good. Satyaveda's fawning behaviour, his attempts at charming the prince and winning his trust, the subtle yet elaborate ploy of separating him, Atulyateja, from Ghatakarpara by sending him to oversee the battle preparations in Madhyamika and Gosringa — everything meticulously executed to isolate Ghatakarpara, so that he could be plucked and handed to the barbarians like a ripe fruit.

Had he paid closer attention to what was happening at the dinner table, none of this would have...

"What is the meaning of this, commander? Are your men out of their stupid minds?"

Atulyateja turned to observe Satyaveda stomp into the hall. The governor was attired in official clothes, but these were crushed from being sat around in. He also seemed to have misplaced his turban, so that the bald patch on his head gave him an even more scrawny and vulture-like appearance. He ranted in his nasal voice all the way from the door to Atulyateja's side, his face contorting in outrage that almost succeeded in masking the fear in his eyes.

"How dare they put me under house arrest? Me, Governor of Malawa! Under whose silly orders are they acting? I wished to step out, but your men forced me back inside at sword-point. Do you understand what I am saying? I was prevented from dispensing my duties as governor, you understand? *An act of treason against the representative of the crown.* I will have this reported, and you can have it from me that those responsible will pay a hefty price." Switching suddenly to third person, he added darkly, "I will teach those who mess around with Governor Satyaveda a lesson they won't easily forget."

"Are you done? May I speak now?"

Atulyateja did not use any official form of address, and his tone was calm but neutral. If Satyaveda noticed this, he showed no sign of it. "You may speak if it is to offer an apology for this appalling behaviour," he said, forcing a coldness into his voice that didn't fool the commander one bit.

"There is nothing to apologize for. The men were acting on *my* orders."

"What...? Why? Have you lost your..." The governor stopped as Atulyateja raised a hand, demanding silence.

"You were placed under house arrest because I did not want you preventing us from... *interrogating* Chirayu."

The garrison commander had smartly switched 'questioning' with a more intimidating 'interrogating' at the last moment, and he was happy to see Satyaveda pale a little.

"Chira— Why has Chirayu been arrested, and what has that got to do with me?"

"Chirayu is your assistant, isn't he?"

"So?"

"Assistants like Chirayu have lots of interesting stories. I also placed you under house arrest so that you could not leave the garrison until I had finished questioning the merchant Aatreya and his men, who include a fool by the name of Kubja."

"Who is... who *are* these people?" Satyaveda bluffed and blustered. "Have you gone completely insane? Why are you telling me...?"

"Aatreya is the merchant in whose company you spend hours betting on cock fights that are held illegally in the northern limits of Udaypuri. Aatreya is the man whose daughter Prince Ghatakarpara fell in love with, a situation you came to know of and used to your advantage to get the prince kidnapped and handed over to the Sakas. No, no... don't waste your breath denying this. Aatreya told us all of this, among a lot of other things. As did Chirayu in his confession. And Kubja is one of the prince's kidnappers, a complete idiot who was stupid enough to steal something that belonged to Ghatakarpara and gift it to his wife — which is how everyone involved in this affair has finally been nabbed. And that includes you, you understand?"

The governor had turned ashen, but there was still some fight left in him. "Lies, these are all lies. Some enemy of mine is trying to set me up. I have nothing to do with any of this…"

"Quiet!" The garrison commander stepped closer to Satyaveda, and the traitor quailed.

"The other afternoon, *you* did not grant me immediate permission to launch a hunt for Ghatakarpara, because you were buying time for your cronies to move the prince from wherever they were hiding him into the mountains, and from there into the Marusthali. Instead of facilitating a search that may have resulted in the prince's quick rescue, you deliberately hindered the process. Before that, *you* had Chirayu bribe the guards in Sristhali with promotions, so that they would look the other way when Chirayu brought the snake to the Huna scout's cell. In your capacity as Governor of Malawa, using the means and powers vested in you, *you* have been aiding and abetting our enemies in various ways, Satyaveda. You abused the authority of your office, and your actions have all been schemes and designs against the throne of Avanti — *acts of treason committed by a representative of the crown.*"

Satyaveda had put his hands together in supplication and was whimpering, mumbling unintelligibly under his breath. He appeared to be crumpling at the joints, bending and breaking as if the glue that had held him up all this while was loosening and giving way. His face was contorted with fear, shame and anguish, but even though he looked closely, Atulyateja saw no sign of remorse.

Disgusted by the man, the garrison commander inclined his head at one of his soldiers, who was bearing a set of shackles. As the soldier slapped the chains on Satyaveda's hands, Atulyateja said, "I remove you from your position as Governor of Malawa and arrest you on charges of treason. Further, I will petition the court of Ujjayini to send you into the Forest of the Exiles for conspiring against the kingdom of Avanti."

"No, please, no!" Satyaveda's eyes went wild at the mention of exile. "I didn't know what I was doing. I must not have been in my senses... You must listen to me. No, not treason... please... I beg you."

For a moment, Atulyateja watched his prisoner with contempt. Then, he stepped even closer to whisper into Satyaveda's ear. "I am guaranteeing nothing, because no one is going to take a lenient view of you," he said. "But maybe, *just maybe,* there is a tiny chance of not ending up in the Dandaka — if you can tell me exactly where in the desert the Sakas have taken Prince Ghatakarpara."

* * *

"The Halahala is in Borderworld?"

A hush had fallen over the Court of the Golden Triad, and only the torchlit shadows shifted this way and that in small, erratic movements, as a draught rose out of the valley outside and blundered through the hall, nudging past the assembled asura generals, looking for a way out. Holika, who had almost ceased breathing, came down the last few steps from the black crystal throne of Patala to stand before Shukracharya, her eyes pools of ice blue, wide with almost childlike amazement.

"*Really?*" she asked again, searching the high priest's face.

"The bones had been telling me as much for a while now," Shukracharya nodded with a rueful pull of the face. "Sadly, I misinterpreted what they were alluding to."

"For the second time, mahaguru."

The words, raw-edged with the stirring of displeasure, rumbled deep in Hiranyaksha's throat. Shukracharya looked over Holika's shoulder to see the asura lord lean forward on his throne, an elbow on one knee, the other fist resting on the other thigh, a frown forming under the heavy ram horns curling up from his forehead.

"Unfortunately, yes," said the high priest, biting back a retort that he knew would have been ill timed. He hated being reminded of how he had misread the bones the last time, when they had warned him about the yaksha coming to take Vishakha's life. And now this terrible mix-up over the dagger's hiding place. He realized that Hiranyaksha was justified in feeling let down.

Swallowing his pride, Shukracharya lifted his chin in the direction of the asura lord. "I just failed to connect the field of endless pyres with Borderworld, and the banyan with Betaal's abode. It never once crossed my mind that the human king might have access to the Ghoulmaster himself."

"But how, mahaguru?" Holika placed a pacifying hand on Shukracharya's forearm. "How did the human king get Betaal to keep Veeshada's dagger? What influence does Vikramaditya exert over the Ghoulmaster?"

The high priest turned to consider the small gathering of asura generals. The hour was late, else the court would have been full of keen and inquisitive asuras, he knew. His own sons Chandasura and Amarka were in the crowd. "It's a story that goes all the way back to the king's childhood."

For a moment, Shukracharya let his words hang in the ensuing silence, which echoed with the faraway roar of the Patala Ganga, plunging and snarling past the black crystal palace in a petulant and perpetual loop of damnation.

"It all began with a severe bout of brain fever that afflicted Vikramaditya when he was a little boy," Shukracharya launched into the account, turning back to face the asura sibling-consorts. "The fever was particularly virulent, and despite everything the palace *vaidyas* did, late one night, the boy died — briefly."

"Briefly?" Hiranyaksha echoed the word in befuddlement. "What do you mean?"

"Well, he died, but he came back. Or rather, he was brought back by the Ghoulmaster. The Ghoulmaster caught the boy stumbling through Borderworld, but realizing that his time hadn't come, he led the boy back from Borderworld to his home in Ujjayini."

Shukracharya paused to look at the faces that had drawn around him in a tightening circle of curiosity and interest. "That was quite a remarkable event in itself," he said, "but nothing compared to what happened years later, when the Ghoulmaster was taken captive."

"Betaal, a prisoner?" gasped an asura general. "How did that happen?"

"By way of a Huna sorcerer." Seeing the blank expressions around him, Shukracharya paused. "The Hunas are also humans, desert dwellers. They want to capture Sindhuvarta — they've been wanting to for years now. In fact, they had overrun large parts of Sindhuvarta before they were driven back into the desert."

"The sorcerer of the desert dwellers is capable of taking Betaal captive, and yet, they were driven out of Sindhuvarta?" Holika shook her head in incomprehension. "How?"

"The Hunas were driven back by Vikramaditya and his Council of Nine."

Again, a moment's silence as the asuras weighed the import of what had been said.

"How was the Ghoulmaster set free of the Huna sorcerer's clutches, father?" asked Amarka.

"When the Hunas invaded and conquered large parts of Sindhuvarta, the local kingdoms were offering them stiff resistance. Vikramaditya had just become the king of Avanti and leader of the Sindhuvarta alliance when the Huna sorcerer captured Betaal. The sorcerer's objective was to sacrifice Betaal and take control of Borderworld, which would provide the Hunas a ready army of undead warriors to be deployed against Sindhuvarta's forces. The undead are hard to kill, and those who died fighting the undead would be revived and would return as part of the undead troops."

"A masterstroke," Hiranyaksha smiled grimly in appreciation. "A constantly replenishing army with no casualties among your own soldiers. Every general's dream. No way the desert dwellers could have lost from there, had they succeeded. What stopped them?"

"Betaal," Shukracharya replied. "And Vikramaditya."

"What the Hunas didn't realize when taking the Ghoulmaster prisoner was his sheer will to survive," the high priest continued. "Betaal knew his time was running out, but he had the presence of mind to reach out to the one he had rescued as a boy — the human king. He haunted Vikramaditya's sleep until the king took notice and told the king about his predicament, as well as what his death meant to the kingdoms of Sindhuvarta. He also told Vikramaditya that there was only one way out of the situation — Vikramaditya had to rescue him from the sorcerer's clutches and take him back to Borderworld. And the human king was the only one who could do this…"

"…as he was the only one alive who knew the route into and out of Borderworld," Holika finished triumphantly. "He had done this journey before as a boy."

"Precisely," said the high priest. "To cut the story short, Vikramaditya and his army, which included the councilors Vararuchi, Varahamihira, Amara Simha and Kalidasa, attacked the Hunas who were holding the Ghoulmaster captive. The king and his councilors fought like men possessed. Kalidasa killed the sorcerer, so that Vikramaditya could free Betaal and return him to the safety of Borderworld. The Hunas' plans and ambitions were torn to shreds, and the battle really broke the resolve of the invaders. From then on, the tide of the war turned firmly in favour of Sindhuvarta's defenders."

"And the Ghoulmaster owed a debt to the human king from that time, which is why he agreed to keep Veeshada's dagger," Hiranyaksha concluded.

"How does the human king enter and come out of Borderworld, mahaguru?" asked an asura.

"With the help of his extremely clever and talented chief councilor, Acharya Vetala Bhatta. The Acharya has a way of playing with minds. He creates a conduit for his king to slip in and out of Borderworld." Shukracharya paused and looked around the assembly meaningfully. "Which is what we will do as well — create a conduit to enter Borderworld."

"To take the Halahala from Betaal, mahaguru?" Anticipation kindled in the depths of the Witch Queen's cold eyes. A restive murmur broke out as excitement caught and leaped from one asura to the next and knitted possibilities over their heads.

"Yes," the high priest spoke above the din. "Indra is basking in the glow of what he has achieved — dividing the human brothers and setting them up for confrontation. That doesn't matter any longer, for *we* know the dagger is not in Ujjayini under the protection of the Nine Pearls. But Indra doesn't know that. He will be watching Vikramaditya and keeping an eye out for us, expecting us to show up in Sindhuvarta. The human king thinks the Halahala is safe as long as it is in Borderworld, and anyway, between a disgruntled Vararuchi, a vengeful Kalidasa and the Hunas, he has plenty to deal with. Neither he nor Indra expects us to go into Borderworld. Nor does the Ghoulmaster. If we move swiftly, Veeshada's dagger is ours for the taking."

"Let us move swiftly then, mahaguru." The asura lord's eyes were molten gold and smouldering as they assessed the high priest. "Tell us how we can find our way into Borderworld. How do we, the living, enter the realm of the passing?"

"Entering is relatively simple; it is the coming back that can be tricky," Shukracharya said. "It can be accomplished nonetheless. The human king does it easily, and I myself have been there." Turning around, he cast his eye over the gathered generals. "What I need to figure out is how to take an army of a hundred asuras along, and bring all of them safely back from Borderworld."

* * *

Amara Simha's face was a deep tone of red in the light of the torches, though it was hard to say whether it was on account of the torchlight, or because he was trembling with barely contained fury.

"*The treacherous snake*," he spat. "The cunning, conniving, worthless piece of scum! How dare he plot against Avanti... how did the thought even *cross* his filthy mind? The kidnapping of a councilor, the king's own nephew. What audacity! Hold him tight here," he pointed at Atulyateja to stress his point. "I will have him hanged for what he has done."

"Satyaveda is firmly under lock and key, councilor," the garrison commander assured, adding with a chuckle, "And the only one liable to set him free by smuggling a cobra into his cell is also in prison." Pausing to sober up, he said, "Should you wish to see him, I can have him presented to you."

"Much as I would love to look the vermin in the eye and spit on his face, now is not the time. Ghatakarpara is our priority." Amara Simha shook his head as if dismissing a thought. "I'm also afraid if I find Satyaveda in front of me, I won't be able to stop myself from tearing his head off. The prince is like a son to me. If *anything* happens to Ghatakarpara, I shall skin the man alive, I swear."

"The prince will be safe, councilor," the garrison commander assessed Amara Simha, who was yet to dismount from his horse. Ranged behind the councilor was the force of *samsaptakas* under Angamitra's command, all tough and dusty men waiting for a command to ride back into the dark. And in their midst, though Atulyateja didn't know this yet, were the Huna scout and the interpreter who had come along on this expedition. "We will find him. But do come inside. You can't stay out here all night. Have all of you eaten?"

"We must begin our search for Ghatakarpara," Amara Simha replied, not moving, not responding to Atulyateja's invitation. He peered into the darkness of the garrison's courtyard from under his bushy, red eyebrows. "There's no time to lose."

The councilor and the *samsaptakas* had ridden with very few halts in between, and their arrival in the middle of the night had taken the garrison by surprise. Amara Simha had already got some wind of the happenings in the garrison town, and he hadn't budged from his saddle as Atulyateja brought him up to date on the ex-governor's treachery, summarizing the events that had led to the arrest of Chirayu, Aatreya and everyone else who had played a part in Ghatakarpara's kidnapping.

"Wait until it is light, councilor," the garrison commander suggested, eyeing the tired faces before him. "You have ridden hard, and there is more riding ahead of you. Your horses need rest too. Stretch yourselves a bit, catch a little sleep if you can. Do come."

The offer was tempting and sensible, and Atulyateja was persuasive. A quarter of an hour later, washed and in a fresh set of clothes, Amara Simha found himself at a table with the garrison commander, Angamitra, Dattaka and a pitcher of firewater for company. Dattaka filled the four cups, and once they had quenched a bit of their thirst, the brawny councilor stared across the table at Atulyateja.

"Where, according to Satyaveda, have the Sakas taken Ghatakarpara?"

"To their fortress in the town of Ki'barr."

"Ki'barr," the councilor repeated. He nodded at Angamitra. "Will you fetch the scout and the interpreter, please?"

Once the *samsaptaka* had left, Amara Simha had another question lined up.

"Any idea since when Satyaveda has been playing us?"

"I haven't got around to questioning him in such great detail, councilor," Atulyateja replied. "I thought it would be pertinent to ask the palace before interrogating him. I intended sending a message to Ujjayini in the morning, but now that you're here…"

"Let the palace know of his arrest, but otherwise, you are free to interrogate him," said Amara Simha. "Find out everything you can — since when he has been in the pay of the Hunas and Sakas, who his contacts are, what sort of information he has passed on so far, whether there are other Huna or Saka spies this side of the border… everything of consequence."

"I definitely shall, but in my understanding, he had no direct contact with the savages. All information was passed through Aatreya, who was the intermediary."

"Hmm…" The councilor took a gulp from his cup. "And it is this merchant's daughter who alerted us to the kidnapping?"

"She did, though she had no clue about what she was leading us into. She didn't even know her father was involved in the racket. Poor girl… she only wanted the prince — I mean, the soldier she has fallen in love with — to be found."

"Does she *now* know the truth about her beloved soldier?"

Atulyateja nodded. "It came as a shock to her. Everything has been a shock for her."

They were silent for a few moments.

"And Ghatakarpara?" Amara Simha looked quizzically

at the garrison commander. "Was he serious about this girl?"

"I don't know, councilor. But if there is anything I know about my friend, it is that he is not shallow. He would never play with a woman's feelings or take her for a ride. Ghatakarpara is a man of honour, and he wouldn't give his word lightly. If the girl thinks he loves her, it's because he has given her reason to think so."

"So, he reciprocates her feelings," Amara Simha sighed. "Damn, how this complicates matters! Did he even realize what he was getting into? He is a scion of the Aditya dynasty — how is he ever going to be with the daughter of a merchant... *now* the daughter of a traitor? How is this not going to end in heartbreak?" He set the cup down on the table hard, his voice ringing with with anger and anguish. "Why do young people not think before falling in love? Why can't they see the pain that they are inviting upon themselves? Why does love hanker for so much sorrow and punishment? Why is love so foolish?"

Amara Simha sat staring morosely at the table, while Dattaka and Atulyateja looked at one another, at a loss for words. At last, the councilor stirred and looked at Dattaka.

"You did well by solving the mystery surrounding the Huna scout's death. Now I can proudly say that a relation of mine helped nab the traitor Satyaveda." He smiled at the young commander. "Well done! A promotion is in order."

"Thank you for trusting me to solve the scout's murder, councilor," Dattaka answered, glowing with pride.

Given the lateness of the hour, it took Angamitra a little longer than usual to shoo the Huna scout into the room. The scout looked frightened at having been woken up and marched so late in the night, and when he caught Amara Simha staring balefully at him, he shrank and whimpered unintelligibly. The interpreter followed a few moments later, blinking and rubbing the sleep from his eyes.

"Forgive me for having disturbed your sleep," Amara

Simha addressed the interpreter. "But there is something I need you to ask this fellow."

The interpreter nodded.

"Ask him if he knows where the town of Ki'barr is."

The interpreter put forth the question, and the scout replied with a nod. Without being prompted, he pointed westward and said a couple of words.

"That way," said the interpreter, pointing in the same direction.

"Ask him how far the town is from here."

Again, the interpreter and the Huna prisoner exchanged words.

"He says it will take us three days to get there."

Amara Simha drained his firewater and rose from the table. "Tell him that he has two days on the outside to get us there. *Two days*." He raised his index and middle fingers to stress his point. "If we are not there by the evening of the day after, I will wring his neck and kill him. Tell him that."

The interpreter spoke, and the Huna turned pale, and paler still, until it looked like he would faint. Finally, he turned to the councilor and nodded weakly.

"Good that we understand each other," said Amara Simha.

Addressing the others in the room, he added, "I suggest we all catch what little sleep we can. Once the sun is up, we shall depart for the Fortress of Ki'barr."

Yah'bre

Hearing the stomp of approaching feet and voices raised in anger, Ghatakarpara braced himself.

What came through the door of his cell would probably be ugly, but the important bit was that somebody was finally taking notice of him.

That way, it had been a calculated risk.

A key was rammed into the lock, and the next instant, the door swung wildly on its hinges, kicked in by a foot wearing a rough shoe made of horsehide. A leg followed the foot through the widening crack, followed by a tall, bearded man with a swarthy complexion. The elderly woman charged with minding the prince entered next, joined by two other men, both bearded and bearing swords.

The group's leader glared at Ghatakarpara, then dropped his gaze to the earthenware pitcher that lay in many pieces by the wall next to the door. The woman took up a shrill rant; it struck the prince that this was the first time he had heard her utter a word in the two days they had been acquainted as captive and jailor. Not that he understood anything of what she was saying, for her dialect was alien to him. Listening to her nagging, grating tone, he immediately wished she would go back to being quiet, but there was no letting up as the woman railed and pointed vigorously from Ghatakarpara to the shattered pitcher to a bruise on her forearm near the wrist.

Seeing that the woman would go on forever if given the choice, the leader raised a hand, calling for silence. Eyes fixed on Ghatakarpara, he drew a short sword and approached, and then, moving quickly, he grabbed the prince by his shackled wrists. Simultaneously, he put the blade to Ghatakarpara's throat and pulled him close; the sword nicked the prince's skin, drawing a trickle of blood.

"Why hit?" he growled, thrusting his face down into Ghatakarpara's. The prince noticed that the man's beard had flecks of grey and he was missing a tooth, so the air whistled through the gap as he drew breath.

"What want, uh?" The man said, struggling to thread words in Avanti. He jerked his head at the woman and the broken pitcher to make himself understood. "Uh?"

Ghatakarpara sneaked a glance at his minder, who stood nursing her wrist and looking at him with resentful eyes. The two men who had accompanied the leader stood by her side, waiting and watching. Ghatakarpara gave the woman a sour, vindictive smile.

"If you are asking why I threw the pitcher at her," he replied, turning back to the leader, the smile still in place, "it was to see if she could do anything apart from bringing me food and water. Looking at the speed with which she fetched you all, I realize she can."

"You think funny?" the leader scowled, bearing down on the prince. "You think funny on us? You... *but'ut yei* or be dead." Not finding the correct equivalent in Avanti, he substituted with words from his strange tongue, but the way he drew the sword across the prince's throat, miming the slashing motion, needed no translating.

"I don't think funny on you," Ghatakarpara said a trifle too smugly, knowing he was pushing his luck, but wanting to show them that he wasn't the sort to be rattled easily. "On the contrary, I want to have a serious talk with you about your own safety and well-being."

The leader blinked, trying to understand what had been said and failing miserably. He shot a glance over his shoulder at his men, whose faces were blank too. Reassured that he was still their linguistic superior, he turned back to Ghatakarpara.

"What speak?" he asked, shaking his head to show that he didn't comprehend.

"You should let me go," Ghatakarpara sighed, deciding to keep it simple. "Otherwise, you will all be destroyed, I assure you."

"Oh." This time the man understood and grinned. "Oh. I so afraid." He gave a mock shiver and grinned even wider.

"Nice. I would like to see that grin when the weight of Avanti's forces is breathing down your backs and you bandits have nowhere to run."

The man ogled in confusion. "What?"

"Yes, I bet that possibility didn't even strike you," Ghatakarpara smiled. "Of course, why would it? You have no way of knowing who I am or who my uncle is."

"We know. You Gharakapara. Your uncle Avanti king. What think? We Saka foolish, don't know?"

"Wha... what did you say?" The prince's mouth fell open. "You are Sakas?"

"Yes, Sakas."

The man nodded grimly, then realizing that it had only now dawned on their prisoner, he grinned. "We know you. You no know us. You still think funny on us, uh?" It wasn't humanly possible to grin any wider, but the prince thought his captor just did. "We will *pak'ui se...*" again a substitution. Then, slowly, searching for the right words, "You... we will give to uncle... for land in Avanti he give us. Okay?"

Ghatakarpara understood, and his heart sank. From the moment he had returned to consciousness and realized that he was being held hostage, he had thought that his captors were mountain bandits, and that he was being held in one of their hideouts along the frontier between Gosringa and the kingdom of Matsya. The assumption had been formed on the back of the conversation between his attackers that evening outside Udaypuri — his assailants had spoken in dialects of Avanti, the hotchpotch lingo of the bandits. And even after figuring out that he was being kept a prisoner, it had never once crossed the prince's mind that his captors might know of his identity, or that they could be planning to leverage him to extract a ransom out of Avanti.

They won't pay if he's dead. They want him alive. The prince suddenly remembered overhearing this as he lay with his senses slowly ebbing out of him. The men who had attacked him, he now understood, were locals from around Udaypuri, hired to kidnap him and hand him over alive to the Sakas. Ghatakarpara also realized that had the man leaning over him not referred to himself as a Saka, he would probably never have guessed his captors were savages from the Marusthali — for he had come to expect all savages to sport the *hriiz* on their foreheads. Whereas, he now remembered, even though the Hunas and Sakas had a common religion, unlike the Hunas, wearing a *hriiz* was not binding on the Sakas.

"What do you think Samrat Vikramaditya to be?" the prince scoffed, even though he felt a lot less confident. "My uncle will not trade with filth like you."

"No?"

The leer vanished abruptly, replaced with a hard, brutal sneer. Lifting Ghatakarpara's shackled hand, the man brought his sword's point to rest near the base of the prince's index finger. Tracing a light path, he drew a faint line across the base of all four fingers, nicking the skin just enough to get the blood to swell out in trickling droplets.

"No? We send one finger. Then we send one finger. Then one finger. He trade, no? I think he trade, Prince Gharakapara."

Ghatakarpara was undecided whether to headbutt his captor or drive a knee into his groin — both were attractive options and easily achievable under the circumstances — and had wisely concluded that neither would serve much purpose as long as he was in chains, when the man unexpectedly shoved him away. The prince staggered back in surprise. As he fought to retrieve his balance, the Saka pointed his sword straight at the prince's face, his arm rigid and extended.

"You *s'apale*... be nice." He pointed to the woman and shook his head in a warning. "Not hit... *s'apale*. You hit, one finger to uncle — I cut."

Turning on his heel and sheathing his sword in one fluid motion, the leader snapped something at the woman and his two companions and marched out of the cell. One of the men followed without a moment's delay, but the other stood and stared at Ghatakarpara insolently. The prince understood that from now on, he would be under watch, the one surveying him from the door being the first to be saddled with the task.

As the woman made her way to the door, Ghatakarpara called after her. "I want water."

The woman paused, glanced at the sentry, then turned to the prince with a malicious glint in her eye. She surveyed the broken pitcher and discovered that one broken piece miraculously held a shallow amount of water, an inch deep and as wide as a human palm. With sadistic intent, she kicked and nudged the broken piece in Ghatakarpara's direction, the water inside it sloshing and tipping and spilling over the uneven edges. When the piece was within the prince's reach, the woman turned and left the cell. The door shut with a bang, the lock turned heavily and the shuffling of footsteps faded into silence.

Ghatakarpara watched the piece of broken pottery come to a wobbling halt with less than enough water in it to quench a bird's thirst. His mind was not on the water, though, but on the implications of what he had learned. The Sakas knew who he was; they had probably always known, which was why they had had him kidnapped with the aim of ransoming him to Avanti. He guessed that the savages would use him to negotiate an entry into Sindhuvarta, and in addition, would bargain for some territorial control over Avanti and Matsya. There was no immediate threat to his life, but the Sakas could carry out their threat of mutilation should Avanti offer resistance. Yet, the prince was aware that his uncles as well as the rest of the council would not want him harmed in any way — which meant that most of the Sakas' demands would be met.

And that, he decided, was unacceptable.

He would not be the reason for the savages getting a foothold in Sindhuvarta once again. He would not let the barbarians win so easily. If only he had the key to his shackles and the door...

The prince blinked and stared at the jagged piece of earthenware, lying where his minder had kicked it. The piece had begun quivering on its own accord, and as he watched, the ounce of water inside it rose into the air, looping and defying gravity, stretching in strange, elliptical shapes. There was hardly enough water there, still the globule shifted and moulded itself — and in the twinkling of the eye, it had eerily formed the shape of a small key.

It hung in the air a foot off the ground, shifting and dripping, but somehow holding its shape, as if by some exotic magic. A crude but distinct key shape, elastic and wobbling.

Mesmerized, Ghatakarpara dropped to a crouch and crept forward, reaching for the key with his manacled hands. He touched its surface tenderly, expecting it to break into a shower of droplets and collapse to the ground. Instead, the water shifted thickly mid-air, as though held by a magnetic force. Losing the shape of a key, the globule slipped between his fingers and ran heavily into the cup of his right palm, where it pooled, not one drop spilling to the floor.

Ghatakarpara stared thoughtfully at his palm for a moment, before tossing the water into the air. Up it went in an arcing splash, breaking into a dozen globules of varying sizes, and these were all still rising when the prince tried staying them with his mind. Immediately, the globules and droplets eased to a halt, suspended two feet over his head, bobbing dreamily. One by one, the prince willed the globules to loosen and fall, and one by one each globule plopped into his palm, settling obediently to form a pool once again.

Ghatakarpara stared thoughtfully into his palm for a long time.

* * *

"I always thought he was a bit of a fool, but I find it hard to believe that Satyaveda betrayed our trust and sold his loyalty to the barbarians."

"I don't."

"No?" Dhanavantri faced Varahamihira in surprise. "How come?"

"Satyaveda always had a vicious streak. He was vindictive, not the sort to let go of a grudge. You remember the time he was a courtier here and one of the palace guards failed to greet him…"

"Oh yes," the physician nodded, catching on. "It was

dark and raining, and the guard said he didn't see Satyaveda standing in the shadows, but Satyaveda insisted the man had deliberately ignored him."

"Right, and look at the furore Satyaveda raised. He wanted the poor guard stripped of his rank and punished for disrespecting the throne. He petitioned every courtier, every palace official to support his demand. He came to me, urging me to take the matter up with the rest of the council..."

"He came to me too," said Dhanavantri. "He just couldn't see that this was too petty an issue. Yes, you are right. He is the sort to nurse ill feelings."

"If he could feel so severely slighted at a guard failing to greet him, imagine how badly he must have taken the fact that he had been passed over for a seat at this table." Varahamihira tapped the heavy council table with a forefinger and looked from the physician to Vikramaditya. "With a grand-uncle who was a chief councilor and a father who was a councilor, Satyaveda probably imagined a seat would be kept vacant for him here. And when things didn't materialize as he had hoped, he turned bitterly against the throne."

"Does the message say how long he has been in the pay of the barbarians?" Kshapanaka asked from across the table.

The samrat shuffled through the small stack of palm leaves and shook his head. "This was sent by Commander Atulyateja at first light, as soon as the *suryayantras* became operational," he said. "We will learn more once he starts interrogating Satyaveda and the rest of the ring."

"By the looks of it, Satyaveda and this merchant... what's his name?" Dhanavantri paused.

"Aatreya."

"Aatreya. Satyaveda and Aatreya were running the ring. Satyaveda must have been sourcing information from inside the garrison, and Aatreya must have been passing it on to the Sakas. That's how the savages would have known about Ghatakarpara."

As the king and Varahamihira nodded, Kshapanaka spoke. "Atulyateja's message mentions a girl who helped uncover the plot."

Vikramaditya glanced down at the palm leaves again. "Yes, Aparupa." His eyebrows rose in surprise. "Apparently, she is Aatreya's daughter."

"What exactly was her role?"

"It doesn't say," the samrat replied. "But we must find out more about her. If she has helped in bringing the plot into the open, she must be rewarded."

"The head of the Sristhali command centre, Dattaka, too," Varahamihira added. "He's the one who exposed Satyaveda's hand in the murder of that Huna scout."

"Yes," Vikramaditya said. "Atulyateja's note mentions that Amara Simha has already recommended Dattaka for a promotion."

A short pause followed, broken by Kshapanaka.

"The message says that Amara Simha departed for the Saka settlement of Ki'barr this morning, and that the town is a two-to-three-day ride. I expect it will be a week before we hear about what happened at Ki'barr."

There was apprehension in the councilor's voice, which was understandable. Not once had anyone from Avanti ever set foot in the inhospitable Marusthali before; and here, a band of warriors was venturing into the Great Desert to take on the Sakas for whom the desert had been home for generations. The odds were heavily against Avanti's raiders.

"I can tell you what will happen right now," Dhanavantri flashed a smile aimed at lightening the mood. "Amara Simha will walk into the town and half its population will fall dead at the sight of him. The other half, unluckily, will try to offer some resistance and learn the hard way not to cross Amara Simha again — *if* they manage to get out of Ki'barr alive, that is."

The samrat and Varahamihira smiled at the physician's words, but Kshapanaka looked at Dhanavantri with a strange light in her eyes.

"I believe you," she said, the anxiety no longer there. "If Amara Simha can do what he did when the serpent Ahi attacked me, he can tear apart the Saka township with his bare hands."

There was something reassuring in Kshapanaka's tone that topped even Dhanavantri's lighthearted banter, and the tense atmosphere around the council table lifted. Vikramaditya looked at his councilors with the intent to speak, but the chamber door opened just then to admit Shanku.

"Greetings, Samrat," the girl said with a bow. "I bring you news from the men who went to Lava in search of the fugitive Greeshma."

"Ah yes, Greeshma," the king exclaimed. "What's the news, Shankubala?"

"He has been found, your honour."

Vikramaditya's face brightened and the councilors smiled at one another.

"First Satyaveda and now this. Finally, a day of good tidings," said Varahamihira.

Not getting the reference to Satyaveda, Shanku glanced at the lame councilor in confusion, then turned back to the king.

"Yes. He wasn't in Bhiwaha as fath— as we had been told, but the men asked around and discovered that he was hiding some distance down the Lava-Madhyamika road."

"And he is in their custody?"

"Yes. He is being brought to Ujjayini. They should be here by this evening."

"Excellent! Let's just hope he can guide us to the danavas now."

The samrat began pushing his chair away from the table with the intention of rising, but stopped on seeing Varahamihira sit up in his seat and look searchingly around the table.

"Where is Harihara?" the councilor asked abruptly. "I see he hasn't joined us today."

"He left for Mahishmati this morning," the king said.

Varahamihira rubbed his chin in contemplation. "He had become a bit of a permanent fixture here over the last two days, I thought." A pause, before his eyes travelled between Dhanavantri and the samrat, curious. "Why was he here in the first place?"

Everyone looked at everyone else, and nobody spoke. Finally, with a light shrug, Vikramaditya said, "A courtesy visit. He had heard about... all the developments in Avanti, so..."

The samrat let his words dwindle in the hope that the topic would end there, but the physician pounced on them with the ferocity of a cat pinning down its prey.

"So, he came to take stock of the situation for himself instead of depending on the rumours of traders and travellers," Dhanavantri said hotly. "He kept hovering around the palace like a bee around a pot of honey. All greed, no shame. His behaviour was more in keeping with that of a scout than of a king. Useless fellow!"

The unexpectedness of the rant took everyone aback, but while eyebrows did rise, no one came to Harihara's defence. In fact, everyone seemed to tacitly concur with the physician's opinion. Seeing no one had anything else to add, Vikramaditya got to his feet.

"That's all for now. I must go and inform Pralupi about the progress Amara Simha has made."

Dhanavantri looked sharply at the king. "I could get someone to deliver the message to her."

"I know." Interpreting the physician's gesture correctly, Vikramaditya offered a small smile of gratitude. "But I think she would appreciate it if I told her."

Reaching Pralupi's chambers and finding the door partially open, the samrat coughed and cleared his throat loudly. He then rapped on the door and waited for a response. When none came, he called out, "Sister? It's me, Vikrama."

Even after calling twice, when Pralupi did not respond, the king pushed the door open and stepped into an antechamber. From there, one door led to the right towards the bedchamber, while another gave way to a broad balcony to the left. Vikramaditya called once more at the bedroom door, then turned and went onto the balcony, which was cleverly landscaped to resemble a forest pond. Green grass grew underfoot and stretched all the way to a small pond that was fed by a small, bubbling waterfall, and where two ducks paddled silently. Overhead was a trellis of branches, housing cages with parrots, bulbuls and mynahs. A stone pathway cut through the grass and led to the far railing, which overlooked the palace lake.

Vikramaditya picked his way down this pathway, peering right and left to see if he could catch sight of his sister lounging on one of the stone benches. However, Pralupi was nowhere to be seen. The king was about to turn back when, out of the corner of his eye, he spied a figure stepping out from behind a clump of ornamental bamboo.

Believing it to be Pralupi, the samrat swung around — and saw that it was a young woman carrying a basket full of dried twigs and fallen leaves. Sensing that she was not alone, the woman looked up at the same time, and their eyes met and held for the briefest of moments. The woman then dropped her gaze, her long eyelashes coming down like heavy curtains over her eyes.

"Salutations," she said in a breezy whisper that carried only to where the king stood. Bowing her head at the same time, she draped her hands over the basket, which she hitched coyly to her waist.

"I... came looking for sister. Where is she?" Vikramaditya looked around, then back at the woman. "And who are you?"

"I am Mithyamayi, Princess Pralupi's maid."

"I've never seen you before." The samrat raised one eyebrow. "A maid, you say?"

"Yes," the woman blushed gently at the king's words. "I'm new to the city, my king."

"I see. And where can I find the princess?"

"I am here."

Vikramaditya turned to find Pralupi leaning against the doorpost that gave into the balcony. Her manner was cold and remote, and she regarded him with a strange mixture of hostility and disinterest.

"What did you want?"

The samrat was about to speak, but he paused and glanced briefly over his shoulder towards Mithyamayi.

"It's alright," said Pralupi. "She's just a maid."

Vikramaditya took a deep breath. "I'm here to tell you that Amara Simha reached the garrison of Udaypuri last night. They have learned that Ghatakarpara is being held by the Sakas in a fortress in the town of Ki'barr in the Great Desert. Amara Simha and the *samsaptakas* have left for Ki'barr this morning to rescue Ghatakarpara."

Pushing herself off the doorpost, Pralupi nodded and walked up to her brother. She walked past him without a word and headed for the pond, where she stood gazing into the depths of the water.

"Anything else, brother?" she asked pointedly.

The samrat frowned, shook his head and was about to turn and leave when Pralupi spoke again.

"You haven't changed your mind?"

For a moment, Vikramaditya looked puzzled, before comprehension dawned. "No, and I am not going to."

He strode away before he could be engaged in another exhausting argument.

Her mouth twisting with the sour taste of disappointment, Pralupi sat on a bench by the pond. Glancing up at Mithyamayi, the princess was surprised to see her maid eyeing the retreating figure of her brother. Mithyamayi stared boldly after Vikramaditya until the king had walked out of the door and disappeared from her line of vision.

Observing her maid with narrowed eyes, a ghost of a smile crept across Pralupi's lips as an entirely new possibility slowly dawned on her.

* * *

The sun was a great bangle in the sky, a quarter of the way up and burning down on the small procession of a dozen horsemen making its way across the flat desert. Draped in cotton shawls to protect themselves from the sun and the hot wind, led by Kalidasa and chief Khash'i Dur in front, they made slow, trudging progress to conserve energy and keep the precious water in their horses' bodies from burning up too quickly.

In the Marusthali, the elements were unrelenting in their severity, Kalidasa thought to himself, forcing his mind to remain active lest he fall asleep to the monotonous plodding of his horse's hooves. The day's heat was always punishing; the nights were invariably cold; wind and dust continually scoured the land and its people, and rain was a rarity. On his way to Mun'h, he had seen evidence of the harshness that the desert inflicted on its people, but he had assumed conditions would be better in the larger urban settlements. In this, he had been proved wrong — life in towns like Mun'h was just as hard, and if anything, with larger populations, the shortage of water was even more acute. Despite wells being guarded fiercely and water rights being enforced vigorously, fights over water were routine, constantly testing the leadership skills of the *shy'ors*. Water theft, Kalidasa had learned, was severely punishable, with offenders being exiled into the desert to die of dehydration.

Thinking of the innumerable women he had seen traversing miles of desert to fetch two miserly sheepskin bags of water from a faraway well, the giant couldn't help observing how unfair life was for Huna women as compared to the one led by the womenfolk of Sindhuvarta. In Sindhuvarta, water was in such abundance that women had all the time to indulge their passion for the arts. Here, the only time the women had to themselves was during their long treks in search of water; they put this to use by composing songs that were laments to dashed dreams. Kalidasa could easily see why the Hunas were obsessed by what they called *zaa'ri ulla* — the land of plenty.

"We discovered the land of plenty maybe a generation ago, when someone decided to go east," Khash'i Dur had said as they had sat around a fire the previous evening, partaking a meal of steamed rice and lentils. "It took courage to cross the mountains, but whoever it was came back to tell of a land that was green with grass and blue with water."

That early pioneer's account of Sindhuvarta inspired a handful of Huna households to follow in his footsteps, and they eventually came and pitched their tents in what were then the principalities of Salwa and Gosringa. Even while living on the fringes, the settlers thrived, and their tidings brought more Huna families into Sindhuvarta. But as their numbers swelled, they became more conspicuous, drawing the attention of the native rulers of the land.

"We did not mean them any harm," the *shy'or* had spoken through mouthfuls of rice. "We only wanted to live without scrounging for water every day. They had so much of it and we had so little, yet they were unwilling to share. The people of *zaa'ri ulla* despised us, called us names, and the kings sent their soldiers to harass us and drive us out of our settlements."

Still, the lure of water and a gentler life goaded more Hunas to cross the Arbudas, and slowly, their population increased and spread to the erstwhile kingdoms of Nishada and Kunti. But the influx of a Huna populace only served to threaten the natives even further, fuelling their antipathy, and the conflict of cultures resulted in incidents of violence.

"They mocked *hriiz* and attacked our people. We were forced to retaliate," Khash'i Dur had explained. "Then their soldiers started committing atrocities on our women. They took our women as slaves and put the heads of our menfolk on stakes in the mountain paths as a warning to those of us who intended crossing over. Our children were orphaned and left to die of cold and starvation. Some of the survivors brought the dead children back, and when we saw their small, shrivelled bodies, we knew there was no space for compromise, no room for mercy."

The account was a familiar one. A clash of outward differences in language, customs and religion; a deeper conflict over control of land and power; a sense of victimhood on both sides, leading to a hardening of stances — Kalidasa understood that perpetrator and victim were interchangeable here, depending on who was telling the story. But the outcome was that the Hunas and Sakas, who had suffered similar persecution in Sindhuvarta, struck an alliance and took to the warpath to seek vengeance against a common enemy. And thus, the first organized raids on the kingdoms of Sindhuvarta had begun, culminating in the conquest of *zaa'ri ulla.*

"With the blessings of *hriiz* and your help, we will take *zaa'ri ulla* again," Khash'i Dur had said with confidence. Smiling secretively, he had added, "This time, we also have the *yah'bre* to help us in the noble fight."

"You mentioned the *yah'bre* before. What are they?" Kalidasa had been curious.

"Tomorrow morning, Thra'akha," the *shy'or* had chuckled. "Tomorrow morning, we will join the *droiba* and you will see for yourself."

Thus, here they were, labouring through the morning heat, bound for wherever the *droiba* was at the moment. They had left Mun'h right after daybreak; but as far as Kalidasa could tell, they were still nowhere close to anywhere. Whichever way he looked, all he saw was baked and scarred desert.

"Now that you are back among us, you should take a Huna as your wife."

Kalidasa stirred from the depths of his ruminations and turned to find Khash'i Dur by his side. He had been so lost in his thoughts that he had failed to notice the chieftain ride up to him.

"What kind of a woman would you want, Thra'akha?" the *shy'or* asked.

Kalidasa gave a noncommittal shrug.

"Mmm, you are choosy, I see. Or are you just shy?" Khash'i Dur threw his head back and laughed. "Never mind, we will find someone suitable for the son of Zho E'rami. I am sure there won't be a dearth of prospective brides." He winked and laughed again. "Huna women are the best women under the sun."

The giant offered a polite smile and turned away.

He had never quite known how he had taken a liking to her. For a long time, he only knew her as the Warden's daughter, and it wasn't until the Acharya spotted her talent for throwing knives and *chakrams*, and included her among the children being tutored at the palace, that he came to know her name — Shankubala, though she preferred just Shanku. Even after she came to the palace, they hardly spoke to each other, and he guessed that was how things would have been had Vikramaditya not opted to make Shanku a councilor. Despite being together in the council, they spoke sparingly, finding their comfort in silences, and Kalidasa wondered how they had understood so much about one another while saying so little.

I would ask you to come with me, except that I know you won't.

All these years and you choose this moment to bring that up? Shanku had answered as they had ridden side by side on the day he had left Ujjayini and the palace.

He realized that he should have brought it up a long time ago. If he had, she might have been here, with him. Instead, he had stayed silent, and she was in Ujjayini.

Kalidasa turned back to consider Khash'i Dur.

"You are obviously very proud of your Huna heritage," he said. "Then, if I may ask, why do you insist on speaking to me in Avanti instead of our native language?"

Khash'i Dur studied the giant as he rode alongside. "By speaking in Avanti," he said, "I am making myself proficient in the tongue of the people I will rule when I have invaded and conquered Sindhuvarta. When you know the language of the people you have conquered and subjugated, you rob them of their ability to plot and conspire against you. Because language, my friend, is information, and information is power."

Another couple of miles, and the group finally reached an encampment of four goat-hide tents laid out in a rough circle around the ruins of the previous night's fire. There were half a dozen Huna warriors on guard, and they welcomed the *shy'or* and the *mahek* — the nickname the men had given Kalidasa, which translated as 'storm' — and informed them that the shaman had just left for the desert.

"We've arrived just in time," Khash'i Dur beamed at Kalidasa. "If we hurry, you'll see the whole thing. Come."

A fire had been lit, and the smoke from it was already slithering and coiling around the *droiba* when Kalidasa and the *shy'or* reached the consecrated spot, marked by the skulls of four mountain goats laid out in four corners. The *droiba* walked around the fire muttering under his breath, and at the same time, he kept pouring a fistful of sand from one hand into the other. The hot wind blew from the west, flapping at their clothes and sending eddies of smoke into the white-blue sky.

For a long while, nothing seemed to happen. But just as Kalidasa was beginning to tire, the shaman stopped his pacing and faced the desert. Clutching the sand tightly, he walked into the desert, the smoke following him, clinging to his body, a patchy, murky python form. He kept walking until his features could no longer be made out, and then he stopped.

Kalidasa watched closely as the shaman divided the sand between his fists. Then, in a sudden, impulsive move, the *droiba* flung the sand from both fists into the wind. The same instant, the smoke that was wrapped around him appeared to leap into the air, as if chasing the thrown sand. And a moment later, the entire desert floor around the *droiba* heaved... spun... and rose in a wailing pillar of dust, swallowing the shaman whole.

"Will he be alright?" Kalidasa whispered into the chieftain's ear.

The *shy'or* merely nodded, but there was enough conviction there to allay the giant's qualms. As if to reassure him further, the twirling pillar of dust shifted and moved into the desert, leaving the *droiba* standing unharmed and smokeless in its wake. The *droiba* watched the churning pillar, and like everyone else, so did Kalidasa —

— and he saw the pillar tear into two. Both parts twisted and danced away from each other, and as they spun, they became less particulate and assumed structure, gradually morphing into colossal dust giants that towered a hundred feet into the air, raining debris over the desert, their rudimentary mouths opening like caverns to reveal roiling thunderclouds within, lit at the edges by flashes of blue lightning. At the same time, a bellowing rage issued from those mouths, sounding to Kalidasa like the lowing of a dozen irate bulls.

Kalidasa remembered a portent that the Mother Oracle had shared with the samrat a long time back, when the council had sought news of the Hunas. The oracle had said that she had overheard the birds speaking of a wall of dust rising far away in the west, and everyone in the council had assumed it was the dust kicked up by an army on the move. Everyone had been so wrong.

Yah'bre.

Not dust-souls as he had originally thought, Kalidasa shook his head. His grasp over the Huna tongue was still rusty. *Bre* did mean 'souls', but now he remembered that it also meant 'spirits'. *Yah'bre.* Dust-spirits. Malevolent beings from the Huna hell, hard to control, but loyal and powerful weapons in the hands of one who knew how to bend them to his will.

The *droiba* turned and headed in their direction, and behind him, the *yah'bre* came like obedient dogs, rolling and growling and glowering, tons of mud, sand, anger and violence. They came after their master, who had summoned them to do his bidding.

"Look at them," the *shy'or* gushed like a proud parent, grabbing Kalidasa's arm in his excitement, his scarred face wreathed in delight and suddenly handsome. "Just look at them. Such magnificence."

With the blessings of hriiz *and your help, we will take* zaa'ri ulla *again*. That was what Khash'i Dur had said over dinner last night. Kalidasa now saw that the chieftain's confidence wasn't misplaced. The *yah'bre* were equipped to rain havoc on behalf of the Hunas.

Kalidasa smiled to himself at the thought of taking the *yah'bre* into Sindhuvarta.

Greeshma

He slunk away under cover of night like a dog with its tail tucked between its legs."

Indra took a deep pull from his goblet of *soma*, letting the cool, spicy liquid scald his lips and throat as it went down. In an almost instantaneous reaction, the wine rushed to his head, flushing him with a giddy sense of well-being. He placed the goblet back on his lips for a second draught, his mind only partly on Brihaspati's ceaseless prattle.

"The worm had the audacity to try and befriend Prince Jayanta right under my nose — as if I would allow that," the chamberlain went on, puffing up with pride at having seen through his old rival's game. "He was eyeing the mantras to awaken Ahi, that much I guessed fairly early."

"And the mantras are safe, I assume," Indra broke away from his drink long enough to look at the guru for reassurance.

"Oh, absolutely," Brihaspati tittered, clasping his hands to contain his joy, but it still spilled over in a breathless giggle. "I had Jayanta hand them over as soon as we learned of their existence. I bet Shukracharya was trying to plot a way to get Jayanta to pinch the mantras back from me."

"And he left just like that? Without as much as a goodbye?"

"Oh, he was so ashamed at having been unmasked, he couldn't have lived with the indignity of looking me in the eye. Running away into the night was the best he could do." Brihaspati waved a disdainful hand in front of his face. "This, after lying about how he was waiting for your return, so that the two of you could decide what to do next."

"He wasn't really lying about that," said the deva lord absent-mindedly. "We were supposed to share notes once I came back from Sindhuvarta."

"Oh," Brihaspati said for the third time. His enthusiasm a little punctured, he folded himself into a crushed silence.

Seeing he finally had some room to enter the conversation, Narada looked at Indra. "How was the visit to Sindhuvarta, lord?"

"Exactly as Shukracharya had predicted," Indra replied, rising and going over to one of the large windows that looked out over Amaravati.

He recalled the shock on Vikramaditya's face when he had introduced Gandharvasena as his real father, and thinking back to that moment, the deva lord felt a deep sense of satisfaction at having shaken the king's self-assuredness. But the triumph had been fleeting, gone before he could savour it properly; Vikramaditya had recovered quickly and well to stand before him, unbowed.

"Vikramaditya is tough, arrogant and uncompromising," he said. "He wouldn't accept Gandharvasena as his father, he refused to call his mother to vouch for his paternity, he refused to accept any help from me... *he refused to entertain me in any way*. He defied me the whole time, and he had the temerity to demand that I leave his city."

"It must be the deva blood in him that makes him so headstrong, lord," said Narada.

Indra didn't answer immediately. He drained his goblet, then wiped his lips and beard with the back of his hand. When he turned and addressed the diplomat, his voice was hard as granite. "He may have my blood coursing through his veins, but that won't stop me from showing him his place. I go wherever I want and stay for as long as it pleases me, and nobody tells me to leave. Not even my grandson."

Narada waited for Indra to replenish his goblet. "And what about the purpose of your visit, lord?" he asked. "Did your revelation bring about the rift between the king and his half-brother, as Shukracharya had predicted?"

"Humph," Brihaspati snorted at the mention of the high priest, but neither of the other devas paid him any attention.

"It was too soon for me to say, but if Shukracharya thinks a rift can be brought about, I suppose it can." The deva lord ignored the chamberlain, who was shaking his head in a silent show of disagreement. "We should know soon enough. Matali is in the palace, and we are due to hear from him shortly."

"Has Matali found out the Halahala's whereabouts?"

Indra shook his head and emptied the contents of the goblet down his gullet. "But I am certain that he will. And when he does, I want us to be ready."

Indra looked at Narada, who nodded in agreement.

"We are almost ready, lord," said the diplomat. "I had anticipated this, so in your absence, I have had everyone prepare for battle. Besides the Ashvins, the Maruts and Agneyi and her fire-wraiths, the regular deva divisions have been put on alert. Summons have been sent to Tribhanu to put his kinnara regiments at our service, and I have intimated Takshaka to spare us his naga divisions as well."

"Wonderful," said Indra. "When will the kinnaras and nagas join us?"

"I would expect them here in a couple of days, lord."

"Good. I can't rid myself of the suspicion that Shukracharya's stealthy departure is due to some change in the nature of the standoff between us and Vikramaditya." Seeing Brihaspati shake his head fervently, Indra raised a patient hand. "Yes, gurudev, I am certain you shamed him into flight as well, but we must never underestimate Shukracharya. Something about the way he left tells me that we must keep a close eye on Vikramaditya and Ujjayini."

Pausing to fill his goblet again, Indra looked up at his councilors. "I can feel it in my bones that any time now, the asuras are going to make a play for Veeshada's dagger. Come what may, we have to beat them to it."

* * *

Tormented by his thoughts, he had barely slept a wink all night. Every muscle in his body was now dulled with tiredness, and his eyelids were heavy and gritty when he blinked against the bright, mid-morning sun. His head felt weighty, as if it would tip over, and he was sure he could easily topple into sleep. But the moment he lay down, sleep fled his pillow, and he was left staring blankly at the ceiling and listening to the Queen Mother's voice chiding him.

You are never going to be the king of Avanti, so stop treating this palace like it's your own and learn to conduct yourself with the dignity expected from a soldier. If you can't do that, go back to the gutter you came from.

Look at you, all covered in mud and trailing muck all over the place. One would be forgiven for thinking you are some stupid commoner kid lost in the palace — which is, of course, the sad truth about you.

Vararuchi sniffed and turned away from the glare of the sun to look at the activity in the courtyard below. Soldiers of

the Imperial Army were filing into rows under the command
of the young captain Pulyama, who was issuing drill orders.
The soldiers were fully armed, as if readying for battle. The
garrison's gate was being fortified, and the councilor noticed
that additional soldiers had been posted on sentry duty. Seeing
all this, a part of him raised a small voice of alarm, but he
quelled it without a second thought.

King Mahendraditya is my father.

*I believe you. But I want to hear the Queen Mother say
so as well.*

She will not.

Why is that?

*Because I won't let her. And because she is not answerable
to you either.*

But she is answerable to the people of Avanti, Vikrama,
Vararuchi thought to himself. The Queen Mother is answerable
to her people. *And so are you.* You cannot stop the people from
demanding answers. The people always come first, Vikrama.
None of us is above the people.

On hearing the clomp of feet on the wooden stairs behind
him, Vararuchi turned to see Sharamana climbing up the
steps, two at a time. Behind him came two other figures, but
Sharamana's bulk hid them until they had joined Vararuchi on
the terrace of the garrison's central tower.

"Suhasa, my friend. And Commander Ajanya," the
councilor smiled at the newcomers with genuine pleasure. "It
has been a long while. I am glad you came."

"Salutations, councilor," said Suhasa, the older of the two.
Both men sported curling moustaches, though while Suhasa's
was white, Ajanya's was still mostly black.

"Sharamana told us we were needed, so here we are,"
Suhasa added, taking Vararuchi in an immense bear hug that
spoke of rare familiarity and fellowship.

"Thank you," Vararuchi stepped out of the hug and nodded

to Ajanya. "Avanti thanks both of you." He glanced in the direction of the courtyard. "Your men?" he asked, looking back at Suhasa and Ajanya with raised eyebrows.

"At your service. Here and at our own garrisons," replied Ajanya in a voice that was reassuringly deep.

"At Avanti's service," Vararuchi corrected good-naturedly. The fatigue that had been clinging to him moments ago had dissipated. "Shall we go downstairs?"

Seated at a table with glasses of refreshing buttermilk at their elbows, the councilor assessed the three officers of the Imperial Army. His expression was grim, his eyes watching the three men carefully. "Are you aware of the circumstances that have led to us meeting here?" he asked Ajanya and Suhasa.

Suhasa nodded as he sipped from his glass and wiped the froth from his moustache. "Sharamana gave us a broad overview," he said, continuing to stroke his moustache.

"And the two of you... *agree* with me?" Vararuchi looked from Suhasa to Ajanya.

"From the time we fought by your side to drive the savages out, we have always agreed with you, councilor," Suhasa answered.

Seeing Ajanya incline his head, Vararuchi heaved a sigh of relief. Planting his elbows on the table, he steepled his fingers and spoke thoughtfully.

"You are familiar with the threat from the Great Desert — the return of the Huna and Saka hordes. It hasn't been a month since I fought to save Dvarka from the Hunas. The armies of Sindhuvarta lost many men in Dvarka, and we will lose more when the Hunas come over the Arbudas. Losing men to war is inevitable, but losing them to foolish sentiment is unpardonable. By letting Kalidasa cross to the Huna side, we have paved the way for such losses, friends. For the sake of his friendship, our Samrat has gambled with our soldiers' lives."

The three officers shifted in their seats, exchanged glances and nodded cautiously. They were not stupid. They knew Vararuchi's incitement was tantamount to treason. Vararuchi was the samrat's councilor.

And his half-brother.

"I would never have let Kalidasa leave the palace, but he was allowed to go. As a consequence, countless soldiers of the Imperial Army and the Frontier Guard will die on account of Kalidasa's treachery. I am powerless to stop that from happening now, but I demand that the throne justify its actions to the soldiers whose lives it has so willfully compromised. The throne cannot throw its soldiers into death's path without telling them why they should die for the throne's mistakes."

"I am fully with you on the absurdity of the whole thing, councilor," said Ajanya. "As a commander in the Imperial Army, I know my men's lives are at great risk because Coun—" he stopped and corrected himself, "because Kalidasa can give the Hunas every little bit of information about our troops."

"You said that you demand that the throne justify its actions…" Leaning his forearms on the table, Suhasa scrutinized Vararuchi. "What exactly do you want the throne to do or say?"

Drinking deeply from his glass, the councilor leaned back. He shot a quick glance at Sharamana. "In usual circumstances, I would not be sitting here and talking to all of you about this; I would be speaking to the Samrat, and getting him to talk to you, so that you could convey his message to your men and allay their fears. But that Samrat is no longer in the palace. The Samrat who is now in the palace does not talk to his people. Forget his people, he does not talk to his councilors any more. You know about Ghatakarpara, I'm sure," he paused, and as the men nodded, he pointed to Sharamana. "I learned about his disappearance from the commander here, not from the palace. Not… one… word."

Suhasa, Ajanya and Sharamana looked at one another with troubled frowns. This was disturbing.

"In these circumstances, do I expect the Samrat to take a sympathetic view of what happens to your soldiers? *No*," Vararuchi was emphatic. "Do I expect the Samrat to justify his actions? *No*. The Samrat does not care any longer." He stopped and suddenly pressed forward, staring into the men's faces, one by one, until he was sure he had their full attention.

"You must be familiar with what happened in Ujjayini two mornings ago." He paused to see if the men had understood what he was referring to. "The visit from Indra…" he prompted.

"Yes, yes," Suhasa nodded.

"Do you know the details of what transpired? What Indra said to the Samrat… about the Queen Mother?"

The three officers looked distinctly uncomfortable. But seeing that Vararuchi was waiting for a response from them, Suhasa gave a weak nod.

"Well, after such a big accusation has been hurled at the palace, what would you expect the Queen Mother to do?" The councilor kept switching from one face to the next, forcing the men to confront his questions. "I would expect the Queen Mother to make a public rebuttal of Indra's claims. Would that be a fair expectation?" He looked at the men, seeking their support, and they nodded. "Isn't that the least that the palace owes the people of Avanti? But no. Two days after Indra's visit and the charges he levelled, there is complete silence from the palace. Why isn't the Queen Mother telling her people the truth? Is it because she has something to hide? In which case, don't her people deserve to know what she is hiding?"

Vararuchi leaned back once again, giving room for his questions to stew in the officers' minds. When he thought they had had enough time to ponder, he returned his elbows to the table. "Let me tell you something else. Yesterday morning,

I went to the Samrat and suggested that the Queen Mother address the people about the charges Indra has made. But the Samrat refused to listen to me. He kept insisting that King Mahendraditya was his father, and there was no need to drag the Queen Mother into this. I want to believe the Samrat, but the Queen Mother needs to convince me. All she has to do is refute Indra, but she refuses to clear the air. Why?"

In the small, stuffy room, the seeds that Vararuchi had sown were taking root and sprouting in the silence. The sound of battle drills and practice fights came from the one open window.

"What do you propose to do, councilor?" Suhasa asked finally.

"As I said before, do I expect this new Samrat to speak up? No. This Samrat thinks he is not answerable to the people. The Queen Mother thinks *she* is not answerable to the people either. But they are. We are the people, and we insist on knowing the truth — the truth about the Samrat's birth. The truth about who his father is. We want to know whether the man sitting on the throne of the Adityas is an Aditya. We want answers."

"And how will you get the Samrat and the Queen Mother to answer us?"

"Here is what I propose to do, Commander Ajanya." The councilor motioned with his hand for the men to draw closer. Dropping his voice to a conspiratorial whisper, he added, "For this, I will need your complete support."

* * *

When they brought Greeshma into the Throne Room, Shanku was struck by the man's bulk. He was nearly a hand taller than the soldiers escorting him and had the girth to match. He was mildly disheveled, his scruffy grey beard and whiskers lending him a ferocious look. Shanku couldn't help thinking of the frightening figure he must have presented to wayfarers in his days as a highwayman in the dense forests of Nishada.

"Greeshma," said Vikramaditya, leaning forward on his throne. "Greeshma the Wild."

"Yes… Samrat." The old bandit looked at the men who had accompanied him with surly eyes. Catching one of them jerk his head sternly, Greeshma bowed and joined his hands in a *pranaam*. "Salutations, my king."

"Salutations," the king replied. "So, you were once a highwayman, is it?"

The Throne Room was occupied by the samrat, the four councilors and a select set of courtiers. Greeshma's eyes darted from one face to the next as he wondered where the king's question was leading him and what was in store for him.

"I was, your honour," the answer came at last. "But I was an honourable one."

"Honourable?" Vikramaditya smiled in amusement. "Where is the honour in robbery?"

"I meant I had nothing to do with what happened to the woman, the bride… if that is what this is about. That was the work of the three depraved men I once thought of as brothers." His mouth twisted in dislike at the thought. "Those three deserved to die for what they did, but not the rest of them."

"In the Dandaka, you mean?"

"Yes, your honour. The others were sentenced for no fault of theirs. And they died for no fault of theirs."

Vikramaditya was silent for a moment. "Tell us about the Dandaka."

Shanku was certain she saw Greeshma turn a shade paler in the light of the countless lamps illuminating the Throne Room. He shuffled and cleared his throat nervously.

"It is not a place I would ever want to return to," he said at last.

"Why is that?"

The bandit looked around at the expectant faces staring at him. "I will get the hundred gold coins on offer, will I not?" he asked.

"The throne will never renege on its promise," said the samrat. "Now tell us about the Dandaka."

"It is a place of infinite terror. Miles and miles and miles of forest with death stalking you wherever you go. Tigers, leopards, wild boar, pythons, venomous cobras and vipers, crocodiles, scorpions... everything out to get you. And if not those, then the mosquitoes that are always swarming around, thick in the air. The forest is forever damp, and sunlight hardly ever touches the ground. Death and danger lurk in every bush and behind every tree trunk. I have seen one of my men being plucked from the ground by a python up in a tree. I have seen another being dragged screaming into the undergrowth by something that we later discovered had chewed his head right off. I have seen a man gored to death by a wild boar the size of a bull." He closed his eyes and shuddered. "It feels horrible to know you are being hunted as prey. You hear the tigers snarling in the night; you see a leopard disappearing into the bushes. And you know what you hear and see is watching you, waiting for the right moment to strike."

"Then you must have finally understood what the victims of your banditry would have felt while passing through the forests you terrorized," said Varahamihira.

"We hunted, but we never killed..." Greeshma looked at the councilor, and realizing he was addressing someone of authority, he added, "... your honour. We always spared lives. But in the Dandaka, every day was a struggle for survival. Every day, for four years, I fought to live for just one more day."

"What do you know of Janasthana and the danavas?"

Vikramaditya had thrown the question suddenly, without

warning, and Shanku saw the old bandit reel. He blinked and swallowed.

"If you were inside the Dandaka for four years, you must have come across them."

"They…" Greeshma turned even paler. "They are worse than the beasts I told you about. They are fast like the wind and ruthless like lightning. And they are fiercely protective of their city. Once, we ventured too close, and they attacked us. We fled, but they managed taking two of us captive. We returned a week later, hopeful of rescuing those two somehow, but the sight that greeted us was of them nailed to the trees by the city gate. Nailed with arrows, and half-eaten by wild animals and birds. They are savages."

"Is there anything you learned about the danavas… their city, their ruler…?"

"We once met an old man from Kosala, another exile who, god knows how, had survived in the Dandaka for years. He had built a hut for himself high in a tree, maybe that's how. But he was very ill — you can't escape disease by climbing a tree, you see. He was happy to see us, and we spent a few days with him before he died."

Greeshma stopped talking and stared glumly in front of him, his mind on the old man. The samrat didn't prod the bandit out of respect for that death from so many years ago; instead, he sat on his throne, waiting for Greeshma to return on his own accord.

"According to the old man, the city of the danavas is run by magic," the bandit spoke at last. "It seems that the danavas are masters of magic. They can make trees and stones do impossible things, he said. The old man also told us there is no magician among the danavas greater than their king, Shalivahana."

Shalivahana, Shanku whispered to herself, committing the name to memory.

"And the way to Janasthana… can you find it through the jungle?" asked the king.

"It is not easy, but it can —" Greeshma stopped suddenly, looking apprehensive. "Why do you ask, your honour?"

"Because you will guide us to the city."

"No, no… No, your honour." Waving his hands in protest, Greeshma began backing away. His face was now white, his eyes wide with fear. "I am not going back into the Forest of the Exiles, please… I won't go."

He ran into the drawn swords of his guards and stopped short. Turning back to the samrat, he spoke in a pained voice.

"I thought this was about the gold coins, your honour," he complained. "Nobody told me I was supposed to go back into the Dandaka. I am being cheated here…"

"No one is cheating you, Greeshma," Vikramaditya's voice cut through the rant. "You will get the hundred gold coins, as promised. In fact, you will get the coins *before* you take us in. All we want from you is to be our guide to Janasthana. Take us in, and bring us back out."

"What use are the gold coins to me if I die there? No, your honour," the bandit gave his shaggy head a stubborn shake. "I cannot do this. Going into the Forest of the Exiles is insanity. Why would you want to go in there? I don't want any gold coins. Find someone else to lead you to Janasthana."

"You refuse?" the samrat asked shrewdly.

Greeshma shook his head again, leaving no doubt regarding his refusal.

"Very well. In which case, you will be sent back to the Dandaka anyway." Seeing the startled look on the highwayman's face, Vikramaditya smiled thinly. "You were sentenced to the Forest of the Exiles *for life*, but you managed to escape. Now that you have been caught, you will be sent back there to complete the rest of your sentence — which, in your case, will be until the day you die."

"No, your honour, please," Greeshma entreated. "Please don't do that."

"I am offering you a way out," said the samrat, suddenly reasonable. "Take us to Janasthana."

Seeing the bandit shake his head, Vikramaditya continued, "One way or the other, you are going into the Dandaka. If you take us with you and bring us back, you come out of there alive *and* you have a reward of a hundred gold coins. Otherwise, you go in, you stay there and you die there. So, what do you say?"

"This is so unfair..." Greeshma began, but the king snapped at him, cutting him short.

"This is the only way, Greeshma. Yes, or no?"

With a great deal of reluctance, the bandit finally nodded, his shoulders slumped in defeat.

"Good. One more question. Do you know what language the danavas converse in?"

"The time we got too close to Janasthana and they attacked us, they were screaming... in *Avanti*." Despite himself, Greeshma looked up in surprise, as if the novelty of that discovery had just struck him. The colour drained from his face at the memory. "I understood them. They were screaming and urging each other to kill us all and spare no one."

"Thank you. You may leave now."

Watching him hang his head and drag his feet as he was ushered out, Shanku reckoned that in his mind, Greeshma was already a man condemned to his death.

When they had the Throne Room to themselves again, Vikramaditya took in the councilors and courtiers in a sweeping glance. "That's done," he said with a mild note of triumph. "Now to decide who will undertake the journey to Janasthana."

Before anyone could say a word, Kshapanaka stepped forward. "I will," she offered.

The samrat looked at her, but Dhanavantri spoke first. "I was thinking this would be a good time to call Vararuchi back," he said, casting a quick look at Vikramaditya. "From what Greeshma tells us, the forest is full of dangers..."

"Pardon me, but are you saying because it is full of dangers, *I* shouldn't be the one going in?" asked Kshapanaka. "Is it because I am not equipped to deal with dangers, or is it because I am a woman, and you somehow think a woman can't be trusted to do this?"

"That is not what I meant at all, Kshapanaka," the physician's shoulders sagged in dismay. "I know you are more than capable of doing this..."

"Good," Kshapanaka interrupted and looked at the king. "Then that's decided."

Vikramaditya was still considering her decision when Shanku took a step forward. "I never ask for anything, Samrat, but I am making an exception now."

As the king turned to her in surprise, the girl drew a deep breath. "The thought of approaching the danavas came from my grandmother, the oracle. The lead to Greeshma came from my father. Something tells me that destiny has linked my family and me to this journey. Allow me to go and meet Shalivahana and enlist the help of the danavas." She turned to Kshapanaka. "Give me this one, sister, please."

Placing a hand on Shanku's shoulder, Kshapanaka smiled and looked up at the samrat. "I trust Shanku's ability to tackle the dangers of the Dandaka," she said. "I propose that she go instead of me."

"We owe the Mother Oracle and your father our gratitude, Shankubala," Vikramaditya said. "They have both earned the throne's respect. The throne now entrusts you with the responsibility to go to Janasthana and strike an alliance with the danavas on its behalf. You will have a garrison at your command."

"I don't need a garrison, Samrat. I need no more than six hardy men and Greeshma."

Eyebrows rose in surprise around the room. "Councilor," one of the elderly courtiers intervened. "You heard what Greeshma had to say about how vicious the danavas are and how they protect their city. What protection can six men offer against a city full of danavas?"

"If you are going in peace, why would you take an army along, sir?" Shanku asked. "The Acharya has gone to Odra with a dozen men; why should it be different for the danavas? If the danavas see an army marching at them, they are bound to feel threatened and will attack us. We will have to defend ourselves and there will be unnecessary bloodshed. No, the smaller the group, the better. Six men with courage in their hearts and faith in me. That's all I need."

Vikramaditya looked over to Varahamihira. "Have the six best men handpicked for this mission." Turning back to Shanku, he asked, "When do you propose to leave?"

"Tomorrow, if it can't be earlier."

Rebellion

The ground along the margins of the road and in the open spaces between the barracks, stables, armouries and outhouses was covered with a heavy sprinkling of frost, but the road itself was muddy brown, churned by horses' hooves and the tramp of soldiers' feet. A wet chill hung in the still, early morning air like an invisible pall, weighing down miserably on the shoulders of King Baanahasta and Shashivardhan as they rode into the garrison of Kasavati on the northwestern fringes of Matsya.

Hunched inside a crude cloak made from the pelt of a large animal, Baanahasta cocked a weary eye at the moody sky and shivered, already missing the warmth and cheer of Viratapuri. Such was the desolation of the northwest, it felt as if they had journeyed to the other end of the earth. And if *he* felt that way about Kasavati, he wondered how Shashivardhan, born and bred in the sunny plains of Vatsa, would respond to the place. Baanahasta was inclined to think that the prince might be harbouring second thoughts about volunteering to serve on Matsya's frontier.

The king sneaked a glance at Shashivardhan, who sat awkwardly on his saddle, sniffling and wiping his nose on the sleeve of his woollen tunic, his face red with the cold. Baanahasta still couldn't believe the prince was serious about joining in the defence of Matsya. Even if he was, the king didn't think it was such a good idea — he didn't want his best friend's only son, now also the king designate of Vatsa, dying in this stretch of hilly wilderness populated by opium and saffron farmers and bands of wandering outlaws. But then his eyes strayed to the bulk of Piyusha, the prince's bodyguard, and the nine other soldiers who formed Shashivardhan's escort. Baanahasta conceded that the prince might have a chance of returning to Kausambi as long as he didn't do anything terribly heroic or utterly foolish.

Picking a haphazard course between military buildings and the few houses and establishments owned by the townsfolk of Kasavati, the cavalcade reached an open square, at one end of which sat the squat headquarters of Kasavati's garrison commander. News of their arrival had reached the garrison belatedly, and as they made their way across the square, a flurry of activity ensued as squires and servants rushed out to meet them from all directions. Baanahasta and Shashivardhan had almost reached the garrison commander's quarters when the man himself stumbled out, bleary eyed and red faced.

"Salutations, my king," he said, shuffling down two short steps and bowing deeply. "I was up until late last night, and I didn't expect to see you so early in the day. Had I known..."

"We decided to ride through the night rather than spend it in a cold, flimsy tent," Baanahasta interrupted as he alighted from his horse. Handing the reins over to a waiting squire, he stretched his lean frame and cast a critical look around the garrison. Then, turning to Shashivardhan, who had climbed off his mount, he said, "Prince, this is Commander Adri, in charge of the garrison. Commander, as you know, the prince is joining you here. I hope you have taken steps to make his stay comfortable."

"Indeed, your honour, indeed," the garrison commander said, bowing hurriedly to Shashivardhan. "The garrison of Kasavati is honoured by your visit, Prince. Your first trip to these parts, if I'm not mistaken?" He stepped forward to take the reins from Shashivardhan.

Shashivardhan joined Baanahasta, who continued with his inspection of the garrison. The king's gaze settled on a rabble of hastily erected tents jutting out into one corner of the square.

"Our allies' troops, I presume?" he asked.

"Yes, your honour," Adri answered. "From King Bhoomipala's court, a hundred units of Kosala's heavy cavalry." Waving his hand around, he added, "We also have five hundred of their infantry and a few hundred more from the Anartas."

"Make sure they are all fed well and properly looked after," Baanahasta indicated the tents as he began climbing the steps to the building. "Provide them with extra rugs and furs. They come from warmer climates and are unused to this cold. They may be soldiers, but they are also our guests."

Nodding vigorously, the garrison commander ushered his king and Shashivardhan into a square room where a log fire burned in one corner. The room was dark and smoky but relatively warm, which was all that mattered. Casting his damp cloak aside, Baanahasta lowered himself into a chair, and Shashivardhan followed suit. His bodyguard, Piyusha, entered and stationed himself at the door, and in a moment, they were joined by three officers of the garrison. As one of the officers unfurled a map of blue satin on the table, the garrison commander pressed jars of firewater into the visitors' hands. Taking a long pull from his jar, Baanahasta felt the liquid light up and warm him. Clearing his throat, he looked sharply at the men.

"What's the latest?" he asked, the fire playing across his dark, angular features.

"Three watchtowers were attacked and burned down to the north..." one of the officers began, but the king cut him short.

"Wait, this was last week, right?"

"No, your honour," a second officer answered, placing a finger on the painted map of Kasavati and its vicinity. "The watchtowers that were destroyed last week were here, to the southwest. The three to the north were attacked over the last two days."

There was a moment's silence as the man's words sank in.

"Did we lose any of our men in these attacks?" Baanahasta tried his best to keep the unease out of his voice.

"No, your honour. None of the towers were manned at the time of the attacks."

"Anything else?"

"Early yesterday morning, a patrol of twenty men was ambushed a few miles west of here," Adri spoke. "It was a small skirmish that didn't last long." There was an ominous pause. "We lost two men, your honour, while five more were injured."

The king's jaw tensed in anger. "What about the attackers? Any of them killed or captured?"

"I'm afraid not, your honour. They were archers on horses, as usual. They escaped before our soldiers could retaliate."

"Could they have been bandits, the attackers, I mean? I'm told there are lots of bandits in these parts."

Heads turned to consider Shashivardhan, who had spoken for the first time since entering the garrison. Baanahasta had observed the prince empty his jar of firewater in one straight gulp; he suspected the drink had loosened the young man's tongue.

"Bandits don't like to draw the attention of law keepers if it can be helped, your honour," Adri replied. "Ambushing patrols and killing soldiers is a very bad way of conducting business, for it only earns the wrath of the law keepers."

"We took a close look at the arrows that were shot at the patrol, your honour," one of the officers added in a quiet voice. "They were definitely of Saka origin."

"Oh," the prince subsided. He picked up his empty jar, stared into it and put it back on the table. Adri immediately refilled the jar from a pitcher. Baanahasta made a mental note to tell the garrison commander to go easy with the firewater when Shashivardhan was around.

"What else do we have?" he asked.

"That is all as of now, your honour."

The king stared down at the map, tugging his pointed beard in concentration. Watchtowers destroyed to the southwest and the north, and a patrol attacked to the west. The attacks were scattered across a wide arc, forcing the defence to spread itself thin, making the entire region porous and vulnerable.

"What I don't get," said Shashivardhan, his voice beginning to slur at the edges, "is the strategy of the Sakas. I mean, they are burning our watchtowers and attacking our troops, but they aren't invading us yet. Why? Are they afraid of us?"

"Theirs is the raider's strategy," said Baanahasta, sighing inwardly. Here was a man who had volunteered to fight the savages without even knowing the basics of warfare. There was very little to hope for.

"What's that?"

"When you capture territory, you have to secure it with troops. The more territory you capture, the greater the efforts you need to make to keep it, and the fewer troops you have at your disposal. Move troops, and you risk losing captured territory. So, once you capture territory, from being an attacker, you become a defender. But if your strategy is *raiding*, you are constantly mobile, never tied to defending a territory, always in attacker mode. You are nimble, while your rival is stodgy and can't move easily. You are free to trouble your rival wherever it pleases you, as you don't have the burden of committing troops to hold territory. As a raider, you can bully, harass and generally frustrate a defending force — you can drive a rival up the wall."

"I see." Shashivardhan nodded. Draining his jar, he leaned back. The fire and the firewater seemed to have taken effect, and he appeared to have lost interest in the discussion.

Baanahasta returned to the map with worried eyes. What he hadn't told Shashivardhan was that by engaging in light attacks, the intruders were toying with Sindhuvarta's troops, keeping them on tenterhooks before full-scale bloodshed exploded upon them.

"Have the watchtowers rebuilt and manned by larger units, night and day," he said. "And increase the strength of the patrols to thirty men, with at least half a dozen cavalrymen in each."

"I have already given orders for the watchtowers to be rebuilt, your honour, and work is underway," the garrison commander replied. "We have also started moving troops to forward positions. But we need more men in each outpost. We are desperately falling short of soldiers."

"Five hundred soldiers and a hundred archers have been commissioned to join your garrison. They should be here in a couple of days."

"I fear that won't suffice, your honour. We need at least twice that number and some cavalry support to guard these hills."

Baanahasta heaved a sigh and leaned back in his chair. "Matsya has a long border with four garrisons, and I have four garrison commanders asking me for two times as many soldiers as I can give them. I am trying my best with what I have, commander. I hope you will try as well."

Adri dropped his eyes and nodded. A small snore issued from across the table where Shashivardhan was seated.

The king swivelled in his chair so he could look at Piyusha. "Thank you for coming here with the prince, captain. This land may be cold and hostile, but you have my word that the soldiers of Matsya will never be lacking in warmth and brotherhood."

"We are proud to fight alongside your men," the bodyguard answered.

"Fight bravely then, and fight for Sindhuvarta." Pushing his chair back, Baanahasta rose to his feet and addressed Adri. "Once the prince is rested, I would like to ride out to the watchtowers that were attacked. Let us start with the ones to the north."

The garrison commander bowed as Baanahasta made for the door. The king wanted to get to the frontlines, so that his army — and the units from Vatsa, Kosala and the Anartas — could see him riding across the wild hills and talking to the soldiers, instead of issuing orders from the comfort of a garrison. Word would spread, the soldiers' morale would get a boost, and when the time came, he hoped the men would put more heart into the fight.

Emerging on to the verandah, Baanahasta raised his head and breathed in the cold, clear air as he surveyed the hills rolling and rising westward to meet the Arbuda Mountains. Gazing west, he thought of the report he had received just as he was leaving Viratapuri — a disturbing piece of news about Kalidasa having fallen out with Vikramaditya and having left the palace of Ujjayini. The report was sketchy, but it said something about Kalidasa being of Huna origin and of him heading west to the frontier. Baanahasta had made no mention of this to Shashivardhan — he didn't want to burden the prince's mind any further — but now that he was alone, he couldn't help worrying about the impact of that report.

If Kalidasa was indeed a Huna, and if he did cross over to the side of the savages, the fate of the coming war was already sealed in favour of the savages, he thought glumly. So, who was he kidding by riding around the hills and boosting his troops' morale? And why was he allowing an alcoholic prince to pretend he was being useful with the sword?

Baanahasta realized that with every passing day, he was less and less confident about defending his kingdom and Sindhuvarta.

* * *

"Tchk, tchk."

The driver of the foremost bullock cart flicked the reins impatiently, and the beasts responded by throwing their weight against the yoke so that the cart, nearly buried under a mountain of household goods, juddered and groaned. The huge wooden wheels moved almost imperceptibly at first, then slowly gained momentum, and the whole teetering structure took to the road. Four more carts, all similarly laden with an assortment of belongings, followed the first, forming a trundling caravan of tired creaks and squeaks. The families that were moving out came last, their shoulders stooped as if everyone was bearing a burden of memories, and everyone invariably stopped once to cast forlorn glances at what they were letting go of.

Observing this sorry march of people and bullock carts from a nearby embankment, Vikramaditya sighed unhappily. He sat astride his horse, flanked by Kshapanaka to his left and a senior captain of the City Watch to his right. "Have your men faced any resistance from the people, any unwillingness to cooperate?" he asked the captain.

"It depends, your honour," the captain shrugged his lean shoulders. "In some places, it has been without incident — we tell them the orders from the palace, they understand and make it easy for us. But in others, there is stubbornness, a refusal to see reason." He pointed at the five departing carts with his chin. "Four of those households had no problem, but the old man in the fifth was impossible. He kept going on about how people had never been inconvenienced like this before, not even during the last Huna invasion. It was a struggle getting him to leave with the rest of the family."

"Remember that no force should be used," the king reminded. "No one likes the uncertainty of having to leave their homes behind. Let us not add to their pain."

"The men have been made aware of your concerns, my king. They will be careful."

"How many households have been relocated so far?" asked Kshapanaka.

"I don't have this morning's figures, councilor, but from yesterday afternoon to late last night, we had moved nearly twenty families."

"Just twenty?" Kshapanaka looked a little worried. "From all over the city?"

"Not all, councilor. We started with the districts to the north and northwest. That was all we were to cover yesterday. The twenty are only from those parts."

Kshapanaka looked relieved.

Vikramaditya squinted at the overcast sky. There was a hint of rain in the breeze. "Those who have been evacuated... do they have another place to stay? Or are they being moved to the temporary camps?"

"Most of them have somewhere to stay," the captain replied. "Only a few are headed for the camps."

"Who has been put in charge of the camps?" the samrat asked Kshapanaka.

"The commander of the City Watch. But I am overseeing the arrangements. I intend visiting the camps later in the afternoon and tomorrow to see that all arrangements are in place."

"That's good. Make sure the camps have an adequate supply of tents. No one should be without shelter, especially if it rains. Also ensure there is enough food and water."

"I have seen to it, but I will check again."

Vikramaditya turned to the captain. "Send an update to the palace in the evening with the number of families evacuated today."

"Yes, your honour."

The king and Kshapanaka nudged their horses around and descended into a quiet side street. The breeze picked up and the branches of the trees overhead swayed, sending a shower of leaves down on the samrat and Kshapanaka. As they rode on, the devastated colony of ironmongers came into view. Some restoration work had begun, but much was still the way it had been the day after Ahi's attack.

"What is the state of our iron reserves, do you know?" Vikramaditya remarked.

"Varahamihira would have the latest figures, but I suspect it is not too good," came the gloomy reply.

"I wonder how the Acharya has fared in Odra. By now he should have met Queen Abhirami." The samrat paused to reach up and snap a leaf from the overhanging bough of a *tamalpatra* tree. As he crushed the leaf in his fingers and inhaled its aroma, he added, "I hope he has been able to convince her to trade with us."

Kshapanaka nodded but didn't reply. They rode on in silence, exiting the side street and turning into Ujjayini's main north-south avenue, where the day's bustle had begun.

"It just dawned on me that with Shanku on her way to Janasthana, we are down to four councilors," Kshapanaka said suddenly. "From nine to four."

Vikramaditya nodded. "It crossed my mind last night. Which is why I am hoping that the Acharya is done with his mission to Odra and is on his way back."

"We should call Vararuchi back too." Kshapanaka looked sideways at her king.

"We must," the answer came after a moment's thought. "I shall have a message sent to him as soon as we get back to the palace."

They had barely ridden a hundred paces when a horseman of the Palace Guards came into view at the far end of the avenue. He was riding at a gallop, and seeing him charging down the street, Vikramaditya and Kshapanaka tensed, spurring their mounts forward to meet the guard midway. As they drew near one another, the samrat recognized the rider as Vismaya. When the king and the councilor were within hailing distance, Vismaya reined in his horse and dismounted.

"What is the cause for your hurry?" the king asked.

"Your honour, Councilor Dhanavantri and Councilor Varahamihira have sent me to fetch you."

"Why?" Vikramaditya and Kshapanaka glanced at one another in alarm. Only something terribly important and sensitive would have warranted that the chief of the guards be sent.

"Your honour... they..." the Vismaya paused, as if searching for the right words.

"Go on," Kshapanaka urged impatiently.

The chief of the guards shuffled his feet apologetically. "It..." he looked quickly around to make sure no one was within earshot, and just to be sure, he dropped his voice. "It is about Councilor Vararuchi."

"What about him?" The samrat looked puzzled, then anxious. "Is he alright?"

"Yes, your honour. It is just that... he has... he seems to have demanded that you step down as king of Avanti."

Vikramaditya and Kshapanaka blinked at Vismaya, too stunned to even comprehend the full import of what they had heard. They turned slowly, like puppets in the hands of the master puppeteers of Malawa and Gosringa, to look at one another with wide eyes, and then looked back at the chief of the Palace Guards, who stood before them with his head bowed.

"*He demands that I step down as king of Avanti?*" the words came out slowly, each one weighed down with doubt and incredulity.

"Yes, Samrat."

* * *

Bhoomipala paced the length of the upper floor verandah, his shoulders hunched, his hands behind him, a thunderstorm brewing over his head judging by the frown on his face. His courtiers Kadru, Kirtana and Adheepa had been joined by two other palace officials, and the five men stood to one side, following the king with their eyes, their own expressions dark and troubled.

"I should never have gambled with his life. Never, never, never..." the king muttered moodily to himself through his beard. "I knew the risks involved but I took a chance, which I should never have done with Pallavan. It is all my fault," he shook his head in despair.

"Please stop blaming yourself, your honour," Kadru entreated. "What had to happen has happened. It is not your fault that Councilor Pallavan is dead."

"But it is," Bhoomipala insisted, still pacing furiously. "*I* gave him permission to go to Girivraja to bring the Magadhan royal council around to seeing the truth about Shoorasena. If *I* hadn't let him go, he wouldn't have been captured in the first place. And *I* thought up the stupid idea of substituting the musician with the prisoner — I should have known someone would see through the subterfuge and Pallavan might have to pay for it with his life." A broken sob of frustration and guilt escaped the king's lips. He brought his hands up to his face, staring at the open palms in misery. "Pallavan's blood is on my hands."

"It is *not*, my king." Adheepa, the elderly general of Kosala's army, stepped firmly into Bhoomipala's path. "Pallavan's blood is on Shoorasena's hands, your honour. And Shoorasena will have to pay for it. Kosala will settle this debt at all costs. This debt will bring Shoorasena to his knees."

The general's words were combative, forceful and inspiring, and Bhoomipala saw his courtiers square their shoulders and thrust their chests out in implicit support. The king looked into Adheepa's eyes and found a resolve there that he hadn't seen in many years. He gripped the general's shoulder and gave it a squeeze, signalling his thanks.

"What do you propose, general?" the king asked.

"War."

Bhoomipala looked at the rest of the courtiers and saw that none of them had anything else to suggest. He turned and walked to the verandah's railing. Leaning against it, he considered the sweep of the Ajiravati, flowing down from the mountains to the north in a rush to get to the plains, where it then spread and lolled in the sun like a lazy, overfed crocodile. Lazy and overfed. That described Kosala well, he realized. His kingdom had been blessed with the Ajiravati, which kept the soil rich and fertile, and the grateful land had been throwing up its bounty year after year. Even during the peak of the Huna-Saka invasion, the intruders had never occupied Kosala, and the kingdom had been spared the worst of their barbarism. Cocooned by Vatsa, Matsya and Avanti to the west and Magadha in the east, Kosala had had it easy for years — but the chill of uncertainty was now blowing in the wind.

"Our best soldiers are in Matsya, defending the frontier." Bhoomipala turned back to Adheepa. "Can we afford a war with an enemy who is many times stronger in number and capability?"

"There are times when it is important to look beyond the cost of war and assess the cost of peace — which can be even steeper than the cost of war, your honour," the general replied. "What is the point of peace if it robs us of our dignity and self-esteem, my king? Pallavan has been killed by Shoorasena's troops, and if we don't hit back, what message are we sending to the people of Kosala? That the lives of Kosala's citizens count for nothing? That anyone is free to take our lives and we won't raise a finger in our defence? Let our willingness to fight be determined by what is right, not by whether victory is achievable."

"I agree, your honour," said Kirtana, stepping forward to stand by Adheepa's side. "I have always been cautious of war, but if we don't act against this aggression, we will come across as weak and ineffective, and we shall risk losing the trust of our people."

Bhoomipala nodded. "I agree, not because I am worried about what the people would think but because I want Pallavan avenged as well. Fight we must, and fight we will." He paused and scratched his beard in thought. "But that doesn't take away from the fact that Magadha is a superior fighting force. What can we do to even the odds a little; from whom can we seek assistance?"

"I don't think we should seek aid from anyone — we will end up being disappointed," said Kadru. Seeing the others looking at him in confusion, he added, "Our allies have all committed troops to the defence of Sindhuvarta, as we have, so I doubt any of them would have soldiers to spare for our fight with Magadha. We could try sending a request to Avanti, maybe asking if they could lend us Councilor Amara Simha or Councilor Vararuchi, but as they are dealing with deva and asura attacks, I don't think our request will be entertained."

"Anyway, with Councilor Kalidasa supposedly leaving the court, Avanti is dealing with its own turmoil," added Kirtana.

"Any truth in that news, your honour?" one of the other courtiers asked nervously. "There are rumours going around that Councilor Kalidasa is a Huna spy, and that..."

"If rumours are to be believed, one could believe anything," Bhoomipala cautioned sharply, though at the back of his mind, he too was worried about the happenings in Ujjayini and their implications for everyone in Sindhuvarta. Still, he had to keep his men in check. "We don't yet know how much of what is being spoken about is true, but it does seem that Kalidasa is not with Samrat Vikramaditya any more. Why this is so, what happens next... these are questions to which we don't have answers yet. But I agree with the councilors," he pointed to Kadru and Kirtana. "We can't approach our allies for help; it looks like we will have to go into this battle alone."

The courtiers all looked at one another, suddenly dispirited.

"We are not really alone, my king. We have the musician, who was witness to the murder of King Siddhasena," Adheepa reminded them. "We must get his story into the open as soon as possible. Let the news spread to Magadha quickly to sow doubt in people's minds. We must adopt any method that can potentially weaken Shoorasena. Which also brings me to the Kikata resistance. Ever since Shoorasena has used the killing of King Siddhasena to fan hatred against the Kikatas, the Kikatas have been regrouping to form a defence against attacks on members of the tribe. That regrouping has now taken the form of an armed resistance against Magadha, I am told. We can reach out to the leaders of the Kikata resistance and see how we can help each other."

"This is very good news, general." Feeling a little relieved, Bhoomipala let out a huge sigh. "Do we know who the leaders of the Kikatas are and how we can get in touch with them?"

"From what I have gathered, the resistance has taken root in the forests to the southwest of Magadha, along the base of the Riksha Mountains. I shall start making enquiries about their leaders, and try and establish contact with them."

"Do that, and yes, let us start spreading the news about what Gajaketu witnessed that morning on the steps of the palace of Girivraja." Bhoomipala stuck his beard into the air in defiance. "Let us prepare for war against Shoorasena. Let us avenge Pallavan."

* * *

"He made the demand while addressing a section of the Imperial Army at the garrison of Musili early this morning. There were three garrison commanders with him, and the men he addressed were under their command."

"What exactly did he say in his address?"

Dhanavantri cleared his throat delicately. "According to the early reports that came in this morning, Vararuchi wants you to step down from the throne because you..." he paused, "... because *he claims* you are not an Aditya by blood, and only an Aditya can inherit the throne of Avanti."

The king looked away from the physician, his gaze going to the curtains flapping in the chill wind that was driving a drizzle over the lake, so that the lake's surface broke into a dance between the raindrops and the ripples. There were just the four of them — the samrat, Dhanavantri, Varahamihira and Kshapanaka — huddled at the near end of the council table.

In the absence of the other six councilors, the table seemed to expand in size, a lavish, barren, predatory expanse of bronze, gold, coral and lapis lazuli that dwarfed everything else in the room. Struck by the steady erosion of the council's strength, a shiver went through Kshapanaka, and she crossed her arms against the wind whipping through the windows.

"But his demand is conditional, Vikrama," said Varahamihira. "He has apparently said he wants the Queen Mother to issue a public declaration, refuting the allegations made by Indra. As long as the Queen Mother will vouch for your Aditya bloodline..."

"...I can continue as king," the samrat finished the sentence for the councilor. He hadn't turned from the window, and his eyes had a faraway look. "I know."

Vikramaditya remained lost in thought, and the three councilors said nothing. At last, Varahamihira broke the silence. "Perhaps the Queen Mother can be persuaded..."

"No, she won't."

The samrat turned sharply on Varahamihira and shook his head. "I have given her my word that she will not be subjected to questioning."

"She only has to..." the lame councilor began, but he was interrupted once again.

"She will not lie, and I will not let her demean herself in everyone's eyes by telling the truth."

The councilors looked at one another as the full import of Vikramaditya's words sunk in. The king turned and went to the window, where the drizzle slanted into the room. Leaning out, he let the fine droplets fall on his upturned face, stinging his flesh. He closed his eyes for a moment, allowing the wind and water to soothe his burning skin.

"I do not care who my real father is. I consider none but Mahendraditya to be my father." Wiping the water off his face, the samrat faced his councilors again. "But does that give me the legitimacy to rule Avanti, the legitimacy that Vararuchi asks for? Maybe not. If only an Aditya can rule Avanti, I can't because I am not one."

"Please tell me you're not thinking of agreeing to the demand," Dhanavantri's voice rose in apprehension.

"Don't take hasty decisions, Vikrama..." Varahamihira, for his part, began.

"No, I am *not* stepping down," the samrat clarified.

He approached the table. "Under different circumstances, I would have. But now, there are far too many threats facing Avanti for it to be without a king, even for a short while. I have pledged to protect my people. With the savages and the devas and asuras due to arrive anytime, I will not abandon my people just because I am no longer *rightfully* their king. That is one reason."

Sitting down, the king waved his hand, inviting the others to sit as well. "Moreover, if I give in to Vararuchi's demands, I virtually put the Queen Mother on trial and judge her on behalf of everyone else. In one stroke, I drag her dignity through the streets of Ujjayini; I can't do that. I gave father my word that I would uphold mother's honour. I have promised the Queen Mother the same."

"We understand, Vikrama," said Varahamihira.

"If I needed a third reason for not stepping down, it is the impropriety of Vararuchi's actions — what he has done in Musili amounts to treason." The samrat's expression turned hard and uncompromising. "When he came to me demanding that the Queen Mother issue a rebuttal to Indra's charges, I tried reasoning with him, but he wouldn't listen. I understand he is upset; he loved father dearly, and Indra's slur must have hurt. It hurt me too. It still does. But the situation called for a dialogue — not a rebellion."

"Which is why I wanted someone to go after him that morning, Vikrama," said Dhanavantri. "Someone who could have spoken to him, addressed his grievance. But you wanted him to be left alone."

"He didn't seem to want to talk that morning," the king replied. "But you are right. Perhaps I shouldn't have stopped you." He was pensive for a moment. "Also, that day, I thought I knew Vararuchi well. The Vararuchi I knew is not this one. The one I knew would never think of challenging the palace by rallying troops in his support."

"Why Musili?" Kshapanaka asked curiously. "It's not even a proper garrison."

"Perhaps because Sharamana is commander of that garrison," the physician shrugged. "He is Vararuchi's old loyalist, as are Suhasa and Ajanya, the other commanders whose backing Vararuchi seems to have. All of them fought closely with Vararuchi in the campaign against the Hunas and Sakas."

"Is that the only reason why they have thrown their weight behind Vararuchi?" Kshapanaka asked, confounded by the possibility.

"We don't know," said Varahamihira. "I suspect he must have played on their fears or pandered to their egoes in some way. We'll know better once we get more information." He paused and looked at his companions with raised eyebrows. "The question is, what do we do next? How do we respond to this?"

"We should engage Vararuchi in a dialogue," said Dhanavantri.

"Not immediately," said Vikramaditya, disagreeing before anyone could say a word. "We will first send him a message, telling him to take his demands back and disband the men he has assembled. *Unconditionally*. Only when he agrees will the throne engage in a dialogue with him."

"He is your brother, Vikrama."

"That thought doesn't seem to have held *him* back."

Kshapanaka and Varahamihira exchanged unsure glances. "In my opinion, we should talk to him before the situation gets completely out of hand," the physician dug in adamantly.

"Rallying troops and making inciting speeches against the throne is an act of treason," the king looked at the three councilors closely. "Vararuchi was aware of that, *and* of its consequences, yet he went ahead. He needs to be reminded that such acts will not be tolerated. We must make it clear that the throne will not be bullied or threatened into a dialogue. Vararuchi has to put a stop to his rebellion — anything less is unacceptable to me as king of Avanti."

Escape

The broad stone terrace offered an unobstructed view of Uttara Tosali, which sloped gently towards the bay where the little lights of boats and fishing vessels bobbed in the swell of the incoming currents. The city itself stretched out on both sides of the palace, the left arm curving outwards into the sea to form a headland, marked by the pinnacle of a temple dedicated to Uttara Tosali's presiding deity.

All this Vetala Bhatta took in with a sweep of his eye as he leaned into the cool night breeze and sipped *soma* from a flagon made of a dark, aromatic wood that lifted the flavour of the wine. He had washed and bathed for the first time since crossing the Riksha Mountains, and he was attired in a clean set of clothes that gave off the scent of sandalwood. Yet, for all the creature comforts at his disposal, a frown was pinned on the Acharya's face, his shoulders under the shawl were bunched with stress, and he shifted from one leg to the other in a growing display of impatience.

They had finally ridden into Uttara Tosali just as the sun was setting, and much to the chief councilor's relief, the guard master at the city's gates had been warm and welcoming, making their transit through the city and into the palace an easy affair. Even at the palace, they were treated with the utmost respect, and the Acharya was beginning to hope for a successful meeting with Abhirami when he learned that the queen was not in the city — she had left for Tosali five days ago to celebrate a harvest festival with her brother Veerayanka, and it would be a couple of days before she returned to Odra.

Vetala Bhatta's solution to this was simple. He was willing to take the road to Tosali and meet Abhirami there, and if he encountered the queen on her way back somewhere midway, so much the better. But the good ministers of Odra had patiently explained to him that their queen was making the journey by sea, so it was best if the Acharya awaited her in Uttara Tosali. So here he was, sipping a fragrant wine and grinding his teeth at the unforeseen delay, while cursing every precious moment they had lost inside the Ghost Marsh.

On hearing a door open to his left, the councilor turned to see a figure come out onto the terrace. The Acharya was expecting an official of Odra or a palace hand, so he was surprised to note that the approaching figure seemed vaguely familiar to him. It was when the man smiled and raised a hand in salutation that Vetala Bhatta finally placed him, staring at him in complete astonishment.

"Greetings, raj-guru," the man smiled, bowing.

"Chancellor Sudasan, what are you doing here?" Vetala Bhatta blurted out.

The chief of the old republic of Vanga didn't answer immediately. Instead, he walked up to the Acharya and bowed formally once again. "I was told that you were here," he said. "You arrived in the evening, isn't it?"

"Yes." The raj-guru stared at the noble face in front of him, full of dignity, yet bearing the weight of all that Vanga had endured in the recent past. "You were the last person I expected to see here."

"Hah, it is a long story," Sudasan sighed. "You must have heard about the massacre in Tamralipti." When Vetala Bhatta shook his head, the chancellor said, "Once Bhadraka and the other two chiefs switched their loyalties, Vanga fell easily to Shoorasena's forces led by Kapila. The Magadhan general Daipayana then rounded up seventeen members of our Grand Assembly with Bhadraka's help, and had all of them hanged in the main market of Tamralipti."

"Coldblooded murder," the chief councilor stared, horrified.

The chancellor nodded. "The rest of us fled Tamralipti. We hid in the marshland to the east, but when we learned that they were searching for us, we realized we would eventually be discovered. We decided to seek asylum somewhere, and the only choices we had were Pragjyotishpura, the kingdoms of Sribhoja and Srivijaya, or here. So, here we are."

"And Queen Abhirami has granted you asylum?" The Acharya's face was hopeful. He knew that if she had, it meant Odra and Kalinga were thawing to outsiders, which was a good sign.

"Not yet. Like you, we arrived after she had left for King Veerayanka's court. We too are waiting for her to return, so that she can decide our fate." Sudasan licked his lips nervously. "I do hope she takes a sympathetic view of our situation."

"I see." Vetala Bhatta tried not to let his disappointment show. He was about to sip his wine when, noticing that the chancellor's hands were empty and remembering his manners, he said, "Where's your flagon? Shall I call for some *soma* for you?"

"No, no, I am fine," Sudasan shook his head. Then, looking curiously at the raj-guru, "What brings *you* to Odra?"

"Like yours, a long story," the Acharya replied. He then told the chancellor about the growing shortage of iron in

Sindhuvarta, Ahi's attack on the ironmongers' colony in Ujjayini and the fears of a severe crunch in iron ore supplies. "The Samrat wants to establish a trade treaty between Avanti and Odra and Kalinga to purchase iron ore as well as use the ports of Tosali and Uttara Tosali to keep up the trade with Sribhoja and Srivijaya."

"I see."

Sudasan was silent for a while, gazing at the city's lights and the moon reflected in the bay. At last, he turned to Vetala Bhatta. "What makes you think Abhirami and Veerayanka will agree to a trade alliance with Avanti?"

There was a challenge in the chancellor's tone and a note of skepticism, which suddenly angered the raj-guru. "The same thing that makes you think they will agree to grant you political asylum — *hope*."

The words hit hard and Sudasan dropped his eyes, looking crushed. Regretting his harshness, Vetala Bhatta placed a hand on the chancellor's shoulder. "I shouldn't have said that. The idea was not to hurt you. I think it was the fatigue and stress talking."

"It is alright, raj-guru," Sudasan smiled. "I asked for it, so please don't apologize."

The Acharya finished the *soma* and turned back to look at the bay. Watching him chew on his lips and drum on the parapet with his fingers, the chancellor asked, "Is something else troubling you?"

"I must get back to Ujjayini. The city is under constant threat, the people are living in great fear, and the Samrat and his council are under a lot of pressure. I was hoping to sort out the trade alliance swiftly and get back, but it looks like I will have to wait for a few days now." He smacked the parapet hard with the flat of his hand. "I wish I could go to Tosali to meet the queen, but these people don't seem keen on it."

It was Sudasan's turn to place a comforting hand on Vetala

Bhatta's shoulder. "It can be frustrating, but time and destiny travel at their own pace, raj-guru. We can only be patient and accept whatever is outside our control with grace."

The Acharya was silent for a long time before he finally sighed and nodded at the chancellor. Both men turned back to the watch the moon turn molten silver and come ashore, riding on the tides.

* * *

Everything is crafted in the mind before it is crafted by the fingers.

Ghatakarpara remembered the old woodcraftsman's instructions to him and Atulyateja as they had sat hunched in his little shop that hot summer many years ago, knives in hand, learning how to whittle bamboo flutes and carve ironwood birds' nests, while the Kshipra flowed passively outside.

If you can't see it in your mind, having the nimblest of fingers is useless. That is the problem with him... pointing to Atulyateja ... *he doesn't see, so he can't make.*

Feeling the weight of the key in his palm — hard and ice-cold, but already starting to melt from the heat transmitted by his hand — the prince wondered if he had seen it right in his mind. He hoped he had. His escape depended on it.

He picked up the slippery key delicately with his other hand, its icy chill numbing his fingertips. Squinting at it by the moonlight coming in from the high window, he reworked the water melting off it, fusing it back onto the key as ice. Once the key had been reconstituted to his satisfaction, he slid it carefully into the lock that chained his wrists to one another and the wall bracket.

Since the morning of his confrontation with his captors — and since discovering that he could do some deft tricks with water — Ghatakarpara had spent nearly every waking moment trying to gain mastery over this new skill. He hadn't the faintest idea how and from where this mysterious talent had surfaced, but he quickly realized that the more he worked on it, the better he got at moulding water. By the afternoon of that first day, he was being able to design wobbly models of simple objects like jars and small saucers, and by nightfall, he had graduated to creating crude but identifiable animal shapes. Resuming at daybreak, he worked through the morning, achieving the breakthrough of fashioning water into ice or steam, and then turning ice and steam back into water. From afternoon onwards, he had focused solely on making, unmaking and then remaking the three tools he needed to break out of captivity.

Still working on the key with his mind, feeling the pressure of its grooves against the tumblers, the prince turned it gently in the lock. There was a moment's resistance — a heart-stopping moment when Ghatakarpara thought his efforts weren't going to pay off — and then the lock clicked open, the chains slipped free and slid to the floor. Their heavy clatter on the stone floor felt loud enough to rouse the dead, but though the prince waited to hear approaching footsteps, no one came to investigate. He had been an exceptionally good prisoner for the last two days, always quiet and eating and drinking without complaint; he guessed the Sakas had decided he didn't need close monitoring after all.

Rubbing his wrists and flexing his arms to get the circulation going, he beckoned to the ice key with his fingers. The key instantly thinned out and liquefied, but instead of answering to gravity and splashing to the floor, it rose as a globule of water and hung before the prince, catching the moonlight like a blob of quicksilver, rippling and oscillating softly in the flow of air currents.

Ghatakarpara turned his attention to the door. He had observed his minders lock it many times and had come to the conclusion that the key that opened his chains and the one that fitted the door's lock were the same. He had also figured out that though the door had bolts, his minders rarely used them, relying solely on the lock instead. That night, after dinner had been served, the prince had paid special attention to how the woman closed the door after her, and he had been relieved to hear only the key turning in the lock.

The water globule turned to ice, which Ghatakarpara then moulded into a key again — the more often he did it, the better and faster he got at it, he realized. Inserting the ice key into the keyhole, the prince once again turned it; the lock opened. Sliding the key out, he breathed in deeply, opened the door a crack and peeped out, half expecting to find a guard or two on the other side.

The passage outside was dark but empty.

Easing the door open, the prince stepped through, locking it carefully behind him. He tiptoed out of the passage and slipped past a succession of rooms, some empty, some with slumbering forms inside. Seeing that no guards were stationed anywhere, it occurred to Ghatakarpara that the Sakas had entirely discounted the possibility of him attempting an escape — or of someone coming from outside to rescue him. The former, he understood; he had been on his best behaviour since discovering his magic touch with water, and to the Sakas, his self-absorption must have felt like docility and obedience. The latter worried him, though — if the Sakas thought no one could come for him, where exactly was he?

Logic said he was somewhere in the Marusthali in a Saka stronghold. But was he in a city or some remote, impossible-to-find hideaway? And the Marusthali was vast, which meant he could be anywhere, hundreds of miles from the safety of Sindhuvarta. All he knew was that if he succeeded in breaking out, he would have to strike out east for the Arbudas.

But that came much later. First, he had to get out of

wherever he was — and he hadn't the remotest idea about the geography of this place. All he was familiar with was the small patch of sky seen through the barred window.

Stepping over a family of sleeping Sakas, Ghatakarpara reached what he assumed was the building's main entrance. Fumbling in the dark, he found the latch, opened the door and stepped into a deserted alley that was lined with dark mud-brick houses on both sides. The alley wound down a small rise, and at its end, the prince came upon an open rectangle that looked like a market. The town — for it was a town, he could now tell by the number of roofs glistening in the moonlight — was asleep, with not a soul about, and Ghatakarpara was beginning to feel pleased with himself...

...when a dog suddenly took to barking at him from across the open marketplace.

The animal was a stray and a poorly fed one at that, but its bark was full-blooded in the still of the night. On and on it yapped at him, full of outrage, the noise echoing off the town's buildings and scurrying down streets. The prince cursed and tried to slip into the shadows, staying quiet and immobile, but the dog was not to be fooled. It could smell him, it knew he was still there, so it barked its head off.

Ghatakarpara understood that the dog had the potential to spoil his plans. In no mood to run into any curious Saka sentries, he twirled his fingers around the water globule he was carrying in his hand. Kneading the globule, he shaped it into hard, frozen ball of ice, which he flung at the dog. The projectile struck the dog, which gave a frightened yelp of surprise. Turning around, it fled into the shadows. The prince waited for a few moments to see if the mutt would return, his fingers already toying with a fresh ball of water that had almost magically appeared in his hands.

When he was certain that the dog was not coming back, Ghatakarpara slipped from cover. Still hugging the shadows, he walked down one broken street and then the next, weaving a way downhill until he reached a high wooden stockade. On observing how the stockade skirted a wide section of the town, it struck the prince that he had probably reached the town's limits, and that he only had to get beyond the fence to be free. He darted a glance over his shoulder, making sure he was alone. Keeping the stockade to his left, he then began walking, looking for a way over or under it.

He came upon the gap in the stockade without warning. The fence took a sudden turn to the left, and following it, Ghatakarpara found himself staring at the space left by a pair of missing logs, a space wide enough for him to slip through. He guessed the gap hadn't been fixed because the townsfolk were using it as a shortcut.

Twisting sideways, the prince squeezed through the gap. He had one leg and half his body out on the other side and was pulling the rest of himself out when a figure materialized just outside the gap. Startled, he looked up, and the figure stared back at him.

"*Kadeh?*" the man said. From the intonation, Ghatakarpara figured a question had been posed.

Not knowing what had been asked or what to say in reply, hanging stupidly half in and half out of the fence, the prince simply gawked at the man, painfully conscious of the fact that the moonlight was fully on him. His head still hurt a little from the wound, and now the pain seemed to flare, as if in response to an alarm that had gone off in his brain.

"*Hei'isa... ghu'r...*" the man said, his tone suddenly alert, and Ghatakarpara saw him reach for the sword swinging at his waist.

"Bad idea," the prince muttered, stepping free of the fence. He held a short dagger in his hand, which glistened wet and white in the moonlight.

The man was taller than Ghatakarpara, giving him superior

reach, but the prince was much quicker. Even as the man drew his sword and swung it in a great curving arc, Ghatakarpara had narrowed the distance between them, ducking low under the man's slashing arm and then coming up swiftly. He pulled in close, grabbing the man's free hand and twisting it sharply so that the man yelled in pain.

That moment of pain, of distraction, was all the prince needed. As the Saka fought to free his hand from the vice-like grip, Ghatakarpara stepped even closer and drove the ice dagger into the man's midriff, just under his ribcage. The dagger eased in, and the man opened his mouth to scream, but the prince let go of his hand and clamped the man's mouth shut instead. The man sagged to the ground moaning, his eyes wide in agony, and Ghatakarpara dropped to his knees as well, still pushing the dagger deep into the man's side. Hot blood flowed over the prince's fingers and he knew the dagger would melt quickly.

The Saka coughed into Ghatakarpara's hand and gave a strangled retch. The dagger was gone, water mixed with blood. It crossed the prince's mind that he could take the man's sword and put an end to his agony, but seeing the man was already losing consciousness, he decided against it. He had a more important thing to do, anyway.

He scrambled to his feet and looked around. There was no one. The coast was clear.

Ghatakarpara leaped over the Saka and ran blindly into the night, his stubby shadow sticking to him, chasing him over the flat, sandy desert.

* * *

Which father — the one who came yesterday or the one whose ashes we scattered in the holy Kshipra? Which one?

I heard how you refused Indra the opportunity to question

me in front of everyone. You stood up… you saved me the
humiliation. But now you will have to do that again and again.

Vikramaditya stroked Vishakha's hand, white and inert
between his, tracing a fine pattern along the network of veins
with his finger. Outside the queen's window, the rain that had
finally arrived that evening pattered on the leaves of the nearby
trees. The night was dark, the moon hidden behind clouds.
Except for the king and queen, the bedchamber was empty,
the matron and the maids having withdrawn to an adjoining
chamber out of respect for their samrat.

I can't serve this palace any longer. I can no longer swear
allegiance to the throne that was responsible for my family's
death. My duty towards Avanti ends here.

The king took a deep breath and looked at Vishakha's
face, wondering what he expected to see there. A spark of
recognition? A glimpse of understanding? A flare of sympathy?

Will it be alright if I never remember? Or will it all come
to a hopeless, grinding halt?

You did remember, my love, the samrat said, speaking to
Vishakha in his head. *But then you went away again.*

As did everyone else.

Walking into the council chamber earlier that evening,
he had been struck by the number of vacant chairs around
the council table. With only Dhanavantri, Kshapanaka and
Varahamihira left in Ujjayini, his council was threadbare. He
had no idea of the fate that had befallen Ghatakarpara, and he
didn't know what destiny had in store for the Acharya, Amara
Simha and now Shanku. The Council of Nine had once been
strong, resolute and unshakeable, an embodiment of Ujjayini's
resolve and preeminence. But now, it lay in tatters, torn from
within and without, much like his beloved city.

He was trying his utmost to hold everything together,
but he was failing miserably. The council was coming apart.
The palace was coming apart. The city was coming apart.

Everyone and everything was drifting away from everyone and everything else.

One by one, you have all gone away. Each of you who was dear to me.

Vikramaditya raised the queen's hand to his lips and kissed it gently.

On whose shoulder do I lean now, in whose arms do I seek comfort? Where am I to go now, Vishakha? Where?

* * *

The sparks from the bonfire spat and rose in spirals like so many fireflies fleeing the flames, pinpoints of orange light swirling dervish-like in the desert wind to the clapping of hands and the gentle plucking of the *khi'nor* strings. One of the men played a small flute at a high-pitched melancholic note, while a pair of women sang a tuneless song whose words escaped Kalidasa but left him thinking of wide blue skies and blue mountains in the distance, hidden in haze.

Dinner had yet to be served, but no one in the fort of Mun'h seemed much inclined to eating, what with *in'tah*, the local brew made from fermented rice water, in free flow. Kalidasa's pewter jar had already been refilled thrice, and he was beginning to feel a little light-headed as he sat by himself in one corner of the fort's open courtyard and took in the merrymaking.

Soon after their return to Mun'h from witnessing the *droiba* conjure up the *yah'bre*, Khash'i Dur had sent a dozen messengers out to different corners of the horizon. In response to his summons, from that morning, large and small groups of Hunas had begun assembling outside Mun'h. These were different Huna tribes, Kalidasa learned, each headed by a minor *shy'or* who owed allegiance to Khash'i Dur. A couple of Saka chieftains had also come from nearby with their own bands of warriors, so they could take Khash'i Dur's battle plans back to their own war-chiefs. The more important of the Huna *shy'ors* were introduced to Kalidasa, and all of them had a good word for Zho E'rami. And without fail, all of them were grateful to him for returning to the fold.

More would come from all over the desert over the next few days, Khash'i Dur had told him. More than a dozen tribes, all armed and united under the banner of the *hriiz*, all prepared for the long march east, over the mountains and into *zaa'ri ulla*, the land of plenty.

A new song broke out, a ribald duet between the men and the two women, loaded with innuendo. There was much hugging and backslapping as tribes met, and the night filled with the clinking of pewter jars, the rumble of familiar laughter and the sighs of nostalgia — sounds of old friendship that thankfully never changed, thought Kalidasa.

A fourth round of *in'tah* had just been tipped into his jar when Kalidasa felt a hand on his shoulder. Looking around, he saw Khash'i Dur, who motioned with his other hand, asking Kalidasa to come with him. Nudging and smiling their way through corridors packed with happy tribesmen, Kalidasa and the *shy'or* climbed a staircase that brought them to a secluded balcony, where three senior Huna chieftains lounged on sheepskin blankets. They greeted Kalidasa as if they had known him forever, making room for him on the blankets. The *droiba* sat drooping in one corner, eyes shut, though Kalidasa very much doubted he was asleep.

When Khash'i Dur had ensured that Kalidasa was comfortable and his jar was full, he lowered himself to the blankets as well. "As you know," he said, addressing Kalidasa in Avanti, "We are assembling for the march into Sindhuvarta."

Kalidasa inclined his head.

"There is obviously a lot that you know about Sindhuvarta and its kingdoms that we know nothing of. Avanti, of course, is of particular interest to us, because it leads the alliance of Sindhuvarta's kingdoms. We are interested in Avanti and in Vikramaditya. Tell us about him. Tell us about the others in his council as well. Tell us everything that we should know before we set foot on Avanti's soil."

Kalidasa nodded and took a big gulp from his jar. Then, in slow and halting Huna, he spoke about Avanti, Vikramaditya and the council.

He spoke late into the night and told the Huna chiefs everything.

* * *

A shadow slipped through the galleries of Ujjayini's palace, unseen because of the lateness of the hour, and because the shadow did a very good job of staying undetected from the eyes of any palace guards who happened by. It slipped from one patch of darkness to another, from one recessed alcove to the next, sometimes even disappearing altogether when crossing a pool of light, so that none but the alertest of guards would even have sensed anything strange in the shifting play of brightness and dark caused by the torches guttering in their brackets in the breeze.

The shadow moved up a staircase and down one gallery before turning into a passage that led towards Pralupi's chambers. In the seclusion of the passage, the shadow became more stable, as if now confident of not being discovered, and as it passed under the weak glow of the lamp illuminating the passage, its face showed fleetingly.

Vismaya.

The chief of the Palace Guards reached the end of the passage, where the door to Pralupi's chambers blocked his way. He stopped in front of the door, as if undecided — and then he slipped *right through the closed door*, oozing through the dark and heavy wood, so that one moment he was outside the door and the next he was through to the other side.

Once inside the princess' chambers, Vismaya looked from side to side, unsure about which way to go. Peering through the crack in the door to the right, he drew back and struck out to the left, across the landscaped balcony with its forest pond and waterfall. Disturbed by the presence of a trespasser, the birds in the cages overhead shifted in their perches and ruffled their feathers, and one of the ducks gave an annoyed quack.

"Careful or you'll wake the birds, and they'll end up waking the princess."

Vismaya turned towards the voice and saw Mithyamayi step out of the far corner of the balcony. "We don't want the king's sister discovering the truth about us, do we?" she said as she approached him.

The chief of the guards shook his head.

"What brings you here at this late hour, Matali?"

Vismaya's face underwent a subtle transition, and for the briefest of moments, it took on the hooded features of the deva, his eyes droopy and cold, his mouth turned down in a ruthless half-snarl. Then he was back to being Vismaya, his eyes keen above his disfigured nose over a short, grey beard.

"I have a message from our lord, Indra," he said in an undertone. "He wants to know what progress you have made in discovering the whereabouts of Veeshada's dagger."

The woman stared at the deva, and the deva stared back. The balcony was still. The birds had gone back to sleep in their cages.

"What am I to tell him, Urvashi?"

"Tell him I haven't found the right opportunity yet. It has been only two days since I entered the palace, and I am yet to gain the princess' confidence."

Matali nodded. "I would suggest you move a whole lot

quicker at gaining everyone's confidence. Our lord is running out of patience."

"He wouldn't be if *you* had done your job and discovered where the dagger is hidden. It's because you couldn't that I had to come here as Mithyamayi..."

"I tried; I am still trying," Matali interrupted with a low snarl.

"Good, that makes two of us. Let us *both* work quicker and harder."

With a curt nod, the deva turned to depart. But checking himself, he looked back.

"Just out of curiosity, what is this right opportunity that you are waiting for, Urvashi?"

The apsara tilted her head, and her eyes caught the light from a lamp hanging in one corner of the balcony. In them, Matali saw a cold, manipulative gleam, fleeting like lightning on the far horizon.

"The opportunity to get to know the Samrat better," she replied, the mildest hint of seduction in the velvety folds of her voice.

Departure

Amara Simha and the *samsaptakas* had advanced towards the settlement of Ki'barr at a crawl, literally inching along under the night sky, chary of alerting any lookouts that the town's guardians might have posted.

The moment they had spotted the town on the horizon, Amara Simha knew it wasn't going to be easy taking it. To begin with, Ki'barr was situated in the middle of a flat stretch of desert, with not a single knoll, dune or straggle of desert trees to offer him and his men concealment. They had had to stay out of the town's field of vision, baking in the desert heat and waiting for night to fall. But as soon as the sun set, the moon had sailed out, so again, they hadn't dared to get too close for fear of being sighted.

They had waited until the middle of the night to make a move, but because they were still too far out in the desert, rushing the town was useless as the beat of the hooves and the dust that the horses kicked up would effectively serve as an alarm, giving the townsfolk enough time to mount a defence. Amara Simha feared the Saka arrows in particular; caught in a hail of those lethal missiles, he knew they stood no chance of breaching Ki'barr. Thus, they had shuffled forward, careful not to give themselves away.

When they were no more than half a mile from the stockade that surrounded the town, the burly councilor reined in his horse. Hefting his broad battle-axe, he cast a sideways glance at Angamitra, who nodded in response. Amara Simha turned and looked at the *samsaptakas* riding behind him, raising his axe high and giving it a fierce shake. Even in the tepid moonlight, his eyes blazed and his lips mouthed a silent battle-cry. In response, the *samsaptakas* raised their own weapons, all silent but volcanic in their readiness to do battle.

Amara Simha turned and faced Ki'barr. Behind him, the Warriors of the Oath did the same. The councilor suddenly dipped his head and spurred his mount into a gallop, and the attack on Ki'barr got underway.

Whether it was complacency on the part of the Sakas — who had never anticipated an attack on them so deep in the desert — or plain providence, the fact that they had managed stealing so close to the town unseen gave the raiders an upper hand early in the battle. The Huna scout they had with them had given them a broad idea of what to expect in a Saka fort's layout, and Amara Simha and the *samsaptakas* made a beeline for the one main gate in the stockade. The gate was manned by a pair of guards who were easily brushed aside, and before they knew it, the attackers were inside Ki'barr.

Conscious of the fact that he had no idea where to look for Ghatakarpara in an alien town — assuming Satyaveda had not lied, and Ghatakarpara was still here and had not been moved elsewhere — Amara Simha's strategy to get to the prince was simple. He had instructed the *samsaptakas* to be merciless on the Sakas, hitting them hard, stunning them into submission, so that they would be happy to part with their hostage as long as they were left alone. And that was what the attackers did.

From street to street, building to building, the *samsaptakas* slipped freely, not caring in which direction they went as long as they found Sakas to kill. Most of the townsfolk and soldiers were still rubbing the sleep from their eyes and wondering what had happened when they were cut down in their doorways and in the streets outside their homes. The raiders were ruthless in their efficiency, and soon, the alleyways of Ki'barr were full of people running for their lives, the air over the town shivering with the screams of the dying.

Knowing that the biggest house in the village is invariably the headman's, Amara Simha made for the largest building in Ki'barr, a two-storey structure at the town's centre. His approach was noticed; the four Saka guards who came out to stop him fell trying. Onwards he pressed, but the closer he got, the more resistance he met with. The attack had started a while ago, and the Saka warriors had had time to regroup. They now came out screaming, their long swords waving in the moonlight. Amara Simha was beset by six of them, and this lot was hardier and fought with more purpose, cutting and slashing at the councilor, halting his march.

Amara Simha parried their attack and countered it with a fierce push of his own. Swords met the axe, causing sparks to fly, and blood splattered to the ground as blades slipped past defences. The Sakas lost three men to the councilor's fury, but reinforcements arrived to take him on. More and more men joined in, trying to cut him down from all sides, and one of the swords succeeded in opening a long gash down his left shoulder and across the back.

Pain blossomed and rushed to Amara Simha's head. At that instant, he felt a hot flush on his cheeks and sensed a surge of something wild and deeply primitive in his veins — a sudden taste for blood, an overriding desire to hunt and kill prey.

In a flash, he realized that the prey was right in front of him. Cowering. Frantically backing away. Moaning in terror.

The Saka warriors were now staggering away from him, tripping and stepping over one another in desperation, scrambling and clawing to stay out of his grasp. Their eyes were fixed on him, petrified, their resolve to fight giving way in a most abrupt and unbecoming fashion, so that they either dropped their weapons in dread or forgot all about using them in their fright.

Vaguely puzzled by their behaviour — and puzzled that his canines were suddenly long and sharp in his mouth — Amara Simha stretched a hand to grab the savage closest to him. That was when he noticed that his arm was covered in fine golden-brown fur, while at his fingertips, long, curving black claws had sprouted again. Before he knew it, his hand struck the warrior he had been reaching for in the back, the claws digging deep, mauling and mangling the flesh. The soldier screamed in pain.

The scent of blood, hot and freshly let, came to Amara Simha in a blooming tide, and the councilor felt his mouth salivate as he struck the soldier a second time, in the back of the head. The man's head caved in under the force of the blow, and even as he went down, Amara Simha leaped towards his next victim. With a primal snarl, he ripped the second warrior's legs from under him, bringing him down hard before driving his claws into the man's neck and snapping his vertebra. Blood sprayed from the wound, drenching the councilor's rough, dark mane in fine droplets.

Amara Simha roared in pleasure at the exhilaration of the hunt. The roar of a lion.

The Sakas were now fleeing at the sight of him, clearing a path to the large house. Axe in one hand, his transformation into man-lion complete, the councilor leaped and bounded to the door of the house. With another hearty roar, he hammered the door down and stepped inside, only to be assailed by a pair of guards. The first Amara Simha smote with his left hand, sending him flying; the second he grabbed by the neck, lifting him into the air, before bringing him down to the ground hard on his back. As the man cried out in agony, the man-lion bent over him, pinning him to the ground and snarling into his face in acute rage. The lust for blood thrummed and keened in the councilor's ears, matched by a gnawing, gluttonous urge to maim and dismember.

There was an outbreak of panicked voices from overhead, followed by the frenzied rush of feet down a flight of stairs. Amara Simha sprang to his feet and faced the stairs, his axe in a half-swing, ready to meet the next wave of attack. But instead of soldiers, two young women came into view, both scared and trembling so hard that they could barely stay on their feet. Behind them came a middle-aged man carrying a child of about three, and after him, an old man with a long, white beard. Five pairs of eyes stared at the man-lion in abject fear — and then the women slowly came down the last few steps, quaking and sobbing. Dropping to their knees, they joined their hands in supplication, words tumbling out of their mouths, none of which made sense to Amara Simha though he understood their intent. The two men joined the women in beseeching him, the middle-aged man making the small child get down on its knees and put its hands together in a pathetic plea for mercy.

The sight of the child kneeling before him, its hands joined, staring up at him in wonder and incomprehension, filled Amara Simha with shame and revulsion. Unable to look the child in the eye, unwilling to do what the mad voices in his head were urging him to do, he let his arm drop reluctantly and turned wearily away from the terrified family.

For now, the killing was over. The town's surrender was complete.

* * *

The asura army numbered a couple of hundred, their solemn faces lit by torchlight, their horns polished black and shiny with oil, the jagged javelins they carried twinkling with fire, their shadows splashed on the walls of the large cavern where they were assembled. Before them, on a rising piece of granite that served as a platform, stood Hiranyaksha, his face flush with pride, eyes glowing with hope and anticipation.

"You have put yourselves in the hands of the mahaguru," he said, surveying the army. "Have faith in him and he will guide you into Borderworld and bring you back. Fight well, brothers and sisters. Fight for Patala."

"For Patala," the crowd roared back, banging their spears on the floor and dislodging the bats roosting in the darkness. As the cavern filled with skittering and screeching, the asura lord turned to Shukracharya.

"Veeshada's dagger will soon be ours," he said, with a smile on his face. "I wish you could be back with it before brother returns, so we can gift it to him."

"I shall try," the high priest replied. "Though I can't say for certain because our entry into Borderworld might take a while, whereas Hiranyakashipu is due to return any time now. Still, I will try."

"I am sure you will," Hiranyaksha paused. "Brother will be eager to meet you."

"I am keen to see him as well. It has been so long. But our meeting might take longer than expected."

"Why is that, mahaguru?" Hiranyaksha peered curiously at the high priest.

Shukracharya stepped in front of the asura lord and faced him.

"If Hiranyakashipu returns in my absence, I have an urgent errand for him. This errand might delay my meeting him. If I am not around, I want you to tell him what I want done."

Hiranyaksha bowed. "What is it that you want of him, mahaguru?"

"I want him to go to Devaloka."

Seeing the surprise on the asura lord's face, Shukracharya nodded, his eye flashing in cold anger as a bitter memory was stoked. "There is a small matter of my prestige at stake, and I want the score settled."

* * *

"Is this some sort of a joke?" Amara Simha fumed. "Does this fool expect me to fall for his tricks? Tell him he has one last chance to tell us the truth."

The interpreter who had accompanied them turned to the Saka, the *shy'or* of Ki'barr. The two conversed for a while, the man frightened but insistent in his tone, shifting from foot to foot, shooting uneasy glances at the councilor, as if half-expecting him to turn back into the man-lion at any moment. Finally, with a helpless shrug, the interpreter looked at the councilor.

"He maintains he has no clue about what has happened to the prince. He says the prince has been in this cell ever since they brought him here, and he swears the prince was here earlier in the night. They checked on him, it seems."

"He was locked up in this cell?

"Yes."

"So where is he now?" Amara Simha peered theatrically into the shadows of the cell, which was empty except for the goat-hair blankets, a mud pitcher and the unlocked fetters lying on the floor. "I don't see him here... or there." He looked up at the narrow window and the rectangular patch of night sky outside. "He couldn't have gone out that way either. And he definitely couldn't have slipped out of the keyhole." He swung around to glare into the Saka chief's face, which was sick with fear in the torchlight. "Where is the prince, my friend? I see you have one tooth missing, so I can ask you that question another thirty-one times. I promise you it will be very painful."

If not from the words, the man understood the threat from the councilor's expression. He grabbed the interpreter's arm and babbled desperately, trying his best to convince him that he was telling the truth.

"He swears the prince has not been moved out and that he was here a few hours ago."

"Yet, he is not here when we walk in, and the door is locked from the outside." The councilor eyed the Saka suspiciously. "And the two keys to the cell were where they were supposed to be."

"Your honour," the interpreter paused, then decided to continue. "If he were lying, why would he bring us to this empty cell, knowing fully well that the situation wouldn't make him look good in our eyes? He would have to be really stupid to bring us here if he knew the prince was not in the cell."

Exasperated, Amara Simha drew a deep breath. "If *he* doesn't know where the prince is, *who* is supposed to know? He is the chief of this godforsaken place, isn't he?" Shaking his head, he snapped angrily, "I've had enough. I want some answers, and I'm going to get them one way or the other. Let us string this fellow up in the courtyard."

As a couple of *samsaptakas* took him by the arms and started hauling him away, the Saka let out a stream of protests, pleading and yowling at the top of his voice. Amara Simha and the interpreter followed, and the small group eventually emerged into a small courtyard, where a stake was driven into the ground. The *samsaptakas* were still tying the *shy'or* to the stake when an old woman appeared at a door, flailing her hands at Amara Simha as she beat her chest and pointed at the man.

"Stop," the interpreter said to the two *samsaptakas*.

He posed some questions to the woman, for which she had ready answers, wailing and gesticulating all the time she spoke. On hearing what she had to say, the Saka chief sagged with relief and even managed giving Amara Simha a broken, conciliatory smile. At last, the interpreter turned to the councilor.

"She says a Saka soldier was found lying unconscious outside the stockade. He'd suffered a bad stab wound, it seems. While it looked like he had been injured in our attack, he's just regained consciousness and says that he was struck while trying to stop the prince from escaping."

"He tried to stop Ghatakarpara? Where? When?"

"In the middle of the night. Near a gap in the stockade. It seems they had a scuffle, and the prince stabbed him."

Reaching over his shoulder, Amara Simha probed the bloodied bandage covering the cut on his back. A *samsaptaka* with rudimentary skills had washed and treated the wound with a crude turmeric preparation that had helped staunch the bleeding, but the cut hurt very much, especially when he strained his back muscles.

"How did the prince get out of his cell?" he asked, bringing his hand away and examining it closely, relieved to see there were no traces of fresh blood on his fingers.

"No idea, but this man is certain it was the prince." The interpreter exchanged a few words with the woman and nodded. "He is certain because he was one of those who brought the prince here from over the Arbudas and through the desert."

"Does he know what happened to the prince after he was stabbed?"

The interpreter and the woman spoke again.

"He says the prince left him bleeding on the ground and ran into the desert."

Amara Simha looked up at the sky, slowly growing lighter from the east. In a short while, the blazing desert sun would be up. He looked down at the prince's sun-crest medallion lying flat on his palm, which they had recovered from the chief's possession.

"Ghatakarpara is smart enough to head in an easterly direction," he said, closing his fingers over the medallion and tucking it into his waistband. "He has a few hours' head start, but I gather he is on foot, while we have horses." He flicked his fingers at one of the *samsaptakas*, urging speed.

"Find Angamitra and ask him to get everyone together quickly. Load up on food and water. We begin our ride to save the prince before the sun fully clears the horizon."

* * *

A small puff of mist detached itself from the larger pall hanging over Lake Alaka and drifted towards a patch of wooded land on the other side of the stretch of placid water.

As it drew near land, its composition changed. It grew denser and more angular, transforming from within, and once it was on firm land, feet emerged from its opacity, followed by the knees, a waist, two hands and then the rest of the body. Moments later, a fully formed yaksha strode away from the lake and down the misty pathway, the last few trails of mist running out from between his fingers and blowing away into the wind.

The yaksha entered another bank of the mist, so it was impossible to tell which way he was headed, but he strode confidently along, until the mist suddenly parted and fell away like a veil to reveal a large glistening pool at his feet. The pool was made of nacre, and at its centre was an alabaster pavilion, connected to the pool's rim with swinging bamboo bridges. Inside the pavilion, Kubera sat in the company of two other yakshas, both playing a morning raga on their *vamsis*. The melodious notes of the two flutes sprang and riffled the air at the precise moment the curtains of mist had parted for the visiting yaksha.

The yaksha waited for the music to finish before clearing his throat to let his master know of his arrival. Kubera turned his heavy, bearded face in the yaksha's direction, and recognizing his visitor, waved a fat hand, calling him over. At the same time, the yaksha lord inclined his head at the two musicians, who got to their feet and withdrew soundlessly. Only when he and the newly arrived yaksha were alone did Kubera nod.

"Tell me what you have learned about the human king."

The yaksha spoke for long and without interruption, and by the time he was done, a mild sunlight was nudging its way through the mist and little arcs of rainbows flashed here and there like colourful illusions. Kubera listened to the yaksha's account, latching onto every word. When the narration was finally over, he leaned back on the white silken bolsters and stroked his beard pensively.

"So, Vikramaditya is Indra's grandson," he remarked.

"He is, my lord. The human king refuses to accept Gandharvasena as his father, though. He told Indra as much to his face before literally throwing him out of his city."

"I would have loved to see Indra's face when that happened," Kubera said, grinning and smacking his thigh in delight. "Being shown the door by your own grandson — impressive." His voice acquired a shade of respect and admiration at that last word, which could only have been for Vikramaditya.

"The human king has a will of iron, my lord."

"Hmm. And all of this has to do with Veeshada's dagger." The yaksha lord shook his head in amazement. "The Omniscient One picked a *human* to protect the Halahala."

"He is the Wielder of the Hellfires, lord," the yaksha

reminded. "I saw Diti's devilish creations burning in his hands as he faced Indra. And his councilors are the bearers of the Nine Sacred Pearls."

"The Wielder of the Hellfires who also has possession of the Halahala." Kubera shook his head again, marvelling at what he was hearing. "The Hellfires and the Halahala — two things that both the asuras and devas have always hankered after, but to no avail. How it must gall them to see both in the possession of a human king! I'm not the least bit surprised that Shukracharya and Indra set their differences aside to plot Vikramaditya's downfall."

The yaksha did not respond, and for a while, Kubera was silent, still in thought.

"So, from what you have seen, is Shukracharya's plan to break the power of the Nine Pearls by dividing the king and his councilors, taking effect?" he asked.

"Yes, my lord. One of the councilors has already left the king's service and gone over to the side of Avanti's enemies. And now, because Vikramaditya is really Gandharvasena's son, the king's half-brother has risen against him over the right to rule the kingdom — I was there in the central hallway of the palace, hiding behind some drapes, when the half-brother challenged the king. I overheard their argument and knew this would not end well for the human king. It didn't."

"Interesting." Heaving a deep sigh, Kubera rose from the cushions and walked to the edge of the pavilion to lean on the railings and stare into the clear water. "Very interesting."

The yaksha kept quiet.

"And where exactly is Veeshada's dagger?" Kubera turned around, his eyes bright and sparking with possibilities.

"I don't know, lord. It is a secret because no one in the council talks about it, ever."

"Fair enough. You may go."

In the solitude of the pool, Kubera went over everything

that he had been told about the king and his councilors. The longer the yaksha thought about it, the more it seemed to him that the devas and asuras were likely to prevail over the human king; that in their fight for the Halahala, Vikramaditya would be the first casualty.

The time was ripe for the yakshas to make their own move, he decided.

* * *

The sun had been up for a while now, but it was concealed by the high cliffs that lined the northern bank of the Payoshni, so that the narrow pass that led from the garrison to the river was still in shadow. The small group of eight people walked through the pass, watched keenly by the soldiers of Heheya, who stood within the garrison, craning their necks to catch a last glimpse of the party that was setting out on what was plainly a hopeless endeavour, doomed to fail.

The eight travellers, accompanied by a boatman from the garrison, reached the river, where the boat had been drawn up on a spit of land. With help from two of the soldiers in the group, the boatman pushed the boat into the water, and everyone climbed carefully into the craft. At a signal from the young girl, the boatman picked up the bargepole and punted the boat away from land and into the currents.

Shanku looked away from the boatman at the six soldiers accompanying her on the mission, and then at Greeshma. The six soldiers were all young and eager, flawless examples of military discipline, whereas the fugitive was old and a little slovenly, slumped unhappily in the middle of the boat. From the time they had left Ujjayini, it had become clear to Shanku that the men did not like Greeshma, and in turn, the old bandit despised them. And her. And this mission that he had been forced into.

With a sigh, she turned to gaze in the direction of Payoshni Pass and the garrison beyond, but the massive wooden gates that had been erected at the pass — after the attack by the blind rakshasa and the pishachas, the head of the garrison had told her — were already shut; later, they would open a fraction to let the boatman back in. She raised her eyes to the sky, light blue with clouds like fine brushstrokes. That was the sky she was leaving behind, a familiar sky.

Use your gift, my child.

That was what the oracle had said when she had gone to seek her blessings.

Her father had cried big tears, afraid that he would never see her again. Cursing her for having volunteered to go, and cursing himself for having told the crown about Greeshma. Wanting to go along with her, and cursing her when she put her foot down.

He had given her his blessings all the same, and had told her that he loved her.

That was the sky she was leaving behind.

Shanku blinked and turned, and this time, she faced straight ahead into the thick wall of trees slowly approaching the boat. The trees grew tall and close to one another, and the spaces between them were dark and gloomy. A dank and heavy mist wound through those spaces, grey and ghostlike, coiling around the tree trunks and forming garlands between trees, creeping through the foliage overhead and seeping through the undergrowth, its finger-like tendrils beckoning the boat, luring them into the darkness.

Above all, there was the silence. Stale and deathly.

Listening to the muddy river slushing against the bargepole and the hull of the boat, Shanku stared at the Forest of the Exiles.

End of Book 3

COMING SOON

VIKRAMADITYA VEERGATHA
BOOK 4

THE

WRATH
OF THE
HELLFIRES